Emma Lorant lives in Somerset. *Lullaby of Fear* is her second novel, and her first, *Cradle of Secrets*, was also published by Headline.

Lullaby of Fear

Emma Lorant

First published in Great Britain in 1994
by HEADLINE BOOK PUBLISHING

First published in paperback in 1994
by HEADLINE BOOK PUBLISHING

A HEADLINE FEATURE paperback

10 9 8 7 6 5 4 3 2 1

ISBN 0 7472 4564 9

Typeset by
Letterpart Limited, Reigate, Surrey

Printed and bound in Great Britain by
Cox & Wyman Ltd., Reading, Berks.

HEADLINE BOOK PUBLISHING
A division of Hodder Headline PLC
338 Euston Road
London NW1 3BH

To the memory of
Jeremy Fredric Warburg
without whom this book could not
have come into being

ACKNOWLEDGEMENTS

Thanks are due to everyone who helped with this book.

First and foremost, to Dr Richard Warburg, whose assistance with genetics has been invaluable.

Also to Nickie Bertolotti, Joy Cotter and Gillian Geering for reading the early drafts; Dietger Bansberg and Katharina Bosch for commenting on German usage; Dr Daryl Cantor and Dr Leonard McEwen for their help with medical matters; Chris Dyer for his advice on sailing; David Hartshorne of Cellmark Diagnostics, and Jackie Bennett of Scotland Yard's Specialist Operations press desk for their guidance on various aspects of genetic profiling; the Royal Society for the Protection of Birds.

Thanks also to many others, too numerous to name, for their generous contributions.

Any errors are, of course, the author's.

1

As soon as she touched the present her godmother had given her, Mary Fullbridey felt its power, sensed that it held the start of a whole new life. What Mary did not, could not, know was that its work had already begun.

'I've brought it all the way from Austria,' Gabriela Adler explained. 'From a pure source high in the Alps, above the village of St Walter.'

Mary felt the cocoon shape move as though it were alive. But that was just a trick of her imagination. When she looked again she saw she was holding a quite ordinary, stainless steel tube.

'Thank you, Aunt Rilla,' she murmured. Rilla, short for Gabriela, was the name her godmother liked her to use.

Her sensitive fingers twined round the shiny phial and tensed. Mary stared at the likeness reflecting back at her, moved the little cylinder from hand to hand and breathed in hard. The glinting image shifted into distortions which held her, drew her into themselves. Round, surprised eyes looked out at her – and yet they were not hers. She shook her head, fascinated by the way her mirrored hair tumbled beside widened temples and cheeks and on past a determined chin. There was no doubt that the features were hers, yet they seemed alien.

'I scooped some up for you from the chapel of my old convent school,' Aunt Rilla told her. 'I bring a little holy water back every time I visit. Mother Theresia has given me special permission to do so.'

'I shall always treasure it.' Mary's lips smiled gratitude but her eyes edged away, clouded up. She twisted the slim tube, spellbound by the chance indentations which contorted her face even more.

Daddy insisted that Catholics went in for superstitious practices. He'd be terribly upset if he found out about this present. The Fullbrideys were Nonconformists, and it was only because Aunt Rilla was Mummy's special friend and had no children of her own that she was allowed to be an honorary godmother.

'The mountain spring supplies our water,' Aunt Rilla went on, unaware of Mary's uneasiness. 'A little of it is blessed, a pinch of salt added and it is put in the stoup near the entrance of the chapel.' Her gentle eyes enveloped Mary with their warmth, made her feel loved. 'Holy water is a reminder of our baptism, and a symbol of purity. Do not use it in vain, Mary, but if you have a sincere wish, a need, dab a drop on your finger. It helps to open up a channel of communication with God. You know He will always hear a genuine prayer.' She took the child's hands in hers and squeezed them tight over the little phial. 'He may not answer you in the way you expect,' she said softly, 'but answer you He will.'

A chill of cold moved from the cylinder through Mary's fingers, coursed through her palms and up her arms. She shivered as she felt her blood cool, slow down. As soon as Aunt Rilla left her bedroom she hid the phial behind her dressing-table mirror, almost forgot it.

Then Bridget began to mope, look thin. At first Mary thought she was going to die, but then she remembered the holy water. This was her chance to try it out. She'd sprinkle some into Bridget's drinking bottle. One drop at a time, no more. There was so very little of it anyway. And she would pray for her pet to get well.

It really worked: Bridget began to look better from the very first day. And when Mary went down to see her before school she was completely cured, all cuddly as she used to be and almost twice the size she had been the month before.

Now, back from school, Mary looked forward to playing with her. She skipped through the open french windows of the living room and brandished her school boater in happy greeting. But Mummy was on the telephone, busy counselling one of her clients. Mary could tell from the way her mother flicked a carefully manicured hand over her neat blouse and skirt to indicate she was to change, then waved her dismissively away. The young girl raced upstairs, she slipped thankfully out of the high-necked cotton blouse and straight linen skirt that distinguished Highgate Ladies' pupils from the contemporary world, and changed into T-shirt and jeans. She could hardly wait to be with Bridget and tell her about the school disco Miss Johnson had announced.

The sultry May afternoon was black with thunderclouds dulling the daylight. Lighthearted, Mary ran down the long garden path, free to do as she pleased until dinner. She'd tell Bridget the good news about the party before she told either of her parents. Bridget would understand how wonderful it was going to be.

3

The phial, almost empty now, was in the pocket of her jeans so that Mummy wouldn't see it. Just one more drop, just to make sure that her pet really was herself again and stayed that way.

Mary suddenly stood still, half-way towards the big oak, and listened hard. Why was everything so quiet, so eerie? Why couldn't she see Bridget hopping towards her the way she always did? A spark of sunlight, finding a chink in the suffocating banks of cloud, winked conspiratorially at Mary, glinted into her eyes, lulled her into pleasurable expectation. She could already feel the welcoming twitch of Bridget's soft pink nose, the silky nibble as she searched for the greens Mary always brought.

'A rabbit? You want to have a *rabbit* for a pet?' Daddy had demanded at the shop, an exaggerated look of amazement twisting dark eyebrows upwards. His pink scalp gleamed through thinning hair which thickened sideways into pepper and salt, making puffed sails above his ears. Devil's wings, Mary had thought, his eyebrows little dark horns meeting over the long, thin nose as he frowned distaste.

'Such a good choice,' Aunt Rilla had put in quickly, soothingly. 'How clever of Mary to think of a pet which won't affect her mother's asthma.' Her godmother had smiled disarmingly at Daddy.

'I suppose there's that,' Daddy, nostrils widened, had agreed. 'Just the one, remember. I said you could have one pet and no more.'

'Yes, Daddy.'

'Yes, what?'

'Yes, thank you, Daddy.'

Mary shrugged off the memory and moved on, opened the gate to the rabbit enclosure and walked through. A streak of lightning lit up the ancient oak, showing branches densed black with birds. The sudden flurry of wings made her duck. A flock of starlings, fooled into early roosting by leaden skies, now thronged massed bodies into writhing ribbons. They changed shape as though programmed. Two overshadowing flaps, a giant vampire about to pounce, plunged a cold stab of terror into Mary as she bolted towards Bridget's hutch at the far end. She slackened into relief as she saw it had not been struck. Thunder roared and the clouds streamed an intense summer rain. Only the lush oakleaf umbrella kept Mary from getting drenched.

A cold wind began to stir. Mary's hazel eyes glowed gold as they searched eagerly within the wire mesh partition. No sign of the fluffy body, no sound of hind legs thumping a greeting. Bridget must have scuttled into the night compartment. Mary opened that side of the hutch and peered into the gloom.

At first she could see nothing: no fuzz of long angora hair, no movement. The eager anticipation of a few minutes before gave way to dread as her eyes adjusted to the murky light. Bridget was there – but hunched away, pricked ears alert to danger. Mary reached her hand inside, feeling for the downy body, wanting to fondle her pet. Anxious fingers felt tufts of matted fur separated from the doe. Was she unwell again, in spite of the holy water? Skin clammy with foreboding, Mary searched the dark, felt her fingertips brush over warm, naked skin. She recoiled as though stung.

'What's wrong, Bridget? Look what I've brought you.' Mary put her hand inside the hutch again to offer the carrot-tops she stored above it. The rabbit did not come over to her and Mary's heart teetered with fear. Exploring further she put her whole arm inside. Her

5

bare skin was scratched by hay, then brushed against small, warm, throbbing, hairless bumps. Had Bridget caught the dreaded myxomatosis? She couldn't have done; she'd been vaccinated.

There was a sudden pounding as the rabbit hopped in agitation. Mary could just see a separate body moving by the soft fur. A mouse? A shrew? Had something dangerous got in with her pet?

A predator would have scurried away, not moved towards the rabbit. Bridget was being protective, keeping her body between Mary and the moving, pulsating mass. A tiny, mewling sound flooded back memories of her best friend Kate's pedigree Orange Rex doe and her new babies. A litter – Bridget had had kittens! The soft, round, naked balls were baby rabbits which Bridget was shielding from the outside world.

A thrill overwhelmed the fourteen-year-old. Daddy had decreed only one pet, and Bridget had fooled him, had produced a brood and fuddled rigid rules. Mary gurgled sweet nothings at the angora. Eyes grown accustomed to the blur made out three baby rabbits. Bridget huffed long hairs over them to warm them. The little ones moved their blind heads, eager mouths seeking their mother's teats.

Mary drew away, laid the rest of the fresh carrot-tops beside the doe and softly closed both night and day doors.

She dashed headlong back into her parents' house, and paused in the hall. 'Mummy! Guess what,' she shouted her delight. 'Bridget's had babies. Three of them!'

Anne Fullbridey's controlled, made-up face appeared at the dining room door, a damask tablecloth in her hand. 'What *are* you shrieking about, Mary? You know she can't have young; she hasn't been mated.' The smooth forehead darted anxiously towards her daughter and creased into frown lines.

'But she has, Mummy. Honestly!' Mary rushed at her, her feet twirling pirouettes on the polished floor. 'Just come and see.' Her eyes shone joy. 'It's like a miracle.'

'You know I'm in the middle of laying the table,' Anne began, when a familiar figure, taller than Anne, dark, emerged from behind her and walked towards Mary with her arms outstretched.

'Hello there, Goddaughter,' Gabriela said softly. 'Such a big surprise.' Her strong German accent emphasised the last word.

'Aunt Rilla,' Mary enthused, running up and hugging her, kissing her on both cheeks. 'I didn't know you were here already. Come down and see. Bridget's had babies.'

'I will investigate.' Gabriela smiled at Anne. 'You finish the preparations and I try to sort out what is going on.'

'You are a dear.' Anne flirted her elaborately negligent hair upwards with pink-nailed fingertips and drifted away. 'Mary's so crazy about that rabbit she'd make more appear out of thin air.'

The rain had stopped, the sky still overcast, a few shafts of evening sunlight glistening through. 'Look, Mary.' Gabriela pointed to the sky. A double rainbow arched above the oak's glistening leaves. 'The colours always show up so brilliantly against the grey.' She took Mary's hand and swung it as they walked. 'You must have a magic rabbit which lives at the rainbow's end,' she teased as she and Mary tripped towards the hutch.

7

Gabriela unfastened the door of the day compartment. The inside, still dim in spite of slanting evening sun, showed a trough of hay, a water bottle, a mineral lick and a good straw cover on the floor – but no Bridget. Their heads craned towards the opening to the night compartment at the side. The doe came forward and pressed furry beige against the opening, intent on blocking their view.

'She's got a nest at the back; bits of her fur all matted up,' Mary squeaked.

'Shh, Mary. Keep your voice very low and calm. If we frighten her, she might cull her babies.'

'Cull? You mean . . .'

'She might kill them,' Gabriela whispered. 'Out of fear. I'll open the door and you hold her. Be careful. Just stroke her gently, the way you always do.'

'I'd better shut the gate, in case I let go of her.'

'That is a good idea,' Gabriela murmured, and waited.

'All set.' Mary used both hands to draw Bridget out and cradled the rabbit to herself while Gabriela peered into the back.

'I won't touch them, Mary. Bridget might not like that. But you are quite right. She has had – what do you call rabbit babies in English?'

'Kittens,' Mary whispered. 'Kate Brenman says they're called kittens.'

'Bridget has had kittens. More than three. I think I can see four young ones altogether.'

'I knew I couldn't have got it wrong!'

The brisk snap of the enclosure gate opening made them jump. Bridget's strong claws dug into Mary's shoulder as Thomas Fullbridey, his glasses glinting back what light there was, strode up to them.

8

'What's all this nonsense?' his strong voice barked.

Mary clutched her pet tight, fluttered kisses on her long ears, murmured endearments. She turned towards her father. 'Please, Daddy. Keep your voice low. You'll frighten her,' she breathed. 'Look. Isn't it wonderful? Bridget's had four babies.'

'Produced a litter? Can't have. Allbrights assured me the animal's never been mated.' Thomas did not lower his voice. 'She'll have to go straight back.' Cold, loud, condemning.

'But Daddy . . .'

His hard, determined lips pressed tight, taut hands flipping grass cuttings from his trousers. 'It really is absurd. They gave me a firm assurance that she had not been near a buck. It even says so on her pedigree.'

'Rabbits reach sexual maturity at a very early age.' Gabriela walked up, put a calming hand on the doe in Mary's arms. 'As soon as three months, you know. Perhaps they did not realise . . .'

'Presumably Allbrights are privy to that piece of essential information,' Thomas exploded as Bridget lurched in Mary's arms. 'At any rate, that's their problem.' He turned to his daughter. 'I said *one* pet. Have you been letting her exercise with Kate's animals?'

'No, Daddy. How could I? Bridget's much too heavy for me to carry her all the way to Kate's.'

'That place is more like a warren than a house,' Thomas said sourly. 'Did Kate bring a rabbit over here, by any chance?'

'She showed me one of her Orange Rex kittens,' Mary said reluctantly. 'Only three weeks old, so tiny he fitted into her pocket. He'd just opened his eyes.'

'A buck? And he was with the doe?'

9

'No, Daddy, honestly. We showed him to Bridget through the wire, that's all. And he was just a baby.'

Thomas had stalked over to the hutch and was staring inside it. 'Breed like rabbits is right.' Voice hoarse with suppressed anger, he turned again to his daughter. 'But they can't breed without a male.'

'Actually,' Gabriela said reflectively, 'that isn't necessarily so, Thomas. Rabbits are almost always on heat. Given the correct stimulus, they can conceive.'

'Does that mean there's something wrong with Bridget?' Mary asked, her eyes clamped on her godmother. 'She's going to die?'

'No, Mary. Bridget and her babies will be fine.'

'That's utter nonsense, Gabriela.' Thomas's brusque snarl of dismissal brought a restraining hand from Gabriela and a retreat from Mary, who felt the sharp edge of his voice sear through her.

'Softly, Thomas. You'll make the doe cannibalistic.'

He brushed Gabriela's hand away. 'Asexual reproduction doesn't apply to mammals,' he grumbled, softening his voice a little. 'Only to the lower life forms.' An irritated look took in the enclosure, the rabbit, the hutch, finishing on Mary. 'And a few insects.'

'Not always, Thomas–' Gabriela began.

'In any case, they're going back to Allbrights in the morning,' he announced, voice rising again. 'And that is final. Now come back to the house at once, Mary. Your mother's about to serve dinner and you're still in jeans.' He darted a final look of disgust at the rabbit hutch, turned on his heel and strode away.

Mary's slight shoulders stooped as her tears began to fall. Gabriela gently detached Bridget from her, replaced her in the hutch and locked the door. She put comforting arms round Mary's shoulders and

10

hugged her. 'We'll see what we can do,' she whispered, using her right hand to brush back the long, honey-blonde hair and offering a handkerchief. 'Come along now.'

'They're going to kill them,' Mary sobbed. 'They're going to kill Bridget's babies.'

'I'll see they don't,' Gabriela promised, cuddling her. 'Even if I have to take Bridget and her kittens over myself.'

'You'd do that?' Mary looked up through her tears. 'You'd really do that, Aunt Rilla? You'd let her keep her babies?'

'Of course I would, Mary. Bridget is a beautiful rabbit, and she has done nothing wrong. I shall be delighted to offer her and her little family a home.' Gabriela cupped Mary's face in her hands. 'And you can come and see them whenever you like.' She smiled. 'I'll give you a copy of our house key so you can visit her any time. After all, we're only a few hundred yards along the road.'

Mary's eyes shone their gratitude. 'Thank you, Aunt Rilla,' she gulped. She twisted her body, sprinted away, unaware of Gabriela's gaze following her, of the yearning in the dark eyes.

Bursting into the living room, the child grasped her father's arm. 'It's all right, Daddy. Don't ring the pet shop. Bridget doesn't have to go back. Aunt Rilla is going to look after her.'

Thomas turned slowly from the drinks cabinet and watched as Gabriela puffed into the room. 'You really want to take that animal on?'

'And her little brood.' Gabriela gasped, out of breath trying to keep up with Mary, glowing at the sight of the beaming face.

11

'Ready for a drink?' Thomas asked gruffly. 'I think you could use a stiff one, by the look of you.'

Gabriela nodded, the jet pageboy swinging forward on her flushed face.

'I know how to do it, Daddy. Aunt Rilla likes rum and Coke.'

'Mary and I can share the Coke.' Gabriela's eyes, almond-shaped, slanted very slightly above high cheekbones, their brown irises soft and melting at her goddaughter. 'We can drink to the health of the new mother and her children,' she announced gaily.

'Then you are in luck. I have brought just the thing,' a baritone thick with German intonations announced.

'Liebling, you were here already and I didn't even see you!' Gabriela went over to her husband and embraced him.

'He was about to prise you loose from the wretched rabbits,' Anne said, bringing in cheese straws. 'He was afraid you'd never leave even rabbit babies for something as boring as our company.'

Thomas poured a thick, pale-coloured liquid into a glass and handed it to Mary. 'Drink up, then change.' He turned to her godmother. 'You know we don't allow the child to have cola drinks, Gabriela. Freshly made juice is so much healthier for her. This is our very own brew.'

'The bubbly isn't chilled,' Michael Adler said, flourishing a bottle of Veuve Clicquot, 'but I have just finished my Lebanon assignment. I shall spend a whole week at home, so I thought we should celebrate.'

Gabriela grinned. 'I think we can wait a short time for it to cool. A chance for you to get used to the idea, Liebling. We are about to take on a whole family. It is an important step. Celebration is quite in order.'

2

Mary leant against the marble of the Adam fireplace, trying to cool her overheated body. She felt elated, savouring the sensation of being part of the real world at last. Slight, ethereal, the normally smooth alabaster of her skin shone damp and flushed, hazel eyes limpid, pools of enjoyment.

This was her first disco, her initiation into the fun, bright lights and loud music her parents frowned on. To her surprise they had given their consent for her to go – perhaps it was to make up for banning Bridget and her babies from their home.

What astonished her even more was that it was all happening at Highgate Ladies. The moment Miss Johnson had announced the disco to celebrate the school's fiftieth anniversary, an acute awareness had triggered in Mary's mind. There was a click, a knowing that this was her first chance to leave childhood behind. This evening would be the turning point. The disco was bound to be quite different from the birthday parties her mother had always given for her, which were never entirely for friends of Mary's age.

'Just encourages them to nonsense,' Anne was fond of declaiming. 'A mix of ages is good for everyone.'

'For you girls only,' the headmistress's voice had

boomed into Mary's consciousness only two weeks ago. 'And I expect you to be properly turned out. Dresses or skirts, no boots or stiletto heels.' Resonant, clipped, Miss Johnson always made sure no one could fail to hear her. 'This is a young ladies' establishment,' she had reminded them, emphasising the words severely by stomping her stick on the platform.

'As though we could forget,' Kate Brenman, standing next to Mary, had whispered.

'We all know that girls suffer from competition with boys at puberty,' Miss Johnson had continued. 'Your parents send you here to avoid too much involvement with the opposite sex at this delicate stage of your development.' She had tossed a cashmere shawl over her shoulder, hiding evidence of the dowager's hump which spoiled her upright stance.

A titter had run through the hall at the mention of the word sex. Mary had felt a quiver of excitement, had sensed the swifter flow of blood in her young limbs. Kate had grinned and nudged her. The friendly brush of Kate's bare leg against her own had made Mary tingle with expectations of pleasures she was, as yet, entirely unconscious of.

'You may invite suitable guests: younger sisters, cousins, that sort of thing. No brothers or other boys. And you may play dance music. We'll take up the rugs and let you enjoy the Regency heritage.' The headmistress had pointed her stick towards the magnificent floor of the huge entrance hall stretching away from her, past the ornate fireplace and on to the sweeping staircase leading to her study on the mezzanine above.

A soft murmur had begun to trickle forwards from the back, an eddy of heads bending towards each other. The stick had thumped down hard as Miss Johnson had

made herself clear. 'Saturday, 12 June, between seven and eleven.' A twist of the thin lips showed she was about to make a joke. 'In the evening. Make sure those times are kept to.'

'Well, there's a thing then,' Kate had said. 'Fancy old Johnny coming round to that.'

'I won't be able to go,' Mary had wailed, eyes starting to fill. She had been sure Daddy would stop her. He'd dream up something: the car was being serviced so he couldn't drive her, someone had to stay in to answer the phone, Mummy had a headache and needed Mary there.

'Why ever not?'

'I don't know how to disco,' she'd evaded the issue.

'Course you do!' Kate had spun her round, showed her how to wiggle her hips. 'Comes naturally. We'll work out a couple of fancy twirls when you come to the house.' Kate's older brothers always practised with her to the latest hits.

That evening Mary had sprinkled the rest of the holy water on her hair and prayed to be allowed to go. And the magic had worked again, just as it had for Bridget. Except that her pet wasn't with *her* any more, but with Aunt Rilla.

The longed-for day was here. The party was in full swing. Madonna, the singer on the tape, voiced pulsating lyrics telling of love – of frankly sexual love. The enticing, captivating huskiness had seduced Mary's body into movements, gyrations, whose very existence she had never been aware of before. Deep, vocal calls had fired through her developing figure so that she twisted, instinctively, into the sinuous, rhythmic vibrations of a dance she had no idea she was capable of carrying out. The feeling of elation, of a throbbing

sensation creeping upwards between her thighs, of her bosom swelling, tightened her throat with anticipations of delight. It seemed to fire her body until she felt it was hot enough to scorch whatever it touched.

She danced primarily with Kate; she was, after all, her best friend. And Kate – skilled, confident Kate – was careful to include the two of them with other groups of dancers, pushing her this way and that, showing off what to do and when to do it. Mary was surprised at the intensity of Kate's dancing, at the tempestuous response to the beat of the music.

Both girls loved music, enjoyed blending their voices, singing in the school choir where Kate's deep contralto contrasted well with Mary's fluting soprano. But this was different. This music, basic, raw, pulsated to the rhythm of life: life in the present, which was not in the least like the time-tested, refined cadence of classical music. Here was all the overpowering, thumping discordance of sounds still immature, still unexpected. Not that Mary was unappreciative of the past. It was simply that this was her first taste of the excitement of the untried, the new, the unexplored. She relished it.

'I'm getting really thirsty. And so are you, judging by that red face,' Kate said, playfully pushing Mary towards the side.

Mary teetered precariously, then smiled agreement and was about to head for the juice bar stacked with junk fizzies.

'I'll get the drinks,' Kate said, manoeuvring Mary towards the fireplace at the far end of the hall. 'You seem a bit hot and overdone. Better cool off. Coke OK? Or are you going to stick to orange juice?'

'Coke.' Mary giggled, reeling against the mantelpiece, appreciating the cold marble against her hot

flesh. 'A really large glass of Coke. With loads of ice.'

She watched Kate go. Her tall, slim figure was sleekly sinuous in heavy satin, the fuchsia antique nightdress topped by a long-sleeved, tied lace blouse. She looked wonderful. Kate hobbled her platforms away, then scudded expertly between the wheeling dancers to reach the long table laden with drinks. She shimmied with whirling friends while she snaked towards the hi-fi and turned up the sound.

Mary began to beat her foot in time to the throbbing music, began to hum, thought about imitating the singer. A few notes emerged, then she realised she did not know the tune well enough to carry on and self-consciousness took over. Dreamily she thought about Miss Turner, and what she'd said.

The shy student teacher had praised her voice, had told her to treasure it, to make something of it. 'Don't count out pop,' she'd said. 'That's music too.' Jilly Turner had not succeeded in helping Mary develop her voice to any great extent, but she had made her feel joyful about her talent, had urged her to find a teacher qualified in voice.

Thomas Fullbridey would not tolerate any such suggestion. 'You're at an excellent school,' he'd preached at Mary severely. 'Highgate Ladies is one of the top girls' independent schools. How could you possibly need more than they are able to supply?'

Mary closed her eyes to blot out the memory of her father. As she stretched tall, enjoying so many sensations new to her, her mouth curved upwards. She felt a cool breeze caress her, pushed languid, sweltering arms behind her ears, held soft, honey-blonde locks away from her neck, leant further back against the marble and arched her back.

17

The breeze turned into a cold, harsh eddy of alien air, a draught that swirled unexpectedly towards her and lifted up the translucent chiffon of her dress. Mummy, coming into her bedroom as she was dressing, had insisted she wore a slip and bra. Kate had laughed at that as soon as she'd arrived at school, had persuaded her to sneak to the cloakroom to take off the slip – and the pearl necklace Daddy had given her. Instead Kate had put a blue ribbon around Mary's throat, matching the cornflowers in her dress, long ends dangling, A small, tight, crochet skull-cap Kate had brought was pulled down over Mary's forehead, hair spreading out from under it.

The continuing cold alerted Mary to a fundamental change in the room, the situation. She opened her eyes, then broadened them as far as they would go. The front door stood ajar; several youths crowded on the threshold, smirking their eyes around the hall full of twirling girls, sniffing their noses into an atmosphere soaked in hormonal vapour.

A tall, assertive boy strutted in on the right – dark complexion, close-cropped hair, thick neck – and caught Mary's stare and open mouth. Mesmerised, she could not take her eyes off him, found herself locked into his gaze. He yelled something she could not understand, roughly shouldered through the dancing girls on the floor and zoomed in on her. He beckoned the other youths to follow.

The music blared on, the loud beat overpowering all other noise. But the dancing girls near the boys stood rigid. The others, now sensing intrusion, stopped too. Their heads craned in unison towards the uninvited guests, their eyes gawped at the band of youths now stalking Mary.

Kate was still standing by the hi-fi near the front door. Courageously she moved forward, put out a restraining arm. A boy jerked it away, tossing her to one side and into a pair of petrified dancers.

The other girls watched, mouths open, remaining where they were, unable to move. Their eyes riveted on the dark shapes penetrating their school, girlish features hardened into horror as the youths crashed across the hall, trampled past the staircase leading to Miss Johnson's study and crossed to the fireplace. Eight bare-armed boys, muscles rippling beyond shiny black leather, stud-booted their way over the parquet. Glints from the fire sparkled into gold ear ornaments, rings flashed like knuckle-dusters on their hands, the leader's nose-stud accentuated a determined mouth.

They stomped up to Mary, surrounded her. The dark one – yelled to as 'Ard Card' by his companions – grinned tobacco-stained teeth at the young girl now cringing against the marble, caught between the fire and the boys.

'Wanna drag?' He held out a partly-smoked cigarette.

Mary tried, unsuccessfully, to melt further into the side of the fireplace. She dropped her eyes.

'Drink?' Ard Card persisted, jerking off the crochet cap.

Mary's head dropped lower, her hair, free-flowing for the party, covering her face in mute uncooperation.

'Bugger you!' Ard Card pulled the ribbon ends, forcing Mary's hands up to guard her throat.

'Yer means . . .' one of the other thugs immediately took up, cackling.

Ard Card turned towards him, grinned. 'One way to get somethink in on 'er.'

He turned back to Mary and grabbed a handful of her

19

hair, pulled it up and back, compelling her to look at him.

Mary's unfocused eyes met dark, intense ones. Their penetrating stare signalled the boy's intention, their hardness mirrored the hardness of his hands and body.

With a throb of anger at this violation, a spark of fury, Mary twisted her body away, then felt herself dragged back again by her hair. 'Fuck off!' Her lips formed words she had never uttered before, hardly realised she knew.

'Atta girl!'

'Let me go!' Her hands pulled at the strong, tough hold as the other youths began to grab her arms and legs.

'You foul . . . !' A grimy hand slapped her face, clamped over her mouth. She tried to bite it, could only grasp at the leather, wrenching her teeth.

Two more youths each grabbed an arm, another ripped off her shoes, clawed her tights down, then moved his hands up to her groin. An icy numbness crept over Mary as her flesh started to cool, to shrink away.

The other girls began to find their voices. A cacophony of screams overcame the sound of the music, pierced Mary's ears, swelled until she thought her head would burst.

There seemed to be nothing but the screeching wail of female voices, a piercing, thin, distracting sound that stabbed the air but failed to stop the tearing, searching hands, the grunting, thrusting legs. Rapacious fingers tore the flowered chiffon, stripped the clinging material from her squirming, silent body trying to slip through flailing arms and legs. Mary felt her dress leaving her body, felt the fine silk of her bra split, felt her shoulders and her breasts bared.

An exploding rat-a-bong of wood against metal rounded into a boom, and a loud, staccato voice overwhelmed the din. '*What* is going on here?'

It seemed to Mary that time crawled, almost stood still. What her brain knew to be swift movement slowed down to deliberate, unhurried action. One by one the voices of her schoolfellows fell silent, the group of youths stood still, drew apart, showed Mary a glimpse of a sea of girls beyond.

As though in unison, arms pointed towards her, accusing, menacing. Mary began to howl, to shriek, to precipitate an anguished sound she could not connect with herself.

Black-leathered bodies, bare arms, returned to the attack. Mary felt herself grasped under her armpits, shoulders propelled back, breasts displayed, only a brief pair of panties between her and complete nakedness.

A crash of hard mahogany splintering glass above her showered particles of chandelier in attack. There was a momentary lull as shrapnels of crystal cascaded down. Another clang of wood on steel reverberated through as Miss Johnson, ungainly legs clomping the stairs, used the brief quiet to advance.

The walking stick, whose last impact with the gong had forced the hush, advanced rapidly and sizzled down hard across an exposed, quivering snake of pink threatening Mary. The whoosh of displaced air sounded like a hiss. The boy screamed agony as he vaulted back.

A black shape emerged from Miss Johnson's other hand. Mary's mind conjured up a gun, then realised the portable phone in her headmistress's hand had found voice.

A murderous howl of redoubled anguish ricocheted against the cold marble, the wooden slats of floor, re-echoed from columns to plastered ceiling, as the wounded youth felt his pain.

'Emergency services; which—'

'Police!' Miss Johnson yelled at the mouthpiece.

The phone spluttered: '. . . address?'

'38 Flinsgate Road, Highgate. Attempted rape!'

'A squad car is on its way,' the voice replied, calm, in charge. 'With you in two minutes.'

Ard Card, his hand still on Mary's pants pulling them down, turned round as he let go. 'Scarper!' he bellowed out. 'She's got the frigging fuzz.'

A bevy of teachers now stampeded down the stairs and into the hall. Chairs were used as weapons as they began to assault the retreating boys.

Miss Johnson, her stick abandoned, was approaching Mary, a dark, wide shape held out ahead of her.

'No. Noooo!' Mary cried out, flinching back, sobs shaking her as she pulled her hair around herself.

'All right now, Mary. They've gone, I'm only trying to cover you.'

A sudden movement as the terrified girl ducked under Miss Johnson's arm and ran for the open door.

Another teacher sprinted ahead of her and blocked her exit. Younger, spryer than Miss Johnson, Miss Turner took the cashmere shawl and wrapped it round the shivering girl. Mary was weeping now, unable to stop the convulsions of her shoulders, the shaking of her whole body.

But there was no sound; the young girl was weeping silently. Thudding noises filled her ears, coursing blood needled through her eyes. And through it all she could hear the clipped, distinctive tones of her headmistress.

'I expect you to come right away, Dr Harrison.'

A blurred, crackling sound. Each tiny crack seemed

to vibrate, to infiltrate Mary's body, her very being.

'This *is* an emergency. The girl is terrified . . .'

Mary could hear the voice at the other end clearly, a man's voice. A deep, rumbling voice whose intonations cut through her as though they were made of sharpened steel.

'Just keep her warm; nothing to worry about. I'll be there right away.' A cough. 'Better inform the parents,' the voice went on, low and trenchant.

Mary shuddered, convulsed into the filmy shawl as she realised Miss Turner was pulling the heavy front door shut, bolting the stable door. Almost immediately there was a loud rapping.

'Police.'

Mary's heart lurched as Miss Johnson put the chain on the door, then opened it an inch or two.

A uniformed arm pushed through identification as Mary lost consciousness.

3

Mary, in that limbo between sleeping and waking, became aware of feeling numb. A hard, inflexible surface under her made her body ache. The lids of her eyes seemed glued together. She gave up the effort of lifting them and tried to work out why she was lying on something so unyielding. As consciousness came to the surface of her mind, she realised she was not on her bed, not even in her home. Some protective instinct warned her to keep her eyes shut and to listen to what was going on around her.

Almost at once awareness blasted into her brain: she was not alone. The buzz of several people talking lapped over her, propelled fear into her mind, tightened her muscles and made her hold her breath. She tensed herself still.

She made out her father's voice: dominating, reverberating, angry tones kept under tight control. 'There was *no one* with Mary?' Thomas Fullbridey demanded.

'All the other girls were with her,' she recognised Miss Johnson, courteous, steely, pointing out. 'Her fellow students and their guests. I would hardly describe that as no one with her.'

'Other girls.' The heavy, wounded tone Daddy always used when she had dared to go against even his smallest wish. 'Other *children*; you are saying I entrusted my daughter not to you, or to your staff, but to a bunch of young people gathered together for a party which, I had been given to understand, was going to be strictly supervised?'

'I accept that they were in my care, Mr Fullbridey. I take complete responsibility,' Miss Johnson acknowledged. 'My full complement of staff, and myself, were present in this room. It is, after all, directly by the flight of stairs which leads down to the hall.' She paused. 'We were seeing to it that the girls had a little leeway, some innocent enjoyment. This is a school, you know, not a prison. The girls must be allowed some freedom to prepare them for adult life. Naturally we looked in on them from time to time.'

Mary had finally worked out where the people she could hear talking must be: assembled in Miss Johnson's study. Gathered, no doubt, around the twin-pedestal writing-desk which was her pride and joy.

Cautiously she tried opening her eyes. Still gluey, they finally responded. She saw she was lying on the elegant chaise-longue, its solid contours digging into her. What had she done? She shut her eyes again to try to figure out what had been happening.

'They feel inhibited if the staff watch as they dance,' Miss Turner's piping voice agreed with Miss Johnson. A beat of pulsing music insinuated itself into Mary's mind, and she remembered. Disco dancing; they had been disco dancing . . .

'And that is paramount, is it? What the girls feel?' Anne Fullbridey's angry voice this time.

So both her parents were here and they sounded equally outraged, distressed. It must be serious.

'It does seem to me,' a male voice Mary did not

25

recognise intruded into the conversation, 'that apportioning blame is not going to solve the real problems we need to address here. A young, sheltered girl has been assaulted. She is evidently traumatised to some degree. I've given her a mild sedative, but she's likely to come round quite soon. Let's concentrate on her well-being.'

That sounded like a doctor. Sedated? She'd been sedated? That would explain her lying prone. But why? What could have happened? Mary's eyes, open wide at last, fluttered around the beautiful room. The familiar surroundings brought back memories of the last time she had been in here, especially summoned to attend. A sunny morning, a beaming headmistress who had waved her to a seat.

'Miss Turner tells me your singing lessons are going very well, Mary. She feels you have a quite exceptional voice, and that she has come to the end of the help she can give you. Are you interested in developing your gift professionally, my dear?'

Mary had admired the elegant room, its huge casement windows open wide and leading to the balcony overlooking the garden at the back. 'I'm not quite sure,' she'd murmured, unable to adjust to the unexpected question.

'It is very hard work,' Miss Johnson had continued smoothly. 'No doubt you're aware of that. You would have to study music from an academic point of view.' The headmistress had actually walked round her desk and placed an encouraging hand on her shoulder. 'And you'd have to learn to sing in German, Italian, French. It's a very tough career. Do you think you'd be interested in such a possibility, Mary?'

This room was Miss Johnson's throne-room. It was

from here she reigned. And from here, Mary remembered suddenly, that she had emerged clumping from mezzanine to ground floor, thumping her stick, insisting on knowing what was going on.

Going on at the party, the disco . . . What *had* been going on? The chiffon dress; had Miss Johnson noticed that she'd taken off her slip and considered it unseemly? Was she about to be expelled?

Mary lowered her lids again and allowed the flow of conversation to mull around her. She picked out stray phrases, sensed memory spearing through a clearing mind, tried to stop the pain of recollection washing over her. The images, so violent, so unbelievable, she pushed below her consciousness as soon as they tried to surface. What she did note was that she was dressed in her tennis outfit topped with the warm school jumper, a rug pulled over her legs, something soft under her head.

A throb stirred through her forehead and reached back into her skull. She breathed deeply, trying to calm herself before she allowed the people around her to realise she was awake. As she lay back listening, feeling apart, she felt divorced from the girl she remembered herself to have been, felt stripped of her previous identity, naked, fragile and vulnerable. It was as though she had been propelled into a different world, a new existence.

Persistent images returned. She remembered Miss Johnson – decrepit, limping Miss Johnson – tramping down the wide marble staircase to rescue her. Miss Johnson had saved her, had been the one who had wielded the stick normally proclaiming her infirmity, and used it as a weapon. She had braved the gatecrashers, smashed her beloved chandelier and so rained broken glass on the coarse youths who were tormenting

Mary. How could her father scold Miss Johnson? Why wasn't he thanking her?

'We take considerable precautions, as you know, to keep the girls quite safe. There were no alcoholic drinks, no drugs. I did not allow any young men – not even the girls' brothers – to attend the party. Perhaps it would have been better if I had. And the front door was locked.' Miss Johnson tapped her stick against the Aubusson. It made a muted, muffled noise. 'The police tell me a plastic strip was used to slip the lock. I'd no idea we were so easily assailable.'

'It's standard practice.' Thomas Fullbridey's cold voice.

Mary opened her eyes, sat up, allowed the cushion behind her head to fall to the floor.

'How are you feeling now, Mary?' The doctor's voice, low and male, projected towards her as he strode over. The decisive, masculine gait, the assertive look in his eyes, the hairy hands – it seemed to Mary that she was about to choke. She put her own hand up to her throat – the ribbon was still there. She tried to tear it off, cringed away, could not produce a response from her vocal chords. There was no sound at all. They simply did not function. She put shielding arms in front of her, eyes pleading, waving him away.

He stopped. 'Are you in pain?'

Mary shook her head, made no sound. Tears began to fall. Slowly at first, then the trickle turned into a steady stream.

'Something we can get you? A hot drink?'

Once more the shaking of the head.

The doctor turned to Miss Johnson. 'Are there normally these problems? Is she particularly highly strung?'

28

'Mary is not hysterical, Dr Harrison. And she isn't deaf. She has had a horrific, grotesque experience. It may take a little time for her to come to terms with it.'

'But nothing actually happened,' the doctor said irritably.

Mary looked over to see the headmistress turn and smile briefly at her. 'Is there anything you'd like to say, Mary? Anything you would like us to do?'

Mary pointed to her throat.

Miss Johnson walked over, sat down beside her and unwound the ribbon, slid it away. 'I think she's telling us she cannot find her voice,' she explained. 'I think what Mary needs now; most of all, is her own bed. And rest. We can discuss the whys and wherefores some other time.'

'You can't dismiss everything as easily as that, Miss Johnson. We shall seriously have to consider removing Mary from the school,' Thomas intoned.

'That is your privilege.'

Why was Daddy arguing with Miss Johnson instead of coming to sit by his little girl? Why wasn't Mummy holding her, hugging her? She was their daughter, their only child.

'When you rang us up you told us nothing very terrible had happened, that Dr Harrison had sedated Mary because she was upset. It seems to me there's more to it than that. She cannot speak,' he continued, more threatening now. 'She hasn't said anything at all.' He stared at his daughter across the room.

Nothing terrible? Mary could not remember precisely what had happened, but it had been horrific. Rough boys, black leather clothes, studded boots . . .

'Nothing to worry about,' Dr Harrison tried to reassure Thomas. 'A hysterical reaction – in the medical sense – to perceived trauma. She'll have forgotten it all by tomorrow morning.'

The doctor's tone implied that she was making a fuss about nothing. She shivered, and Miss Johnson pulled the rug from her legs up around her shoulders, patting her.

Violent scenes were coming back. Strange boys had crowded round her, grabbed her, pulled at her clothes. Her pretty dress, the new dress Kate had helped Mummy and her choose, had been torn, ripped from her body in full view of her schoolfellows and the gatecrashers. She gagged.

'Make sure she's kept warm.' Dr Harrison turned to Anne Fullbridey. 'She's obviously in shock.' He took out his prescription pad and wrote rapidly. 'It's just a passing phase. Let her have one of these if she's still disturbed tomorrow.'

'It is two hours since the incident. Not exactly a passing phase,' Thomas pointed out.

'If you will just allow Mary to rest, Mr Fullbridey, I'm sure everything will be back to normal very soon,' Miss Johnson tried to soothe him.

'I can only hope you're right.'

Mary saw him turn and watch them both as her mother came over to help her stand. She shivered as the rug slid off her shoulders, leaving her in only the T-shirt and shorts overlapped by the school jumper. Mummy, her arm around her waist, pulled her towards the door. The tennis shoes squeaked unpleasantly across the uncarpeted section of the floor.

'And, in particular, I hope her singing voice has not been affected. I would certainly have to take action about that.' Thomas walked towards his family and extended an arm for Mary to hold on to.

Supported now on both sides by her parents, Mary walked down the beautiful staircase, out of the heavy front door. She left the school without looking back.

4

St Paul's Cathedral was crowded. The Vienna Boys Choir was a favourite of Mary's, and she had been thrilled when Aunt Rilla had invited her to a concert there.

'So good of you to spend so much of your time with Mary,' Mummy had greeted Aunt Rilla earlier that day. 'I don't know what we would have done without your help.'

'How are you feeling, Mary?' Aunt Rilla's hopeful question had brought back the infuriating fact that she still could not speak. A tear had trembled in her left eye, caught on the lashes, dropped down. She'd fumbled unhappily for a Kleenex. 'You're still so upset?'

Not upset, exactly. Frustrated that she could not even control her body, could not use the voice which, she'd been told, was such a special gift.

'It's really worrying us, Rilla. She still hasn't spoken a single word since that dreadful night. And that was nearly three weeks ago.' Mummy had smiled that swift, nervous smile of hers and turned away. 'Nothing, not even good night or good morning. Not a single syllable. Thomas keeps saying she's being wilful,' Mummy had said, frowning. 'But I know the problem goes much deeper than that. Mary is a quiet girl, but this is different.'

'Why don't we try to talk about it?' Aunt Rilla had perched herself opposite Mary on the window seat and prompted her with a smile.

Her head raised to look at her godmother, she'd merely shaken it and allowed her gaze to drift back to the roses colouring the garden.

'I have a surprise for you,' Aunt Rilla's voice had been full of empathy. 'I told you the Vienna Sängerknaben are over on a tour. Well, there's a concert at St Paul's tonight. Tickets are almost impossible to come by, but Michael knows one of the boys' fathers. He was able to get three excellent seats. Would you like to join us?'

Mary, now sitting between the Adlers in the beautiful old cathedral, began to feel safe, cossetted. A glow of comfort, of well-being, spread through her as the organ music swelled into the domed ceiling. Then the combination of soaring trebles coursed through her, reminded her of her own voice, of her own joy at using it. She shook as she realised the enormity of what had happened to her. A vital part of her had been silenced since that terrible night.

She strained her ears and allowed the glorious sounds to permeate her mind, her soul, felt her spirits lift, felt herself moved to use her vocal cords, impelled to push air across them, twang them into expression. Her throat muscles tensed, bunched, then softened and gave way. A welling, tickling feeling gave Mary hope that she would be able to make a sound, that this beautiful music would turn out to be the key.

She was supposed to be a singer, after all. During the last song the audience would, she knew, be invited to join in with the choir. Let that be when my voice comes back to me, she prayed. Here, in this sublime setting, with Aunt Rilla and Uncle Michael on either side.

The moment came, the audience rose and Mary rose with them, her mouth open, eager to join in. A sudden, unexpected explosion rasped a grating sound which contrasted hideously with her companions' melodious singing. Impulsively they hugged her tight, sang out loud to drown any imperfections. Mary's eyes shut with frustration and shame.

'So your voice came back, just like that!' Gabriela thrilled at Mary as soon as they were outside the cathedral.

No further sound came out of Mary's throat. They watched as it constricted just the way it had done before. Gabriela turned, trying to hide the pain in her eyes, the moistness. Even Michael's sympathetic gaze had trouble watching Mary's efforts.

'Try to sing again, Mary,' Gabriela whispered.

Mary opened and shut her mouth, swallowed saliva, gulped, tried again. There was nothing, not even a rasp.

'Let's all sing together,' Michael suggested, beginning with the first bars of the chorus of 'Edelweiss'. Gabriela joined in as they walked towards the place where their car was parked, singing in unison with her husband.

And Mary walked silently between them. Slowly the Adlers' joyful singing faded away. They began to chat amiably across Mary, tried to draw her in, found only pressure from her arms in response to yes or no.

'Let's have an ice cream,' Michael suggested. 'It lubricates the throat and won't spoil the dinner your mother's getting ready for us.'

Mary held back, shook her head. They walked in silence to the car, and drove Mary home with the radio

34

blaring to cover the lack of conversation.

'What Mary needs is a complete change of scene,' Michael boomed around the Fullbridey dinner table. 'My editor is sending me on a new assignment in the Middle East tomorrow. I shall be away a whole month, so Gabriela is going to spend a couple of weeks with her mother in Austria. Why not let Mary go with her?'

Mary's head shot up and her eyes grew round, intense. She focused on her mother, whose lips compressed into a tight line as her eyes flinted at her husband. He, in turn, appeared distant, aloof.

Michael glanced at his wife, and shrugged.

'Perhaps you are worried about who will look after Bridget,' Gabriela suggested, smiling at Mary. 'There is no need. Our neighbour has offered to look after her – she'll feed her twice a day, and exercise her. And I've found homes for each of the babies, so they won't be a problem.' She grinned enthusiastically. 'It's quite extraordinary: the kittens have almost exactly the same markings as Bridget, and they're all does, so there was real competition for them.'

'Ah, yes.' Michael grinned. 'I forgot about the rabbit family. But not my Rilla; she would never forget such an important detail.' He laughed, and put a hand over his wife's. 'So she will have the chance to enjoy our beautiful Salzkammergut while I work my fingers to the bone tapping out scoops on my notebook computer.' He paused. 'Well, what do you think of the idea? A change of scene would be an excellent opportunity to help Mary forget.'

Mary's eyes glowed. Thomas, about to pour the Bordeaux, jolted red wine on to the damask tablecloth. 'Sorry,' he muttered, milling sea salt over the stain.

'It will not leave a mark if it's rinsed in cold water first,' Gabriela encouraged him.

'I'm sure you remember our telling you where Rilla's mother lives,' Michael went on, absently pouring ordinary salt on the stain.

'The eminent Erika Lager. You know that Rilla goes back every October, and this year she went at Easter, too. Her mother had a very painful attack of arthritis.'

Mary nodded, eyes shining, but there was no response from her parents.

'St Walter,' Michael went on, his voice carrying a honeyed tone. 'It's an enchanting mountain village about forty kilometres from Salzburg.'

'I remember *that*, Michael. Just didn't know what Salzkammergut meant,' Thomas explained, a pained look on his face. 'Anyway, I thought Salzburg was in the Salzburgerland.' He glowered as he started to pour the wine again.

'You are quite right. It is.' Michael smiled. 'The village is in the neighbouring province. Land of the salt chambers. Salt mines, in other words.'

'The infamous salt mines!' Thomas roared, discharging tension.

'The Romans were responsible for the abominable goings on.' Michael grinned at him. 'Nothing to do with us Austrians.' He drained the contents of his glass.

'We do know that, Michael.' Thomas looked at the empty glass. 'That Bordeaux clearly went down well, even though it's French. More?'

'Thanks. I didn't mean to preach.' He smiled, displaying even white teeth, a twinkle in his eye. The German accent which sometimes made Gabriela sound severe took on a softness when voiced in Michael's charming baritone. 'Erika – busy lady – can never be prised away from her laboratory for more than a few days, so she visits us only for long weekends.' He looked at Gabriela, his eyes full of understanding. 'Wedded to her work.'

'Laboratory? That's new to me. I thought she was a doctor.' Thomas poured more Bordeaux, this time all of it into Gabriela's glass.

'She is also a research scientist.' Gabriela sounded unsure, a slight hesitation in her voice. 'She is very gifted. In fact she started her scientific career at a very early age, helping her father with his work. She was a child prodigy, you see, even before the war. Then the Nazis took a great interest in my grandfather's work.' She looked at the Fullbrideys. 'His name was Helmut Fluge. You may have heard of him?' There was no sign that the Fullbrideys recognised the name. 'No? Anyway, after a time the Nazis insisted my grandfather continue his research in Berlin. That was in 1943, when my mother was only fifteen. They sent her, too, as his assistant.'

'So why is she hiding away in St Walter? Shouldn't she be leading some important team in a large university set-up?' Anne asked.

'She prefers to work on her own. Says she hates committee decisions. And, as both my grandfather and my father died during the war, she also had to be the breadwinner of the family. The doctoring could be combined with bringing me up. She had to do that as well after my grandmother died.'

'What area of research?' Thomas put down the wine and prepared to carve more beef. 'Well done for you, Gabriela?'

'Lovely.' Gabriela held her plate out. 'The roast beef is superb, Anne. Good English cooking can stand

37

comparison with any on the continent.'

'Genetics,' Michael explained. 'Her speciality is chromosomal mutations. She is searching for chemicals – like nucleic acids – to overcome genetically transmitted degenerative disease.'

Mary wrote a single word on the pad beside her and moved it over to Gabriela. 'Chromosome?'

'Chromosomes are chains of genes which are structures within a cell's nucleus,' Michael explained. 'They all look very similar through a microscope, but they can readily be stained with certain dyes to show up quite startling differences. This is what gave them their name. It actually means coloured bodies.'

Mary was listening intently.

'A human being has forty-six chromosomes,' Michael continued, 'arranged in corresponding pairs of twenty-three, usually at the centre of each of our cells. They are the units of inheritance, with one of each pair inherited from the mother, the other from the father.'

'We know that each of these chromosomes contains a tightly twisted molecule formed from two strands held together in a double helix. The DNA uniquely represents the genetic code for each human being.' Gabriela took over, drawing long, twirling ribbons, marking the lengths with different patterns across their width. 'Imagine these diagrams are stained representations of chromosomes. I am illustrating them with their genetic coding crudely shown by the patterns. Yes?'

Mary nodded, and wrote 'gene?' on the pad.

Gabriela smiled ruefully. 'I think I'll let Michael explain the rest of it. I am not that good academically, and I might get it wrong.'

'She has such a hang-up about that,' Michael said, a cloud over his eyes. 'Her mother's brilliance, all those stories about her as a child prodigy, have given Gabriela an inferiority complex. Totally inappropriate. My Rilla is very gifted in her own way.' He frowned. 'A gene is the basic unit of heredity, a section of chromosomal material.' He pulled the drawing towards himself and drew lines to cut the ribbons into portions. 'This one, say.' He isolated a small section by drawing thick lines on either side of it.

Gabriela smiled at Mary, passing back the pad. 'They have not taught you any of that in biology?'

Mary shook her head.

'Science teaching was not Highgate Ladies' forte, I'm afraid,' Thomas explained. 'We've been looking into several other schools.'

'To make it clearer,' Michael went on, 'a chromosome acts as a replicator, something which reproduces the sets of genes along its length.' He had turned to Mary to explain. 'What Erika Lager is trying to achieve is the understanding of specific genetic units. In that way she hopes to cut out, or insert, chromosomal material to combat genetically transmitted disease such as muscular dystrophy and cystic fibrosis. And the same method can, potentially, be used to alleviate acquired diseases; ghastly things like the HIV virus.'

'That's quite ambitious,' Anne said.

'My mother is very ambitious, there is no doubt. That is how I knew about Bridget. She stimulates asexual reproduction in mice and rabbits so that she has numbers of animals with very similar genetic coding. To test her theories on, you see.'

'Histological work?' Anne asked, getting a little edgy.

'No,' Gabriela said quickly. 'As a matter of fact all her animals are very well treated and looked after, never killed. She does not need to do histological tests, she simply examines the animals' DNA. Because she works on the cure of diseases, the animals are living proof.'

'So that's what made you think Mary's rabbit could reproduce on its own,' Thomas said irritably. 'You had the advantage of me there.' He paused. 'And does your mother consider commercial applications? Has she thought about patenting her work?'

'She isn't really interested in that,' Gabriela said. 'She never has been. She's much more concerned to have things going the way she wants in her laboratory.' she grinned. 'Last time I was there, when she couldn't get about the way she usually does, she, had to let the woman who looks after the animals, Resi Glockner, deal with her laboratory equipment. A perfectly nice village woman who has been with her for years. My mother got into quite a state, particularly about the phials. Apparently Resi got the cleaned and uncleaned ones muddled up, and it affected some of the data Mutter was putting into her computer. There was absolute hell to pay.' She laughed. 'She cares only about results; I think she's happy to leave the applications to others.'

'Lucky them,' Thomas said.

'But in spite of being so clever, a doctor *and* a research scientist, she wasn't able to help you, Rilla?'

'I'm afraid not.' Gabriela's eyes were bleak. She looked towards Anne. 'Fertility isn't her field.' The corners of her mouth drooped as she pushed the meat around her plate.

'Sorry, stupid of me to bring it up. I didn't mean to raise old ghosts.'

'No need.' Gabriela rolled her napkin in her fingers. 'The funny thing is,' she went on, her voice high but under control, 'that there *is* a connection with fertility in the village. There's a shrine in a grotto, on the mountain above my old convent in St Walter. They have a festival there, every October, called the Mothering of the Brides. Almost all the girls from the surrounding districts, the ones who married during the year before, come to the shrine and take part in a special ritual.'

'One of your masses, you mean,' Thomas dismissed it.

'There is more to it than that. They drink a few drops of the spring water which collects in a stone trough in the grotto. It's said to have some particular ingredient which makes women fertile. As well as being blessed, and therefore holy. It is from the same source that supplies the drinking water in the village, but that doesn't have the same effect.'

'And have you tried it?' Anne asked, brought out of English reticence by her curiosity. 'You've kept it very quiet if you have.'

'Of course she has,' Thomas butted in. 'That's the secret of your annual pilgrimage home every October, isn't it? Not to your mother – to the shrine.'

'Quite right. I have never mentioned it to you before because we don't like to advertise it. And also because I was sure you would consider it a popish superstition,' Gabriela added, smiling. 'In fact I have never missed a year since I was married.' She sighed.

'And are there miracles?'

'Hard to tell with the brides. But quite a few local women who didn't go as brides, and who haven't conceived in their first years of marriage, go as well. So yes, there have been some indications that women previously infertile have conceived.'

'Do they keep official records?' Thomas looked up, curious enough to ask.

Gabriela looked surprised. 'Well, yes. Reverend Mother has kept them since 1956.' A sad look veiled her eyes. 'I remember the year because it was the one after my grandmother died. She was the one who kept them until then.'

'In 1955? Really? She must have been quite young.'

'Only forty-seven. I adored her, you know. She looked after me when my mother went to medical school.'

'So what happened?'

'I was only ten, so my memories are bound to be garbled. Anyway, some dreadful infection took hold in the village. I contracted it and became very ill – unfortunately my ovaries were involved. And then my grandmother, who'd been looking after me, was also struck down with the horrible thing. She was very devout, always helped with the Oktoberfest. Well, she went up to the grotto the afternoon before the Sunday it takes place, just to check that everything was as it should be. She must have succumbed then, felt dizzy. The access is quite steep, you see. She slipped on her way back.' Gabriela stopped, breathed deep. 'Stumbled over the side of a path she knew like the back of her hand. Crashed down and couldn't stop. Dead when they got to her.'

'Oh, Rilla. How awful,' Anne said.

Mary had put her hand across the table and placed it over Gabriela's, her eyes full of tears.

Gabriela cleared her throat. 'My mother was up there with her, but she couldn't save her.' Her eyes were moist. 'My grandmother was a skilled climber, brought up to it, but it was a very virulent sort of bug. I know I

42

was quite delirious with it. That's what must have happened to her.'

'You were obviously very fond of her,' Anne said softly. 'You've told me before, but I've forgotten. What was her name?'

'Heidi; Heidi Fluge,' Gabriela said, squaring her shoulders. 'She was just wonderful about the festival, there's always so much to organise. She saw to everything for the nuns and, as I said, kept the records. Though not in any sense official, apparently they showed reasonable grounds for believing something more than mass hysteria was going on.'

'Women labelled infertile by their doctors became pregnant?'

'The figure is put as high as eighty per cent. But there's no medical corroboration; the convent doesn't want publicity.'

'Even so, word must have got around. The place must be getting swamped.'

'That's why we try to keep it quiet. Please don't mention it to anyone.' Gabriela smiled.

'But it isn't a hundred per cent effective, is it?'

'You mean because it hasn't worked for me?'

'Quite,' Thomas agreed. 'So it could be something other than a miracle. A physical cause.'

'Or a lack of faith on my part,' Gabriela said sadly. 'Some things even miracles can't overcome.'

Michael put his hand out. 'And there are compensations. Rilla has the chance to revisit childhood haunts every year.' His smile took them all in. 'She loves that old school, you know. You would not believe it possible, but she simply adores going back, talking to the old nuns, gossiping with childhood friends.'

43

Mary was listening intently, her eyes fastened on her godmother.

'So what do you think? How about Mary having an alpine holiday?' Michael pressed. 'You'd love to show her round, wouldn't you, Schatzi?' His brown eyes grew tender as he pronounced the Austrian endearment: it was clear he thought of her as his greatest treasure.

'I do agree that it's a good idea,' Gabriela backed him up. 'I hope you do not mind, but I told Mary's story to my mother. She was most concerned when she heard it.' Gabriela paused, then decided to carry on. 'She has a certain amount of experience in that area. The war, you know. Such terrible things happened when the Russians came, when they took over parts of Vienna and all that. She and my grandmother comforted several girls at that time. They came to the mountains to recuperate.'

'But she isn't a psychiatrist,' Thomas said. 'That really would be stretching her capacities.'

'No, no, nothing like that. She merely offered friendship. Counselling, if you like. Rather like Anne and her marriage guidance, but without the official status. Just a friendly ear, really. Anyway, it was Mutter's idea to suggest that Mary come with me. She was most keen to invite her to stay.'

'That would be something of an imposition, surely,' Anne said. 'Does she have enough room?'

'More than enough. She lives in the rambling old hunting lodge my grandparents bought before the war. It is called the Franzjosephschanze – the Franz Joseph Lodge. In fact it was used by the Hapsburg entourage in Franz Joseph's heyday. They particularly liked the area for hunting, their favourite sport. Their trophies are still hanging on the walls.'

'Really? How grand!' Anne said at once. 'You

haven't mentioned that before, either,' she reproached Gabriela.

'Austria is a republic now. We do not talk about our past.'

'We wouldn't want to abuse your mother's hospitality,' Thomas broke in, urbane. 'But why don't I arrange for the three of us take a holiday in Salzburg, and maybe meet you there? You could introduce us to your mother then.' The words were clipped to preclude any argument.

Mary's eyes, full of anticipation, went blank.

'That would be lovely,' Gabriela said, deflated, disappointed.

Michael turned towards Mary and smiled at her as though to say it would all work out. 'So: how have you got on with your search for a new school?' he asked Thomas.

'Not too well, actually. Most of them simply refuse to believe that Mary could have any talents at all. As far as they're concerned, she's dumb in every sense of the word. We've shown them her past reports, given them the psychiatrist's assessment. Dr Grossmann assures us her voice will come back very soon.' He took a sip of wine, tasted it slowly and carefully. 'They're polite but guarded.'

'You mean they won't take her?' Gabriela looked appalled.

'They don't say that. Some are quite short of pupils. I'm the one who has the misgivings. If they can't cope at this stage, what are they going to do when she's there, and her voice doesn't come back for a while? Useless, in my view.'

'I will take you round my old school,' Gabriela told them, eyes shining. 'I am sure they would not have such hang-ups. Mother Theresia is wonderful. She is still the Reverend Mother though she's over ninety. If her headmistress was not able to make better assessments than that, she would lose her job.'

'They employ secular teachers?'

'Yes, indeed. All highly qualified women. Most of the nuns are too old to teach, though a couple still do. We do not have private schools in Austria, you see. Everyone has to pass the state exams. The Convent of the Immaculate Conception takes mostly boarders; paying pupils. But you can get in only if you pass the national entrance test, or come from abroad.'

'One of the best schools in Austria,' Michael put in. 'Very highly regarded. The University of Vienna takes many girls from there. And Professor Lager teaches biology. Quite a feather in their cap.'

'Gabriela's mother is a professor?'

'Honorary. University of Indiana.' He turned to Mary. 'And they specialise in music. Proximity to Salzburg, I suppose.'

'They supply a steady stream of singers for the female choirs,' Gabriela told them proudly. 'And they turn out some spectacular soloists, including players of the spinet. To perform original Mozart, for instance.'

'It does sound a fascinating place,' Thomas agreed. 'I'll look into holiday dates on Monday.'

5

The small, round, marble-topped tables at the Salzburg coffee house were crowded together. Mary watched ample Austrians fork cream-oozing cakes into their mouths, slurp from solid cups overflowing with whipped cream and listened to the guttural sounds all round her. The smell of coffee mingled with that of smoked Havana and the pungent aftermath of cheap cigarettes. There was an impressive display of international news-papers – *Die Presse*, the *International Herald Tribune*, *The Times*, *Le Monde* – ingeniously supported on long, narrow wooden poles. Many were held upright and spread open, successfully hiding their readers' faces.

'Gabriela did say three, didn't she?' Thomas said petulantly to Anne, his eyes whisking past Mary. 'I know she said the Winkler because I wrote it down.' He ducked his head to look sideways at a woman on his right to check whether Gabriela was hidden behind the newsprint. Mary shook her head to show she was not, and indicated that she had looked at the others with the same result. 'It's half past,' he said, looking severely at his watch. 'Did we get the wrong day? She's usually so punctual.'

'Her mother is a doctor,' Anne reminded him. 'Per-haps she was called out at the last moment.' She turned

47

solicitously to Mary. 'Another Mozartkugel?'

The special cake, its outer sponge casing shaped rather like a large potato and covered in a sprinkling of cocoa to represent the colour, was filled with a melting mixture of egg yolk, chocolate and butter. Mary had dutifully eaten most of one, though she found it too rich for her taste. She smiled at her mother now, indicated a few mouthfuls still left on her plate, and shrugged to imply the pastry was too filling to eat more.

'Well, I'll have another while we're waiting.' Anne licked her lips in satisfaction. 'They really are delicious.'

Mary saw Thomas eye her mother, then beckon to the waiter. As she followed his hand, she saw a woman in a dirndl smiling at her. At first she did not recognise her godmother, she looked so different dressed in the traditional Austrian dress. A white cotton blouse with huge sleeves edged in lace puffed out from a tight-fitting, sleeveless bodice. The round neckline was ruched with a soft blue silk contrasting with the deep blue of the heavier bodice material, while the delicate flower print on the cotton dirndl skirt was reminiscent of an alpine meadow in full flower. The lighter colouring of the apron covered the front of the skirt and gave Gabriela a gay and youthful air. It also made her look shorter.

'Sorry to be late,' she breathed at them. 'My mother will be along in just a moment. She had to take something to the laboratory.' Gabriela pulled out a chair and sat down.

'Was she called out?'

'Called out? You mean for an emergency?' Gabriela laughed. 'Not exactly. She is, as usual, working on some project. Apparently there was a breakthrough this morning. Also as usual.' She grinned. 'That happens quite often, though in the end one discovers it is some tiny part of an enormous whole. Anyway, I could not extricate her from her concoctions. We had to wait for Helden to assemble chemicals while Mutter put data into the computer. She has taken the latest batch to be kept safe at the genetics department of the university. She uses that to corroborate the date of a test result.'

'I thought she worked on her own?' Thomas waved at a waiter, who ignored him.

'She does,' Gabriela said, puzzled. 'Oh, you mean Helden. She is one of a steady stream of teenage assistants who help with the more monotonous chores. Mutter selects the brightest girls from her classes at the convent. It is considered a great honour to be chosen. Helden Elisabeth has been helping ever since her sister Helga . . .' Gabriela's voice tailed off vaguely, her eyes staring over Mary's head, then she pulled herself back and cleared her throat. 'Helden Elisabeth's been helping Mutter for a couple of years. Being local makes her particularly valuable because she is there in the school holidays.'

'You call the girls by their surnames?' Thomas was intrigued.

'We use the surname, then add the Christian name after it if several girls from the same family are at the school.'

'What will you have, Gabriela?' Thomas asked.

'Coffee would be lovely. A small black one.'

Thomas signalled for the waiter again, but he did not respond.

'Herr Ober!' Gabriela's clipped tones brought the man running.

'Kaffee,' Thomas began. 'And a Mozartkugel for you, too?'

49

'Perhaps later.'

'Eine Melange, Gnä' Frau?'

'Einen kleinen Schwarzen.' Gabriela turned back to Thomas. 'I'll have to give you a report on the different types of coffee you can order. A Melange is a large cup of relatively weak coffee mixed with hot milk frothed like the Italian cappuccino. Ein kleiner Schwarzer is strong, black coffee served in a demitasse. Ein kleiner Brauner is the same thing with a little milk added. Substitute the word grosser for kleiner and you're presented with a large cup of the same thing.' She smiled around the Fullbrideys. 'And there's the famous Viennese coffee: "*Kaffee mit Schlag*". Schlag is short for Schlagobers, Austrian for whipped cream. So there you are. The most important phrases for your holiday.'

Gabriela's back was to the door. Mary watched as a small, jittery woman approached the back of her godmother's chair and put manipulative fingers on her shoulders. They looked as though they were digging deep. The nails were lacquered a fiery red. 'Bin endlich da,' she said. 'I have finally arrived.'

Gabriela turned right round, then stood. 'This is my mother,' she introduced her. 'Professor Erika Lager.'

The two women were startlingly different. Gabriela's tall, wide-shouldered frame towered over her diminutive mother. The daughter's sallow complexion contrasted strangely with her mother's Dresden pink and white.

'I have heard so much about you.' Erika shook hands with both Thomas and Anne. She was pencil slim, and smart in a formal suit lightened by a cream silk blouse. One of the ubiquitous deep olive green hats, with what looked like a feather set in the ribbon around the crown, was jammed tightly on to her head. She had cocked it

50

rakishly to one side, bright eyes gleaming. Gabriela had already told Mary that the decoration was not a feather, but chamois hair.

Mary stood politely and smiled, extending a hand.

'So this is Mary,' Erika said, the bright eyes alert. 'I have looked forward to meeting you very much.' Small, clawlike fingers wound themselves round Mary's right hand, and clasped it in both of hers. She was surprised at how rough the skin felt, the fingers curved, the palms coarse with what appeared to be deep scars. Perhaps she had had an accident in her laboratory. 'I hear you have the lovely voice.'

Mary smiled uncomfortably, wondering when it would be right for her to withdraw her hand. Erika looked deeply into her eyes, approaching even nearer as she did so. Mary, unnerved, drew back and nodded her head in an attempt to stem the onslaught.

'So, you cannot speak.' Erika's abrupt announcement took them all by surprise. 'But Gabriela said just once you produced a little sound when trying to sing. It will pass. You will be well very soon.' A statement, not a suggestion. The little woman leaned on the small table, a look of pain crossing her face. She recovered, signalled imperiously to the hovering waiter and summoned another chair. She settled into Gabriela's, though Thomas, standing, had offered her his.

'I never drink coffee. It is a poison,' Erika announced. 'Ich nehm ein Glas Gumpoldskirchner,' she told the waiter. 'A glass or two of wine a day is very good for your health,' she went on, addressing Anne. 'No more, of course. But all this coffee, and these cakes, are bad for you. They give you heart disease.'

'They are on holiday, Mutter,' her daughter reminded her. 'Do not lecture at them and spoil their fun.'

'I do not spoil their fun, I just warn them what will happen if they are not careful,' Erika insisted.

'Your English is marvellous,' Thomas complimented her. 'It really puts us all to shame. Where did you learn to speak so well?'

'I attend conferences in my field all over the world. Many are held in the United States. No one can afford not to speak English if they wish to confer with colleagues abroad.'

'Gabriela told us you are doing research into genetically transmitted diseases,' Anne put in.

'I am doing research into the use of genetic coding to modify undesirable inherited traits,' Erika said severely. 'That can include haemophilia, cystic fibrosis, Down's syndrome, anything of that sort. I have published a number of papers on my speciality. The whole orientation in the handling of antisocial behaviour has changed since the discovery of DNA. We are in the process of . . .'

A feeling of unease passed through Mary. This woman sounded as domineering as her father.

'They want to know the best things to do while they are here, Mutter,' Gabriela diverted her.

The little woman's face turned towards her daughter as she drew in her breath. When she spoke again her voice had lost the excitement of a few moments before. 'So, ja,' she said indifferently. 'Gabriela is not intellectually gifted. Such matters do not interest her.' The glittering eyes lost their sparkle. 'What are you planning for your holiday? The Festspiele are not till August. But there is still excellent music in the town. We have wonderful choirs in all our churches. You can listen to a different solemn mass each Sunday – several, if you wish.'

52

'We aren't Catholics, I'm afraid,' Anne told her. 'Not even Church of England. We're Nonconformists.'

'It is not necessary. I am not Catholic either. You can still go.'

'Die Fromm!' Gabriela suddenly yelled out. 'That is Greti Fromm over there.' She smiled at the others. 'I have not seen her for years. She used to be in my class at school.' She stood up and waved to a young girl sitting across the room. 'Greti! Where have you suddenly sprung from?'

'Gabriela, I beg of you. You are making a spectacle! That young girl thinks you are crazy. Greti Fromm is your age,' Erika hissed at her daughter. But she looked at the girl with narrowed eyes.

Gabriela glanced at her mother, frowned, and sat down again. The girl, a sullen look on her face, had turned round to stare towards their table without any sign of recognition. There was no doubt that she was only in her teens.

'Entschuldigung,' Gabriela said quietly, surprised. 'I am sorry. I made a mistake.' Her frownlines deepened. 'It is quite extraordinary. That girl is the image of a former schoolfellow. I would have staked my life on it: same eyes, same nose, same chin; even the way she sits and throws back her hair, the way she uses her hands. It is uncanny.' She smiled, embarrassed. 'My mother is quite right. That is a young girl, not a woman of a certain age.' She turned to Anne. 'Greti Fromm was at school with me. She emigrated to the United States in the sixties. I heard she married there.'

As her godmother was apologising, Mary noticed that Erika was still scrutinising the young girl. She saw the intensity return to her eyes, saw the hands clench the stem of the wineglass she was drinking from.

Gabriela also followed her mother's gaze. 'You know, I last saw Greti at the October festival about sixteen years ago.' She paused, and looked at Erika. 'She was quite upset that she hadn't been able to conceive and the American doctors were not able to help her. Perhaps the festival performed its miracle and this child is the result.' A wan smile scurried across her lips. She sipped from the tumbler of water brought with her coffee, then crashed it down. 'Mein Gott noch einmal! That's Greti, there,' she whispered. 'I was right; the girl must be her daughter. How incredible. I would never have recognised that fat lady as my old schoolfellow.' She grinned. 'American flab is different from solid Austrian fat.'

Mary saw a look of satisfaction, of knowing, pass over Erika Lager's features. A slight smile flickered as she continued to stare at the young girl. That was not, in itself, unusual; Mary had already noticed that staring was quite common in Austria, apparently not considered rude. The sound of scraping chairs drew her attention away from Erika. A very well endowed middle-aged lady waddled her way to join the young girl and sat down heavily.

Erika seemed mesmerised by mother and daughter. 'Why don't you ask them over?' she said, blinking at Gabriela.

The teenager was nodding her head in their direction. The woman looked up and caught Gabriela's eye. Slow recognition seemed to dawn on her, her eyes rounded, then crinkled into a smile. She stood and waved.

'Die Lager!' she shouted across the room. 'Gabriela Lager.'

Mary watched the glittering look of triumph in Erika's eyes. It seemed oddly inappropriate. She turned to her daughter, all smiles, the severity of just a few moments ago completely gone. 'Na, Rilla. Go and invite them over. They speak English, after all. Maybe Greti is here to show her daughter her roots. It would be most interesting for the Fullbrideys to meet them.'

'Would you mind?' Gabriela raised her eyebrows questioningly at her friends. 'I can arrange to see Greti some other time . . .'

'Naturally they will not mind.' Erika said. 'Herr Ober!'

The waiter came running. Another small round table and two more chairs were added almost instantly.

'Of course, Gabriela,' Anne said, staring at Erika's animated face. 'We'd be delighted to meet an old schoolfriend of yours.'

The two of them came over, introductions were completed. Greti had married Sam Cohen, and her daughter Jenny was fifteen. 'So good to see you again, Professor Lager,' Greti said to Erika. 'Isn't it wonderful that Jenny came about through the festival? I shall never forget that you suggested I try it. I am so grateful.' She sat down next to Gabriela and smiled happily at her. 'As I remember it, you're married to a journalist?'

'A foreign correspondent, yes. I hardly see him.'

'And this is your daughter?'

'My goddaughter, Greti. Mary is Thomas and Anne's daughter,' Gabriela said. 'I have no children.'

A shadow crossed over Greti's face. 'Like me before my little miracle.' She put fat fingers on her daughter's arm as Jenny leaned away, then, resigned, bit into a slice of Apfelstrudel. 'It's all coming back to me now. You had that terrible infection of the ovaries. You were only a child, as I recall.' She munched reflectively. 'The same year your poor grandmother died. Some dreadful bug was going round.' She turned to her daughter. 'I've told you about the shrine, haven't I, Jenny?'

'Jeez, Mom.' The girl looked away. 'Only a hundred times! Can I get a soda here?'

'Not soda,' Erika said promptly. 'But how about a Spritzer and an ice-cream? Put them together, it is the nearest we can offer.'

Jenny stared at Erika without bothering to reply. 'They don't have burgers either, Mom. When can we head back home?'

'You do not like Austrian food?' Erika asked, her eyes concentrated on the girl.

Jenny stared back. 'I don't like Austria, period,' she announced. 'Mom said it would be great.'

'The mountains do not interest you?'

Jenny simply turned her back.

'Jenny, Professor Lager is speaking with you.' Greti nudged her daughter.

'What about the music, Jenny? Do you like that?' Erika persisted.

'You gotta be kidding.'

'I think the Fullbrideys wanted to see St Walter, Mutter,' Gabriela broke in. 'I've told them all about it.'

'It is a fine example of an alpine village,' Erika agreed. 'Many excellent walks start from St Walter as a base.' Her small, bright eyes darted around the table. 'Has Gabriela told you? The convent runs a summer school next month. German for foreigners. You are interested in that for Jenny?'

'For *Mary*, Mutter!' Gabriela almost shouted. 'We discussed telling the Fullbrideys about it for Mary.'

'Naturally for Mary, Gabriela. I thought you had already mentioned it to your friends. But perhaps Jenny would like to come as well. The two are not exclusive.'

'Summer school? No, actually we had no idea,' Thomas rumbled at her. 'You mean they run a sort of camp in the summer holidays?'

'Certainly not. It is a summer teaching course in German language and music. Students come from schools all over the world, and even from universities. The convent employs first-class music teachers. They prepare local talent for the Mozarteum.' Erika saw there was no flicker of recognition at the word. 'Like the Guildhall School of Music and Drama in London,' she added. 'So a promising talent can be given an excellent assessment during the summer session. That is why so many come here.'

Mary's expression, lustreless throughout most of the day, had suddenly become transformed. She looked at her mother, tugged at her arm.

'Do they teach singing?' Anne asked, glancing at Mary severely.

'Most certainly. The summer intake is not as carefully selected as the year-round students, but the teachers are still first class.'

'In fact,' Gabriela interrupted her mother, 'Joseph Helden, one of the local boys, is going to teach Austrian folk songs this year. He has done a lot of research in that field. He is quite outstanding, and . . .'

'This place is co-ed?' Jenny showed interest for the first time.

Erika looked at Jenny, her bright eyes hard. Mary noticed her nostrils flare in distaste.

'Jenny, honey, didn't I tell you?'

'It is a convent,' Erika said. 'They allow only carefully selected girls in their school.'

Jenny turned away, mumbling, 'Wouldn't you know,' under her breath.

57

'Young Helden also shepherds during the summer months,' Erika said, dismissing that. 'He does not have all that much time. And there are far better singing teachers. The distinguished Katharina Weisskopf, for example.'

'My mother prefers female voices,' Gabriela broke in. 'It is a prejudice. Joseph works terribly hard in the summer. He also takes parties climbing . . .'

'This cool guy . . . Would he take me?' Jenny demanded.

'If you stayed as a summer guest on his parents' farm,' Gabriela explained. 'Or you can hire him. He tries to make enough money so that he can study music in Salzburg during the rest of the year.'

'We could arrange for you both to attend the summer school.' Erika turned back to Mary, her casual tone belied by the grip with which she held her wine glass. 'Reverend Mother is an old friend, and will accept my recommendations. You would like me to arrange it?'

'Really, Mutter, I have already spoken to her about Mary.' Gabriela sounded piqued. She turned to the Fullbrideys. 'Maybe you would like to spend a few days at the Braune Rössl, right on the Kernsee and only a relatively short drive from St Walter? I expect you've heard of Kernkirchen; it's a popular holiday resort.'

'The Salzkammergut is the lake district of Austria,' Erika took over from her daughter. 'Glacier lakes, formed in the ice age. The problem is that the water is cold even in summer. And the weather is treacherous. A storm can blow up in minutes. But do not worry about that. We have a most efficient rescue service.'

'We have not had a drowning for many years,' Gabriela hastened to add.

'Would Joseph rescue us?' Jenny asked, eyes bright.

'That is Kurt Miller's job.' Gabriela drank the rest of her coffee and slapped her cup down on its saucer. 'He's the head lifeguard. There are several other young men, but Miller is the one who is in charge of the Kernkirchen lakeside during the summer.'

'Would that be Johann Miller's son, by any chance? He was such a heart-throb. I remember him.' Greti smiled at her daughter.

'One of Miller's sons; he has four altogether. Kurt is a marvellous swimmer and the best sailor, and very good with horses besides. He's extremely gifted as far as sport is concerned.'

'Sounds a good deal,' Jenny said.

'I think you would not enjoy one of our storms, Jenny, even in the company of a strong young man. They are not immune to the elements,' Erika said coldly.

Jenny narrowed her eyes and turned her attention to what was left of her mother's Apfelstrudel.

Mary looked up to see Erika Lager staring at her again. 'So, Mary. You would enjoy some weeks here?'

She nodded vigorous assent.

Jenny turned to Mary in her turn. 'What do you say, Mary? Shall we go for the local guys?' She grinned. 'One thing I like about Austria is the guys. They sure are hunks.'

6

Once off the Autobahn system which had infiltrated even the mountainous regions of the Salzkammergut, Thomas Fullbridey gave the marked road map to his wife. She directed him faultlessly.

The drive to St Walter was spectacular. Mary watched as massive horns of mountain overshadowed their path, turned daylight into dusk. She looked ahead, saw stolid giants of stone poke ice-tipped fingers into steely blue and point towards the sun. She shivered; then her eye caught the waving green of fir, took in the softening of the unrelenting stone. She watched the awesome beauty, breathed relief as white-laced sky turned purple shadows into gentle mauve.

'A right turn to Kernkirchen, then follow the road for about four miles, then another turn to the right,' Anne read out to Thomas.

'And that's it?'

'That's St Walter. Then we have to find the convent.'

'Isn't it in the village?'

'Not far outside. Only half a mile or so as the crow flies, but much further driving via the hairpin bends.' Anne put her finger on her place in the map and levelled thoughtful eyes at her husband, then smiled at Mary sitting behind him. 'The convent's actually shown on

60

this map. A rather large building. Gabriela told me it was purpose-built for the Little Sisters in the fifteenth century. Not like England, where the dissolution of the monasteries still has consequences. Austria is a Catholic country, so the buildings their religious orders live in are often the original ones, and quite magnificent.'

Mary, relaxing in the back of the car, watched as deciduous trees gave way to conifers, felt a lurch in her stomach as the spectacular views of diminishing lakes seen from high altitudes gave her a taste of vertigo.

'Turn right on the next side road across the Lödnacher Bach valley and on into St Walter,' Anne directed.

It was raining. In fact it had been raining most of the time they had so far spent in Austria. The mountains caught the clouds and precipitated the moisture. The area was not noted for its sunny climate. A sign, isolated on the far side of the mountain road, announced St Walter.

'This it?' Thomas asked his wife. 'I don't see any buildings.'

'They always mark the town boundary a short distance from the actual buildings,' Anne reminded him. As though to prove her right, clusters of typical mountain houses magically appeared around the next bend. Wide, shallow roofs allowed the snow to lie, wooden frameworks gave warmth and adaptability. An imposing tidiness. There was no litter, each house had clean net curtains and almost every one displayed neat window-boxes full of colour.

'Now where?'

'Just follow the road through the village to the square. Turn left off the main road and uphill from there.'

'Looks like a rather minor road.'

'That's all there is. It must be right.'

They drove on in silence. Mary stared at hay meadows bright with flowers, adjusted her eyes to the sudden pitch into dense pine forests dark enough for her father to feel he had to turn on the headlights.

'I hope they checked the brakes thoroughly. These zigzags are quite steep,' he muttered, feeling the car sliding over odd pebbles on the road.

'It's not far now. Just past that mill and then the first turning on the left after that.'

The Mercedes Thomas had hired purred along the road. They turned left, climbed up a single-lane track hewn out of rock and extending for several hundred yards and arrived at a surprisingly spacious gravelled drive. This fronted a magnificent stone building. The main part, straight and uncompromising, spread on both sides of an imposing wooden door recessed behind a portico held up by stone pillars. Ten huge windows looked out from either side on the ground floor, repeated on the two floors above. All had slatted green shutters, most of them folded back against the walls. Some were shut, the slats clearly used to keep out the sun now shining hot. Mary looked at them uneasily. She felt uncomfortable, as though the windows were eyes observing her, judging her actions.

She shook herself and looked again. The central room, above the door, was sheltered behind a balcony built over the portico. Its wide stone balustrade was intricately carved. A separate building to the left, evidently a small church or a chapel because of the bell-tower rising above it, was separated by a covered way from the main building. The area on the right side was hidden behind an enormous stone wall interrupted by a narrow but magnificent wrought-iron gate. Beyond it the Fullbrideys could see enticing glimpses of a spacious garden. And beyond the buildings and garden was the steeply rising mountainside. Thomas drove slowly around the car park, then turned the car to face the building. Neither he nor Anne spoke as they took in the scene in front of them.

'Breathtaking,' Anne announced at last.

'Utterly,' Thomas agreed.

Heavy double front doors opened wide and Gabriela walked towards them. 'You've found us,' she said, smiling invitingly, opening the passenger door and helping Anne out. 'And in good time. I was looking out for you from Reverend Mother's room. That's the one behind the balcony,' she said, turning to embrace Mary, now out of the car and looking around. 'The hub of the convent.'

'The Little Sisters are certainly off the beaten track.' Anne smiled. 'But we found a good map.'

'I will show you round first, then we will meet Mother Theresia. I've just left her to take her nap; she needs one morning and afternoon, but otherwise she is still going strong. She will be ninety-one this year. It must be the virtuous life.'

Gabriela led them through long, wide corridors which led to immaculate classrooms. The desks were banked, as in a university auditorium, arranged on a series of platforms set one behind the other so that even the pupils at the back would easily hear, and see, the teacher. Huge blackboards filled the whole expanse of the front of the room, modern lighting showed off the highly polished floors. Progressing to the second floor they noticed that the enormous front windows displayed magnificent views. Glorious alpine meadows showed a backdrop of pine forest and some of the Alps' finest snowcapped peaks.

'It's very modern,' Thomas said, almost in awe. 'And very quiet.'

'The nuns are forward-looking,' Gabriela explained. 'And, as I mentioned before, most of the teachers here are lay and highly qualified. This is a first-class school. I don't think you could better it even in Vienna.' Gabriela turned to the Fullbrideys, looking meaningfully at them. 'Or London, for that matter.'

'It's certainly impressive,' Anne agreed. 'So that's why you're so well educated.'

'I am not a particularly good example.' Gabriela smiled. 'Especially with my mother's high achievements to live up to. Somehow I was always in the bottom half of the class. However, even that was quite good. Standards are very high in Austria,' Gabriela assured them. 'They have to be. We are a small country, and we have to survive in a hostile world. We were not on the right side during the war, remember.'

'Judging by the exchange rate, you've done pretty well,' Thomas chuckled at her. 'An economic miracle. Just like Germany.'

'Not really,' Gabriela said sharply. 'Austrians are quite different from Germans. For a start, not so many of us embraced Nazism. Well, maybe in Vienna, but not here, not in the mountains. Members of the party were quite few and far between.'

'I suppose you did escape all that, in any case,' Thomas agreed.

'Personally, I did. I was born after the war. But the Nazis were very much in evidence in St Walter. They even built a cog railway behind the convent.'

'A cog railway? For the nuns to go up the mountain?'

Gabriela laughed. 'Not for the nuns. For them. They took to the idea of the Oktoberfest. Perhaps it reminded them of the beer festival in Munich! Increasing the fertility of Aryan stock and all that. They encouraged SS officers with attendant girlfriends, I gather. The little carriage was to transport the Nazis and their lady friends as near as possible to the grotto. It wouldn't have been easy for them to negotiate the mountain route. Most city people are not up to that.'

Progress around the school was relatively slow. Every time they met a nun Gabriela would stop, smile and make a sort of half-curtsy, half-bow. The nuns wore the traditional habit: white coifs and wimples covering the head, completely covering hair and shadowing the face, black robes, a large crucifix attached to a chain round the neck, a rosary strung from the waist. There were no young faces, and only a sprinkling of the late middle-aged. It seemed that even in Austria the vocation for the religious life was becoming rare. The older faces showed smile-lines grooved deep, serene expressions in the eyes. None of them said anything; Gabriela had explained that the Little Sisters were a semi-enclosed order, and spoke only if it was necessary. Their expressive eyes were adept at conveying information. It fascinated Mary, made her feel at ease. For the first time since she had lost her voice, she felt able to communicate with others.

One of the sisters, rather unexpectedly, asked Mary a question. 'You come to our summer school?' The sweet smile, its innocence as clear as that of a baby, moved Mary to try to speak. It did not work.

'This is Sister Christa,' Gabriela introduced her to the Fullbrideys. 'She is in charge of the admittances.' She turned to the nun, spoke volubly in German. Sister

Christa, listening intently, smiled back, nodded, but made no further comment. She bowed goodbye.

'She spoke because that is part of her job,' Gabriela whispered at the Fullbrideys. 'But you will notice that she became silent as soon as it was clear that Mary was not one of the scheduled students.'

Mary drank it all in, intrigued. Somehow, though she could not understand the German and could not express herself vocally at all, she felt comfortable among these quiet women. Their gentle bearing, their hushed, assured walk, the folded arms across the chest, the high-held, placid heads seemed to denote a calm, and wise, acceptance of life.

'No married women are allowed to enter the order,' Gabriela had explained to them. 'The postulants are all young girls, all virgins.'

'You mean they wouldn't take anyone who wasn't?'

'I do not know whether that question is actually asked. I think it unlikely that anyone who did not have a vocation from an early age would ask to join an order like this. And the catechism does stress the sinfulness of fornication.'

'Gabriela,' Thomas began.

Gabriela grinned at Anne. Thomas's assumption that Mary was entirely ignorant – he called it innocent – of any knowledge about sex verged on the obsessive. 'All postulants know that they will be asked to take vows of chastity, poverty and obedience,' she went on smoothly. 'That is emphasised when the girls first come here.'

'Young people cannot understand those precepts at such a tender age.'

'That is the point, Thomas. The ecclesiastical authorities make quite sure the girls know what they are letting themselves in for,' Gabriela said sharply. 'They ask a great many questions over the first three years, before the girls are even allowed to take the preliminary vows. The community cannot afford to take in anyone who would not fit in. It is far too intimate a life for that.'

'Surely a number of girls have unhappy love affairs and take this as the easy option?'

'The Church is always careful to weed those out. As I said, this is a strict order. No men are allowed beyond the public rooms and the chapel, not even a doctor, unless they have special dispensation from the Bishop. Even the nuns' domestic quarters are out of bounds for most women. Just a few are given special permission to pass through. Cleaners, for instance, now that so many of the nuns are old and frail. And the girl who looks after the grotto.'

Mary felt a glow through her body, sensed that the place was made for her. She smiled at Gabriela and took her hand. Her eyes, more expressive than before, glowed enjoyment, even excitement.

Gabriela acknowledged with a squeeze of her fingers the first sign that her young friend was beginning to come back into the world. 'The chapel is for the convent's use,' she explained as they approached a wide door set apart on the side of the school building. 'The village has its own church, and its own parish priest. Pfarrer Eisenberger is the chaplain here. It is usual to address him as Hochwürden – a rather old-fashioned form of address, but then he is old. Getting on for eighty.'

'There can't be much for him to do.'

'The spiritual well-being of the nuns and teaching the Catholic girls the catechism.'

'Aren't they all Catholics?'

'Most of them are. But there are other denominations; Protestants, Jews, even a Buddhist, I believe. They are all required to leave the room during catechism classes. The convent does not see it as its mission to convert their non-Catholic students.'

'Really? I thought all Christians, particularly Catholics, were supposed to be missionaries?'

'Reverend Mother takes the view that example is the best persuasion. The rest she leaves to God.'

'A refreshingly simple attitude,' Thomas approved. 'I've always found it a problem, dealing with religious institutions. They are so bigoted about their own point of view.'

'It is a form of self-preservation. We live in a secular world and the girls have to go out into it. Reverend Mother maintains that the more pressure is put on them to conform, the less likely they are to carry their religion through their lives. She insists that only those girls who actually wish to do so attend early morning mass or benediction on Sundays.'

'You mean they need not go to services at all?'

'All Catholics are obliged to go to mass on Sundays and attend mass on holidays of obligation. The rest is up to them.'

'Holidays of obligation?'

'Special holy days set aside in the liturgical year. The next one is the fifteenth of August, a national holiday. Everything in the whole of Austria shuts down.' She smiled. 'Well, excluding hotels and restaurants. Our tourist trade could not cope with that!'

'So what happens?'

'There are extensive celebrations. The faithful process, carrying a statue of the Virgin Mary. It is the day of her Assumption into heaven.'

'Popish rubbish,' Thomas muttered under his breath.

A soft, slanting sunlight shone through the stained glass on to the pews. There were hard wooden benches with no kneelers. The nuns, whatever their age, apparently managed the rigours of religious observance without the comforts normally considered necessary.

The organ in the loft began to sound, softly at first, crescendoing into magnificence. A Bach prelude echoed from walls depicting the stations of the cross and from the exuberant Gothic triptych at the front. The crucifix beyond the altar was also sumptuous. A modern piece, it showed a twisted contortion of metals to signify the crown of thorns within the body of the crucified Christ. It hung opulently behind the undying flame.

The music coursed through Mary. Leaving her parents and Gabriela at the back she walked up to the high altar, turned round and looked towards the sound.

A straight, strong back was moving to and fro. A shock of straight sun-bleached hair cut short moved with the body. One hand, raised to turn the pages of the music, was firm and large. A checked shirt and jeans suggested a young man. In the convent, in the chapel?

Gabriela walked down the aisle to join Mary, genuflected, then looked up at the organ. 'That's Joseph Helden,' she whispered. 'The one who teaches folk singing at the summer school. He is allowed to practise here and in the music room whenever he is at home. His parents are too poor to be able to afford an instrument. And in return he plays the organ here on the Sundays and holy days he can be here. During term time he is in Salzburg.'

The organist, unaware that he had an audience, began to play, and then sing, Schubert's Ave Maria. His voice, a pure tenor, floated around the chapel, softly, gently, lovingly. It sounded very young.

Mary could feel a sort of tickle in her throat, almost a caress, as she breathed in. Her vocal chords began to loosen. As the music continued, she could no longer restrain herself. '*Dominus tecum*,' she joined in, whispering to start with, then gaining strength.

'*Et benedicta tu in mulieribus*' the two sang together: 'And blessed are you among women.'

She continued to sing as the young man played and sang with her. At the end, he stopped and turned. A gentle, smiling young face. He waved to her and put his hands together in a silent clap.

Mary did not see, or hear, the small figure heavily draped in black gliding into the chapel. She did not even hear the clink of the rosary as Mother Theresia approached the altar and Mary standing in front of it.

'That was beautiful, mein Kind. You have a most beautiful voice.'

Mary, her eyes still lingering on the young man who now stood looking down at her, turned in the direction of the voice. She focused on the shrivelled face, the clear grey eyes.

'Thank you,' she said. And there was not a single tremor, not a moment of hesitation as she spoke.

7

'Why not let her go to the summer school, Anne? Surely that can't do any harm.'

Mary was sitting at the piano in the music room in her parents' house, ostensibly learning a part she was to sing with the local operatic society in October. Hearing her godmother's clipped tones coming from the hall, she stopped and listened to what Gabriela was saying. Though she had tried to cajole her parents into letting her go to the summer school scheduled to start the following week, she had not had any success.

'Mary has just been through a terrible trauma,' Anne intoned, her voice low, but Mary could still hear it.

'Really, Anne,' Gabriela's reply took on a stronger tone, 'you are being over-cautious.' She hesitated. 'It would be so good for Mary to enjoy the company of other young people. You know the Brenmans have gone off to their Devon cottage. What do you expect Mary to do with herself all day? After all, you are out seeing clients most of the time.'

'At the moment she's busy preparing for a small part in *The Mikado*.' There was a silence. Mary hastily played a few notes on the piano. 'I really would not like to expose her to an alien – I mean a foreign – country at this stage.'

71

'It is not as drastic as all that. You saw how Mary and Mother Theresia took to each other. And perhaps you have forgotten that Mary got her voice back in the chapel. What could be more auspicious than that?'

'Coincidence,' Anne said, obstinate.

'Even if it were, Mary clearly loved the school, the atmosphere, everything about it. Being away from London will give her a proper chance to get over that frightful happening. She will meet young people from all over the world, get a smattering of German . . .'

Mary got up and walked out into the hall. 'I want to go, Mummy,' she said. Her voice sounded resolute and clear. 'I'm fourteen, I can work these things out for myself. Daddy's already decided I'm not to go back to Highgate Ladies, whatever Miss Johnson says. And I don't want to go back.' She put her arms round her mother's neck. 'The summer school would be perfect for showing us what to look for in a new school,' she said pleadingly. 'I've told you over and over what's really important to me. Miss Turner said my voice is special. I'd like to meet the right singing teacher to give me a professional evaluation.'

'You may never use your voice, Mary. You know very well that it takes more than just a promising talent.'

Gabriela could not contain herself. 'Um Gottes willen, Anne. You know Mary has a wonderful voice. It is not merely *promising*. She has an exceptionally clear tone and a beautiful timbre. In the right hands this basic instrument could be formed into a potentially magnificent one. Such a rare attribute, it would be a crime not to try to develop it.' She walked over to Mary and kissed her, turned determinedly back to Anne. 'And Mary needs to experience for herself whether she is prepared to do the work involved.'

'Exactly; the work involved. It takes years of study.'

'So what? You will not have to make any sacrifices to support her while she is training. You and Thomas can easily afford it.'

'I wasn't talking about money,' Anne said stiffly. 'I was talking about commitment.'

'Yours, you mean?'

'You are being deliberately obtuse, Gabriela! I'm talking about Mary's commitment. And there is all the travelling. She will need someone to be with her. I have a career myself, you know. I can't just abandon all that.'

Mary looked at Gabriela, opened her mouth, then shut it again. She hunched her shoulders, began to scuff the highly polished hall floor.

Gabriela hesitated, then drew in a deep breath. 'I would be willing to go on trips with Mary. I am used to travelling. I often went with Michael in the past.' Her eyes challenged Anne. 'That is, if you trust me to look after her.'

'Naturally I trust you. But what about your teaching, Gabriela?'

'I only work as a supply teacher. The job is not of special interest to me. Supporting Mary, helping to launch her on a fine career, would give me enormous pleasure. I can go back to teaching German any time.' There was a sadness in the tall woman's bearing, a yearning in her voice. 'Helping Mary develop her talent would be a privilege.'

'Couldn't I just try the summer school, Mummy? It's only for a month.' There was a tremble, a hint of huskiness.

'And my mother would keep an eye on Mary. She offered without my prompting her. She was as taken with Mary as Mother Theresia was. I know Mutter's

73

manner is a little brusque but I am sure you noticed how much she liked Mary. I expect you remember she asked if she could approach Reverend Mother for you.'

'She seemed to be much more taken with that ghastly Jenny.'

A momentary shadow flitted across Gabriela's face. 'Whatever interest Mutter showed in Jenny wasn't meant to detract from Mary. My mother is keen to help any bright young girl achieve her potential. She happens to think America is stultifying for young minds. That's why she was so keen to persuade Jenny.' Gabriela thought for a moment. 'And I suppose she was rather struck by the fact that Jenny was conceived after her mother attended the October festival. It is one of the most clear-cut examples we have. The records of that time show only the number of women attending and the consequent births. There is no mention of infertility among the local girls. In Greti's case we know she'd had all kinds of fertility treatment in the States. She bored my mother endlessly with the gory details. After all, she used to be one of my mother's patients.' She paused. 'It's funny, Mutter has always pooh-poohed the grotto claims before, but this time she had to admit it was more than simple coincidence or a put-up job. We don't need medical records to know Jenny isn't adopted, or from a donor ovum – she looks so like her mother it's positively uncanny.'

'She could be a test-tube baby,' Anne said.

'Greti told my mother she'd tried that method and it hadn't worked. Why would she lie?'

'Miracles are so much more satisfactory – and unusual, I suppose.' Anne laughed, but her attitude was clearly softening. 'So you would specifically arrange for Erika to take Mary under her wing?'

'She can do better than that. She can introduce Mary to Elisabeth Helden. She's the girl I told you about, the one who helps my mother in the lab.'

'You know her, do you?'

'Of course. Her mother, Friedl Maier – she's Friedl Helden now – and I were best friends at school, in the same class. We were, are, very close. I was even . . .' There was a pause, then Gabriela cleared her throat. 'Anyway, she married a local farmer. They work a traditional farmstead, and struggle to do the best for their family. Salt of the earth.'

Gabriela turned to smile at Mary. 'Elisabeth assists my mother – she inputs data into the computers, checks up on the mice and rabbits. And her English is very good. I have often helped her practise.'

Mary could hardly contain herself. 'Do let me go, Mummy.'

'I'll discuss it with Daddy tonight,' Anne promised. 'Now I really have to go. Since you're a lady of leisure in the holidays, Rilla, why don't you two spend the day together? I might not be back until late.'

Mary and Gabriela looked at each other guiltily. They had already planned to attend that day's free lunchtime concert in the Wigmore Hall, then to go back to the Adlers' house to play with Bridget. And Gabriela had started to coach Mary in the rudiments of German.

Mary walked nervously up to the minibus waiting outside Salzburg airport. There was no lettering on it, no one in the driving seat, nothing to distinguish the vehicle except that it was the only minibus waiting there. Another girl, her pink leggings covered by an enormous T-shirt with I LOVE LOVE printed in large black letters, kicked irritably at a duffle-bag sitting forlornly on the pavement.

Mary put her case down next to the bag. 'You're Jenny, aren't you?'

The girl swept her eyes over Mary, examined the neat summer dress and sensible sandals, her expression bored. 'I guess. You been sent to meet me? Where's the driver?'

'I think we've met before. In July; afternoon tea at the Winkler, with our parents.'

'Sure thing.' A flicker of recognition, then frustration set in again and Jenny put some chewing-gum in her mouth.

'Is this the summer-school bus, d'you know?'

'Beats me.'

'Perhaps they're waiting for another flight to come in, from Switzerland or somewhere.'

'Wir sprechen jetzt Deutsch,' a male voice announced, striding up to the vehicle, opening the back and piling the girls' luggage in. 'We only speak German now.'

Jenny's bored eyes glinted into friendliness. As the young man stood aside to motion her through the opened minibus door she stumbled against him. 'Gee,' she said. 'What's your name?'

He caught her, held out stiff arms until she stood upright again. 'Joseph Helden. Und wie heissen Sie?'

'I guess I didn't quite catch that,' Jenny said.

'He wants to know your name,' Mary translated.

'Oh, sure. Jenny Cohen.' She swung herself past Joseph into the bus, provocatively wiggling her behind.

He did not even glance after her. He had already turned to Mary, his dark eyes on hers. 'Ave Maria,' he said softly. 'I remember your name is Mary.' He smiled,

76

held out a hand. 'The step is very high. I help you.'

'Danke,' Mary whispered rather than spoke. Her hand, sweating cold with nervousness, trembled on the handrail as Joseph's strong grip helped her up the steep steps. She tumbled through into the bus and sank into the seat next to Jenny.

'I guess you've scored already.'

'We wait for one more,' Joseph said, calm, assured. 'She is coming now.'

'Must be his date,' Jenny said dully. 'Wouldn't you know?'

A smiling, buxom, picture-postcard-pretty girl in a dirndl, her hands full of parcels, her face red, climbed sweatily into the bus. Joseph made no attempt to help her. She threw a small package at him, speaking rapidly in German. Then she looked at the two girls sitting together and levered herself into the seat behind Mary.

'Are you Mary Fullbridey?' Her voice had a German accent with that softness characteristic of alpine German.

'Yes,' Mary said cautiously, looking at the girl. She could not remember having seen her before. 'How do you know?'

'I am Elisabeth Helden,' the girl announced. 'Frau Professor Lager asked me to introduce myself to you. I think you know her.'

'We have met a few times,' Mary agreed. She felt irritable, tried to subdue a sense of being watched, having a spy set over her. 'This is Jenny Cohen,' she said. 'Jenny comes from America.'

'Hello, Jenny.'

'Joseph your steady?' Jenny asked, taking a bag of peanuts out of her handbag and starting to munch.

'Want some?' She held the bag out to Mary. 'The airline gave them out.'

'No, thank you.'

'Steady?' Elisabeth asked. 'Steady what?'

'Is he your boyfriend, for chrissake? You heard of that?'

'Joseph is my brother,' Elisabeth said. 'I do not often get to Salzburg. I live on a farm on the alp. He offered me a lift when he knew he had to fetch you from the airport.'

'OK, OK. It's no big deal.' Jenny pulled her Walkman headphones on and stared out of the bus window.

Mary and Elisabeth looked at one another, began to grin.

'They told me to take you to your dormitory and to show you round the convent,' Elisabeth said. 'Is that what you would like to do?'

'It's very kind of you. Professor Lager's daughter showed me and my parents round. Gabriela Adler is my godmother.'

'Really?' Elisabeth's polite smile became friendly. 'She was my sister Helga's godmother, too.'

'*Was* she?' Mary said, eyes wide, surprised. 'She didn't tell us that. How old's your sister?'

'She died,' Elisabeth said softly, her eyes moistening. 'She fell off when she was exercising a horse.'

'I'm sorry, Elisabeth. I didn't know.'

Elisabeth's face crumpled, then brightened. 'Over two years ago now, but it's still hard for us all. She and I were best friends. Tante Rilla was always very nice to her, and to me. She brought us things from England.' She smiled sadly. 'We don't see much of her any more. I think she, too, is sad.'

'She brings me things from Austria,' Mary said

eagerly. 'And she's been wonderful, telling me all about the convent.'

'She did?'

'And she brought me some holy water from the chapel. I gave some to my rabbit.'

'Really? Your rabbit needed it?'

'She was ill. I thought she was going to die. So I gave her some water, just a drop or two, and she was better in days.'

'You mean she drank it?' Elisabeth stared at her.

'Yes; isn't that all right?'

'It is unusual. So she was cured by a miracle?'

'I suppose it must have been.'

Elisabeth's eyes relaxed, then grinned. 'Very good. I think we can find something more interesting to do than show you what you know already.'

'More interesting?'

'Come back here and sit with me,' Elisabeth said, dismissing Jenny with a brief nod.

Mary looked at the body slumped in its seat next to hers. The jaws were chomping. She moved back to sit next to her new friend.

'I'll show you where the shrine is,' Elisabeth whispered in her ear, watching Jenny in front. 'And tell you the story. It's really super.' She motioned Mary further back, then followed her. 'I'm the only one who can show you the old way to the grotto.'

'Grotto? What grotto?'

'A sort of cave up in the mountain. That's where the shrine is.'

'You mean where my holy water came from?'

'No; that was from the chapel. No one is allowed to take water from the grotto.'

'Where is it, then?'

'Ssh, not so loud. It is a very secret place. The grotto water is only for the brides. I am the one who makes sure everything is all right for the Oktoberfest. I go up every Saturday during the summer.'

'Really? What do you have to do?'

'I examine the path the brides walk on. Only I am allowed. I make sure it is completely safe and the ropes the brides hold on to are not frayed. There have been accidents in the past.'

'You mean people have been injured?'

'Sometimes. One year someone was killed. Tante Rilla's grandmother. She fell to her death. So now we have ropes fixed to the side of the path. And I make sure the grotto water is clear and pure.'

'Just you?'

'My brother Joseph also helps, but not in the grotto. Only women are allowed in there, apart from priests. Joseph is supposed to make sure the source of the water above the grotto is not interfered with. That is high up on the mountain.'

'Aunt Rilla said he was a really good climber.'

'He is up on the alp in any case. He does some shepherding jobs during the summer months.'

'So what does he have to do?'

'The stream which feeds the grotto trough just trickles in. The thawing winter snows bring most of the water. In dry weather it can take several weeks to fill up after the brides have drunk from it. He has to make sure the water can get through all right.'

'Your English is terribly good,' Mary said, almost enviously. 'How did you learn?'

'We're taught during the school year,' Elisabeth passed it off. 'And I join in the summer school, helping out. I learn a lot from the other girls, you know. They're supposed to learn German, but they teach me loads of English.'

'Your accent sounds faintly American,' Mary said thoughtfully.

'OK – American. They're the ones who can afford to come.'

'To the summer school?'

'It counts towards their grades. But the convent is very choosy, so there aren't all that many.' She brought her face close to Mary's ear again. 'They have very bad manners. Mother Theresia does not like that.' She withdrew and spoke in her normal voice. 'I mean at home. My mother has summer tourists in the house.'

'Bed and breakfast?'

'And an evening meal. We live on a farm, you see. They call it remote, but it's only eight kilometres from the village. Our guests like hiking, and they come back hungry and tired. They love my mother's cooking. I often take them, show them the best walks and where the finest alpine flowers are.'

'Will you really take me and show me what you do?' Mary asked, eyes bright. 'Aunt Rilla has told me a bit about the festival. I would love to see the grotto.'

8

'Keep a look-out while I unlock the door,' Elisabeth whispered as she tiptoed ahead of Mary along the corridor beyond the classrooms. This led to the Little Sisters' domestic quarters.

Mary craned her neck backwards and forwards along the passage which faced the mountainside. Though there were windows, there was virtually no light. The mountain itself obscured it. And no sound; nothing, no one to see.

'Hurry in right after me!' Elisabeth ordered. She slipped through the door and into the inner sanctum. This area of the convent was kept separate from the outside world. It was strictly private, reserved for the nuns and carefully selected laity. Elisabeth had Reverend Mother's special permission to enter the hall beyond the corridor door, but no other part. And she was allowed to do this only on Saturdays.

The french windows opposite the door leading to the outside world gave access to the nuns' private garden. On turning left, this was simply a narrow alley between the convent buildings and the mountainside. The official path to the grotto, the one Elisabeth was supposed to use, was reached by turning right. But there was also an old unused track up the mountain hidden behind the deep green foliage of several gloomy rhododendron bushes on the left.

Mary slipped nervously into the sanctum after Elisabeth. The froufrou of a heavy skirt coming towards her, the tiny tinkle of the rosary beads, the squeak of leather on quarry tiles, made Mary dart behind the drawn-back curtains which guarded the french windows. In her haste to hide, she almost skidded on a rug spread on the highly polished floor. There was a shuffling sound as friction retained the rug askew.

'Good afternoon, Sister.' Elisabeth sprinted back from the window and curtsied elaborately to Sister Wilhelmina while kicking the rug back into place. The old lady's rheumy eyes, bent down towards the floor, trying to work out what was happening, lifted and swivelled vaguely towards Elisabeth's head. The heavy coif nodded solemnly with the effort. At last the eyes made contact, the mouth curved a faint smile, the fragile old hand waved and the old nun shuffled on.

Elisabeth motioned to Mary not to stir. She unbolted the heavy french windows and swung one side outwards, looked around from left to right, from back to front. Then she beckoned Mary through. 'Run,' she said softly.

Mary scurried out, made for the bushes and dived straight under the shelter of the dark rhododendron leaves. She waited, panting.

French windows fastened after her, Elisabeth stood on the small cinder path and looked around, then up at the windows of the convent. Nothing stirred, not even a bird. Satisfied, she too darted under the shrubs. The two girls muffled their giggles with their hands.

'Poor old thing couldn't make out what was happening.'

'I know. She thought she saw the rug move, then decided it was just me being clumsy. Or her eyes letting her down.'

'I was sure she'd see my shoes peeping out from under those curtains.'

'She's half blind.' Elisabeth turned round, taking Mary's hand. 'Just follow right behind me,' she said conspiratorially. 'It isn't all that difficult.'

'Doesn't look as though many people use this path,' Mary said, pushing obtruding vegetation aside.

'I usually go the easy way. We aren't really allowed to do this,' she flung over her shoulder at Mary as she led the way up a precipitous mountain trail. 'Our botany teacher would kill me if she knew. She says it disturbs the local flora and fauna if people use a track.'

'But I thought walking was one of the big sports here.'

'That's the whole point. No one's allowed to go through the private parts of the convent, and the nuns are too old. Fräulein Bader thinks this bit of mountainside should be kept as a sanctuary.'

'So how are you supposed to get to the grotto?'

'Along the side of the train track, of course.'

'Train? There's a train up the mountain?'

'Not an ordinary one, a cog railway.'

'Oh, yes. Aunt Rilla told us about that.'

'Only since the war. The Germans built it.' Elisabeth's voice became scornful. 'All because of one of the village women. She wanted to make herself important – a local celebrity. My grandmother goes on about it even now. Frau Miller; she started a branch of the Order of German Women. She said the grotto water was important, that it would increase the number of children born to the right people.' She turned back towards Mary and grinned. 'That's all boring stuff. Point is it takes much longer to go that way, and the kitchen nuns could spot us from their windows if we did. I told you, I'm not supposed to let **you** come.'

'Why not?'

'Because I have to go through the private part of the convent. They only open it for the festival. They let me do it because none of the nuns is supposed to leave the convent buildings. Anyway, none of them is young enough to do the chores.'

'You mean the nuns used to use this path?' Mary was finding it difficult to keep up with Elisabeth. The track was not only steep, there were small stones which rolled under her shoes and made it hard for them to grip. The leather lace-ups her mother insisted she wore were nothing like as good as Elisabeth's trainers. Mary envied the way her shoes protected her ankles, gripped the earth and cushioned the walker's feet. 'How could they have managed in their habits?'

'Only the postulants were allowed, even in the old days. They sort of hitched the skirts behind their backs.' Elisabeth's voice came floating breathily back to Mary. 'Most of them came from round here. They're used to mountains.'

There was a hush as both girls negotiated a short, stiff climb which settled into a relatively easy zigzag after twenty metres.

'Sister Paula used to oversee the arrangements. She's too old now, just like the rest of them.' A short lull in Elisabeth's chatter as she stopped and watched Mary. 'Anyway, only a few postulants apply. Reverend Mother turns them all down. There aren't any novices at all. That's why I'm in charge,' Elisabeth declared. 'They trust me.'

Mary puffed with the exertion.

'Sorry. I'm going too fast.' Elisabeth waited patiently. She seemed to find walking uphill as easy as if she were a mountain goat. 'You aren't acclimatised yet.'

Mary had begun to pant, to fight for oxygen, uneasily aware of feeling faint in the thin air. She gritted her teeth. 'I'll get used to it. Is it still far?'

'Not in distance, but it is steep. It takes me about twenty minutes to get to the platform, but you'll need longer. Look out for loose stones. You need a scrambling technique on this bit. Can you manage?'

'I'll be OK.'

'Watch me. Do exactly what I tell you.' Elisabeth slowed to demonstrate. 'Shorten your stride, and place your heel down hard to get a grip.'

'Like this?'

'Avoid smooth bits. Make sure you find a good foothold.'

Mary grasped at a shrub.

'Don't do that!' Elisabeth shouted, then moderated her tone. 'Grip with your heels. Use your leg muscles to push you up.'

Mary placed her feet carefully. Confidence inspired speed.

'Slow down!' Elisabeth shrilled at her. 'That's dangerous and exhausting. You need a proper rhythm and to stick to that.' There was a silence as Mary concentrated. 'I see you've never climbed before.'

'You're very good at teaching.'

'My mother's paying guests give me good training.' Elisabeth waited for Mary to catch up. 'There is one short, real climb ahead so you'd better practise now.'

'Practise?'

'Learn how to do it. Really watch me. Don't lean your trunk forward; it shifts your centre of gravity. Stay upright, near as you can, and lever upwards with your legs instead of pulling with your hands. Never hurry. I promise I won't run away. Got it?'

'What's the difference between a postulant and a novice?'

'Focus on what you're doing, for goodness' sake!' Elisabeth sounded quite shocked. 'Even a small mistake can lead to a serious accident.'

'I'm all right.'

'Keep your hands below shoulder height, Mary. That's how you can see what's ahead. You've got to use your brain.'

It seemed to Mary that the path was now vertical. A hand veered out to grasp at vegetation.

'Don't *pull* up, Mary. That drags you into the rock and your feet could slip away. *Never* do that.'

Mary stood still, irresolute. 'What am I allowed to do?'

'Use one limb at a time. If you use a hand, keep both feet firm and push up with them. As I told you.'

'I don't think I can do it, Elisabeth.'

'Yes, you can. I teach all those tourists, and they're much slower than you. Look up, Mary. See the path widening out? It gets quite easy.' Elisabeth scrambled on.

Mary put out an arm to grab at a branch, and then remembered. She saw a space, placed her toe into it and was about to lever up when a small stone dislodged, she guessed, by Elisabeth fell alongside her.

'Sorry,' the voice floated down.

'It's . . .' Suddenly the world went black. A cawing, whirring sound erupted from a crevice beside her, a dense shadow blotted out the light. Something brushed past, and Mary gasped as she made out two bright, round eyes. The shape fluttered, then flew away, but a small, grey bundle of fluff fell softly on to her arm. Looking at it, Mary could see blood oozing at one end. She screamed.

'Hold tight!' she heard Elisabeth shout. 'I'm coming back.'

Mary cringed into the rock. The grey blob crawled towards her. She shook it off, gagging into the rockface. It fell, soft thuds going from rock to rock. Another blotting out of light, another swoosh.

'It's only a raven,' Elisabeth's calm voice soothed. 'You startled it, that's all. It dropped its prey. A nestling of some sort.'

Mary was crying, heaving against the rock, clinging tight. A huge black bird – a harbinger of death.

'It didn't mean to hurt you. It was scared of you,' Elisabeth, a few feet away, tried to calm her. 'Better rest before we go any further.'

'I can manage,' Mary said, gulping for breath.

'Count to ten, and breathe in deep but not too deep. We'll wait while you get your breath. There used to be an easier path, but they used it for the Zahnradbahn.'

'Zahnradbahn?' Mary gasped, her breath shallow but easier. She tried to take in what Elisabeth had said. 'What's that?'

'I told you, the cog train.'

'What *is* that, anyway?'

'You've never seen one?'

'No.'

'They have a cog and rack mechanism. The wheels aren't round, they're like pointed teeth set in a circle. They fit into the racks on the rail and the cabin's hoisted up the mountain and down again. It's much too steep for an ordinary train.'

'So why are we working so hard? Why didn't we just use that?'

Elisabeth laughed. 'What do you think? It only runs during the festival. Anyway, remember you're not supposed to be here. We'd have been spotted. You OK now? Come on, and I'll show you where the track goes up to.'

They reached the top, then plodded easily along a straighter stretch of path.

'Any other animals liable to attack me?' Mary looked round, noting the deep shadows cast by the vegetation.

'It wasn't . . .'

'All right, all right. So what's a postulant?'

'What? Oh, that. Someone who asks to enter a religious order.'

'Just asks?'

'It's complicated.'

'But I'm interested,' Mary said eagerly. 'What happens then?'

'Do you really want to know all that?'

'I've never come across nuns before.'

'They train to become novices. Sort of nuns on trial.'

'For how long?'

'Depends. The Little Sisters are very strict; takes three years to become a novice, two more to become a nun. Hardly anyone applies nowadays.' Elisabeth scrunched on, then looked sideways at Mary. 'Shall I tell you a secret?'

Mary stopped short and looked at the Austrian girl. 'What?'

'I haven't told anyone else.'

'I know how to keep secrets,' Mary said crossly. 'Go on.'

'I want to become a nun.'

'Do you really?' Mary gasped. 'That's wonderful!'

'You think so?' Elisabeth picked up a small stone and laid it at the side. 'I haven't even told my mother. You won't breathe a word, will you?'

'Cross my heart.' Mary made an exaggerated gesture as Elisabeth laughed.

'I'm praying to Our Lady. She'll let me know me if I have a true vocation. Sister Paula says you can't always tell. So I study as hard as I can, just in case. That's why I help the Frau Professor.'

'Who's that?'

'Frau Professor Lager. I thought you knew each other.' Elisabeth sounded annoyed. 'That's what you said.'

'It's the way you talk about people. I didn't know who you meant.' Mary ran her hands over a pine cone, feeling its stickiness. 'Why don't you just go to university first, train as a scientist?'

'Because miracles are better than science. I want to go on helping with the festival. When the brides drink the grotto water they get pregnant right away. I think that's beautiful.'

'What's so special about it?'

'Loads of modern couples can't have babies, but they do if they come here.'

'That's what Aunt Rilla said.' Mary looked thoughtful. 'Perhaps it's because there's less pollution in mountainous places.'

'Barren women come and get pregnant,' Elisabeth said heatedly. 'It's wonderful to see the babies the next summer. I don't want that to stop.'

'But why do you have to become a nun?'

'Everyone knows the miracles wouldn't happen if the nuns weren't here to organise the festival.'

'Why don't they just use the train to get up here? Can't they manage that?'

'The order is dying out, Mary. Sister Paula is the youngest, and she must be getting on for sixty.'

'You'd be giving up having a family of your own.'

'I know,' Elisabeth looked noble, 'but that's the point. It's meant to be a real sacrifice. If I'm not prepared to give up the world, it isn't a real vocation.' She paused, looking down at the convent roofs. 'I'll have to teach you how to do this last bit. Watch very carefully, and do exactly what I do.'

The path had stopped, and there was an actual mountain climb ahead. Elisabeth pulled a stout rope from the rucksack strapped to her back.

'Fasten this round you. I'll go first and attach the other end to a good support. See these holes in the rocks? Put your feet in them, and your fingers in the cracks. I've done it lots of times, so it's easy. Just one last effort and we're there.'

Mary had not looked back until that moment. As she did, her heart leapt into her throat. The sheer drop behind her caught her unawares.

She froze against the rock she was leaning on and tried to calm her racing pulse. She knew she could go neither up nor down.

Elisabeth had already climbed ahead. 'Is something wrong?' she called back.

'I can't do it!' Mary wailed at her. 'I've got vertigo.'

Elisabeth climbed down to a ledge just above Mary. 'Take a deep breath and hold it,' she said. 'And don't look down. Use the rope to belay. I've hooked it over a crag. Haul yourself up. I'll wait for you and do it again if we have to. Nothing to it.'

Mary's hand gripped the crack. A small stone slipped

91

under her shoe and she cried out.

'I'm going to say a prayer to St Christopher.' Elisabeth's voice was firm and confident. 'He is the patron saint of travellers. He'll give you courage. And, remember: even if you fall, the rope will hold you.'

There was no sound. Mary firmed her footing, took another deep breath in.

'It's quite safe now,' Elisabeth's voice washed down to her. 'Put your hand on the rope and, at the same time, push your foot into the next hole. And lean your weight back on to your feet. That's all you have to do.'

Mary's hand crawled upward, seeking the rope and finding it. As though by magic her foot followed. Her hand went on hauling, feet searching the rock, finding the next foothold, pushing to the next place.

'Just two more steps and you'll be at the top. Everything's easy after that.'

And it was true. Mary found herself standing on a sturdy ledge leading to a landing on its right. This must be where the Zahnradbahn stopped. There were rope barriers along the ledge enclosing it against the drop down.

'Very good; you've mastered the difficult bit. Now just a few minutes' walk and we'll be there.'

A relatively broad and easy path curved round the mountainside. The two girls walked side by side, Mary's eyes searching the area. Soft, woolly foliage peeped out between rocks, a few white petals straggling over the top.

'There's an edelweiss!'

'We have superb flowers. You'll see some gentians growing higher up.' Elisabeth stood looking around her. 'The colour is incredible. If you keep completely still you may even see a chamois.'

92

The path had stopped at a grassy plateau, big enough to hold several people.

'Sit down on this bit of grass. I've brought some water.' Elisabeth delved her hand into the rucksack and brought out a narrow flask. 'We mustn't drink the grotto water. It's needed for the festival. Anyway, no one's allowed to drink it except the brides. I had to take a solemn oath and promise Reverend Mother and the Frau Professor that I would not drink a single drop.'

'You mean it could be dangerous?'

'Don't be so silly! The water is from a pure spring. The point is that it refills very slowly. Only a trickle from high on the mountain. It just drips down, like a tap with a faulty washer.'

'And that's what the brides drink?'

'The priest blesses it, *then* the brides drink it, and they all have babies right away.'

'Do the husbands come as well?'

'No men are allowed in the grotto, except the priest. And a nun dips a tiny cup, like a thimble, in the trough and offers it to the bride.' Elisabeth laughed. 'And I check the path.'

'You're really in charge?'

'Why shouldn't I be?'

'Aren't you a bit young?'

'My older sister Helga used to do it,' Elisabeth said. 'And she taught me.'

'She was the one who had the accident.'

'I told you, it was a riding accident. Nothing to do with the grotto.' Elisabeth walked faster. 'All I have to do is make sure there are no small stones, that the ropes are OK, and that the rack rail is clear of debris. I'm the best qualified person around for that.' Elisabeth looked carefully at Mary. 'An engineer checks the train mechanism a day or two before the festival. So far they've always been men, but they are sending a woman this year. There has to be special dispensation from the Bishop before any man can walk through the part of the convent we went through.'

'You mean men are not even allowed on this path?'

'I've just told you: only clergy and the engineer. And my brother – he helps the brides load and unload off the train by that grassy bit. He's there in case of accidents.'

'So what about the husbands? What do they do?'

'They wait until their wives come down again,' Elisabeth said airily. 'They don't mind.'

'Are we going into the famous grotto now?'

'*You* can't come in,' Elisabeth said, shocked. 'You'll have to wait out here. Only I'm allowed to go inside the grotto.'

9

'My mother phoned Reverend Mother, Mary. She's just told me, she's given permission for you to come to lunch with my family today!'

Elisabeth, trying not to run out of the chapel where she had been attending Sunday mass, came over to Mary. The Austrian girl was dressed in her Sunday dirndl, her face radiant with anticipated pleasure. Mary had wanted to join her for mass, to take part in singing the church music which appealed so much to her, but loyalty to her father's feelings had, so far, prevented her.

'How kind of your mother, Elisabeth.' Mary was flattered at the interest the Heldens were taking in her, yet nervous about meeting a local family who would speak only German, and a very regional type of German at that. Elisabeth's people were traditional farming stock. Their language could be hard for someone from Salzburg to understand, let alone a foreigner.

'They call me Lisl at home; it's an Austrian shortening for Elisabeth. You can call me that, if you like.'

'All right, Lisl.'

'It's pronounced Liesl – a long *i* sound.'

'Leesl,' Mary tried out. 'Are you sure it isn't too much trouble for your mother?'

'Trouble? She always cooks for an army. And both my parents are longing to meet you. They'll have gone to high mass in St Walter, and they'll pick us up on their way back after that. It's a bit too far to ask you to walk.'

'Can we all fit into the car? I thought you said . . .'

'The grannies are staying at home, and Joseph's going straight from here, up on to the alp. Ursel and the two of us can squash into the back. Let's go outside and meet them. They'll be here any minute now.'

'Shouldn't I change my clothes?'

'Whatever for? Come on, Mary. I can hear the Beetle groaning now, that sound is unmistakable.' She laughed, opened the convent door and pulled Mary outside.

A large, greying woman was getting out of a Nile-green Volkswagen as Elisabeth rushed towards her. Mary followed sedately behind.

Mother and daughter embraced, and Frau Helden turned round. 'Hello, Mary,' she said, taking her hand and shaking it enthusiastically. 'Lisl has told us much of you. This is Herr Helden.'

'Freut mich.' Albert Helden, now standing beside his car, clicked his heels and held out his hand. 'We are most honoured.'

'You've seen Ursel in the refectory,' Lisl said as her sister dashed out of the convent building to join them.

Friedl Helden's large, florid face had soft brown eyes. The greying hair and deep lines, the calloused skin of her hands, told their story of a life spent in hard physical work. 'You sit in the back, yes?' she said, pulling the passenger seat-back forward. Her daughter Ursel darted through. She looked exactly like a younger version of Lisl and both, in turn, had exactly the same doe-like eyes, wide cheekbones and curly light-brown hair as their mother. Mary got dutifully into the car.

'You like horses, Mary? You ride?' Albert Helden asked.

'I like all animals,' Mary said, 'but I've never had the chance to get to know any horses.'

'We show you,' he said confidently. 'We have good ponies.'

'Was fällt dir ein!' Mary heard Frau Helden hiss at her husband. 'Hat das eine Malheur nicht gereicht?'

'Mary's German is very good, Mutti,' Lisl put in quickly. For some reason Frau Helden appeared to think her husband would bring bad luck on them. Mary remembered that their daughter Helga had died after a riding accident, so perhaps she was referring to that.

Lisl's mother settled herself in the passenger seat, then turned right round to face Mary, her voice soft again. 'First we will have our Mittagessen. A special treat because we have a glut of Marillen this year. Perhaps not what you are used to, Mary, but it is an Austrian speciality. Have you ever eaten Marillen-knödeln?'

'I'm afraid not . . .'

'She won't even know what Marillen are,' Lisl explained. 'That's the Austrian for apricots. Our tree is loaded this year. Anyway, we halve the fruit, take out the stone, replace it with a lump of sugar, wrap a potato dough all round the fruit and roll it into a dumpling. Then we chuck a whole lot of them into an enormous pot of boiling water. They sink, and when they rise to the top we know they're done. Delicious!'

'And we sprinkle breadcrumbs fried in butter over them,' Frau Helden went on. 'And then we dry them off in the oven for a few minutes. That adds a wonderful crust.'

'What these women always leave out is the most important part,' Herr Helden boomed, turning his head and grinning at Mary. He seemed to feel his way round the hairpin bend they were negotiating rather than steering round it. 'We organise a competition. The man who can eat the most wins a special prize.'

'You see he doesn't even mention the possibility of a woman winning,' Lisl said. 'Anyway, Vati is bound to win today. His only real rival is Joseph. Sometimes our neighbours join us: Herr Miller and his sons are just as disgusting as my father and brother. That really makes for cut-throat – well, choked throat – war. I'm surprised they haven't burst as yet, the number of dumplings they get through.'

'So what's the highest score?'

'Forty-one,' Lisl said. 'And when you see the size, and have eaten a couple, you'll be impressed.'

'And who's the champion?'

There was a pause. 'Kurt Miller,' Lisl said at last, her eyes blank. 'He's our neighbour's eldest son.'

'All healthy ingredients,' Frau Helden insisted. 'No one can be harmed.' The car drew up at an old farmhouse. 'Well, here we are. Come in, come in. Go right through to the living room.'

'Can't we stay in the kitchen, Mutti? That's what we normally do. Mary is my friend, not just a visitor.'

'Would you mind, Mary?'

'I'd like to do what you always do.'

'Right, Lisl, show your friend round. Ursel and I will get the lunch ready.'

The farmhouse was low and rambling and, though sparklingly clean, had no electricity or central heating. The telephone was the only modern equipment. The Kachelofen in the living room was a splendid example of a tiled wood-burning stove. It stood, reaching almost up to the ceiling, in the far corner of the room. There was what could loosely be described as a chandelier of small paraffin lamps, and several chamois rugs littered the floor.

'I can only let you peep into the guests' bedrooms. They are out during the day, but it would not be right to go in,' Lisl explained.

As the girls walked from room to room Mary could see that each one contained at least one lamp.

'Who cleans the lamps?' she asked Lisl, thinking what hard work it must be to live like this.

'My father, or Joseph. Whoever has the time. They also have to chop the wood for the kitchen range. But at least we never have trouble with power-cuts. We get quite fierce storms up here, you know.'

'There are a lot of antlers around,' Mary said, eyeing the trophies hanging in the living room with a certain amount of nervousness.

'They're from ages ago. Everyone used to hunt in the past, that's what supplied their meat. But that was in the Kaiser's time. You know, before the First World War, right at the beginning of the century.'

'Your family's always lived here?'

'My father's family, yes. His grandmother is still with us, you know. She's over ninety. It was her house, when her husband was alive. Then it became my grand-mother's; she also lives with us. And now it is my mother's turn. After my father dies, my brother's wife will take over from her.'

'How lovely to have so many generations under one roof.'

'We all enjoy it. You hear about how it all used to be, and what your forebears did.'

99

'You've got some lovely old photos here.'

'This is my grandmother – my mother's mother. Wasn't she beautiful?'

'Lovely. And is this the latest family photo?' A huge colour enlargement was hanging on one wall. The present Herr and Frau Helden were standing in the centre, behind the seated great-grandmother and grandmother. Their children ranged around; Joseph behind his father, and three girls. Mary looked at it with the greatest interest.

'It's very good of you, Lisl. You look lovely all dressed up in your Trachtendirndl. Not the one you're wearing today.'

'What do you mean?' Lisl said. 'I only have one dirndl.'

Mary stared at her friend, comparing the photo to her. 'And you look older, somehow – fifteen or sixteen.'

Lisl came over to stand next to Mary and peered at the picture. 'I look younger, Mary. It was taken over two years ago.'

'But . . .' Mary traced a finger on one figure.

Lisl laughed. 'That isn't me, Mary. That's my sister Helga, just before she died. She was four years older than me.'

'So this is you?' Mary said, pointing to another young girl evidently younger than Lisl now, and frowning.

'Yes.'

'Looks much more like Ursel than you.'

'I told you, it was taken in 1991. We have one done every Easter, but my mother couldn't cope the last two years because Helga wasn't with us. So we just had separate photos done.'

'Sorry, I didn't mean to . . .'

'It's all right, I have to get used to it.'

'You girls are all incredibly alike; is this one of Helga?'

'Honestly, Mary. You can see how old it is! That's my mother as a young girl.'

'You're all so very like your mother, too. When she was young, I mean.'

'I suppose so,' Lisl said, taking her friend's arm and moving her away. 'Would you like to see Helga's room? My mother keeps it just the way it always was. Cleans it out and everything, as though she might come back. She was her firstborn, you see.'

'Firstborn? What about Joseph? Isn't he older?'

'He's my half-brother, my father's son by his first wife. She died of leukaemia.'

'Oh.'

'My mother was so thrilled to have Helga. She thought she was infertile, you see. Somehow she can't seem to get over that accident. Don't say anything about it to her.'

'Of course not; how terribly sad.'

'It couldn't be helped, just one of those things. Nobody's fault; Helga was breaking in a new pony. It was one of her special gifts, you know. She was awfully good at it. But she was all stirred up that morning. She'd been up to the grotto – I told you she was in charge of that before me, didn't I? Maybe she found something wrong up there and lost her concentration thinking about it. Anyway, the horse shied and she fell and got concussed.'

'But why did she die?'

'No one knows. The Frau Professor was called in right away, and gave her an injection to make sure everything was all right. But she just seemed to drift off then and there. Went into a coma and never came out of it.' Lisl

101

sighed. 'My father shot the horse. He couldn't bear to see it any more.'

They were in Helga's room. It was small and neat, and very barely furnished. The whitewashed walls held several pictures of saints; a large crucifix hung over the iron bedstead. A chest of drawers did duty as a dressing-table. The centre was taken up with a statue of the Madonna and child, flanked by a candle-holder on one side and a silver-stoppered scent bottle on the other. Helga's silver brush and comb set were neatly stacked at the right end, with a matching mirror on the left.

'Her fiancé gave her the dressing-table set. She was very proud of it. And she always kept holy water in the scent bottle,' Lisl was telling Mary. 'She told me the secret. She wasn't meant to have it here, you see, but she was so devout. Not that she wanted to become a nun, or anything. She was happy to be engaged. She wanted to be like our mother: raise a family, help her husband with his work.'

'She was going to marry a farmer?'

'She was engaged to Kurt Miller. He isn't a farmer yet, he just helps his father at the moment. When he isn't in Kernkirchen, swanning around, that is. But he will inherit the farm eventually, yes.'

'How terrible for him.'

'I suppose so.'

'You don't like him,' Mary said, sensing the hesitation in Lisl's attitude.

'I'm not crazy about his family. I told you about his grandmother. She was the Nazi, the one who got them to build the Zahnradbahn. And Kurt's such a yobbo. He always behaved as though he owned Helga,' she burst out. 'I hated that. I never could understand what she saw in him. They were very much in love, though, so I suppose it would have been all right.'

'What a sad story.'

'Come on, that's enough of doom and gloom. I'll show you our horses. They aren't dangerous, any more than Helga's was.'

The two girls ran out into the farmyard and towards the meadow beyond. A pair of amiable ponies, grazing at the far end, spotted them and cantered up.

'This one is called Minz and the other one Maunz. After one of the stories in *Struwwelpeter*, you know. They were cats, but they did everything together at exactly the same time. And so do these two.'

The two ponies leant over the fence simultaneously, shaking their heads up and down, neighing in unison, proving the point.

'Servus, Lisl. Thought you were buried in that convent of yours.'

'Kurt,' Lisl said, a flat unenthusiastic tone. 'Kurt Miller, Mary. He's the neighbour's son I was telling you about.' She turned her back on him, but he vaulted over the fence separating them, ran in front of her, bowed and handed her a red rose.

'A rose for a beautiful rose,' he said.

'He says that to all the girls,' Lisl shrugged at Mary, flicking the flower back and forth.

'So you're Mary. The English Mary who got her voice back singing with Joseph?'

'Singing the Shubert Ave Maria, yes,' Mary admitted, drawing nearer to Lisl.

'I'm not going to bite you, you know,' Kurt said, looking at her from the top of her head to her shoes muddy with farmyard muck. 'Hold on a minute. I'll be right back.' And he vaulted over the fence again.

'Ignore him, Mary. He just likes to play the local

Casanova. There's always one. Unfortunately he lives on the farm next to us. Their house isn't that far away.'

'You really don't like him, even now.'

'Can't stand the sight of him.'

'What's he done? He seems very keen on you. Is it because he brings it all back again?'

'I suppose it's sad in a way. He's always hanging around. At first he couldn't get over it at all, and now he's transferred his so-called affections to me.'

'Maybe he really means it?'

'It's only because of what you noticed: we're quite alike. He thinks I'm her, now that I'm within a couple of years of the age she was when she . . . when it happened. I'm just some sort of reincarnation for him. It's really creepy. Anyway, you know I don't want to know about a boyfriend.'

'He's very good-looking.'

'So what,' Lisl said crossly. 'What's that got to do with anything? I'm interested in people's souls, not in their bodies.'

'The Blessed Elisabeth,' Kurt said, vaulting back again. He had a yellow rose in his hand. 'Allow me,' he said, and gave a little bow as he handed the rose to Mary. 'Two beautiful girls. That's really made my day for me. Bet your mother's making Marillenknödeln, Lisl. You girls won't be able to get through them on your own. Aren't you going to invite me to lunch? I'll soon demolish them.'

Mary looked at the young man, his grey leather shorts suddenly turned to black, his smile a leer. She fled towards Lisl, grabbed her right arm. Lisl turned away from Kurt and and began to pull Mary after her. She watched, mesmerised, to see what he would do.

His lips parted wider, teeth bared, eyes mocking. He

104

strode over to the girls, took Mary's hand and kissed it. 'Küss die Hand, gnädiges fräulein,' he said, then straightened up. 'It is our custom when we wish to be polite,' he explained. He was about to approach Elisabeth to do the same, but she skipped away, pulling Mary along with her.

'My mother will be serving up,' she said, and closed the farmhouse door on him.

10

'C'm on, Mary. Let's head for the lake. I promised Mom I'd come over after class. It'll be real cool.'

It was the last day of the summer course. The music lessons had already stopped, and this morning had seen the final test for the German lessons. Certificates, and prizes, were to be given out the following morning. The rest of the day was the girls' to spend as they wished.

Mary was feeling adrift, not quite sure what to do with herself. Lisl had gone off to do her chores in the grotto, but Mary had not felt like going with her. The afternoon, so unusually hot and sunny, would be better spent swimming in the lake than climbing the arduous path up to the shrine. She wasn't going to be allowed to go inside, in any case.

She looked at Jenny dressed as skimpily as possible in a remarkably short skirt and a halter top. Her feet, the toenails painted a stylish purple, were slithering in platform sandals. Jenny's search for adventure almost always ended in her finding it, but the mention of 'Mom' made Mary feel relatively secure. 'What were you thinking of doing?' she asked cautiously.

'My Mom's at the Braune Rössl. She naps till three. She'll treat us to something then.'

It sounded reasonably safe, and difficult to get out of

without being rude. 'Shall we go and get our bathing things?' Even Jenny couldn't get into much mischief bathing in the lake with the hundreds of other tourists who'd be crowding it today.

'Let's just paddle. Thought we might come across some of the guys.'

'We're not allowed to get together with any of the local boys, Jen. You know it's strictly forbidden.' They were already away from the convent, beyond the drive and several hundred yards down the track leading to St Walter. It would be impossible to get away from Jenny now.

She clicked her sandal heels together, stood straight and held her hand out in a Hitler salute. 'Streng verboten,' she said, her intonation exactly like her mother's, her accent uncannily accurate. 'Heil, meine Führerin!' She grinned, showing perfect teeth, tossing back gleaming dark-brown curls. Her smile, structured by American dentistry, was strikingly different from her mother's. 'Sure thing. Let's get down to business. Mom let me have some cash. We can go for one of their fanciest boats. Take a real long sail round the Kernsee while she snores. What do you say?'

'D'you know how?' Mary asked.

'Hire a boat? What's to that? You offer money, they produce the boat.' She laughed. 'You don't do that in England?'

'Do you know how to sail, Jenny? It's quite tricky.'

'I guess not. No problem there; we'll pick a crew of guys who can.' Jenny began to walk faster. 'C'mon, let's hustle, otherwise we'll be all day getting there.' She turned impatiently for Mary to catch up. 'I go for the top lifeguard. He can rescue me if a storm blows up.'

'You mean Kurt Miller?' Mary looked horrified. 'He's such a yobbo, Jenny.'

'A schmuck, you mean? Bit of a wiseguy, maybe, but he's pretty dishy.' She grinned.

'Lisl told me his grandmother was a Nazi.'

'Geez, Mary, that was a trillion years ago. Anyway, he'll be my date. We can fix you up with one of his gang. Maybe Joseph'll be around. He has the hots bad for you, he'll come for sure.'

'He's not a lifeguard, Jen. He's . . .' Mary suddenly looked appalled. 'Anyway, *I'm* not asking him.'

'You're such a wimp! OK, I'll suss it out and do the invites. My show, anyway.'

'What about waiting for Lisl Helden?'

Jenny stopped momentarily, looking interested. 'Why, sure, she's local. She know some of the guys? Got a steady?'

'No. She's going to become . . .' Mary stopped herself in time. 'I don't think so. Anyway, she showed me this short-cut.' They had walked beyond the village and Mary pointed to an unmade road hidden behind a rock to the left. She turned into it and Jenny followed. It narrowed to a path leading directly down to the lake.

'Forget it, Dummkopf. Just the four of us,' Jenny said, kicking at small stones in the dust. 'They'd all gabble German. Let's keep it light.'

The Kernsee shimmered invitingly below them. White, triangular flecks showed at least thirty sailboats wisped over the mirroring surface. As they came nearer they could see the lake was still enough to reflect clouds and mountains, a double landscape of breathtaking beauty.

But that beauty was deceptive, Mary remembered.

'The weather can be very treacherous. You do remember that, Jen? It can look perfect, and a storm will suddenly blow up from nowhere. Something to do with currents of hot and cold air getting caught in the mountains.'

'Sure, sure, Mom drones on all the time. Crowd of the lifeguards hang out drinking on the terrace of the Braune Rössl, right?'

'Two always have to be on duty by the jetty, watching the bathers and keeping a look-out for boats in trouble.'

'That has to be a couple of them sitting at that table by the lake,' Jenny said, pointing to two young men sitting at a wooden table by the water. 'Look at those bodies! I guess some of the others are on duty.' She held her hand up to shade her eyes. 'Right. One of them's Kurt. Never seen the other guy before.' Jenny flirted a practised hand through her hair and wetted her lips as she wiggled provocatively between wooden tables towards the young men.

Mary hung back, undecided. Another group of young men at the table she was standing by whistled at her. One of them stood to offer her a seat. 'I'm with friends,' she mumbled, and ran after Jenny.

'Hello, girls!' Kurt beamed as soon as he caught sight of them. 'You have escaped?' He stood and grinned. 'Welcome to the real Austria.' He signalled to a waitress. 'A coffee, yes?'

'Do they have Coke?'

'Of course.' Kurt's hand gestured imperiously.

'Great,' Jenny agreed, sitting down by Kurt and opposite the unknown young man with him. 'You got a name, buster?'

'Fritz Gruber.'

'OK, Fritz. This is Mary and I'm Jen. D'you sail?'

109

'Naturally.'

'Then I guess you're our guy. We want to sail around the lake, best boat you got,' she said, flickering her eyelashes. 'And we need a crew.'

'This afternoon?' Kurt asked.

'Right now,' Jenny said casually. 'My Mom's coming by later. We got about three hours. Plane leaves tomorrow night,' she announced. 'It's now or never.'

'You have not booked, no?' Kurt slitted grey eyes at the girls, looked at Fritz and said something neither girl could follow. 'It is high season, but I fix it. OK?' He vaulted over his bench and walked rapidly towards the jetty.

'There you go,' Jenny said to Mary, smiling, welcoming a Coke brimming with ice. 'I knew it was a good idea.'

'Hello, Mary. You are not with Lisl?'

The familiar voice of Joseph Helden rumbled pleasantly behind Mary. She turned, an uneasy smile on her face, the reddening of a blush confusing her. She shifted closer to Jenny.

'She had to see to the grotto. Jenny and I are going sailing,' she breathed, uncertain.

'It is a lovely day for that,' Joseph agreed. 'You go alone? You are good sailors?'

'Don't know a boom from a rudder,' Jenny announced cheerfully, 'so it's going to be up to the guys here. Kurt's gone to find us a sailboat. You wanna come?'

'The boat is big enough?'

'I told Kurt the fanciest you got around here. I guess that means big enough.'

Fritz rushed some German at Joseph. He looked at Jenny, eyes contemplating her, assessing her. 'You do not mind a high price?'

110

'My Mom said to enjoy.'

'I think Kurt will fetch the *Kleine Austria – Little Austria*. A beautiful boat for beautiful girls,' Joseph added, smiling at Mary. She remembered Lisl had been annoyed when Kurt had said that. Was Joseph also a flirt, or was it just the Austrian way?

'I don't know that I should go,' Mary whispered at Jenny. 'I think the Frau Professor expects me . . .'

'For chrissake's, Mary!' Jenny talked spitfire speed, swallowing words so the Austrians would not be able to understand her. 'You'll be safe enough. The boys are going to have their hands full sailing the damned boat. You're coming,' she finished up, rasping at her. 'I need another chick along. Whadd'ya think it looks like, standing me up?'

'I have arranged it,' Kurt shouted at them, striding from the jetty towards the table, his bronzed body surging with strength. 'We go at once, yes?'

'Joseph is coming too,' Jenny announced, grabbing Joseph's arm.

'Excuse me,' he said, withdrawing from her, mouth curved up but eyes severe. 'I think it would be very unwise to go as you are.'

Jenny stared back, unblinking. 'What's wrong with us?'

'You need something against the cold of the wind – an anorak,' Joseph said, looking at Jenny's skimpy suntop, at Mary's T-shirt, and shaking his head. 'It can be very cold on the lake. And the reflection of the sun will burn you.' He stared at the girls' feet. 'And I had better get some decent deck shoes for you.' Jenny's ungainly sandals sported a tiny leather strap around the ankle, a bar across the foot. 'And lifejackets. I will be back directly.' He headed for the service quarters of the hotel.

Jenny looked after him and shrugged, then turned to Kurt. 'Thought a crew of three might be better than two. Just in case we get one of your famous storms.'

The two young men looked at one another, their eyes meeting. 'I fetch her,' Kurt said. 'Die *Kleine Austria*,' he said to Fritz. 'Erster Anleger, gell?'

'What was that?' Jenny demanded. 'Let's stick to English.'

'I'll take her to the first pier,' Kurt said. 'Fritz will take you to meet me there. Joseph will join us with the gear.'

'I guess we can manage the walk to the pier all by ourselves.' Jenny sounded irritable. 'We hardly need you to steer us on land.' Her lips pouted to a full circle as Kurt's eyes brushed over her, went beyond her and lingered on Mary. 'And Mary's an old hand at sailing. Her dad taught her.'

Mary's mouth opened to deny this, but Fritz was already standing. 'Good,' he put in. 'Too many beginners is dangerous. We go together.'

He interlinked arms with both girls and headed them towards the jetty. Within a few minutes they could see a sloop coming towards them, sail furled, the putter of her motor clear in the swarm of dinghies dotted around the water. Joseph was right. The *Kleine Austria* was a beautiful boat, gliding on the smooth water, rippling the lake.

'All aboard,' Kurt called out, his head thrown back as he manoeuvred the boat smoothly towards them. He threw a line ashore for Fritz to snub around a cleat. The boat came to a soft, gentle stop.

'Fritz will show you what you do, Jenny. I help Mary.' He looked towards Fritz and waved him towards the tiller. 'Also, gemma schon los.' He stopped, guilty at

112

the lapse, and grinned at Jenny. 'Let's go,' he translated for her, putting a hand out for Mary.

She held back. 'We have to wait for Joseph,' she said, eyes hardening, staring at Kurt. 'He said we need lifejackets.'

Kurt held up two. 'All arranged. Do not worry. Fritz and I can swim.'

'Jawohl,' Fritz rumbled as he and Kurt exchanged glances. He put his arm round Jenny's shoulders, unlinking himself from Mary.

'So wartet doch a bissel!' they heard Joseph yelling. 'I am coming as fast as I can.'

Mary, relieved, walked towards Joseph and extended an arm. He placed two anoraks on it. She could see three lifejackets and the laces of two pairs of deck shoes fastened round his neck. As she turned back towards the boat, Jenny was already scrambling over the side with Fritz putting a helping hand on her rear. The skirt was fluttering in the wind.

'I help you on board, Mary,' Kurt purred at her. 'You will be safe with me.'

Mary looked imploringly back at Joseph. He smiled at her and winked. She lowered her eyes, held the anoraks out to Kurt. 'If you could just hold these.' Backing promptly, she allowed Joseph to hand the lifejackets and shoes over to Kurt and climb aboard himself. He held an arm out to her.

Kurt, resigned, began to motor out to open water. He motioned to Fritz, slowed the engine. 'Hoist away,' he called.

'You girls sit down,' Joseph instructed them. 'Put on the shoes and the lifejackets. Then sit still until we're under way.'

Fritz was already freeing the remaining sail tie, while

Kurt trimmed the mainsheet. 'Hard a-lee!'

Joseph took his chance. 'Now, Mary. Over here for the moment.' He sat himself between the two girls, watching with narrowed eyes as Kurt played skipper, coming around into the wind.

They sailed rapidly out to the centre of the lake. The sun, high noon above them, glinted diamonds into the water. Jenny, hot and bemused in the reflection, dipped her hands into the lake, looked up. Kurt, caught unawares, was watching Mary as she fastened her shoes more securely. A trickle of small white clouds cast flitting shadows over the Kernsee, the breeze turned into wind.

'Weather's changing,' Joseph announced. 'You'll need the anoraks.'

Mary gratefully wrapped herself in one, piling the lifejacket on top of it. Jenny ignored what Joseph had said, watching as he moved towards Mary's other side so that she was now between Kurt and Joseph. Both men were looking at the slender, waiflike figure.

She turned to Joseph. 'Have I got it fastened properly?'

Kurt instantly held out an arm. 'Let me help you.' His voice, deep, insistent, was ahead of his arm, now around Mary's shoulders, down to her waist, adjusting the bands. Joseph, outployed, took over the neglected tiller.

'What about me?' Jenny pulled at Kurt's arm, pointed to the lifejacket she had managed to put on upside down.

He turned reluctantly. 'Undo the knot,' he said. 'I help you put it on the correct way.'

The boat was heading straight downwind. The boys began to tack. The unusual, swaying motion showed as discomfort on Jenny's blanched face. She dipped her hand into the water again, dashed it against her cheeks. Kurt, in his element, was showing off to Mary, yelling at Fritz. 'Prepare to gybe!'

Obediently Fritz started to cast off the turns in the jibsheet just as the wind, increasing in force, swung the boat severely enough to make Jenny teeter on unsure legs. She sat down hard.

Kurt grabbed the tiller back from Joseph. The wind began to sough, then whistle. Joseph, sensing danger, bellowed 'Watch your heads!' just as Jenny, unawares, decided to stand up again to move over on Joseph's other side.

'*Duck*, Jenny!' Mary screamed out.

Too late. The fast-moving boom swung tight, crashed into her head. The sickening sound of wood on living tissue shuddered fear through Mary, made her hold her hands over her chest. Jenny crashed down against the cockpit seating, her arms over the backrests, legs levering into the air.

'Verdammte Scheisse!' Joseph jumped over, grabbed the girl's legs and dragged her back on to the deck. She slouched, lay still, her supine body welling blood. Mary could see it was from a cut in the side of Jenny's head.

'Zurückfahren!' Joseph yelled. 'Turn the boat around. Head back!' he yelled at Kurt.

'Arschloch!' Kurt yelled back. 'What the fuck do you think I do?' He had already turned the boat around, was dropping the mainsail, about to start the motor. He handed a loudspeaker to Fritz. 'Alert the lifeguard.'

Joseph crouched down in the cockpit beside Jenny. There was a long gash in her temple. She lay silent, unconscious. 'Take her legs and hold them in case she starts to move; that's to keep the flow of blood down,

115

Mary. Anchor them there while I put pressure on the gash to try to staunch the blood.' He sat down on the bench, put Jenny's head on his lap, drew out a handkerchief, made it into a wad and pressed it to the girl's head.

She opened her eyes. 'What is this? What's going on?' Her voice was soft, hardly audible.

'Lie still, Jenny.'

The blood began to ooze through. 'Something more to stem the blood, Mary.'

Mary put Jenny's legs behind her, sat hard against them. She took off her lifejacket, her anorak, and finally her T-shirt. She did not look up but handed it, without a word, to Joseph. Then she put the anorak back on.

Jenny, becoming aware, looked round, took in the situation, her head on Joseph's lap and smiling up at him. 'OK,' she said. 'OK, big guy. You look after me.'

'Just keep still, Jenny. Do not speak.' He twisted the T-shirt into a ring and placed it over the handkerchief, his hands firm on the wound.

Fritz had already signalled their distress while Kurt started the motor and steered the *Kleine Austria* back.

Ten minutes later they drew in by the pier to find a knot of people standing there. Two young men – the lifeguards on duty – helped to lift Jenny ashore and laid her down.

'She's bleeding badly,' Joseph alerted them. He stepped ashore and placed a small seat cushion under Jenny's head.

They busied around Jenny. Mary stepped ashore and Kurt and Fritz eased the *Kleine Austria* back to her berth.

'We need to keep her warm, and to send for the

116

ambulance right away,' Joseph said, worried eyes on Jenny's white face.

'All been seen to. Frau Professor Lager has been sent for,' one of the lifeguards reassured them. 'She will be here in five minutes.'

Blankets were brought out of the hotel and draped over Jenny. It was one of the longest five minutes Mary could remember. At last Erika Lager's Audi, black and swift, drew up beside them. She placed her bag by Jenny, took one look at the blood-soaked bandaging around her, the face devoid of colour.

'Fetch her mother,' she ordered. 'The child needs an immediate blood transfusion.'

'But, Frau Professor . . .' Mary began.

'No talking, Mary. Help me set up the things I need.' She motioned to Mary to open her bag. 'Take out the needle kit.'

'Helden,' Erika rasped, turning to Joseph. 'Fast as you can, Frau Cohen's room. Drag her down, even if you have to carry her. Tell her her daughter's life is hanging by a thread. We need her to give blood. A vein to vein transfusion.'

'Isn't—' Mary began.

'Move, man!'

Mary watched as Erika put pressure on the wound, rammed her finger expertly on the temple pressure-point to stop the flow through the artery. 'A few stitches while we wait,' she said. Her eyes searched the wounded girl's face, felt the slackening pulse with her other hand.

'Open the bag again, Mary. Take out the antiseptic. Give me the bottle and some clean gauze. Now cut some of that silicone tubing you'll find in there, and sterilise it.'

117

'Tubing?'

The woman crouching over Jenny gave Mary a venomous look. 'Don't argue, girl. The plastic tubing. We have to transfuse directly from mother to daughter.'

'How do you know the blood will match?' she persisted. 'What if it doesn't?' She stared at the still body. 'Jenny could die.'

'Don't argue, girl. Just sterilise the tubing.'

Mary, reluctant, dipped it into the antiseptic fluid.

'Take out two luer needles, the biggest ones, put them at either end and fasten them with the butterfly canulas.'

'Like this?'

'Excellent. Now insert the nylon tap.'

'Tap?'

'That thing there,' Erika said, pointing towards a package. 'I have to be able to gauge the flow.'

'How do you know it will be all right?'

'Do we have any choice?' she snarled, fingers working fast. No sign of Greti Cohen yet. 'Anyway,' she continued, panting, intent, 'I already have Greti's blood group on my files. She was my patient.'

'And Jenny's, too?'

'Yes.' The Frau Professor sat back on her heels. 'You know the school asks for the blood group on your application form.'

'So you've cross-checked them?'

There was no answer. Erika looked at the shaking girl, her eyes pin points of irritation. 'What else can we do, Mary? Jenny will die otherwise. That would be the most terrible tragedy. We must do everything we can to save her.'

It was then that Mary noticed Greti Cohen loping over the concrete towards them. She was wrapped in a

118

vast kimono, slippers covering swollen feet, her bulk urged along by Joseph.

'You can save her life, Greti.' Erika stood up and grabbed at the woman, pushed her up against the bonnet of the car, pulled the kimono back from her neck. 'We don't have time to worry about modesty. Your left arm.'

The shocked Greti leant awkwardly, the wrapper off her shoulders, showing a bulging body clad only in bra and pants.

'I have to do a straight blood transfer to save her. But first I have to inject you with an anticoagulant, so that your blood does not clot and fail to get into her veins. Do I have your permission?'

'Of course, Frau Professor.'

Erika injected her in the left arm. 'I am using heparin, I have some ampoules with me. The effect only lasts a few hours. It will not damage you.'

'Anything, Frau Professor. Anything at all to save my little girl.'

'You have to be higher than Jenny for the blood to flow, Greti. Just sit on the bonnet of my car. I will transfuse from your right arm.' Erika worked swiftly. She inserted one of the luer needles into a vein in Greti's arm, the other into a vein in Jenny's. The blood began to flow.

Greti was weeping, her left hand mopping her eyes. She nodded her head.

'Get something for her to lean against,' Erika shouted. 'This will take at least an hour.'

A mound of mattresses from the lounging chairs on the hotel terrace were placed against the windscreen to support the weeping, heaving Greti. More blankets covered her. The blood seeped slowly, steadily into

119

her daughter's body. Half an hour later they could distinguish the intermittent wailing of the ambulance siren as it drove along the mountain bends towards them.

'It has been a memorable summer,' Reverend Mother Theresia announced as she stood, a little unsteadily, on the platform. The habit seemed to be larger than the woman, obscuring her, weighing her down. 'A time of miracles,' she said. Indifferent heads jerked up. 'By now you will all know that Jenny Cohen is making an excellent recovery after yesterday's accident.' There was a silence as the old nun looked around the room. 'Without the swift and courageous action our Frau Professor Lager took, Jenny would have died. A direct blood transfusion, even between mother and daughter, can have tragic consequences. The Frau Professor was very brave to risk it.'

The voice, a little thin, projected authority towards the back of the large, capacious hall. The impressive space made a brilliant auditorium for the summer students assembled for the final ceremony. Language certificates were about to be handed out, as well as commendations for musical careers. The first winner of the new Folk Singing Competition was also to be announced.

Mary found herself lost in thought. She'd soon be home again, but she wanted to come back. How could she arrange that?

'And now we come to this year's innovation, the St Walter Lieder Prize. Our first course in folk singing has been a wonderful success. Joseph Helden, a member of one of our oldest families, has collected authentic folk songs from the area for several years. Collected them, written down the music and the lyrics, recorded the tunes. It cannot have been easy because these are purely aural traditions. Joseph is the first person to have attempted such a task.'

Mother Theresia peered towards the back of the hall, saw what she was looking for and beckoned towards the platform. Albert and Friedl Helden, sitting on either side of him, pushed Joseph up to standing and out towards the platform.

Worn leather shorts, a loden-green jacket embellished with silver buttons, hand-knitted white knee-socks all helped to give the young man's handsome body an extra fillip as he walked towards the podium. The strong legs, their muscles taut from climbing, sent a frisson around the room of young girls. There was a sigh as he vaulted the platform, ignoring the steps.

Mother Theresia put delicate fingers on his arm, the old face wizened into a beatific smile. 'Joseph has found a way to teach several skills in a delightful manner: singing, German and some unforgettable tunes. We hope this experience will give treasured memories to our visitors from places which may be very different from our alpine regions.'

The applause began, but the Reverend Mother waved it silent. 'Our proximity to Salzburg has made us intensely aware of our musical traditions, yet it fell to such a very young man to try to keep them for future generations. I would like to congratulate him, and to offer our small contribution to his studies.'

A piece of paper, clearly a cheque, was handed over. Joseph took it, read the figures and paled. He could only mutter his thanks.

'And finally, to mark our new venture and to encourage aspiring young singers to spend their summers with us, I am going to announce this year's winner of our Folk Song Competition.

'This is a doubly special occasion because, you see, a second little miracle occurred in this very convent only six short weeks ago. It happened in our chapel. Our excellent student Mary Fullbridey had lost the use of her voice as a result of an unfortunate incident which happened in London in June. Mary came to visit us with her parents in July, and she heard Joseph playing the organ in our chapel. When he sang the first few bars of Schubert's Ave Maria, the miracle occurred. Mary found her voice, mingled it with his to sing that beautiful prayer. It was after that she found her speech had come back to her.'

A ripple of subdued ahhs.

'And now I am so very happy to present Mary with the first prize. I am sure she will sing one of the songs for you.'

Mary sat as though transfixed. *She* had won! It was the answer to a prayer she had not even had time to offer up. Surely Daddy could not fail to let her come back? The girls around Mary stirred and pushed her towards the podium.

'Don't be afraid, Mary. Your voice is one of the most promising I have heard in many years. We hope this will be the beginning of a great career for you. And, if you would like to take it up, we are proud to offer you a place at our school, and a scholarship to train your voice.'

Mary felt the words spurt adrenalin through her veins, air into her lungs. She smiled, stepped towards the platform with confidence and climbed the steps. She took the certificate and looked at the framed picture Sister Paula handed her. A hand-painted copy of the triptych altarpiece in the chapel made her gasp. It depicted the Virgin and Child, with the two central scenes from the Annunciation on either side. Two further scenes, only unveiled on the day of the Mothering of the Brides, scenes which Mary had never seen before, were also shown. They were the birth of Jesus, and the parable of the wise virgins.

The sight of the beautiful grouping released something in Mary. As Joseph walked towards the spinet and strummed the introductory chords of 'Das heilige Wickelkind' – 'Holy Babe', the song Mary had chosen for her audition – she drew in her breath, waited for the right note and began to sing. Her voice, soft to start with, found its strength. She sang the first verse like an angel. Her voice filled the hall, the minds, the souls of everyone there.

There was no sound at first, just a stunned silence. But when the applause did come, shouts of 'encore!' filled the room.

Her eyes met Joseph's. She drew in a breath and began to sing the second verse. There was no longer any doubt in Mary's mind that she should make singing her career.

11

'It's a popish plot,' Thomas Fullbridey announced. Mary watched as he lifted his dessert spoon and fork and brandished them above his placemat. She wondered why adults were allowed such childishness whereas she was reprimanded for the smallest lapse.

The shrewd eyes glinted, looked towards the kitchen, watched for the pudding Gabriela had gone to fetch. Mary eyed her father. She knew he enjoyed Gabriela's Austrian specialities and the wines Michael always produced to set them off. She also knew he found the Adlers' dining room a little cramped. The heavy Biedermeier furniture Gabriela had insisted on bringing over from Austria did little for the small rooms of the Victorian semi. It prevented Thomas from pushing his chair back as far as he liked, and rocking on it. Mary trembled; it was important that her father remained in a good mood.

Michael, his handsome face made even more attractive by the shock of straight brown hair which slipped enticingly over his left eye, was poised over Thomas's glass, about to pour some more Balsac. He had chosen to introduce the heady sweetness of this wine to complement the Salzburger Nockerln Gabriela now set, steaming, on the table. But his face darkened into anger as he stepped back, about to put the bottle down.

'It's an English joke, Schatzi,' Gabriela soothed. 'Thomas knows perfectly well that no one is interested in converting Mary.'

'I d–don't know why you think I would be converted, Daddy,' Mary put in. 'I'm quite capable of having my own ideas.'

Her father looked at her good-humouredly. She knew what that look meant: his little girl needed protecting because she was unable to think for herself. Big Daddy would have to do it for her. Her eyes flashed, but she kept her voice sweet. 'I worked out what happened to Bridget,' she said. 'Without anyone influencing me. I read it up in a b–book I got from the library.'

'Did you now?'

'Written by a professor at Cambridge, a geneticist. He maintains that unfertilised mouse eggs can begin to reproduce themselves if given some sort of electric shock, or dipped in alcohol, or even just warmed or chilled. That's what must have happened to Bridget.'

'Very good, Mary, but there is a slight problem.' Thomas grinned at his daughter. 'I do not believe that Allbrights took the ova from your beloved rabbit, stimulated them and returned them. I think she produced her offspring all by herself. So how do you account for that, eh, my clever little girl?'

'That's what I'm trying to tell you, Daddy. There was a thunderstorm just after Easter. Lightning did strike the hutch – I saw the scorch-marks – that's how I think it happened. The electricity must have gone right through Bridget. Poor little thing must have been terrified. That's why she looked so unwell.'

'Now then, attention if you please. This is the moment we have been waiting for,' Michael announced,

125

drowning out Thomas's reply. He had gone out to the kitchen and returned with an enormous silver ladle.

Gabriela took the ladle and dipped it into the dish. She began to heap deep soup-plates with a buttery mass. 'I don't think I've made this for you before,' she said. 'And we didn't get round to having it in Salzburg. I'm sure you'll love it.' She smiled. 'And it will give Mary a chance to get used to the way Austrians eat. The nuns try to produce American-style food during the summer, but the rest of the year they revert to Austrian staples.'

'I had Marillenknödeln at Lisl's house,' Mary told them. 'They were delicious, but terribly filling.'

'Lisl's house? And who might Lisl be?'

'Elisabeth Helden, Daddy. She's a local girl, the one who helps Professor Lager. Her people live in a beautiful old farmhouse about eight kilometres out of St Walter.'

'And you just went there?'

'No, Daddy. Mother Theresia gave me special permission. And Lisl's parents came over to fetch us.'

'Hmm.'

'This looks pretty substantial.' Anne laughed and tapped her waistline. 'How are we supposed to manage on top of that huge schnitzel?'

'Actually, it's only a soufflé.'

Anne looked unconvinced and Thomas grinned. 'You mean you were so overwhelmed with trying to persuade us to let Mary attend that convent of yours, you let it sink and crack?'

'You'll think it's special pleading,' Michael said. He found it difficult to understand English humour, but trusted Gabriela to have understood Thomas. 'But that's the way it's supposed to be. It splits into Nockerln, which are really small dumplings normally used in soups and stews. The soufflé rises, and then you let it sink in the oven for at least thirty minutes. Then you serve it. Try it.' He looked intently at Thomas. 'I'm trying to convert you to Austrian food,' he said.

Thomas grinned his acceptance of the repartee and put a spoonful into his mouth. His grave, critical eyes took on a dreamy look. 'That really is delicious. I'll take Michael's word for it, Gabriela, about the looks. The taste I can vouch for myself. Marvellous, quite exquisite.'

'If we can go back to the convent for a moment,' Gabriela said softly. 'The order does not see conversion to the faith as its function. The Little Sisters' interest is in helping young musicians to fulfil their potential. That's why they offered Mary the scholarship.'

'Miss Johnson said I really ought . . .' Her godmother looked at Mary warningly. She stopped.

'Yes, Mary? What were the pearls of wisdom from Miss Johnson?'

'Sorry, Daddy, I've forgotten.'

He laughed. 'Well, there you are. Overcome by Gabriela's marvellous cooking.' He smiled expansively around. 'Mary's a good little cook too, you know.'

'I do know, Thomas,' Gabriela agreed. 'Mary is very gifted altogether. But, as I was saying, the convent's mission in life is to further musical talent. That, and the October festival. It's enough to keep a far larger community on its toes, and the order is being depleted by "natural wastage", as we now call it.'

Thomas smiled at Michael to show there was no personal grudge, held out his glass, and pushed his plate towards Gabriela. 'Your dinners are always magnificent, my dear. Now if you were to tell me they'd teach Mary the delights of traditional Austrian cooking at that school, I'd be inclined to forget they're papists.'

'The kitchen nuns are as outstanding in their domain as the teaching nuns in theirs,' Gabriela said gravely. 'I remember my mother telling me how they always managed to produce good, wholesome food even in the middle of the war.'

'So your mother spent the war in Austria.' Thomas looked reflectively at the Adlers. He had not entirely forgotten whose side England had been on.

Catching the hostility, Gabriela smiled again. 'Not all of it. At first she was a student at the convent, in spite of the fact that my paternal grandparents came from Hessen, and were Lutherans.'

'Is she a Catholic now?'

'She told us she wasn't, Thomas. You remember, she said anyone could go to the masses in Salzburg just to listen to the music.'

'She calls herself an agnostic, says it's the only thing a scientist can subscribe to. But the reasons my family managed so well was that my maternal grandmother, Heidi, was a brilliant seamstress. The nuns allowed her to see to the chaplain's vestments. So she and my mother ate their midday meal at the convent on week-days. And they never went short of food.'

'What about your grandfather? Was he in the German army?'

'Not in the army, no. I think I mentioned him before. Helmut Fluge, quite a well-known research scientist.'

'Ah yes, of course you did. Didn't that mean he had to join the Nazi party?' Thomas asked snidely.

Gabriela glanced at Michael. 'Worse than the army, in a way. The Nazis ordered anyone like that to join a special section of the Nazi party – the Union of Nazi Physicians. He also had to belong to the SS, because

128

doctors engaged in important research had military rank.'

'What does essess mean?' Mary wanted to know.

'Short for Schutzstaffel. Known as the Blackshirts,' Michael explained. 'The elite members of the Nazi party had to belong.'

'Eventually they forced him to do his research in Berlin. He was housed in the bunker next to Hitler's, by the Tiergarten. That's how important they thought his work was. My grandmother always told me he resisted that as long as he could. In the end, he had no choice. It was your brain or your life. Worse, actually; your family's life.'

'Now I remember. Your mother went with him,' Anne said. 'So what was so special about what he was doing?'

'I'm not sure, exactly. The one thing which stuck in my mind was the degenerate diseases bit. As far as the Nazi party was concerned that would include tendencies to alcoholism, homosexuality and other "socially undesirable" attributes.'

'You mean they'd abort a foetus simply because they thought it *might* become a homosexual?'

'Without a doubt, if they could pin it down. And even respectable-sounding ideas, such as preventing people being born who happen to have genes which *might* cause a debilitating disease later in life, say. Alzheimer's, for example. The genetic link wasn't known about then, but the Nazis would have had no qualms at all about aborting a foetus which carried such a gene.'

'Stick to the point, Gabriela,' Thomas insisted. 'Do those nuns teach cooking?'

'No. I told you, it's a very strict order. No outsider is allowed in their domestic quarters. I'm afraid they don't teach cooking any more than they preach in order to convert.'

'What Rilla is trying to tell us, Thomas, is that the Reverend Mother will take Mary because of the special circumstances.' Anne handed Thomas some whipped cream for his coffee. 'It's really very good of her.'

'It's not just Rilla,' Michael interrupted. 'I second the idea.' He smiled, the watchful eyes grave behind crinkling skin. 'You know how critical I am, and how inquisitive. I've researched the place thoroughly and, believe me, you couldn't do better.'

'I really want to go, Daddy.'

'I don't want to sound overenthusiastic,' Gabriela's voice had reverted to emphatic Germanic intonations, 'but it's really quite an honour, you know. Normally Mother Theresia would not even consider a girl from London. It's a relatively small school, and the convent prefers to concentrate on the local talents. Especially as the surrounding families are often not that well off. And Mary will need extra help. After all, she isn't fluent in German. She could hold up the other girls in her classes.'

'So why *is* Mother Theresia offering to take her?'

'Well, she won first prize for the folk singing! And Mother Theresia has really taken to her.' Gabriela turned to her goddaughter, and smiled. 'She loved the way Mary conducted herself during the summer course. And naturally she thought very highly of the way she responded to the music, the way she worked so hard, the way she got on so well with Elisabeth Helden right from the start.'

'They seem to think she's perfect!'

'And what is wrong with that?' Gabriela laughed, and

Mary felt the warm thrill of her affection, her encouragement. 'And my mother, too.' Gabriela stopped for a moment as she thought back. 'She spoke most highly of her.'

'I d–did get my voice back in the chapel, Daddy. Doesn't that prove God wants me to go?'

Gabriela shook her head very slightly, trying to warn Mary to leave the negotiations in her hands.

'There you are, then,' Thomas roared. 'It *is* a popish plot!' But he winked at Mary, and laughed to show it was another joke.

'I suppose I was rather taken with that myself,' Anne said, her eyes sad. 'Mary obviously feels at home there. She has had a bit of trouble with her voice again since we got back. She has an occasional stutter when she's under stress.'

'And Mutter was most insistent that I let you know she would keep a special eye out for Mary,' Gabriela added. 'Elisabeth has already taken her over a couple of times to help out in the laboratory.'

'Your mother would actually take Mary on as one of her assistants?'

'Delighted, I understand. She was so impressed with the way Mary kept her head that time with the blood transfusion.'

'Blood transfusion? Mary had a blood transfusion?'

The tension spread all round the room as Thomas looked around the table. Would Daddy ask what she had been doing, going sailing with three boys and Jenny, unsupervised?

'Not Mary, Thomas. The girl you met in Salzburg, Jenny Cohen.'

'Spoilt brat! Up to no good, I suppose.'

Michael got up and lunged for the Balsac bottle.

131

'More wine, Thomas? Your glass is almost empty.'

'If you insist. Lucky we only have to walk down the road. Just hope the police haven't decided to stop pedestrians over the limit!'

Gabriela cleared her throat and began again. 'As I was saying, Mutter would love to have Mary's help.' She turned to Mary. 'That is, if you're willing to take it on?'

Mary was beaming, the crisis clearly over. 'She said I could help to look after the mice and rabbits. Check they are all right, and that.'

'Is there more coffee? Lovely.' Anne also accepted a second helping of Salzburger Nockerln. 'But will Erika have time to think about Mary: will she be able to fit her in with her own schedule?'

'Not a problem if Mary is willing to organise her day. My mother is super efficient, she has it all worked out. Elisabeth can show Mary what to do without taking up my mother's time.' She looked at Thomas. 'That would give Mary a chance to see how research is done, and to get used to a first-class laboratory. Her biology would improve enormously.'

'I suppose we could give it a try for the year, couldn't we, dear? You said you wouldn't send Mary back to Highgate Ladies, and we haven't found anywhere else yet.'

Thomas took a sip of the Balsac, nodded his head at Michael, and took a further one. 'That's true. I had forgotten the school offers an excellent academic programme. All right, we'll try it.' He did not even look at his wife or daughter as he made his pronouncement. 'If it doesn't work out by Christmas, she's coming back.'

The other four exchanged glances, smiled guardedly.

'So let's drink to Mary's singing,' Michael said, raising his glass. 'God works in a mysterious way, Tom. And I don't think you would deny that He is the same God you worship, after all.'

12

'Don't forget we're going up to the grotto,' Lisl whispered to Mary during the last lesson on the third Saturday of the autumn term. They were being instructed in Euclidean geometry, a subject new to Mary but one she enjoyed. 'Then we can be on our own.'

'Helden Elisabeth, you will do three more exercises than the rest of the class. Questions eight, eleven and thirteen.'

'Yes, Sister.' Lisl's eyes dropped demurely to her book.

Sister Marka had chalked three intersecting lines – two of them equal – to represent a triangle on the board. The small waves along the supposedly straight lines gave away her age. Her eyes, however, still flickered sharp understanding. She turned from Lisl to Mary and watched the girl apparently absorbed in her work. Mary had learned to listen without appearing to do so, to trace out parts of circles using her compass, almost on automatic pilot. Sister Marka's instructions presented no problems.

The final bell trilled freedom at two o'clock. Lessons finished an hour early on Saturdays. Lisl and Mary walked sedately out of the classroom, content to wait for the other girls to disperse. They wanted no witnesses to their weekly excursion towards the nuns' inner sanctum.

'Keep a look-out while I make sure there's no one in their hall,' Lisl whispered to Mary as she moved cautiously towards the door blocking the nuns' quarters from the outside world.

She was about to put her key into it when she heard the door being unlocked from the inside. She waited, irresolute, waving to Mary to move away. The door opened and Sister Christa walked through. At first she did not even see Lisl, standing demurely by the side, but when she did she stopped and was moved to speech.

'What are you doing here, Helden?'

Lisl curtsied obsequiously. 'It's my day to see to the grotto, Sister.'

The nun looked at her, then nodded. Mary had retreated into the general corridor and nipped into a classroom to let the nun pass. She emerged after a few moments, carefully approached the forbidden door again and saw Lisl's head peeping round.

'Come on!'

Rapidly, silently, well versed in their conspiracy, they negotiated the nuns' hall, ran out of the french windows and scampered under the dark bushes.

'We'll have to hurry. It gets dark so early now.'

'You're the one who's slow, Lisl. I can go faster if you like.'

'I feel a bit off. Hold on, I'll just drink some water.'

'Are you OK?'

'Just a bit thirsty.'

She moved on, but Mary sensed her friend had to push herself, that she was feeling the rigours of the climb in a way she simply had not done when she had first taken Mary up to the grotto.

'Can you keep a big secret?' Lisl suddenly asked, stopping to regain her breath.

'You've told me already, Lisl. And I haven't breathed a word to a living soul.'

'I've told you?' Lisl stopped stock still.

'About becoming a nun, Lisl. You said you were going to talk to Sister Paula about it. Have you?'

'Oh, that! That's not what I was going to tell you about at all. Something much more important,' Lisl breathed, excited. 'It's really special.' She waited, caught her breath. 'But you mustn't even hint at what I'm going to tell you, or it will all be spoiled.'

'Cross my heart and hope to die,' Mary tittered, putting a hand to her chest and rapidly putting it out again to steady herself.

'What do you mean, "hope to die"?'

'It's nothing, just an old English saying. I won't tell anyone.'

'It could happen to you as well,' Lisl breathed. 'If you do exactly as I say, it could just as soon happen to you.'

'What could?'

'I'll tell you when we get to the easy path.' Lisl climbed on more quickly now, though Mary heard her laboured breathing. 'Can you manage on your own, or do you need help?'

'I'm perfectly OK,' Mary said crossly. 'You're the one who seems to be having problems. And I wish you wouldn't tease. What's this special secret? What happened to you that could happen to me?'

'You'll have to wait.' The two girls climbed on in silence.

Mary had joined Lisl on her weekly trip since the beginning of the autumn term. This was her sixth time

136

up the steep mountain path: three times during the summer session, and twice since then. She was proud of the fact that she could do it in the twenty minutes Lisl had boasted about. True, autumn rains had made the climb easier, given more purchase under foot. In fact Mary had begun to feel quite confident about her mountaineering abilities, and thoroughly enjoyed the clandestine climb. But that was as far as Lisl would let her go. Her friend had never once allowed her into the actual space inside the grotto.

'Right, then. We're on the easy bit. Tell me.'

'Not yet. I want to show you exactly where I saw it,' Lisl puffed behind her, breathing hard, trying to walk fast but not really doing so.

Mary thought it unwise to ask if there was something wrong with her. 'Saw what?' she said instead, just as they arrived at the entrance to the grotto.

There was a sudden whirring as a large, black bird edged its way between the boulders guarding the cave, then spread its wings. It loomed like a giant shadow.

'Is that another raven?' Mary cried out, terrified by the wingspan. 'The last one wasn't nearly as big as that.'

'They're always after nestlings,' Lisl said. 'I think the fledglings try to hide in the grotto because they think they're safe.'

Mary shuddered. 'There won't be any more, will there?'

'Don't think so. Anyway, I'm going to push the stone back so another one would have plenty of space. Then it won't be as frightening.'

One of Lisl's weekly duties was to inspect the grotto for any intrusions, check there was no debris in the water and that the entrance was kept blocked by five weighty stones. They were there to prevent animals from coming in and drinking the precious liquid, even though it was covered by a grid.

'That's odd . . . this isn't exactly how I left it last time.'

'What isn't?'

'That central stone. Mary, look, I always put it back lined up exactly with the two on either side. I'm very careful not to leave any space for even a bird to get through. It's askew. That's how that raven got in.'

'Maybe the wind . . .'

'Too heavy for that. A big animal would have moved it completely, and a little one can't shift it.' Shrugging, Lisl rolled the central boulder aside. 'You're not to come any further, Mary. You promised.' She stood astride the entrance. 'This is where it was.'

'I'm not coming in,' Mary said, petulant. 'This is where *what* was?'

Lisl walked away from the entrance into the dark interior. Mary could just make out a little light coming from the roof, with the figure of Lisl standing to the right of a bulky shape below the daylight. 'I'm standing by the trough,' her voice floated out to Mary. 'Just like that day. I'd picked some flowers for Our Lady, and I was saying a prayer, asking her to help me pass the last violin grade they could teach me at school. That's when I saw her.'

'Saw who?'

'Our Lady. She was so beautiful, Mary.'

Mary watched as a shadowy figure moved rhythmically inside the cave. She heard the sound of sweeping. 'You mean you had a vision?' Mary asked, eager, her feet stepping over the threshold.

'Not one step more, Mary. You promised.'

'Sorry, I forgot. What did she look like?'

'Like nothing I've ever seen before. It was all blue, a beautiful, shimmering sapphire blue – just wonderful. A sort of floating above the water in the trough.'

'Did you talk to her?'

'I couldn't speak, or move, or anything . . .'

'So what did you do?'

'I just looked at her.' Lisl moved nearer the entrance and stopped sweeping. 'She looked at me. I could feel her eyes sort of glow at me, and I knew she was smiling. Then I saw her head move up and down.'

The broom moved again, swift and sure. Stone dust, small rock particles and a few pieces of vegetation were quickly gathered into a heap by the boulder gap.

'Then what happened?'

'I'll tell you later, Mary. I'll just get the old flowers for you to throw away. You go for your walk while I finish here.'

'You're not being fair!'

'I'll tell you later, honestly.'

Mary waited patiently for her friend to bring the withered flowers. 'You've given me the new ones, Lisl!'

'Whatever do you mean? Of course I haven't.'

'These aren't a week old. They can't be the ones we brought last week. The light inside the grotto isn't good enough. You must have swopped them by mistake.'

Lisl stepped out of the grotto and peered at the bunch of flowers now in Mary's hands. They looked as though they had been picked that day. Her mouth drew tight and her nostrils widened, her eyes steely.

'See what I mean?'

Lisl's eyes slid away. 'Maybe it's a sort of miracle, Mary. Perhaps Our Lady chose to keep her flowers fresh.'

139

'You didn't use the grotto water, did you?'

'What a thing to say! That would be terrible. There's hardly enough anyway. You know I always bring a flask.'

'Just trying to work it out.'

'I've got the new ones inside. I don't want those, they'll have to go.'

'But they're still . . .'

'Just get rid of them.'

Mary shuffled away and turned to look at the view below. It was the end of September, the last but one Saturday before the festival. The days were getting shorter and the sun was low, a mist forming in the distance. She hoped Lisl would not be too long. She might have better climbing skills now, but the prospect of scrambling down in mist and almost-dark frightened her.

She put the flowers on a ledge they always used, and looked down. The lights of St Walter blinked at her, their amber glow suggesting warmth and homeliness. The church bell began to chime the hour. Mary's eyes rose, looked over from her vantage point to the side of the mountain. The peak was wreathed in mist, swirling, dull. A shiver coursed through her, the skin on her arms cold and pimply with gooseflesh. Blinking, her eyes swivelled into the haze.

She shuddered, cried out. For there, in front of her, was the silhouette of a figure. She could not make out any features but, somehow, she sensed it was a man. A man she knew. She turned and was about to run when she saw movement out of the corner of her eye. She spun back, twisted her head. The small, tight figure had metamorphised into a looming, menacing giant standing in front of her, unmoving, without a sound. Had the

140

small figure enlarged, changed? Somehow it seemed to have a different build.

Was this a vision? Not of the Virgin Mary. This was a dark, threatening, evil shape. The devil come to haunt her because she had walked through the convent without permission?

She moved her arms to shield her face and saw the figure do the same. Mocking her! Her heart missed a beat, then rocketed into thumps she could not control. She lifted both arms, lowered them. The figure, taunting, grotesque, did the same. What was this ghoul?

'Lisl!' she shrieked. 'It's the devil! He's coming for me!' She hurled herself towards the grotto, about to run inside.

Elisabeth blocked her path. 'What on earth, Mary? I told you . . .'

'He's after me! The devil's after me! He's waiting just outside. Go and see if you don't believe me.' She leaned against one of the rocks blocking the entrance.

Lisl, broom held in front of her, stepped out. The sun, a low ball of red, pushed dim reflections into the murk, a soft, dark cloud ahead of her. She turned; no one, no sound.

'Could you tell whether it was a man or a woman?'

'I think it was a man, I saw light between the legs. Reminded me of someone big and strong.'

'You're sure?'

'I *saw* him.'

'There's nothing, no one, here now,' she said. 'You playing tricks to get into the grotto?'

'He was huge,' Mary gasped. 'Huge enough to stride over from the other mountain. He was in front of me, striding towards me.'

'You're imagining things. I suppose I frightened you

with my story of the vision.' Lisl had walked over to the shivering girl, put her arm around her.

'I saw him. I saw the devil, Lisl!' Mary was sobbing, head on her friend's shoulder, clutching her. 'He's come to get me because I shouldn't be here.'

'There's nothing, Mary, really; no one. Calm down for goodness' sake. We've got to start back, it's getting dark.'

'I can't go out there.'

'We're together, Mary. I'll say a prayer. This is a shrine; the devil can't harm us here.'

Slowly, hesitantly, Lisl persuaded Mary to peer beyond the grotto, to step away from it.

'Sit down,' she said. 'I have to get the boulder back.'

The sun was almost gone, a half-orange sinking behind the mountain. The girls, their backs to it, began the slow descent of the path, hand in hand, towards the mist, the dark.

'What's that?' Mary screamed as she saw a black shape swirling in front of them.

'Oh, that. Is that what you saw?' Lisl laughed relief. 'That's nothing, Mary, nothing but the spectre. Das Brocken Gespenst.'

'Spectre? What spectre?' Mary wailed.

'It happens sometimes. When the setting sun's behind you, and there's a bit of mist.'

'What happens?' Mary cried. 'Why won't you say? It *is* the devil, isn't it?'

'That's our own shadows we're seeing there, that's all,' Lisl soothed, her arm round her friend again. 'I can't see yours and you can't see mine. They look enormous in the mountains, but it's just reflected light. Low-level light, that's all.'

'He was clearer earlier on. Much smaller, and a

different shape. I know I saw the devil!'

'The sun was stronger. You saw your body's shape, just like a giant.'

'I saw it twice! Once it was more or less my size, just a bit bigger. And there was light between its legs. It wasn't me.'

Lisl let her arm slide down to Mary's waist, hugged her along. 'Come *on*, Mary. Believe me, please. It was a reflection of your own shadow. If it gets dark we really will be in trouble, devil or not.'

'I'm never coming up here again,' Mary sobbed. 'It's much too creepy. There's something peculiar going on.'

'Look, Mary. Stand still with your back to the sun and look. See?'

'There's nothing there now. Just a dark cloud.'

'Because the sun has almost gone. You saw your own shadow. Honestly, that's all it was.' Lisl took Mary's hand, icy with sweat. She swung it high. 'Has the shape moved?'

'Yes,' Mary whispered.

'Because it is your shadow.' She pulled her on. 'I know it's frightening, but it's nothing. Honestly. It often happens in the mountains in early autumn. I should have warned you.'

'You're sure?'

'I'm sure. Now let's hurry back. There really will be the devil to pay if we don't show up in time for supper. They'll send a search party out for me.'

'So when she nodded you knew you'd pass?' Mary pressed her friend as they whispered in their dormitory that night.

'Exactly.'

'Shut up, you two. I want to get some sleep.'

'Sorry, Renate.' Mary lowered her voice further. 'And you did?'

'Top marks! You know what it's like. Five examiners sit with their notepads and pencils ready. They always look completely bored. Well, I began to play, and something – some force outside myself – went through my fingers. I began to play in a quite different way from usual. I knew I was doing it but I wasn't sure they'd noticed. So I glanced up and I saw them listening, not taking notes or anything. They were taking in the sounds. All of a sudden the door opened, and I stopped. The chief examiner turned and waved some people into the room, and asked me to go on. After that I just played, I don't know how long, or who was there, or what. Finally one of the examiners came over and laid a hand on my shoulder. "That was beautiful, Helden. We will hear much more of you in the future. Meanwhile we have to make time for the next candidate." And they all clapped, and sent me off. I got the highest distinction.'

'And you think it was a miracle?'

'I *know* it was a miracle. I have never played like that before.'

'It could have been a phenomenon, like the shadows this afternoon. You could just have been inspired to play. You're a talented musician.'

'It was different. My hands were guided by an outside force. I knew when I walked over to the trough and looked up. It was all azure blue. Just like heaven.'

'I don't want to sound like a doubting Thomas, Lisl, but miracles are rather rare.'

'You had one happen to you,' Lisl reminded Mary.

'Down in the chapel. You said you'd lost your voice completely.'

'It almost came back a little bit before. I told you, during the concert with the Vienna Sängerknaben.'

'St Paul's is a church.'

'Only sort of; it was a concert hall that evening. Anyway, the specialist said my voice could come back any time. He said it was impossible to say when, anything could trigger it. So it could just have been the singing.'

'You're so ungrateful, Mary. Aren't you afraid you might lose your voice again?'

'That's pure superstition.' Mary lay back against the pillows. 'Anyway, I started stuttering when I got back to England. It wasn't just a simple miracle. It was psychological. This place is beautiful, inspiring. I love the atmosphere, the way everyone is. Not only Mother Theresia, Frau Professor Lager, too.'

'I thought you said she makes you nervous?'

'Sort of brusque and unpredictable, but I do admire her. It was just fantastic, the way she saved Jenny's life that day.'

'It's her job.'

'She took an awful risk, doing that. If it hadn't worked, she might have been struck off the register.'

Lisl propped herself on her elbow, her head on her upturned hand.

'This is a wonderful place,' Mary said. 'A real shrine. I'm not knocking it. I just don't want to call it a miracle when it isn't. Your pope agrees with that.'

'Lots of people have visions.'

'The brides, you mean?'

Lisl seemed oddly hesitant. 'Well, yes, the brides. But there's nothing to stop you from praying to have a vision yourself. You can sort of make it happen.'

'Why would I want one? I don't want a baby. Not until I'm married, anyway.'

'To help you with your singing,' Lisl answered promptly. 'Then your voice would be as wonderful as my violin playing was that day. And you could have your pick of teachers. Then you'd have the best chance of developing it.' Lisl's voice grew quiet. 'What's wrong with asking Our Lady to intercede for you?'

Mary could hear her father condemning popery. 'That's just superstitious,' she repeated. 'If my voice is good enough, I'll have a career. If it's not, there's no point.'

'Your Shakespeare said it: "There are more things in heaven and earth, Horatio, than are dreamed of in your philosophy." You don't have to be a Catholic to believe that. Buddhists do, so do psychiatrists.'

'I can't pray to the Virgin Mary, Lisl. I don't even believe she was a virgin. After all, she had a son.'

'We do not pray to Our Lady either,' Lisl said crossly. 'We only pray to God. We ask Our Lady to intercede for us.'

'What's the difference?'

'There's all the difference in the world,' Lisl insisted. 'Only God can answer prayers. Even though Mary is the mother of God, she is only a human being, not God. *That's* the difference.'

Mary shrugged. 'Not is, was.'

'She ascended into Heaven, so she *is*.'

'Let's not argue about it.'

'People have visions here because there is a shrine,' Lisl went on. 'And because they drink the holy water.'

'So it's not the prayers, it's the holy water?'

Lisl looked at Mary, and was about to say something more, then changed her mind.

'We'd better get to sleep,' Mary said. 'I can hear Sister Marka doing the rounds. She'll say lights out. And you'll have to say thirty Hail Marys if she catches us.'

13

'Aunt Rilla! I didn't expect to see you till tomorrow. When did you get here?'

'Late last night.' Gabriela turned wistful eyes on her goddaughter and smiled. 'Mary, my dear, I have missed you.' She embraced the young girl warmly, kissed her on both cheeks. 'You look positively blooming.'

'I'm having a wonderful time. Is Uncle Michael here as well?'

'He's gone off to Kuwait for a month.'

'Really?' A mischievous grin. 'I thought no one was allowed to drink alcohol there. How is he going to survive?'

'Apparently he can manage in the cause. He says he's on to a scoop.' Gabriela grasped Mary's shoulders, twirled her round. 'Well, now, let me see. I almost didn't recognise you. Your hair looks most attractive plaited in that Gretchenfrisur. Who taught you how to do it?'

'Lisl.'

'Who else!' Gabriela put her hand gently over the plait wound around Mary's head. 'I did like the way you used to wear it, though. You have such lovely soft waves in your hair. The plait hides that.' She breathed in deeply. 'And I see you're into traditional garb as well.' She looked at Mary's dirndl closely, and frowned.

'I expect you recognise the dirndl. It was Helga's.'

'It was Friedl's,' Gabriela said, a sad look on her face. 'I remember her wearing it when she was a girl.'

'Lisl said it was Helga's,' Mary insisted. 'You must have seen her in it and muddled them up.'

'A very special dirndl, as you can see. One of the original Festendirndl, made for festive wear. You're very lucky, Mary. That gold embroidery on the bodice is just exquisite. Someone as expert as my Oma – my grandmother – must have done that.'

'Lisl said the material is pure silk,' Mary said, smiling.

'I know. Friedl's Sunday best; she used to wear it every week when we were children.'

'But . . .'

'Friedl passed it on to Helga. Realised she'd never fit into it again, I suppose.'

'Lisl said you gave Helga the blouse. It's really pretty.'

'That's right, I did. Another goddaughter; maybe that's what Friedl was thinking of.'

'So that's why she offered it to me. Lisl showed me how her mother keeps all Helga's old clothes in her wardrobe. Later Frau Helden suddenly said she couldn't stand it any more, and asked me if I'd like to have this dirndl and the blouse.'

'Poor Friedl. Such a dreadful, awful thing to happen. I suppose no mother ever gets over the death of a child. And Helga, you know, was one of our festival miracles. I suppose that made it worse, somehow.'

'What do you mean, Aunt Rilla?'

'Friedl also got that dreadful infection, though not as badly as I did. She could hardly fail to, we were best friends, spent all our time together. Well, my mother couldn't do any more for her than she could for me.' Gabriela paused for a moment, sighed. 'So when Friedl first married, the children didn't come. She wasn't very religious then, and she assumed she was infertile. Albert persuaded her to go one October. Helga arrived the next August.'

'Anyway, Lisl didn't say anything about that.'

'Probably doesn't know. Better keep it to yourself. Her mother has had two babies since, and has become very devout.' She looked thoughtful. 'You're very lucky, you know. These Trachtendirndln usually get handed on from mother to daughter.' She sighed. 'All three of her girls look so alike, I suppose she decided she simply could not cope with either of the other two wearing it.' A shrug. 'I remember when Lisl had to change her hairstyle and everything, just so her mother wouldn't jump every time she saw her.' She twirled Mary around. 'Anyway, it suits the high colouring in your cheeks. No one would believe you came over from London only weeks ago.'

'They would as soon as I open my mouth.'

'Your German accent is excellent, my pet, you have such a wonderful ear. If you could only hear some of the much younger children I'm occasionally asked to coach for speech!' She laughed. 'I will have to ask you to demonstrate to them.'

'They're worse than me?'

'Most people find it impossible to change the phonemes they learned in early childhood.'

'Phonemes?'

'The basic sounds of speech. The German *r* compared to the English *r*, for instance. The way of using the mouth to make the sounds is set by the age of three.'

She looked at Mary. 'Perhaps it's because of your musical gifts.'

'Could just be because I like German.' Mary brushed the difficulty aside. 'And I'm enjoying all the maths and science as well, especially the biology. Even Daddy wrote he thinks this is the right place for me, after all.'

'I am so pleased. Michael and I were sure it would be.'

'You staying for the festival, Aunt Rilla? It's on Sunday, you know.'

'I always come specially to join in, Mary. I thought you knew that.'

'Sorry, I forgot.' Mary's eyes blinked. She tried to stop her eyes lighting on the threads of white showing against the black of Gabriela's hair. She looked quite old, maybe even older than Mummy. Too late for babies, anyway. 'So why do you come, Aunt Rilla? Because your mother lives here?' she tried out.

'St Walter is to me what Lourdes is to the sick, Mary. The big difference is that this shrine is open only on the first Sunday in October. So people have to take their chances on that one day.'

'I thought it was mostly for blessing girls who became brides during the year before,' she said. 'So they'll get pregnant right away.' A puzzled frown. 'I thought it only really applied to brides. You mean some of the older women come as well?'

'I've just told you about Friedl Helden, Mary. And you know I've always wanted a child. I haven't entirely given up hope. Anyway, all kinds of women come, my dear. Even mothers beyond childbearing age. Some of them come to give thanks.'

'They can always come to the shrine in the chapel,'

151

Mary said. 'Reverend Mother says everyone is welcome there at any time.'

'Not a single woman has reported becoming pregnant as a result of praying in the chapel.'

'And they always do if they come to the festival?'

'Not always; but usually. No one has told you about it? Not even Lisl?'

'Lisl talks about it all the time. She's the one who looks after the grotto at the moment.' Mary looked nervously away. Had Aunt Rilla guessed she'd been up there? 'She said all the brides get pregnant right away. But having a baby after you get married isn't exactly a miracle, Aunt Rilla.'

Gabriela smiled faintly. 'Naturally not. But one couple in ten – some say as many as one in six – is infertile now, you know. Doesn't that sound different from the grotto record?'

'Maybe people imagine it.'

'Reverend Mother has kept careful records for nearly forty years. My grandmother kept them from after the war until she died. That's over fifty years altogether. The number of resulting births is very striking.'

'It's still not the same as the Lourdes miracles,' Mary said stubbornly.

'There have also been a number of unsubstantiated successes for women who have been infertile for over two years. I know of Friedl Helden, and Jenny's mother. Then there's Ulrike Kramer, Herr Doktor Kramer's daughter-in-law.'

'Who's Herr Doktor Kramer?'

'You haven't met him? He's the doctor from Salzburg; he comes if my mother says they need a second opinion about a girl at the convent. The family live the other side of Salzburg. Ulrike's only child Klara was born after she attended the festival. She'd been married five years by then.' She smiled. 'And if that isn't enough, there are also a few women from Salzburg, patients of the clinic there. Several have become pregnant in the same way. I suppose much of it could be said to be psychological, probably a number of women have simply relaxed and become pregnant because they expected to.' Gabriela paused and looked towards the mountainside and up to where she knew the grotto was. 'It can't just be religious fervour. Friedl was pretty anti when she first conceived. Has to be more than that in her case.'

'It hasn't helped you,' Mary said gently. 'So the miracle doesn't always work.'

'You have the wrong idea, Mary. I keep telling you I had that awful illness, much worse than Friedl.' Gabriela cleared her throat. 'A virus, not a bacterium, so antibiotics had no effect. Both my ovaries were destroyed, so I can't produce any ova to fertilise. Other women are born without wombs, or have had hysterectomies. None of those conceive after coming to St Walter. They are infertile in a different way. They simply do not have the equipment to conceive a child.'

'But you do have a womb, so you don't need a miracle,' Mary said. 'You could have IVF. The Frau Professor told me you won't even consider that.'

'Implanting an egg from another woman is not, in my view, an ethical solution. It would not be my child, and it would not have come about in a natural way.'

'So why do you still come? Doesn't it make you sad?'

'No, Mary. I pray for a child. That is, perhaps, not quite the same thing as praying to conceive.' Mary shuddered. Somehow that sounded ominous. 'I believe that it can be most unwise to insist on one's own answer

153

to a prayer. So I pray for a child, but I do not say how I should come by this child. I leave that to God, and I know that, sooner or later, He will answer my prayer.'

'You're very devout.'

'Faith is a gift from God. I cherish His gift.' Gabriela smiled. 'And that's enough of that. Show me what you have been doing, what songs you have learned. How about my accompanying you on the piano? You can sing a few of those lovely Volkslieder for me.'

'What a shame Lisl isn't here to join in. She had to go to the grotto to prepare for the festival.'

Gabriela's face could not hide her relief. 'That would have been lovely, Mary.'

The procession of brides started out from the parish church of St Walter. It wound slowly towards the convent of the Immaculate Conception. The parish priest, young and vigorous, held high the ornate metal crucifix taken down from its place behind the beautiful Pacher Altar of the convent chapel. A quartet of attendant altar boys flowed lacy white albs behind him, stout mountain boots hidden by black cassocks. They waved braziers to disperse incense. A further eight held an enormous blue canopy above the Bishop, who was seated in a chair carried by four stalwart deacons from the village. The scarlet-gold mitre sat uneasily on his head, the blue of the canopy bobbing on top of it. His holiness used his crosier to poke it free.

Behind the Bishop came an impressive array of clergy dressed for concelebrating mass, and behind them various local dignitaries: the mayor of St Walter together with members of the council, a small steel band. The pilgrims followed behind. Young women, blooming in their bridehood and accompanied by proud-eyed grooms walked, hand in hand, at the head. The smaller following of older women, bleak eyes downcast to rosaries twined between twitching fingers, walked more sedately. Most of these were unaccompanied by husbands. They paired each other or walked with a female friend or relative. Behind them flowed the devout and the merely curious. The river of people began to yawn a wide stretch between the eager young and the resigned middle-aged.

'We're moving very slowly,' Mary grumbled. Instead of the excitement, the feeling of euphoria she had been looking forward to, she felt uneasy, faintly bored, embarrassed. Was it because the people around her were so old? They exuded an odd smell, almost a stench. Was piety odorous?

'No point in rushing,' Gabriela told Mary walking by her side. 'It takes time for the Zahnradbahn cabin to load and unload each cargo of women. Much easier to walk slowly than stand and wait your turn.'

Thin early morning sun glinted October low between dark evergreens lining the road. Autumnal dew, its cold drops sagging spiders' webs out of shape, jewelled their outlines into silver stars. Grey tarmac darkened to black under the tread of hundreds of feet which reverberated their dull shuffling between the mountainsides. Mary felt hemmed in by the jagged peaks, sensed herself penned together with hundreds of other pious sheep. Restlessness stirred, she wondered how she could escape.

It would not be easy. The pilgrims sang their way, encouraged by the band and the church choir relayed by microphones. They would walk, legitimately, through normally forbidden parts of the convent, areas she had trespassed in. Was her unease due to guilt?

155

She projected her mind to the carefully controlled groups of twelve wedded pairs she could imagine streaming through the french windows into the convent garden. Each set of twenty-four would congregate there to await the brides' turn for the Zahnradbahn, while the following pilgrims waited in the car park outside. She could imagine the old chaplain, modest in black soutane, watching out for them, his old head shaking. The Bishop would step down from his throne, enter the newly-cleaned cabin of the train which was to caterpillar its way up the mountainside. Priest and chaplain, bearing the Blessed Sacrament and the undying flame, would follow him. Four of their entourage of altar boys and deacons would fold the canopy and load themselves behind them. Elisabeth Helden, Sister Paula and Sister Marka would go, and so would Joseph Helden. He was, as Lisl had told her, deputed to be in charge of the train at the top landing stage, and the initial outpost of mountain rescue should that be needed. The rest of the clergy would concelebrate mass in the convent garden.

Mary could tell that the first load was ready by the halting of the cavalcade. The engineer had started the mechanism. A hacking, churning sound was followed by a blast, then a plume of thick white smoke rose into the sky.

The waiting pilgrims cheered as they saw the train crawl up the mountainside. They began to sing familiar hymns. Now the foremost of the brides would be lining up into twelves, the first pilgrims to fill the cabin of the little train for this year's festival. It would unload them on to the landing by the path leading up to the grotto. They would follow each other Indian file and allow the descending brides to pass them. Husbands were not allowed. They waited in the garden, then escorted their returned brides through the narrow wrought-iron gate and back to the village.

'It must take a very long time for everyone to get up there and back,' Mary said to Gabriela as they waited in the car park. 'Is it always as slow as this? Lisl said Joseph had worked out how to speed it up.'

'The whole day for a crowd of this size.' Gabriela smiled at her, eyes soft. 'It's highly organised, but even so we have to limit numbers.'

'Lisl told me how they work it. Ten minutes in the train, five minutes changeover from up to down, ten minutes down, and another changeover. And they still have to walk from the train to the grotto and back. She says two hundred is the largest number that could ever be managed, but the nuns prefer a limit of a hundred.'

'My goodness, Mary, what a litany! I haven't worked it out.' Gabriela smiled. 'I just give myself to the occasion.'

'Joseph did,' Mary went on, excited. 'He and Lisl tried to find a quicker way.'

'And did they?'

'He's organised it so the loading and unloading takes only half the time. He's made two sets of steps for them to use.'

'Steps?'

'By the side of the track.'

'How does that help?'

'It's so that the departing brides can leave at the top while the new set files in at the bottom. They use both doors of the little cabin.'

Gabriela looked reflective. 'A loop of brides.' There was a pause. 'It is beginning to sound like EuroDisney,' she suddenly burst out. 'This is a religious festival, not a joyride!'

Mary had not heard such a tone from her godmother before. 'At least it speeds everything up, Aunt Rilla. Don't you get tired, waiting around? There are nearly eighty brides this year, and then all the other ladies.'

'It's never been a problem. And we are just behind them. I expect we'll be through in a couple of hours.'

'It will take at least three, I think. Why don't they let the older women go first?'

'This is the Mothering of the *Brides*, Mary. It is only right that they go first.'

'Do the brides of Christ come to this feast?' Mary asked slyly.

Gabriela turned calm eyes to her. 'In the days when the convent was still flourishing, and there were many postulants and novices and just a few pilgrims, the true brides of Christ, the young nuns after their robing, would act as handmaids for the earthly brides.' Gabriela paused, looking at her rosary. The mother-of-pearl beads glinted in the sun. 'They never drank the water.'

'Really? Why not?'

'Because, symbolically, they are the offspring of the order of the Little Sisters. The nuns do not need to reproduce themselves in a carnal way. So the water is reserved for earthly mothers-to-be.'

Her sweet, melodious voice poured balm on Mary's nervousness. Something about the setting, the atmosphere, had set up resistance in her. She wondered what Daddy would make of it. There was a sense in which she felt these girls and women were lambs being led to slaughter. That was absurd; the pilgrims came because they longed to come. No one put pressure on them, or even encouraged them.

Gabriela placed her hand in Mary's, swung it to and fro. 'I think, my dear, you should not stay to scoff. No

158

one has forced you to attend the festival. Either give it a chance to work for you, or go away. God is not mocked.'

'I'm sorry, Aunt Rilla. It wasn't meant like that.'

As they moved on, the sun began its slow journey upwards, strengthening into darts, then beams, of warmth. The murmurings of prayer, the snatches of hymn, gripped Mary's imagination. She found herself swept along in a drone of spirituality which searched out hidden corners in her unconscious, delved into the past and melded it into the present. Her mind drifted, began to feel the impact of the minds of others around her, began to acquiesce.

At first she merely sang the hymns, allowed the feeling of the crowd to drown physical discomfort and mental boredom. Then Lisl's idea took hold in her mind, intensified. She wanted a vision, too. What better time than today? A vision of the Virgin Mary, the woman who had become a mother without the act Mary could only think of with revulsion. If she, Mary Full-bridey, had a vision, she would see Mary, the Mother of God, as she really was, would know whether these stories her father termed 'popery' were true. A vision could not lie to her.

Time seemed to pass with the speed of light. 'It's my turn now, Mary,' she heard Gabriela say. 'Don't wait for me to come back. It's been four hours already.'

Mary came out of her reverie. 'I thought I was going to go up with you? I thought it was only men who couldn't go?'

'You know it's only for brides or wives; not even widows are allowed. You told me yourself about Joseph's special plan.' She patted Mary's shoulder. 'I'm going up with Magdalena Kobler. She's Ulrike's sister, I

159

told you about her. We were all at school together.'

A woman in her forties Mary had not particularly noticed, strong hints of grey streaking her hair, smiled amply at her. Magdalena was wearing a dirndl in a soft mauve, her abundant bosom swelling over a white apron spotted with roses. Mary looked at the round of belly below and wondered whether the woman was pregnant already, or whether it was simply an overload of Austrian Knödeln which made her look as though she were carrying a child.

Mary had to stifle a giggle at the thought of Magdalena braving the path she and Elisabeth normally used to get to the grotto. And then, unbidden, a feeling of danger for Gabriela flooded over her. 'I thought I might be useful to you coming down,' Mary said anxiously, walking rapidly after her godmother. 'Suppose you fell? You know, like . . .'

Gabriela's teeth bared into what looked like a grimace rather than a smile. 'There is no need to worry, Mary, I have done it many times before, and I am not in my dotage yet.' She sounded irritable. 'In any case, Magdalena and I will look out for each other.'

'I'll wait for you here,' Mary said stubbornly. 'I'll see you back to the house.'

A steady stream of brides who had drunk the magic liquid were ambling back through a lane left open by the pilgrims waiting their turn. The young girls clasped their husbands' arms and seemed to float, starry-eyed, through the waiting crowd. The older women around Mary looked longingly at them, as though somehow they could wrest some of the youth from the young girls who reminded them of themselves only a few years before. Many had tears lurking in the corners of eyes hooded with pain, with faith, with longing. Had they had the vision? Mary wondered. Had Mary, Mother of God, appeared to them? If she had, they would already have had their child, Mary decided. Perhaps the vision was a sign of imminent conception, or of a baby already conceived but not yet known about.

Lisl's clear voice came back to her. She saw her, beckoning her to come into the inner sanctuary of the convent, felt her arm on hers, heard her urging her to climb, heard her whisper: 'I've seen her!' She breathed hard, overcome by the memory. Something was odd about Lisl's vision. How did she come to have it, all by herself? It wasn't during a festival, she wasn't a bride, she wasn't allowed to drink the holy water. The shadow she'd seen outside the grotto filled Mary's mind. It had not been a Brocken Gespenst, not that first dark figure, not the one which moved away from her. Is that what Lisl had seen? A dark, satanic shadow?

'Have you told anyone else?' she had asked Lisl.

'Not even my mother. She might think I was making it up.'

'What about the Frau Professor?'

'Especially not her. She would just ridicule it. So, don't forget, Mary. You promised, it's to be a secret between the two of us.'

'Suppose you have a baby, Lisl?'

'A baby? You are an idiot! Only someone who isn't a Catholic could think that. Visions don't give you babies.'

'What about the brides? They do.'

'The festival is for women who have husbands – that's the whole point. It doesn't happen only at the festival, after all. It's nothing to do with having a vision.'

'You said yourself that many of them have visions.'

'They think they have, a sort of mass hysteria. But I

161

was all by myself, and I wasn't hysterical. I'd just finished my chores, that's all.'

'So what did you see?'

'I felt as though I was floating on air . . .'

'What did you *see*?'

'You're spoiling it, Mary.' Lisl had been near to tears. 'I wish I hadn't told you.'

Mary felt the sun, now high enough to make the enclosed area hot, beat down on her. It shone relentlessly, made her sweat, feel faint. She swayed.

'Trinkens a bissl Wasser,' the woman beside her said, pointing to the flask Gabriela had left with her. 'Drink water. The standing makes you feel unwell.'

'Danke schön.' Mary let the woman uncap the flask, sipped slowly, gratefully. She would escape to her room in the convent. A feeling of something strange, something cataclyptic, came over her. There was to be a miracle, a miraculous birth. She was sure that there would be a child. But would it be a child of God? Mary could not get the image of something dark, something evil, out of her mind.

14

Gabriela walked forward, arm in arm with her friend Magdalena Kobler. As they moved through the cool of the convent corridors she felt her adult life fall away, felt herself drawn back into her early girlhood, into the time her grandmother Heidi was still alive. The stone walls still looked the same, the shining, polished floors had not changed. She had walked here long ago, reverent while carrying the chaplain's vestments stitched in Oma's delicate, tiny silk stitches. She had loved the feel of the brocade and the glittering ophrey banding attached to it with invisible gold threads. Exquisite work, Mother Theresia had always called it.

Oma Heidi; she'd always miss her. Miss the soft body with its open arms ready to comfort her, the gentle smile, the lips brushing their love across her hair, the hugs. No one had been able to replace the beloved grandmother who had also been a mother to her. A stab of grief made her eyes smart as Gabriela remembered herself as a child of ten, a young girl on the brink of womanhood, excited by it, happy, secure. And then tragedy had struck.

She had been so very ill. Oma had made a bed up for her in the living room, so that she could keep an eye on her every minute of the day. And Oma had abandoned her own bedroom to sleep on the hard sofa, to watch over her granddaughter at night. The fever, the delirium, had made Gabriela weak, her bedclothes soggy with sweat. The ordinary sounds of life had taken on a special timbre, a reverberating tone. She had heard loud, booming voices, arguing.

'. . . your father's work, Erika . . .'

'. . . not only *his* . . . *my* work now. I have refined it, extended it, used modern methods undreamed of . . .'

'. . . it's the same work . . . He would never have . . .'

'He would have been proud of me!' the child Gabriela had heard her mother shout out, infuriated. 'What do you know about it? You're just a simpleton.'

'. . . I knew my husband . . .'

She could remember getting better. When she had not sweated quite so much, Oma had decided it would be safe to leave Resi in charge – Resi Glockner, the one who was allowed to clean the convent chapel and the school corridors – for the short time it would take to check the grotto the afternoon before the festival.

Mutter had gone out already. Something terribly important she had to see to, she'd said. She'd had no idea Oma wanted to go out as well.

Mutter had not been with Gabriela, not that day, not any of the days she had been ill. And then she had come back – alone. Gabriela ached as she remembered how she'd heard someone come through the front door, had jumped out of bed to show Oma how well she was, had seen – her mother.

'Rilla! What are you doing up?'

'Where's Omi?'

'You have to be brave, Rilla. Lie down, child.'

'Where's my *Omi*?' Gabriela heard herself screaming.

164

'What have you done with her?' But she already knew the answer.

'I tried to save her, Rilla . . .'

'*Save* her? Save her from what?'

'She should never have gone up'

'*You?*' She remembered she could hardly contain herself. '*You* were up in the grotto?'

She had never forgotten her mother's eyes, staring, glittering, dark. Never forgotten the clawlike hands beating at the air, scrabbling at the curtains, closing them tight.

'I saw her go, Rilla.' The voice low, choking. 'I had to follow her. She was delirious, out of her mind. She didn't know what she was doing . . .'

'She wasn't ill. She was looking after me.'

Her mother had come over to her. 'We must be strong.'

'Don't touch me!'

'The path is so steep, Rilla. She lost her balance and fell. I tried to grab her.'

'She wouldn't fall!'

'Look at my arm, Rilla. Look. It's grazed all the way down. I grabbed her, tried to hold on to her. She dragged me down.' The tears came then. 'So fast,' she'd whispered. 'It was all so fast.'

'Where is she?' Gabriela heard herself sob. 'Where is my Omi?'

'All over in seconds. I'm sorry, my little girl. I am so sorry. I had no choice but to let go.'

At first she had refused to believe what they all said. The chaplain, Reverend Mother, Resi Glockner all told her the same thing. There'd been a terrible accident, Oma Heidi had gone up to the grotto, had felt unwell, had stumbled, slipped, Mutter had grabbed her, had tried to save her. But Oma had been delirious, out of her mind, had fought Mutter off, had hurled herself away. How could she have? Oma was as used to the mountains as she was to her own kitchen.

That terrible virus, they'd said. The one which had robbed Gabriela of her fertility had spread through the brides and other pilgrims that year, had made many seriously ill, had rendered all of them infertile for a year. Nobody's fault. A disease. And it had taken Oma.

Where had it come from? Mutter had had the grotto water tested. It was the only link to everyone who was ill except Gabriela and Friedl – and Oma. No one else in the village had succumbed. But there had been no sign of trouble with the water. A mystery. An unsolved mystery. And since that time the water had been very carefully monitored before each festival, tested against all known pathogens, to make absolutely sure no such terrible catastrophe could ever take place again.

'It's so cool here after that sun blazing down,' Gabriela heard Magdalena say.

Gabriela shook herself out of her memories. Why was she dwelling on childhood scenes, on a past she could not change? 'Amazing how hot it gets even in October. We're lucky the festival isn't held in August,' she burbled. Such rubbish about weather. She still felt displaced in time, saw Magdalena frown at her, felt her pull her along.

'Come *on*, Rilla. Stop dawdling. They're waiting for us to get into the Zahnradbahn.'

As always, Gabriela enjoyed the ride up to the grotto. The sheer drop down the mountainside gave a magnificent view of the convent, of the village of St Walter lying beyond, of the glittering Kernsee below that.

'Even if I didn't come for the festival, I'd come for

166

this view.' Magdalena sighed.

Several pairs of eyes looked at her in disapprobation. They did not approve of chattering while riding in the Zahnradbahn, but Magdalena was undeterred. 'What if they run out of water? There are so many more pilgrims now than there used to be,' she said.

'They built a second trough two years ago,' Gabriela whispered. 'It was handbuilt, to the precise measurements of the first. The spring water is diverted there and trickled into it some weeks beforehand. Helden Lisl saw to it just before the end of the summer term.'

'Same water? I thought there was so little of it.'

'It's all the same. It goes on dripping. They worked out that there's always enough for two troughs.'

'Same size, you mean?'

'Same volume as the original one. For some reason that was considered terribly important.'

'Anyway, I shall know if it's different from the usual. It always tastes odd, quite unlike any other water I've ever tasted.'

'You and your imagination, Magda!'

'I'm not imagining it. It's not how it used to be when we were children. It tasted of mountain, then. Pure, unadulterated mountain.'

'You drank some?' Gabriela gasped, shocked.

'Of course I drank some.' Magda laughed. 'Albert Helden was like a mountain goat, he could climb anywhere. He got some for me.'

'He got you something else. It can't have been from the grotto. He wouldn't have been able to get through the convent.'

'You're such an innocent. He climbed up the alp on the other side, then abseiled down to the grotto. Test of true love, you know. Only Albert, and Johann Miller,

167

could do it.' She grinned. 'I wanted to have the vision, like all the other girls, so I played up to Albert. Johann was sweet on you, he'd have done the same for you. But you never even noticed him. You were so busy thinking they didn't fancy you.'

'They didn't. I looked different to them.'

'That's what they liked. And you were the only one who didn't try to drink it. Always such a goody-goody.' She sighed. 'Those were the days. Until your bossyboots mother said the water had to be tested from then on, every year. Fussy old cow! After that, taking some of the water wasn't just considered a prank, it was a crime against humanity. Well, worse than that, a sacrilege. They said she'd put a curse on you if you did it. Couldn't get the boys to go anywhere near the place after that.'

'Shh,' a woman behind them said. 'This is a time for prayer, not gossip.'

Gabriela laid a hand on Magda's arm, and they stayed silent. They disembarked demurely within moments. 'Up on the right, down on the left.' Joseph Helden directed them. 'And don't forget to hold on to the ropes.'

The two women plodded on in single file, six other pairs of feet behind them, four ahead. The twelve who had just returned from the grotto passing them, twelve others in the grotto drinking the water and praying for a child.

'*In nomine Patris, et Filii, et Spiritus Sancti.*' The convent chaplain dipped a thimble-sized cup into the water of the second trough, motioned to Gabriela to cup her hands, and poured the water in.

Gabriela sucked slowly, deliberately, as she said her annual prayer. 'Thy will, O Lord, not mine, be done. But if you can find it in yourself to give me a child, I will take the greatest care of her.'

It was as though the world stood still. Gabriela felt the water course down her throat, constrict it, suffuse it with energy, vibrate throughout her body, osmotically insinuate itself into her veins. The chaplain pushed his hands out in a gesture of impatience. 'I'm sorry, Father.'

Gabriela stumbled out of the cool of the grotto into the thin noonday sun. The blood in her veins appeared to boil. She gasped, but she had left the flask she normally carried with her with Mary.

She pushed her hair back off her forehead, dislodging the veil she had covered it with. Sweat began to stream down her face, her arms, her legs as she held on to the rope barrier on her left and tried to keep to the rhythm of the other women climbing down the steep path towards the Zahnradbahn.

A rain of small stones, a patter of earth, fell from the mountain above. The line of women ascending heard it, stood still one after the other, waited patiently. Gabriela, deep in the effort of restraining her coursing blood, of trying to control her body, did not hear, did not see. The woman in front had stopped; she tried to stop herself bumping into her, stopped too fast, swung away, jerked at the rope and lost her balance. Her feet slid under her, accelerated by the stones.

'Hold my hand!' Magdalena, behind her, grasped Gabriela's right hand and did her best to pull her back.

The momentum was too great. The rope swayed, Gabriela panted, fell heavily against it, the drop of the mountain gaping up at her. The woman in front of her had turned. She reached her right hand out to the woman opposite her climbing up the path; clasped at Gabriela's skirt and held it tight. Gabriela lost her balance completely, the rope barrier curved out, she fell down hard on to her left knee, her weight sinking on to her foot. There was a crack.

'My ankle! I've twisted my ankle,' she cried.

More arms grabbed at her shoulders, even her hair.

'Keep still! Don't move.'

Gabriela moaned with pain as the weight of her body rested on her ankle. The women in front had continued to move down towards the platform to allow Joseph Helden to hurry to her, a belay rope round his waist.

'First I will strap her ankle,' he told the women around. 'Please just keep very still. Then I will strap her to me. One of you hold me, and one of you hold Frau Kobler. The two of us will help Frau Adler to stand up.'

There was the silence of cooperation of women who understood the danger of mountains. Once Gabriela was standing, attached to Joseph by the rope, he motioned the women who were going up to continue. The path towards the Zahnradbahn was all theirs now. Slowly, patiently, he persuaded Gabriela to lean her weight on him, then hop a short distance on her right foot.

The operation took time. Magdalena went in front, fixing the anchors for the belay rope into the mountain-side as she went down. Slowly, step by step, they reached the landing stage. Gabriela collapsed as soon as they arrived.

'I think she's suffering from sunstroke,' Joseph said as he eased her down. Willing hands helped to load her on the train.

'She looks overheated,' Magdalena said. 'Is there any water?' She shook her dry flask. 'She left hers down there.'

'I have some,' Joseph said. He put some to her lips,

wetted a handkerchief and applied it to Gabriela's neck, and then another to her forehead.

'Give her plenty of air – fan it with your hands to cool her down.'

Gabriela felt light-headed, faint. She had not eaten breakfast, and yet she felt nausea. Was she actually pregnant? Had the miracle finally occurred? Was that why she had stumbled?

'I seem to be surrounded by invalids,' Erika said irritably. 'Helden keeps saying she has some sort of bug, and now you're laid up, Rilla. How on earth did you manage it? You know how dangerous that path can be. I suppose you were in your annual frenzy of religious fervour.'

'I was not in a state, Mutter.' Gabriela kept her tone even. She was, after all, a guest lying on the sofa in her mother's living room. The derision for what her mother chose to call her weakness no longer touched her.

Erika clicked her teeth with annoyance. 'Why do you put yourself through this torture year after year?' The small figure waved her red-tipped claws at Gabriela. 'We all have to make the important decisions of our lives ourselves. You cannot just foist them on to God. I thought I had at least taught you that.'

'You taught me how to do without a mother. If it hadn't been for Oma taking on the role, I wouldn't have had one.'

'My goodness, Rilla, that's history. And mothering was her talent; it wasn't mine.' She stamped across the room, one leg dragging slightly. 'Are you suggesting I neglected you?'

'You gave me all the material things I needed.'

'I taught you how to make the best of what talents you have.'

'Which, in comparison to yours, are practically non-existent.'

'You have your own gifts, Rilla. But they are not analytical thought-processes.'

'You and the other teachers left me in no doubt about that.' Gabriela laughed hollowly. 'And I am not even capable of having a baby.'

'And you blame me for that?'

'You wouldn't take me seriously. You said I was hamming it up.'

'It made no difference, Gabriela. Can't you get that into your head? There was nothing I could do. Once the infection had caught hold, there was absolutely nothing I could do to halt its spread.'

'If you had watched out for me, you would have seen the start of the infection in its early stages. You might have been able to . . .'

'If, if. Your grandmother was looking after that department. I had to get on with teaching and doctoring. Someone had to earn the money, you know.'

'Oma died of that infection.'

'Your grandmother died because she would not listen to reason. You really must face facts, or you will ruin your life completely with your sentimental rewriting of history.' Erika dragged herself to the window, and looked out. 'She was my mother, and I loved her too, you know. I loved her deeply. She was driven to risk her life because of her obsession with that damned festival.' She shrugged. 'Anyway, what could you understand of all that? You were only ten when she threw herself off the mountain, Rilla. She was delirious . . .'

172

'I won't argue with you.' Strange how her grand-mother had had such a similar accident to hers – except that it had been fatal. Why had she fallen today? Why had she felt so odd? Magda said the water was different from years ago. Was that really so?

'Look, Rilla, I have done everything I can to suggest ways of overcoming your infertility. You won't hear of implants, you won't adopt. All you do is traipse up to that grotto every year in hopes of something which simply cannot happen. You have no viable *ova*, Gabriela. You *cannot* conceive a child. Accept it at last and free yourself from this yoke around your neck.'

'I pray for a miracle. Miracles are things which are said to be impossible but happen anyway. I do not ask to conceive – I ask only for a child.'

Erika turned from the window. In the shadow her face looked almost soft, almost as though deep, uncontrollable feelings for her daughter had at last overcome the resentment Gabriela knew she felt. 'All you zealots seem capable of getting drunk on that water.'

'Jesus could *walk* on water! It's nothing to do with the liquid itself. There does not have to be a physical reason for its effect, and there is not meant to be. When some of the women become pregnant we know it is because a miracle has taken place . . .'

'Come now, Rilla! It's because these girls are young and newly married. It is precisely what one would expect.'

'You are being deliberately obtuse.' Gabriela bent down to rub her leg. 'Statistically, far greater numbers than normal get pregnant when they have attended the festival. Even you can't deny that.'

'I don't deny it. It *is* quite extraordinary. Many of

173

these women are my patients, after all, so I'm bound to take an interest. As a matter of fact I think it is an exciting phenomenon. I would go so far as to say that there could be a genetic propensity for exceptional fertility in the area. Remember, the great majority of the brides come from around here, and the same families have lived here for generations.'

There was an air of suppressed fervour about her mother that made Gabriela listen carefully to her. 'Are you making a study of it?'

The small, quick hands snatched up one of Heidi's beautifully embroidered cushions and plumped it up. 'I have too much else to do.' The bright red nail polish she always wore made her fingers look as though they were dripping blood. 'Lean forward,' she ordered her daughter as she arranged the pillow behind her, deft and certain. 'Right.' Roughly she pushed Gabriela's shoulders back. 'Make sure you support that leg up high to keep the circulation flowing. It will take at least two weeks before you can use the ankle properly.' Her words sounded even more clipped than usual. 'I suppose you'd better stay here.'

'So graciously put.' Gabriela adjusted her leg on the footstool her mother had placed for her. 'I don't want to cause problems for you.'

There was a ring at the front door, a knock, and then it opened.

'I expect that's Mary,' Gabriela said, smiling.

'Hello, Frau Professor, Aunt Rilla.' She walked up to the sofa. 'I'm sorry about your accident. Reverend Mother would not let me come yesterday; she said I'd be in the way.' She embraced her godmother. 'I told you I'd go with you.'

'It was sweet of you, Mary, but I did explain. You're

174

not allowed to take part. That is Reverend Mother's rule.'

'Mary, good of you to come,' the Frau Professor said, her words clipped. 'I have a lot of work to do. I'm very near the final solution now.' Her voice lost its harsh intonation as excitment about her research gave it an almost girlish tone. 'I really think I've got there. Just a few more tests on the animals, all the DNA analyses, and I shall be ready to present my paper.' The eyes, so severe just a moment earlier, had melted into eagerness.

'Why not ask Resi Glockner to come in every day?' Gabriela put in. 'Naturally I'll pay for it.'

Erika's small, heavily-lined face grew red, contorted into fury. 'Die Glockner? That stupid lump? Last time I let her near the place she put my research back about two months. She mixed the phials up, for goodness' sake! However often I tell her not to go near it, she slips into that lab and moves everything about. On the pretext of dusting. Who cares about the dust? I'd rather do the cleaning myself than have Glockner messing my work about.'

'Really, Mutter, do calm down. I can always get on to a plane back to London. I've only sprained my ankle, after all.'

'Michael will be away for weeks. You can't possibly live all by yourself. You could injure the ankle permanently if you put a strain on it now.'

'I could come over after school and help every day,' Mary offered shyly. 'It would be easy. Lisl said I could borrow her bike whenever I like. I rode over today.'

'That is good of her.' Gabriela frowned. 'But it's a bit ancient, isn't it? Maybe we should look out for a better one?'

'This one is fine, Aunt Rilla. Really, I enjoy riding this one.'

She smiled. 'If you're sure.'

'You can test me on my German while I do the cooking and all that.'

Erika twisted towards Mary as though about to shout at her. But when she spoke it was in the controlled, careful voice she normally used. 'I thought you were helping *me*, Mary. You know I need all the support I can get at the moment. This year sees the beginning of the second generation.'

'Second generation? What second generation?' Gabriela asked.

Erika pulled in her breath, looked at her daughter. 'My test animals. I now have records of the chromosomal mutations which I contrived in one generation. Their offspring have replicated the change.'

'I see. Just for a moment I thought you were talking about the brides. But that has been going on for many generations.'

'Accurate records have been kept only since 1956,' Erika said irritably. She tightened her lips. 'By Reverend Mother.'

'Is that significant?'

'If one wanted to go in for a scientific study, one would have to start there.'

'I did not know you were looking into generational effects, Mutter,' Gabriela said thoughtfully. 'That's a new departure, surely?'

'Not at all. I have always considered it essential to change the germ line to stamp out genetically transmitted disease. This is the first year I have seen it achieved in the test animals.' Erika's subdued excitement almost broke loose again. 'It is a most inspiring time.'

176

'I thought Lisl had already written up all the rabbit details for you, Frau Professor.'

'She has. But, Mary, the problem is that she isn't feeling at all well. There is still a great deal to do and I do need someone to help me.'

'Just an upset stomach, Frau Professor. But I would be happy to help until . . .'

'I'm afraid it may be more than that. She seems to tire very easily, and she vomited several times the last time she was here.' Erika walked over to her window and began to water the flower boxes. A riot of petunia colours gave the room sparkle. 'I hope it is not catching. I told her not to come for at least one week.' She held the can up, turned to Mary again. 'Did she teach you how to work the computer?'

'I've watched her several times.'

'So I can rely on you to do her inputting of data for me. Is that correct?'

'I can work the computer *and* check the animals,' Mary said confidently, her eyes glowing with anticipation. 'Someone has to make sure their routine isn't changed. Perhaps you could just explain what's happening to Reverend Mother. As long as I can do my homework here, she won't object. Then I can make the supper for you. You won't have any extra work at all, Frau Professor.'

'What did you say was wrong with Lisl?' Gabriela glowered at her mother. 'You don't think perhaps she has that bug . . .' She rubbed her ankle, looked away. 'You know what I mean, the one I got. I was terribly sick as well.'

Erika moved rapidly from one part of the room to another. She was always restless, but today she did not seem able to control her body, to overcome some sort of fervour in her eyes which showed itself in darting movements of her hands, her feet, her head.

'I cannot guarantee that. But why would that suddenly become a problem, and only affect Helden? It is most unlikely. You always fuss about such a possibility. It has not happened again.'

'You know very well what serious consequences it can have, Mutter . . .'

A flash from Erika's eyes silenced her daughter.

'What about a game of German Scrabble, Aunt Rilla?' Mary suggested quickly. 'Then the Frau Professor can carry on with her work.'

'All right, Mary,' Erika snapped. 'Bring it and leave Gabriela to set it up. You help me sort out the computer files. I'll ask Glockner to cook for us at home and bring the food over. Then we can simply heat it up.'

15

Mary, true to her word, cycled from the convent to the Frau Professor's house every day after school. She brought her homework, worked on the computer and checked the animals, then stayed the night. The evenings were drawing in, and neither the Reverend Mother nor Gabriela felt easy about Mary riding back on her own after dark. Not because it was unsafe – the country around St Walter was as safe as anywhere – but the weather was changeable, and the short-cut through the woods was out of bounds. Even the short distance along a tarmac road might cause problems when mist or cloud obscured the way.

'You had your singing lesson today, didn't you, Mary?' Gabriela asked her as soon as she arrived.

'Frau Professor Weisskopf says I'm doing very well.'

'No more than that?'

'She says I have a lot of work to do.'

'Perhaps you shouldn't be so busy here as well, my dear. I'll speak to my mother about it.'

'It's OK, honestly. Lisl will be back to help soon, I expect.' She turned to her godmother, her eyes bright. 'Shall I tell you what I'd really like, Aunt Rilla?'

'I'm listening.'

'I know someone who's had a vision. I'd like to have

one, too.' Mary walked to the large picture window of Erika's house and looked soulfully out. 'She said not to tell anyone who she is, so I can't.' She turned round anxiously. 'You won't say I told you about it, will you?'

'I never betray a confidence.' She paused, rubbing her leg above the bandaged ankle. 'But what makes you so keen to have a vision?'

'You won't laugh at me?'

'I would never laugh at a genuine desire.'

'There is something I'm meant to do,' Mary rushed out. 'Something special which only I can do. I have this feeling about it.'

'You *are* very special, my pet. Of course you are. I think you are quite right – you have a special destiny.'

'But I don't know what it is,' Mary went on breathlessly. 'That's why I need the vision. So I can be sure, so I . . .'

'You don't need visions,' Gabriela said quietly. 'You are a beautiful girl, with a wonderful gift and an enchanting nature.' She smiled. 'Your miracle has already happened.'

'You mean my voice coming back, and the singing,' Mary said dismissively. 'I mean something much more than that. Something quite out of the ordinary, something only I can do.'

'Only you can sing with your voice.'

'Lots of people have good voices. That's just a talent to bring the composer's music to the listener in the best possible way.' She came over and sat on the sofa by Gabriela's outstretched leg. 'Shall I massage your leg?'

'It's almost back to normal, and you're doing enough already.'

'I don't mind.' She rubbed rhythmically between the ankle and the knee. 'What I mean is I think I have a

180

mission in life. Something I am meant to do, something no one has done before.'

'You sound almost like my mother,' Gabriela said sadly. 'She has spent her entire life on her project.'

'I don't mind that; I think that's wonderful.'

'And she still hasn't actually achieved it.'

'But she is just going to, Aunt Rilla. In a very short time . . .'

'She is always "just going to".' Gabriela stopped Mary's hands from massaging her leg. 'Look at me, Mary. Listen. My mother has an exceptional brain. She is a gifted scientist, a very hard worker, an inspired thinker. But she has spent her whole life talking about tomorrow, never today.' She smiled, a wan, wistful smile. 'She had the precious gift of a daughter, something I would give anything for. And she did not even notice it. She preferred to squander her time on research which may never come to anything. She worked all hours and missed my early childhood. She handed me over to her mother to bring up.' Gabriela looked at Mary earnestly. 'Never do that. Even if you have the most wonderful voice anyone has ever had, never give up the gift of motherhood for anything.'

'I won't, Aunt Rilla. I promise you I won't ever do that,' Mary laughed. 'That's not what I mean. I just want to see the vision so that I know exactly what to do.'

'You can't simply order a vision. Try not to let an obsession with visions get in the way of your life.'

'I shouldn't have told you.' Mary tossed her head and moved away. 'I'd better go and ask the Frau Professor what she wants me to do.'

Gabriela sighed. 'And what about Lisl, Mary? How is she now?'

'Still feeling dreadful. I'm very worried about her.

She won't go home; she seems to be afraid to tell her family. I think keeping it a secret is what's making her really ill, not just feeling sick.'

'I shall be flying back soon.'

'I know.'

'Do be careful not to do too much after I've gone. My mother can be something of a slavedriver. You might get ill yourself.'

'Aren't you feeling better yet?' Mary asked Lisl on the Friday two weeks after the festival. Lisl was sitting in the classroom after a maths lesson with Sister Marka, eyes closed, her breathing laboured. 'You don't look as though you can manage to go up to the grotto tomorrow.'

'You always fuss so, Mary. I'll be fine. I'm just a little tired.'

'I'll go with you, make sure you're OK.' She tried to sound jolly. 'We could go on to the Frau Professor's together afterwards.'

'I thought you always stayed the night now.'

'Not after tonight. Aunt Rilla's off first thing tomorrow morning. Do come, Lisl. It'll be like old times.'

'I need another couple of days before I can manage that,' Lisl gasped. Her face white and drawn, her eyes sunk into her head, it seemed to take all her energy just to speak. She took a deep breath in. 'Reverend Mother called the doctor from Salzburg in for a second opinion. I saw him yesterday.'

'You mean after I'd gone to the Frau Professor's?'

'Yes. He says it's just a bug that's going round and I'm particularly affected by it. Nothing to worry about. I don't even have a temperature.'

'You could pray to Our Lady to make it go away.'

Mary's eyes flicked over Lisl's face. It looked leaden, spiritless, quite unlike the girl she knew. 'You haven't seen her again?'

'Only that one time.'

'She didn't appear to me. I prayed for hours during the festival.'

A slight shrug. 'Perhaps it's because you aren't a Catholic.'

'Saul had a vision on the road to Damascus, and he wasn't even a Christian.' Lisl shrugged, eyes listless. 'I've asked Hochwürden to let me sit in on the catechism classes.'

'And?'

'Said I had to have my parents' permission. They'll never give it.' Mary grinned. 'But no one can stop me reading the Jerusalem Bible or the Douay version.' Her eyes brightened. 'You could lend me your catechism.'

A vacant stare, then Lisl lifted the lid of her desk, arm trembling with the effort. She took out a frayed copy of the old-style catechism. 'There's a new one now, but I haven't got it.' She handed over the tattered little booklet and walked slowly to the window, leaned against it and gazed at the magnificent view. Her lips widened, she looked almost like her old self. 'If I tell you another secret, you won't tell anyone?'

'You *have* seen her again!'

'I said I hadn't.' She turned round. 'And I don't expect to. Not unless I go up there and there's been some rain.'

'To the grotto, you mean? Why does it need to rain?'

'There may not be enough water yet.'

'Water?' Mary, leafing through the catechism, looked up sharply. 'You mean you *drank* the holy water? How

183

could you, Lisl? You promised Reverend Mother faith-
fully.'

Tears gathered in Lisl's eyes. 'I know. I just couldn't
help myself.' A forlorn look. 'Only the once, before you
came. Ages ago; beginning of July, before the summer
school. The first trough is full then,' she said, the old
eagerness in her voice. 'That's when I was supposed to
open the valve and let the water flow into the second
trough. Only if there's enough. There was loads this year.
I wasn't doing any harm.'

'But that's what could have made you ill, Lisl.' Mary
rushed over to her friend, put her arms round her shoulders. 'Like the brides that year Aunt Rilla got ill. I expect
that's what it was. Did you tell the doctor?'

'You've got to be joking.' She scowled at Mary. 'I
said they mustn't know.'

'Did you at least tell the Frau Professor?'

'Tell *her*? She'd kill me if she found out! She's worse
than Reverend Mother about that water. And I'll never
speak to you again if you do,' Lisl hissed, shrugging off
Mary's arm. 'Course it wasn't that. It's only water.
Anyway, that was months ago.' Mary looked up at the
sudden silence. 'And I *know* there's nothing wrong with
it because . . .' Her face went white as she gasped for
air. She staggered to a bench and sat down.

'You look really terrible, Lisl. Shall I fetch someone?'

'*No*.' She breathed in hard. 'I'm OK! Just leave me
alone.' She turned her back on Mary.

'I heard Aunt Rilla tell the Frau Professor that you
might have the infection she had.' Mary's voice sounded
anxious. 'Most of the brides got it that year; it's got to
be that water. Tell someone, Lisl – or let me do it.'

'I wish you'd stop all that. I wouldn't have told you if I
thought you'd let me down. Anyway, what do you know

about it?' Her eyes looked strained. 'I only took a few drops; not even as much as the brides.' She swallowed hard. 'You couldn't really call it drinking. My fingers were wet; all I did was lick them dry after I'd undone the valve. D'you think that was awful?'

'Of course I don't. So what happened?'

'I've already told you.'

'Tell me again; so I know what it's like.'

'I felt odd. Light-headed, sort of giddy. I fell on my knees, and prayed. Everything swayed, as though the rock above me had moved, as though it were all sky.'

'As if you were outside?'

'Not outside, not inside. A different world. Swirls and eddies all around me, nothing fixed. I felt myself floating, like zero gravity. I could touch the ceiling, see my body down below . . .'

'I *told* you it was the water.'

'I thought that. But the visions I've heard about were different. They looked like the statues of Our Lady.'

'What happened next?'

'The swirls turned into blue, and when I looked again there was a presence.' Lisl breathed deeply. 'Not something I could see, just feel. A radiance, a glow, the sweetest smile but without a face. I can't describe it.'

'And her body?'

'Not really a body. A kind of tangle of glowing colours floating about. Then they split apart, as though she were about to embrace me. Her smile became even sweeter, she held out her – wings, I suppose. Long, curling, streamer-like things.'

'But why should she appear to *you*?'

'I don't know. It was so beautiful, Mary. I'd give anything to have her appear again. I felt so wonderful, so peaceful, so . . .' Her face was soft, the lines of strain ironed out.

'You think that's what I ought to do?'

'If you really want to see her.'

'Go up to the grotto, scoop up a bit of the water?'

'Just a few drops; that's when it'll happen.' Lisl's face, so white a few moments before, was cherub pink. 'You have to pray as well.'

'I thought you said I had to be a Catholic.'

'Say you'll be one as soon as you can. Not your fault your parents won't let you.'

'When do I get a chance? I'm supposed to go to the Frau Professor's right after school every day. I'm doing your chores as well.'

'Do what you suggested earlier. Explain you'll be along with me later.' Lisl wiped her forehead with a handkerchief. 'Anyway, she can't expect you to spend every minute of your spare time there.'

'What reason could I give for not going ahead of you?'

'The real reason. Tell her you have to help me clean the grotto. She knows it's my job. Just say I'm not well enough to do it on my own. The Frau Professor is even fussier than Reverend Mother about keeping the place spotless. You can say it wouldn't be safe for me to climb up there on my own.'

Mary arrived back at the convent the next morning to find Sister Marka and Renate Scheiderbauer waiting for her by the front door.

'Reverend Mother wishes to see you immediately, Fullbridey.' The nun's voice was low with suppressed excitement, though her eyes were half-lidded to disguise her feelings.

'Before breakfast?'

Sister Marka's eyes slid towards the girl and her lips opened, but she merely nodded her head vigorously and pointed Mary in the direction of Mother Theresia's study. She took the bike and handed it to Renate, then could not resist giving Mary a slight push along the corridor.

Mary looked round, puzzled, and saw the nun already retreating towards the refectory. She walked on, knocked on the study door.

'Herein, come in.'

Reverend Mother was standing with her back to the door. The black habit, the white headdress covered by a black veil nodding on the old nun's head, gave her the stance of a magpie. Mary thought back: magpies were talkative birds, oracular, able to confide secrets to those who could understand them. Was Reverend Mother about to tell her a secret?

The small figure turned, slowly, unsteadily. Mary went over, taking the stick Reverend Mother had left by her desk.

'Thank you. I don't seem able to do without that any more.' She walked stiffly to her chair, sat down, searched Mary's face. 'I understand you have been helping Helden Lisl with the grotto since the beginning of term, Mary.'

'Not helping, Reverend Mother.' Mary dropped her eyes. So Lisl had told her their secret. Why? What else had she said? 'I just climbed up with her and waited for her to finish.'

'You did not enter the grotto?'

'I've never been inside,' Mary said eagerly. 'I'm sorry, Reverend Mother. I know it was wrong to go without permission, but I only went to keep Lisl company.'

'I see.' The stick was put away, the trembling hands placed on the desk. 'It *was* wrong of you, my child. You crossed through the enclosed part of the convent without permission. But that is not what I wanted to talk to you about. Helden is not well.'

'I know, Reverend Mother. I tried to persuade her yesterday. I thought she should ask your permission to stay in bed for a few days. She looked terribly ill.'

'I wanted to tell you what has happened myself. I have had to send her home.' She paused. 'I asked Herr Doktor Kramer to examine her again yesterday.'

'So it is really serious?'

'He thinks she might be suffering from glandular fever, or ME. Both those diseases could show the symptoms afflicting the poor girl.' Keen eyes assessed Mary. 'I wanted you to know that her father collected her last night. That is why I have sent for you; so that you will know exactly what is happening.'

'Is Lisl going to die?' Mary's eyes grew round, her shoulders tensed. 'Is she as ill as that?'

'There is no reason to think along those lines. Glandular fever is debilitating, but people get well again. It may take time.'

'But why has it happened to her?' Mary cried out, tears starting in her eyes. 'She works so hard, and does so much.'

'Too hard, perhaps. I should have seen the danger signs. She has been under great strain practising the violin. I should not have allowed her to attend to the grotto as well as assisting the Frau Professor.'

Whatever they all said, Mary wondered again whether Lisl was ill in the way Aunt Rilla had been. But Lisl wasn't delirious. And if it did turn out she wouldn't be able to have children, Mary assumed it would not really matter. After all, she was going to become a nun. 'You think she will be away for the rest of the term, Reverend Mother?'

'I think we have to assume that.' Gnarled fingers began to strum the desk. 'You have been very good friends, I think.' The old eyes looked at Mary, calm but questioning.

The answer to her prayer for a vision flashed over Mary. She could take over Lisl's duties, look after the holy shrine – and drink the water. 'May I take Lisl's place looking after the grotto while she recovers?'

'I will send for her brother Joseph, Mary. It is not for you to do.'

'But I know just how to, Reverend Mother. Lisl told me exactly what she did,' Mary broke in. The old woman looked at her intently. 'It's Saturday already, he might not be able to get away from his studies in time to climb up to the grotto.' Mary thought hard whether she should mention that Sunday should be kept holy and not used for working, then decided against it. 'And he is a man,' she said instead. 'He would need special dispensation from the Bishop to go through the convent.'

Mother Theresia smiled slightly. 'You want to do this, Mary? You have a calling to do this?'

Mary's eyes filled with tears. 'I would very much like to do it. It would be such an honour.'

'And what about the climb? Can you manage that on your own? You were not brought up in the mountains.'

'I've done it many times now. It's not a problem for me.' She did not mention to Reverend Mother that she and Lisl always used the difficult route. Perhaps she would take the path beside the Zahnradbahn on her own. That would be much easier.

'Then, for this Saturday only, I give you permission,

my child. But you are to go no later than eleven this morning. The days are so short. But after today I shall make other arrangements until Helden is well again. You are not used to bad weather in the mountains.' She looked at Mary again. 'And you, also, may be overtaxing your strength. I will tell the Frau Professor that you may assist her only twice a week. Every day is far too much.'

'Aunt Rilla's ankle is much better, Reverend Mother. She has left to fly back to London this morning. There will not be so much to do.'

As Mary left the sparsely furnished but magnificent room which did duty as the Reverend Mother's office, she wondered whether it was wrong of her to be so ardent for a vision. Ardent enough to disguise the truth about her motives as far as the old nun was concerned. What she was planning couldn't really be wrong. She *had* to make it possible for herself to have the vision. It was the only way she could work out how to order her life. The Virgin Mary would tell her what to do.

It would be all right for a girl like her to drink some of the grotto water – just a tiny bit. She was like Lisl; a virgin, pure, untouched. She never intended to be anything but a virgin.

The very thought of sexual union was repulsive to her. Ard Card and the pinky-purple, engorged penises of the other boys came unbidden into her mind. She tried to shoo them away, gulped hard, substituted instead a vision of the statue of the Blessed Virgin in the chapel, a vision of the Holy Sacrament in the eternal flame.

The Virgin Mary – the symbol of innocence, of purity – would appear to Mary Fullbridey. It would be God's way of showing her where her life's path was to take her. She wondered whether she had a vocation to become a nun. Perhaps at the convent of the Immaculate Conception, just like Lisl. She smiled happily to herself as she thought how she and Lisl would become Little Sisters. They would keep the festival of the Mothering of the Brides going for the convent, for the community. She would use her voice to sing for the greater glory of God. It could not be wrong to have such holy motives.

16

The path was slippery from autumn rain. Mary ground her feet into the surface to find a solid footing, then expertly put her hand out to steady herself. She held her body well away from the mountainside, feeling her centre of gravity holding her upright.

The steepness of the last ten metres gave way to an easier path leading to the railway platform, then on into the relatively gentle incline of the broader section winding up to the grotto. Mary walked confidently along, inspecting the ropes, admiring the scenery.

As she rounded the hairpin bend, she could see that the path had narrowed, and that several of the stakes, together with a section of the rope rail, had fallen away. Perhaps that was the spot where Aunt Rilla had slipped and loosened the surface. There had been storms during the past week. Possibly no one had realised just how much damage had been done, and she would have to report this to Reverend Mother. The task of repairing it would be a large one: several of the village men would be needed to do it.

Mary looked at the narrowed path, the sheer drop, and felt the dizziness of vertigo. 'Don't look down, you silly goose,' she could hear Lisl telling her. 'Look at what you want to do, then do it.'

Should she turn back and alert Reverend Mother right away? If she did, she would never get the chance to have her vision. It would take weeks or, if winter came early, till spring before the mountain path would be repaired. Meanwhile Reverend Mother would ask Joseph to see to the grotto for the remainder of the season. He was the one who had the climbing skills to do it.

So this was her only opportunity. Mary clasped the catechism Lisl had lent her, took out the bookmark of a picture of the Virgin Mary and gazed at it for inspiration.

The certainty grew in her that she should carry on. Slipping the booklet back into her pocket but holding the holy picture in her right hand, Mary inched slowly forward. The path, though narrowed, was still roughly eighteen inches wide. She wondered why she had worried so much. There was no problem about walking up, the only difference was that there was no rope to cordon off the drop of mountain to her right.

Rounding the next bend Mary could see that all was well on that part of the path. The grotto was just ahead, and she approached it eagerly. It was time to dislodge the central boulder guarding the entrance as she had seen Lisl do with such ease.

It was wedged tight. The rains which had washed away the ledge from the mountainside had also sunk the boulder deep into the soil. However much she tugged, Mary could not budge it.

She turned round and looked down towards the convent. What could she do? There must be a way. How would the men move it? They'd use brute force, there would be several of them to apply it, and they were stronger. But she could reason her way to a solution.

Ask the Virgin Mary to guide her just the way Lisl had asked St Christopher to help them on that first climb up to the grotto.

Recent physics lessons came back to her. A lever; she needed to find some sort of lever to apply what force she had to the solid portal. She looked round, hoping for inspiration. Nothing useful: shrubs hugging the mountainside, a mass of cyclamen in shades of rose and purple, small stones which littered the path.

Mary put the holy picture in her pocket, picked several stones up to examine them, saw one shaped like a wedge, used it to scoop soil from in front of the boulder. Still damp, the loose earth came away. She'd use the incline to roll the boulder forward, then lever it sideways to stop it crashing down the mountain. To allow such a thing to happen could spell disaster. Even if it missed the convent, she knew very well a large rock could start an avalanche.

She scraped away, small fingers dirtied, scrabbling, in her eagerness to get into the grotto. The boulder held fast. Mary, discouraged, sat back on her heels and stared at it.

A draught of cold air began to blow out of the cave, a rushing noise as a wind zoomed from inside the grotto through the cracks between and above the boulders and out at Mary. She shivered, chill, beginning to feel numb. A dense cloud formed around her, the vapour heavy and cold as though she were surrounded by ice. Was this the beginning of a vision? Is this what Lisl had described? Why was she surrounded by stolid grey where Lisl had seen blue?

A dazzling brush of bright light radiating outwards from the cave, a hissing noise, a faintly glowing discharge which zigzagged down the mountainside, terrified Mary. She let go of the boulder she had been trying to shift. There was a flash as the rock shattered. Her breath stopped, her heart beat crazily as she was hurled into the cave, fragments of rock exploding round her. She landed on soft mud, felt herself surrounded by debris and water.

An enormous roll of what sounded like thunder reverberated from the rock walls. The grotto was lit with an eerie luminosity which brushed the walls and highlighted the two troughs standing away from them. Her heart leapt. It was a sign. The grotto had been opened for her; she had been given passage to go in, it was ordained.

Cautiously she lifted herself to her knees, looked around, eyes adjusting to the ambient light. The floor of the cave was filmed with water. Fragments of glistening stones shining like jewels caught her eyes. Bright reflections seemed to gleam at her from every angle. The boulder had turned into diamonds. And the trickle above the trough had become a seep of water, oozing through, spattering over small stones and tangled vegetation.

Mary stood up and walked over to the first trough below the opening. The sparkle of stone fragments gleamed brilliantly. The water bubbled, singing to her. Small pebbles, silt, torn vegetation filled the trough and the water shuddered over, a thin layer covering them, glistening different colours.

The second trough was untouched. Its man-made access, a small pipe with a screen to keep any solids away, held barely any water. Another indication. If she had not been meant to drink the water there would not have been any left for her. A sign that she should drink, and drink the water which had been blessed.

Mary sank to her knees. 'If you appear to me I will do whatever you say,' she implored. 'Just once. I just want to see you once.'

She stood, moved the grating and leaning over the second trough, dipped her hand into it. Just one small scoop. Even the brides were allowed only one tiny cupful. She would not break those rules.

She allowed the water to linger on her tongue. The taste was earthy. Presumably it had acquired some of the dilute parts of the mud and rock it had passed over. She savoured it, felt it around her mouth and gums, enjoyed the trickle down her throat and into her stomach. A small, fiery feeling passed from larynx to belly. She looked up. Astonished, she saw the hole in the rockside above the trough open wide, took in the intense blue atmosphere Lisl had described.

It was as though the skies had opened up to transport her to the deep midnight blue of the outer stratosphere. She stared as the dark, almost black, spiralled into deep midnight blue, then yielded to light. A myriad shafts of silvery, spectral light which enlarged from red to blue in a sort of halo, elongated into an upright oval, then spread out and changed to two vast crosses on either side.

Mary gaped. She had not merely had a vision of the Virgin Mary. The Virgin had gone, and left two crosses on either side of her. God the Father, and God the Son. She sank back on to her heels. Her hands, fervently held together, beseeched the image not to disappear. It stayed, and as she fixed her eyes, not daring to blink in case it should melt away, the blazing white merged to a light blue, turning to folds. The top took on the outlines of a veil, hiding a face.

The eyes behind the veil projected twin gleams

towards her. She shivered. Were those the Frau Professor's eyes? They melted into mildness, gentleness. Aunt Rilla's? A yearning look, as though the figure wanted something from her.

'Tell me what you want,' Mary whispered.

There was no answer. The softness merged away, leaving blue swirlings swimming over the trough, then rising high into the mountain through the small aperture above it. She watched till the last vestige of the apparition had gone, gazing up. She felt elated, as though she could do anything she wanted, anything . . .

'Mary? You are all right, Mary?'

She came back into herself as though from a trance. At first she had no idea where she was, or how she had got there. It was cold, so cold. And damp. And dark. Some light was coming from above, some at her back. She felt numb, stiff. Sitting up, shaking her head, she rubbed her arms round herself for warmth. The blood started to circulate more quickly. Where was she? What had happened to her?

Something touched her, a rough, coarse feel. She sprang back, startled.

'It is just my coat, Mary. To warm you.' A male voice, calm but determined. She felt the material hugging her shoulders. 'Can you stand? Shall I help you?'

She could not focus. The figure stood in front of her, silhouetted against the light. Was this what she had seen that day with Lisl? A man, and not a devil? 'Who are you?' Her voice shook.

'Joseph Helden, Mary. Lisl's brother. I think you fainted.'

Lisl's . . . It took a few moments for her to acclimatise herself to the fact that she was still in the grotto.

'What are you doing here?' she whispered.

'I came to look for you. Reverend Mother was terribly worried about you.'

The grotto; she was in the grotto. Time to go. She had to climb down now, down the path without a rope on her left side, the slippery path down the sheer mountainside.

'Can you hear me, Mary?'

She got up, moved forward in a daze towards the light. As she stumbled out she could see that the mountain was shrouded in cloud, visibility low. 'The mists can be very dangerous,' she heard Lisl say. Should she climb down, or shelter for the night? Why had the day turned dark so quickly?

The slosh of water, the crunch of boots behind her made Mary turn. She tensed. 'Who's that? What do you want?'

'It's Joseph, Mary. I have come to help you back to the convent. Don't be afraid. The others will soon be here. I came first, alone, because Reverend Mother rang our house . . .'

Mary felt dizzy. She moved forward to the path, leaned her shoulder against the mountainside on her right and breathed hard. She looked round, then at her watch. Three o'clock. She had set out – she tried to work it out – hours ago. Had she really spent so long here, unaware of the passing of time? She shuddered as she remembered about the vision. The ecstasy had gone, nothing but the cold and damp in her clothes, her hair. And there was a man with her, near her. She leaned away from him, nervous, anxious, afraid. It was a punishment for drinking the water. What should she do?

She scrabbled in her pocket and fished out the

picture of the Virgin. Had she seen her? It bore no resemblance at all to her memory. What had she seen? And had she really seen it? Mary gulped frustration, annoyance with her stupidity, felt the tears fall, her shoulders heave. 'I didn't mean to do anything wrong,' she wailed.

'Everyone is worried sick about you,' Joseph said, standing a little behind her, watching her.

She began to creep slowly down the familiar path, keeping to the rockside, grabbing at vegetation to steady herself. 'I'm sorry.' Her voice sounded odd, singsong. 'The storm has done a lot of damage.' She straightened up, ashamed of her fear, pretending all that had happened had been because she had wished it to.

'So I noticed,' Joseph said drily. 'Um Gottes willen, what were you doing, not turning back? Part of the rope railing is dangling down. Any of us would have turned back at once. Didn't Lisl warn you *on no account* to try and solve problems in the mountains by yourself? I've never heard of anything so stupid.'

'You're by yourself,' she pointed out.

'I've told you, Mary. Don't you remember? I'm only the advance party. Reverend Mother did not worry at first because she thought you were going straight over to the Frau Professor. Then the Frau Professor rang to ask where you'd got to. That really put the wind up Reverend Mother. She phoned my mother in case you had come to us. I was there. Just as well! I said at once I'd go to find out what had happened. The village is gathering a rescue party together.'

She stared at him, trying to understand. 'I'm sorry, Joseph. I just got caught up . . .'

'Caught up?' The young man's earnest face had

subdued its anger. His dark eyes, brown and deep, softened as he looked at the young girl trembling in front of him. He undid a sweater tied around his middle by the arms. 'Put this on under the coat. And sit down. I'm going to get the thermos out.'

'Thank you.'

He lowered the rucksack on his back, took out a thermos, unscrewed the cup and poured hot liquid. 'I grabbed the first thing I could get hold of,' he said. 'Half milk, half coffee on the stove. It's very sweet. My mother always drinks it.'

Mary gulped gratefully.

'So what happened?' He leaned his sturdy frame against the side of the mountain. 'It's getting dark. You must have been up here four hours or more.'

'Nothing . . .' Mary put her hands round the cup, warming them and still clutching the picture of the Virgin Mary.

'Nothing?' Joseph looked at her quizzically. 'I find you coming round from a faint on the grotto floor, and nothing happened?'

Mary just went on drinking the coffee, finished it.

He took the cup and filled it up again. 'You warming up? Have one more drink, and then I think we should get you down. It's getting really dark.' He couldn't resist a grin. 'And the Virgin Mary isn't going to do the climb down for you.'

Her hands clasped round the plastic cup again, knuckles white, but she sipped more coffee and smiled placatingly at Joseph.

'So. Did you . . .?' His head swivelled towards the grotto, eyes focused on the entrance. 'Where's the big stone?'

Mary continued to drink, now gulping the liquid.

'Where's the stone which blocks the grotto, Mary?'

'It rolled away.'

'You mean you found it gone when you got here?'

'Not exactly.'

'Not exactly. So exactly what did happen?'

'I couldn't move it; it was stuck.'

Joseph breathed in deeply. 'Are you telling me you found a way to get it out and it went out of control?'

'In a sort of way.'

'Where is it?'

Mary pointed vaguely in the direction the boulder fragments had taken – into the cave, scattered around down the mountainside.

'You mean it rolled down?' The shock on Joseph's face was unmistakable. 'That could have started an avalanche! My God, girl, you've been here long enough to know that that's the most idiotic thing anyone could do.'

'It didn't roll down, Joseph. I'm not that stupid. It split into fragments. One or two may have rolled down. I didn't mean to . . .'

But he was already on his belly at the side and looking down. 'Where angels fear to tread,' he said. 'Couple of the bigger ones got caught in that scrub. Lucky it's been such a wet season and it's grown so dense. You are an idiot, Mary! You endangered the whole convent.'

'I was only trying to get into the grotto. God moved the boulder for me. . .'

'God?'

'It split into pieces. I told you that.'

'Split?'

'There was a wind, and a crackling sound . . .'

'An electric storm, you mean.' He stared at her, took

201

the cup from her hands. 'Do you mean lightning struck the boulder and hurled the pieces all around? Is that what happened?'

'I didn't see any lightning.'

'What did you see?'

'I don't remember anything about a storm. I just found myself in the grotto.'

'The blast hurled you inside. I wonder if you know just how lucky you've been.' He stared at Mary. 'And precisely what was so urgent about getting into that grotto? Just because Lisl goes on about it, and Reverend Mother lets you do it instead of her, you risked yourself, the convent and even the village?'

'It was nothing to do with Lisl. It was all my idea. I had to get into the grotto.'

'*Had* to?'

'Our Lady told me to.'

'For goodness' sake, Mary, what on earth are you talking about? It doesn't work like that.'

'Why not? What do you know about it?'

'What you are saying is pure superstition. Nothing to do with religion at all. Ask Reverend Mother or any of the priests. Lisl's been filling your mind with her silly notions, hasn't she? She had absolutely no right to.'

'She only told me what had happened to her.'

'Been blathering on about visions to you, hasn't she? Obsessed with that damned festival. Came right out with it to me, as well. She'd had a vision in the summer. There was this apparition of what she took to be the Virgin Mary.'

'She told you?'

'I wormed it out of her. I'm only telling you because I'm sure she did. You two are as thick as thieves.'

202

'I had one, too . . .' she began eagerly, then stopped. 'You won't tell anyone else, will you?' She stared at him. 'Promise?'

'I promise.' Joseph shrugged.

Exhaustion took over, and Mary began to cry.

'Let's get you back down, and into the warm. No damage done, it seems. What you need is a hot bath and an early night.'

'I've got to go to the Frau Professor's.'

'You aren't going anywhere today. That woman makes use of you girls.'

'But Aunt Rilla . . .'

'Frau Adler has gone back to England, Mary. You have forgotten that as well. Anyway, it's disgraceful the way you had to be the one to look after her. She's the Frau Professor's daughter, after all. My mother says she never even looked after her when she was a child. Her grandmother did that, so gentle and kind. Not at all like that awful woman.'

'She's not awful. She's very clever, she does research and everything.'

'She couldn't even save Helga, stupid old witch. And now she's put all kinds of notions into Lisl's head. And she exploits you. I can't stand her.' His eyes glowed dark. 'I'm telling you: she's evil.'

'You're a man. You can't understand.'

'You're trembling, Mary. I'll hold on to you.' Joseph walked over towards Mary and tried to put his arm round her shoulders.

'No!'

He stopped, his mouth open in astonishment. 'What on earth do you think I'm going to do?'

Mary cowered against the mountainside, shoulders shaking, tears streaming down her face.

'All right, all right. You keep to the cliffside. Here, put this rope round you.'

Joseph took ropes out of his rucksack, expertly put them on himself, and motioned to Mary to copy him.

'You go first. If you lose your footing, my body will anchor you.'

'All right,' Mary whispered.

'I'm not about to attack you, Mary.' Joseph approached the girl slowly and circumspectly. 'But I do need to check you've got the fastenings right. I'll walk just behind you in case you slip. OK?'

They inched their way slowly down the path.

'I couldn't start the Zahnradbahn. The mechanism didn't fire. The wet, I suppose. Needs a mechanic. I'll have to help you scramble down beside the track.'

The penetrating sound of a yodel reached through into her consciousness. Someone else was coming towards them.

'Halloooo! Joseph? Bist du da?' A voice from below.

'Hier.' Joseph cupped his hands around his mouth. 'I've got her. We're just starting down.'

The voice continued, began to come nearer, sounding like music in her ears. She was safe now. And she had had her vision. No one could take that from her.

17

'I see you've put on weight, Mary.'

'Really, Mother!' Anne did her best to hide her irritation as she bent away to switch on her Christmas tree lights. She straightened up. 'You sound as though you think Mary has got fat. She looked like a waif when she first went off to Austria.'

The Fullbrideys' tree, a genuine Serbian spruce cultivar – *Picea omorika* – was in the huge earthenware pot where it spent its life. Gilded lights twinkled on and off, demure decorations surrounding them in matching glitter. The green-gold colour scheme looked splendidly opulent in the Fullbrideys' spacious Regency drawing room.

'Well, she looks – different, somehow,' Anne's mother continued, scrutinising Mary, frowning but undeterred. 'Perhaps it's the plait. I can't imagine why you hide your beautiful hair that way.' Her eyes pecked at Mary.

She tossed back the single plait which had snaked over her shoulder and stared at her grandmother.

'I'm not saying she couldn't afford a little extra avoirdupois last summer, but she's certainly going to have to watch it now.' Fiona Dawson held her small finger out to balance the teacup she had just picked up.

'This Williamson & Magor Earl Grey is marvellous, Anne,' she said, sniffing appreciatively. 'I'll have to get some.' Her blue-rinsed hair matched steely-blue irises. She turned majestically to her granddaughter. 'I don't suppose you get any of *that* in Austria, do you, my sweet?'

'They have some lovely herb teas, Grandmama.' Mary picked some golden lametta strands off the floor, put them back on the tree, faced round. 'My favourite is camomile.' Small, even white teeth were flashed towards the pudgy hand, then abruptly sheathed.

'I suppose they lay claim to all kinds of miraculous cures with that,' Fiona went on. She turned to her daughter. 'In my day one's daughters stayed in England to be educated, or ended up in a finishing school in Switzerland. I can't imagine what you and Thomas are thinking of, Anne. Before you know it Mary will start looking like one of their ghastly dumplings.' She stared at her granddaughter again. 'You don't hold yourself very well, you know. Makes you look as though you've got a bit of a tummy. Try balancing a book on the top of your head.'

'Really, mother-in-law.' Thomas stood, and helped himself to a plate. 'Mary was all skin and bones before she left. I suppose you'd like to see her teetering around on high heels? She's not actually aiming to become a fashion model. And her complexion now is fabulous: just look at those roses in her cheeks!'

'She's got the looks for it. What's wrong with being a model?' Fiona sniffed. 'Never thought to see the day when you took the part of foreigners.' She helped herself to another cherry slice and bit a large chunk out of it. 'Those people put whipped cream on everything. Their heart-disease rate must be appalling.'

'Actually, the people in St Walter live to be quite old.' Mary's smile had disappeared. The small line between her eyebrows began to deepen. 'My friend Elisabeth's great-grandmother is nearly ninety. She's a wonderful old lady. She still knits the Trachtenstrümpfe for the whole family.'

'The what?' The slice of cake quivered on the way to Fiona's mouth. 'What a language! Sounds as though you're being sick.'

'Strümpfe means knee-socks, and Tracht means traditional wear, so that word is used for the white knee-socks they wear with the traditional dress of a particular region. Each family has its own unique pattern knitted in, so everyone knows who belongs where.' Mary's eyes were shining. 'Elisabeth's great-grandmother is a wonderful knitter. She made me the pair I'm wearing. Would you like to take a closer look?'

'They still wear native costume? Is that what you've got on now?'

'You make them sound like head-hunters or something, Grandmama. Not native – traditional. It's very practical and saves a lot of money. Some of the clothes are handed down from generation to generation.' She fingered the ruched neckline of the dress she was wearing. 'This dirndl, for instance. Elisabeth's mother gave it to me. The bodice embroidery is worked in gold thread, you know.' Mary stroked the white socks, displaying the pattern against her leg. Intricate knitted lace was interwoven with complicated embossed stitch patterns, finished with a turnover top knitted in green. 'Alpine villagers are still quite poor. They can't afford to buy clothes the way we do.' She picked a book up from the window seat, opened it and took it over to her grandmother. 'Look at this, Grandmama. This is a proper working dirndl. The bodice is laced to allow for a change in size. The shape can look good on anyone – young or old, fat or thin. It's flattering to any female figure.'

'Just as well, the weight some of them get to.' Fiona examined her granddaughter again. 'I've always thought dirndl skirts anything but flattering. Perhaps that's what it is. It doesn't really suit you.'

'And the leather shorts the men wear are brilliant for climbing.'

'You're really sold on the place, aren't you?'

'I've learned more at that school in a single term than in three years at Highgate Ladies.' A spot of bright colour appeared on each cheek. 'I've learned tons of science, especially biology. And my singing teacher is one of the top teachers in the country. My chest has expanded two inches, just from breathing the way she told me to.'

'That's what I said; they're ruining your looks.'

'I need the muscles, Grandmama. You control your voice with your belly muscles, and –'

'Mary promised to sing some Lieder for us,' Anne interrupted hastily. 'Isn't that wonderful? A real treat. And when the Adlers come, a little later on, we can all join in. A medley of English and Austrian Christmas carols.'

'I always like to listen to King's College choir.' Fiona put her cup and saucer delicately back on the coffee table. 'Cambridge, Mary. I don't think your Austrian yokel friends can sing carols in a way which compares to the singing there. They'll be on the box in half an hour. Aren't we going to listen to that?'

'We can do both.' Thomas's firm voice.

'And there's a film I'd like to watch.'

208

'We'll video it and you can see it later,' Anne tried to soothe her mother. 'Come on now, Christmas is for all of us to enjoy. The Adlers always celebrate Christmas Eve rather than Christmas Day. It's the Austrian custom, and it's also Gabriela's birthday. They're off for a fortnight's holiday tomorrow.'

'If Grandmama would rather I didn't sing,' Mary began, edging away towards the window seat, 'I don't mind. I can always sing in church later.'

'Tonight?' Thomas's startled voice boomed loud. 'You mean at the Christmas service tomorrow morning,' he said, the tone adjusted to a softer one, and smiling.

'I meant I can go to midnight mass with Aunt Rilla and Uncle Michael,' Mary said coldly. 'They don't go in for many carols in our church. I enjoy singing at a festive time like Christmas.'

'Of course I'd like to hear you sing, Mary,' Fiona hurried to put in.

'It doesn't matter to me,' Mary said huffily. 'I just thought you might be pleased. I'm working very hard. I'm aiming to try for the Guildhall. It's one of the top music schools in the country.'

'I said I'd like to listen, Mary. We'll forget about the film.' Fiona raised her eyebrows meaningfully at Anne, heaved her ample body around the armchair she was sitting in and scattered crumbs. 'We must all celebrate together, mustn't we? Christmas is a family feast.'

'Christmas is a Christian feast,' Mary's voice rose loud and clear. 'It celebrates the birth of Christ. All the other aspects are purely pagan. Anyway, we're all so spoilt. I don't think we should be giving presents . . . We should give the money to charity.'

'So you don't want what I've chosen for you, Mary? That's what you're saying?'

'That's quite right, thank you, Grandmama. I don't need anything. I'm very well provided for already.'

'As you wish. Just thought you'd like to know that I've got tickets for Garsington Opera – they're doing yet another rarely performed Haydn. I believe they're taking the place of Glyndebourne while that is being rebuilt. A brilliant musical achievement, and very English.' She grinned as she saw Mary's mouth drop open. 'But if you don't want to join me there, I'm sure I can find someone else to take your place.'

Mary assessed her grandmother, tense shoulders easing. 'That is a marvellous present, Grandmama,' she said. 'I didn't realise you'd understood about my music. I didn't even know you went to opera, let alone Glyndebourne.'

Fiona laughed. 'I don't. But your mother talks about your singing all the time,' her hands fluttered to her hair, 'so I thought it would be a good idea if we let you hear work performed in this country. We have a musical tradition too, you know,' she joked. 'We've got to do something to make you aware. Otherwise we'll never get you back here.'

Mary's eyes had begun to shine. 'I think Garsington and Glyndebourne are fantastic. I'd love to take Lisl to something like that next summer. It would be really great, especially sung in English.' She turned to Thomas. 'What d'you think, Daddy? If I ordered tickets now, would you fund them for me until I can save up?'

'Lisl? Who's Lisl? What an odd-sounding name,' Fiona asked.

'It's an Austrian shortening for Elisabeth. My friend,

Elisabeth Helden. The one Daddy said I could have over in the summer hols.'

'The one you met first thing?'

'Yes. She's ill at the moment, but she's bound to be over it by the time I get back.'

'What's wrong with her?'

'Some sort of stomach bug.' She hesitated a moment. 'No one quite knows what it is. The doctor said it might be glandular fever. We get on very well. She was really friendly when I first went there, helped me settle in when I was new.'

'She sounds very sweet.'

'Anyway, she can only stay a week.' Mary turned to her grandmother. 'She always helps at the summer school, you see. Her family isn't particularly well off. There are four children, and both the great-grandmother and the grandmother live with them.'

'Never heard of birth control, I suppose.' Fiona's lips pursed.

'They wanted a large family. Actually, they were disappointed there weren't more, specially boys. They'd help to run the farm, you see.'

'Old-fashioned lot, aren't they?' Anne laughed. 'So Elisabeth has to help support her family? I thought Mother Theresia gave her a free place because she's so gifted at the violin.'

'She has. And Lisl's won a scholarship to study in Salzburg when she's older. She's very gifted in lots of ways. You know she also assists the Frau Professor, and looks after the shrine in the grotto, and . . .'

'Shrine? There's a shrine?' Fiona's voice registered shrill warning.

'Don't get all worked up, Mother. There is a special grotto in the mountain above the convent,' Anne hurried to explain, 'but the nuns are a semi-enclosed order. They only allow it to be used once a year, for a special festival.'

'What sort of festival?'

'It's called the Mothering of the Brides.' Anne's apologetic smile ended in a shrug. 'They think it helps with infertility.'

'You mean they actually encourage them to have babies? Not content with the usual course of things, and banning birth-control . . .'

'Marriage is for the procreation of children,' Mary announced, her eyes slits. 'It seems a perfectly proper festival to me.'

'Bit on the superstitious side,' Thomas put in. 'They even allow older women to attend.'

'Hoping for miracles, you mean?'

'That sort of thing,' Anne agreed. 'No harm in it.'

'What claptrap! Anyway, it isn't always the woman's fault; could be her partner's.' Fiona darted a quick look at Thomas. 'Do they allow men to go as well?'

'They allow the husbands to accompany their wives as far as the convent garden.' Mary's earnest look brought strain back to her eyes. 'They have to wait for them there to take them home. Some of the brides become quite dizzy after drinking the grotto water.'

'You mean there's something in that water?'

'No, Daddy. It's pure mountain water.' A slow, red flush suffused Mary's face, her neck.

He grinned. 'What about minerals, Mary? All water contains some minerals. Particularly mountain water running over rock. The only really pure water would be distilled water.' He put his fingers together carefully, examined them.

'It is completely pure,' Mary said, her eyes becoming

212

bright. 'The water trickles down from a spring high on the alp. Only professional climbers can get up there, so it's quite safe.'

'They could go to the grotto,' Fiona said.

'You can get to that only by going through the convent, and that's not allowed.' Mary flounced down on the sofa.

Anne stood and sat down next to Mary, patted her hand, turned to her mother. 'Well, you know how it is, Mother. The occasion, the prayers, the atmosphere – they do all have consequences. Doesn't have to be anything in the water itself to have an effect. Why don't you sit next to me, Mother? Just be careful what you say when the Adlers arrive. Gabriela twisted her ankle coming down the path from the grotto in October.'

'So it's dangerous, as well?'

'Not really; just a small accident. She must be quite fit again, though. They're off to the Tyrol tomorrow. Michael always insists on a skiing holiday.'

Mary was disappointed. So there wasn't going to be much chance to talk to Aunt Rilla. She wanted to ask her to ring Friedl Helden, see if she could find out what had been happening to Lisl. She had not seen her friend since the day before she had gone up to the grotto by herself, the time she had taken Lisl's place.

'Isn't that the woman who hasn't been able to conceive?'

'That's the one, Mother. So do be tactful.'

There had been no one to discuss the vision with, no one to talk it through. Had she really had a vision? Mary wondered to herself. And, if she had, what exactly had Our Lady asked her to do?

18

'Do you know where Elisabeth is, Sister Marka?' Mary called along the corridor. 'I've been looking all over the school for her.'

Mary had arrived from Salzburg airport half an hour before. It was already late afternoon, and she was longing to see her friend. She had looked for her in the dormitory and every single classroom, but she was nowhere to be found.

Perhaps she had gone up to the grotto. Though the nuns did not answer questions verbally, Mary knew that Sister Marka would nod her head, or point, in the appropriate direction. She did stop, but merely stared at Mary as she came running up to her in the corridor leading to the classrooms, eyes expressing strong disapproval. And she did not respond. Mary remembered to curtsy. The nun, normally so tranquil, acknowledged this but displayed unease by the way she bowed her head. Her wimple obscured most of her face and her eyes slid away.

Mary, already tense, found her nervousness increase until it occurred to her that Sister Marka would not necessarily recognise Elisabeth by her first name. 'I mean Helden; Helden Elisabeth, Sister,' she tried out. She also tried to smile but sensed her features grimace.

'Have you seen her? I can't seem to find her anywhere.'
She made a deliberate attempt to modulate her voice,
though she was beginning to feel really worried about
her friend.

The nun put a finger to her lips, dropped her eyelids
in a gesture of reproach, and walked on. Apparently a
subject as trivial as a student's whereabouts was not
sufficiently important to break the rule of silence.

Mary had looked forward all through the Christmas
holidays to coming back to school. She'd spent some
time with Kate and had been surprised to find she'd
found her company dull, had been bored by her chatter
about a new boyfriend and the disco dances they had
attended. There had been nothing to interest Mary at
home and even playing with Bridget, using the house
key Aunt Rilla had given her to let herself in, had not
held its previous charm. Mary longed to see Lisl again,
to tell her about the vision, to discuss its implications.
She found it really strange that there had been no news
of her friend at all. A formal Christmas card had arrived
on Christmas Eve, signed by Lisl together with the rest
of her family, and nothing further. She hadn't even
answered Mary's letters.

Eventually Mary had pestered her mother to allow
her to ring the Helden household. Frau Helden had
answered the phone each time she'd tried. There had
been voluble evasions in rapid German, a little laughter,
apparent misunderstandings about finding Elisabeth.
She did not seem to understand that Mary was asking
her to come to the phone. It had emerged that Elisabeth
was feeling better, even quite well. Conversation had
shifted abruptly to Joseph. He had helped some of the
village men set another boulder in place to protect the
grotto. They had decided to abandon reconstructive

work until the snows had cleared, as late as May in many years.

'Did Lisl play at the Christmas concert? She practised so hard for that,' Mary had asked, hoping for at least some news of her friend, however oblique.

'She was not well enough at the time.' Friedl Helden had not offered any further information.

'Could I speak to Joseph?'

'*Joseph*?' There had been a lengthy pause. 'He is not here at present.'

Mary had given up. After all, she would be back at school quite soon. She'd find out all about it then.

'Any idea what's happened to Lisl?' Mary now asked Renate Scheiderbauer. Renate, one of the girls in their class, also shared their dormitory.

'Wannheim, d'you mean?' Truculent tone, an impatient shrug of shoulders turning away.

'Helden.' Mary knew the girl must have known exactly whom she meant. The Austrian habit of talking about fellow students by their surnames was still a strain, and she found it difficult to do. It sounded so unfriendly.

'I've no idea.' The girl dropped her eyes, reminding Mary of Sister Marka. 'Helden Ursel's here,' Renate suddenly said, backing away from Mary. 'Ask her.'

But there was no opportunity to do that. As Mary passed the pigeonholes she noticed the sole envelope sitting in the F compartment. She drew it out eagerly. Not Lisl's handwriting, not writing she recognised at all. Large, spidery capitals spelt out MARY FULLBRIDEY.

Perhaps a message from Friedl Helden? Was Lisl seriously ill? Mary tore at the envelope, infuriated by the stiff white paper lined with a flimsy red tissue which made it hard to get at the letter inside.

There was no form of address, no date, no letter heading. The plain white sheet, old-fashioned jagged edging sharp enough to cut, simply read: *Come and see me as soon as possible after your arrival. The matter is of the utmost urgency.*

It was signed: Erika Lager – no final greetings, nothing but the terse message. Was it something to do with Lisl? Had there been an accident? Was Lisl . . .?

The prospect of being told what had been going on by the Frau Professor left Mary faint. She was so brusque, so impersonal. If Lisl had had a serious accident or even died, she was likely to announce it as though she were talking about the unfortunate passing of one of her laboratory animals. Mary baulked at the no-nonsense approach, the lack of warmth, of feeling, she was sure she would find.

She'd try to speak to Mother Theresia first. Walking around on the highly-polished floors, looking through the squeaky clean windows, going into the airy class-rooms just in case she had missed her friend earlier on, she thought of the beginning of last term. How different that had been. She and Lisl had run, giggling, along these long corridors, had laughed and joked, planned their visits to the grotto. Lisl had been so well then, so full of life, so nimble in her climbing. She *couldn't* be really ill. Where was she? What was all the mystery? Why hadn't Frau Helden told her if it was serious?

Mary walked slowly towards Reverend Mother's office and stood, irresolute, outside the door. What could she say? Helden Elisabeth had not been in touch and did Mother Theresia know why? Well, she could ask why Lisl was not at school. She knocked timidly at the door and waited. No reply. She knocked again, louder this time, and heard the soft shuffle of a nun's

217

feet, the subdued rustle of habit skirts.

Not beyond the door, but right behind her in the corridor. She looked up to see Sister Christa coming towards her at the greatest speed ever used by the nuns. Not the slow, deliberate pace they tried to teach the girls. Sister Christa was walking purposefully, evidently using every ounce of willpower to stop herself from hurrying. As soon as she drew level with Mary, she waved her hand in a negative movement and motioned her away from Reverend Mother's door.

'Have you seen Helden, Sister?'

The nun's eyes seemed to sink further behind her wimple, seemed to lose their shine. A kind of veil crossed over them as Sister Christa, like Sister Marka, put her finger to her lips and shook her head.

Mary could only gape at her. Where was Mother Theresia? And then it dawned on Mary that perhaps Reverend Mother was taking a nap. And Lisl was probably already at the Frau Professor's, helping her out, waiting for Mary to turn up. What an idiot she had been not to realise that in the first place.

'You asked me to come and see you, Frau Professor.' Mary had been given permission to call Aunt Rilla's mother Tante Erika, but she could not bring herself to refer to her in that way. She had got used to the Austrian form of address and felt more comfortable using that. At any rate she could not do anything else when at the convent or with Lisl.

'There you are at last,' the Frau Professor greeted her, small hands clutching at Mary's, drawing her into the house. 'You're very late. I expected you an hour ago. I thought the minibus got in at four this afternoon.'

218

'I didn't see your note until half an hour ago.'

'What on earth were you doing all this time? Didn't you pass the pigeonholes?' Her face screwed into peppery lines. 'I urgently need your help, Mary. I have just repeated some very exciting experiments.' She smiled for the first time. 'Every single one has worked out. My records show perfect results.'

Mary wondered again at the frail-looking little woman who demanded such a great deal. There were no questions about what she had done in the holidays, how her parents were, had she seen Aunt Rilla recently. The Frau Professor's work dominated her life, she thought of nothing else. 'You mean the experiment with the rabbits?'

'Exactly. I've been able to make a series of specific ribozymes to act as endoribonucleases in rabbits. They can catalise the cleavage of RNA molecules, thus serving as RNA sequence specific endoribonucleases.'

'I'm not quite sure . . .'

'These ribozymes are produced from a self-splicing RNA. I altered the substrate sequence specificity of a well-known hammerhead ribozyme, allowing a set of sequence-specific endoribonucleases to be produced.'

'So what have you achieved, exactly?' Mary asked, completely bewildered.

The Frau Professor jerked her head up in frustration. 'I thought you understood by now.' She stared at Mary. 'I thought you knew that I have isolated a particular ribozyme which can catalise mitosis – the splitting of cells – in rabbits.'

'But I thought you were working on heritable diseases, Frau Professor? I didn't know you were specifically interested in mitosis . . .'

The little woman stopped, the smile leaving her face, her eyes unfocused. 'Naturally,' she said, fretful, petulance seeping through her voice. 'But I do have to test my results very thoroughly. Desirable changes can be elusive, you know. I need a simple method of reproduction for testing them.' She frowned at Mary. 'Just a means to an end.'

'Of course,' Mary agreed. 'Asexual reproduction in rabbits. But haven't you been doing that for ages?'

'What is this, Mary?' she suddenly snarled. 'Why are you cross-examining me?'

Mary backed away. 'I'm sorry; I was only trying to understand . . .'

The Frau Professor was already busy again, ignoring her.

'So you want me to analyse the data . . .'

'Analyse?' She swung round, eyes glittering. 'Certainly not. It is my work and that is for me to do. All I want you for is to input the data into the computer for me. You'll be told the detailed results in due course, like everybody else.'

'I'm sorry, Frau Professor.'

'I understand. You are as excited as I am.' Softened eyes looked at Mary. 'But you can see that I need a reliable assistant more than ever. I need *you*, there's no one else trained enough, no one else I can possibly trust.'

'You mean as well as Lisl, don't you? Isn't she here?' Mary looked round, expecting to see her friend smiling a greeting, walking through from the laboratory. 'I was sure she would be. I couldn't find her at school, and I looked everywhere.'

'That's what I'm telling you, Mary. Helden hasn't been here for months. I met her mother in the village a week before Christmas. She asked me to call in on them, and I went over to examine the girl. I haven't seen her since.'

'So she's still ill?'

'Ill? What on earth gives you that idea? She isn't ill at all!' the Frau Professor shouted. She shrugged. 'She's malingering. Idiotic girl keeps on about feeling sick, and not up to helping me. But that's nonsense! Just some little stomach upset we all get from time to time. Too much of her mother's heavy cooking, in my opinion. Too much food altogether; she's put on weight. Anyway, that's only a cover.' Her hands flew up into the air. 'She's suddenly decided to chuck up everything I've taught her for that ridiculous boyfriend of hers. Quite unsuitable.'

'Boyfriend? Lisl has a boyfriend?' Mary stared, incredulous, at Erika Lager. 'That can't possibly be true!'

'Can't be true?' Mary followed as she marched into the laboratory, turned to one of her monitors, began to run the cursor down the screen in front of her. 'What can't be true?' she asked absently.

'About Lisl having a boyfriend. She isn't interested in boys.'

A gleeful chuckle greeted the remark. 'All the Helden girls are boy-crazy, Mary. I would have thought you'd have noticed that.'

'No, really. Not Lisl. I know she isn't interested in boys.'

'You know, do you?'

'She told me.'

'And that's good enough for you?'

'She's going to become a nun,' Mary burst out. 'That's why. She can't possibly have a boyfriend.'

221

The shrill, high cackle reverberated round the laboratory. 'A nun?' She laughed again. 'A nun, indeed. That's rich. Your precious would-be nun is involved with one of those oafs who hangs out in Kernkirchen.' The Frau Professor picked up a computer disk, jammed it into a disk drive, then pulled it out again. 'Throwing herself away like that, it really is too bad! That child's got an excellent brain, and a really remarkable talent for playing the violin. What gets into these girls? Why do they do it?'

'Do what, Frau Professor?'

'Chuck up her chances of academic work, give up developing a really rare talent, ruin the possibility of a first-class career – all for some young dolt who happens to tickle her fancy. As though the stupid goose couldn't have her fun with him on the side. Just like that sister of hers,' the Frau Professor fumed, her eyes brilliant with fury. 'Just like that stupid Helga.'

'Helga was engaged, Frau Professor.'

'Exactly. It's what I've been telling you. Helden is going to get married as soon as she's old enough. She's sitting at home sewing for her bottom drawer.' She crashed a pile of printouts into a file. 'A girl living in the last decade of the twentieth century, and all she can think of is getting married. At a time when we are approaching the millenium, the new age of woman, what does our talented Helden choose to do? Rush off with the first thing in trousers that approaches her.'

Before Mary could speak again the Frau Professor pulled her by the arm through the laboratory and into the annexe she had furbished for housing her experimental animals. 'There, you see? Every single one of them has had a litter.'

'But surely that isn't unusual?' Mary asked, 'I

thought it was common knowledge?'

The Frau Professor drew herself up. 'Certainly not, Mary. This is original work; a breakthrough. What I have done is to produce a chemical formula which allows parthenogenic reproduction in rabbits without any surgical intervention.'

'I see. And you think there is a use for this?'

'A use? A commercial application, you mean? The world will be storming my doors as soon as I release the information. That's why I need you, Mary. I know I can rely on you to keep all this to yourself until the time is ripe. Not everyone is going to be delighted with my work. Many people will say it is pernicious and will try to destroy it.'

'I wouldn't tell anyone.'

'I know that, Mary. You're a good girl.'

'But I can't believe Lisl doesn't want to be part of it. She was so excited . . .'

'Have you tried ringing her?'

'I tried from England.'

'Try from here,' She handed Mary the cordless phone. 'Go on, see if you can get anywhere with her. Maybe she'll listen to you. As far as I'm concerned, she's being completely mulish.'

Mary pulled out the aerial and tapped in the Heldens' number.

'Hallo.' The guttural Austrian came sputtering down the line. 'Friedl Helden.'

'Frau Helden? This is Mary Fullbridey speaking.' There was a pause, and then a click as the phone went dead. Mary stared at it in disbelief. 'Hello? Frau Helden? Is that you?'

'She's hung up.' Calm, calculating eyes were turned to Mary. 'She thinks you are calling on my behalf. She doesn't want her precious daughter to have anything further to do with me.'

'Why not?'

'The stupid girl must have given her some garbled version of the work I'm doing, I imagine. Next thing we'll have the animal-lovers breaking in. And you know how careful I always am about the well-being of every single animal. And, most importantly, I do not kill them for histological examination of their tissue. There is no need.'

'They're accusing you of cruelty?'

'Cruelty, witchcraft; you name, they say it.'

'But there was no sign of this last term . . .'

'It's only since Helden decided she's in love with this boy Miller.'

'Miller? You mean Kurt Miller?'

She turned from the file she was labelling. 'There you are, you see. You know she knows him. From her, I take it.'

'Of course I realise she *knows* him, Frau Professor. His family has the farm adjoining hers. And her sister Helga was . . .'

The Frau Professor jerked round, eyes glittering. 'You keep talking about Helga. What exactly do you know about her?'

'Only that she was one of your assistants. She was engaged to Kurt and she had a riding accident and died,' Mary muttered. She felt depressed, let down. 'Lisl always told me she's sorry for Kurt, but she can't stand him. I know he thinks he's in love with her because she reminds him of Helga. He brings her flowers and things, but she . . .'

'Hormones, I suppose. The number of local girls that boy has impregnated is positively stunning. A real stud.'

'There's something wrong here, Frau Professor. Lisl isn't interested in men, really she isn't. She wants to join the order of the Little Sisters and look after the shrine for them. That's what she's set on doing. I just can't believe she could change like that, let alone decide to marry Kurt. We talked about her approaching Reverend Mother first thing this term. There was no way she thought about doing anything else.'

'Do you speak in German to each other?'

'She speaks German, I speak English,' Mary explained. 'But I'm getting round to German.'

'You can't possibly fathom all the nuances of the language yet. And you don't understand the background here.' She smiled, put her hand on Mary's arm. 'Believe me. This is a mountain village, with very narrow views and traditional values. Her parents want Lisl to marry a local man and settle down. Kurt is their neighbour's eldest son, and the perfect match. That's how it is.'

'Perhaps it's her illness. That's got to be it,' Mary insisted. 'She wasn't feeling well, off and on, through most of last term.'

'She wasn't there for most of it. You're talking about the beginning of term, are you? Can you remember exactly when she started feeling off?' The Frau Professor was looking at her with interest. 'Early September, was it?'

'I remember precisely. Not as early as that. It was the Saturday of the week before the festival. She tried to hide it, but she was really weak. I noticed because she found climbing up to the grotto a terrible strain. When I first came she whipped up there like a mountain goat. Then I got better at it than she was.'

'You went up with her, did you, Mary?'

She flushed. 'Yes. Reverend Mother knows.'

'I see.' She looked thoughtful. 'She is not ill, Mary. I examined her thoroughly myself, and so did Herr Doktor Kramer. There is nothing whatever wrong with the girl. You'll have to take my word for that.'

Mary tried hard to accept what the Frau Professor had told her about Lisl but found she simply could not do it. The idea that she had left school of her own free will to marry a man she had clearly disliked only a short time ago did not feel right. Perhaps the Frau Professor was being kind, and Lisl was so ill she was afraid to tell Mary the truth. Each time she'd tried to talk to Ursula about it all she'd run away. The odd conspiracy of silence which surrounded Lisl's absence drowned Mary in depression.

She decided to approach Reverend Mother about visiting the Heldens one Sunday. They had, after all, invited her to lunch only last summer, and had seemed very friendly at the time. Furthermore, Reverend Mother had been happy for her to go.

Mother Theresia did not seem surprised to see her.

'May I have permission to visit the Helden family, Reverend Mother?' she asked right away.

No flicker, no stir from the old face, but the tone was definite. 'I think that would be quite unsuitable, my child.'

'Why would it be unsuitable?' Mary looked across the desk to see a closed, firm expression in the faded eyes. 'Elisabeth Helden was a pupil at this school. I spent most of my time with her when I first came here. Why is she unsuitable now?'

The old nun did not give way. 'Her priorities have changed, Mary. Helden now has a fiancé.'

'You mean she's officially engaged? She's getting married?' In spite of what the Frau Professor had maintained, Mary had convinced herself that, for once, she was mistaken. She was sure that Lisl would be back at school within weeks.

'Yes, Mary. Helden's thoughts are taken up with a young man. Her friendship is no longer right for you. Your interests are quite different from hers now. I cannot allow you to go.'

'But Lisl is ill, Reverend Mother, otherwise she would have been in touch by now.'

'Lisl is not ill, Mary.'

'But you sent her home yourself . . .'

'There is nothing further to discuss.' The old head drooped, hiding the face behind the headdress.

'When is Joseph coming back, Reverend Mother?'

'Joseph?' The headdress lifted and the eyes lit with an unusual flicker of irritation. 'You are referring to Helden Joseph?' The nun looked at her intently. 'Is there a special friendship between him and you?'

'Not at all, Reverend Mother. I hardly know him. I just thought he might give me news of Elisabeth.'

'You will not meet Joseph, Mary. You are in my charge, and I will not permit it.' The hands groped over the desk, turned a page of the calendar. 'In any case he studies in Salzburg. He will not return until the Easter break. When the snows clear he and the other men will straighten out the grotto, restore it to its former state.' A deep look. 'After that I would be most grateful if you will show Renate Scheiderbauer Helden's former duties. She is a local girl and can look after the shrine in the holidays. That is, if you wish to. If not, let me know and I will contact one of our former pupils to show Scheiderbauer what to do.

She is very keen to take it on.'

'I will be honoured to do what I can, Reverend Mother.'

'And your visits to the Frau Professor. You can manage to go on assisting her by yourself? It is not too much for you?'

'No, indeed, Reverend Mother. I learn a great deal and it is not hard.'

19

Now that Lisl was no longer there, Mary's continued visits to Erika Lager grew longer and more intimate. As weeks turned into months Mary found her company stimulating and, increasingly, began to appreciate the older woman's hard working methods, her dedication, her absorption with her cause. There was also the excitement of being involved in original research.

'Do you think it would be possible for me to be a singer *and* a research worker?' Mary asked the Frau Professor tentatively.

'Certainly not. You can see I work every minute of the day.'

'And which do you think is the more important career?'

Erika looked at her intently. 'A beautiful voice is a very unusual gift. It would be a pity to deprive the world of it.' She frowned. 'But if my work really interests you, if you think you might wish to do fundamental research, that is a different matter.'

'You think I could do what you do?'

'Why not? You are getting an excellent grounding from me.' She looked out of her laboratory window. 'That is how I started. I assisted my father from an early age. He was a great scientist, you know. A genius.'

'Aunt Rilla told us that. What field was he working in?'

'Genetics. I followed in his footsteps. The difference is that we have more tools at our disposal now. DNA had not been discovered in his time. Nevertheless, he had a sort of instinct how to proceed. He made great strides.'

'Did he make any big discoveries?' Mary asked eagerly. 'Did he win the Nobel Prize?'

'He died before he had the chance to finish his work. We were under constant bombardment in Berlin. The Nazis insisted he move his researches there.'

'Because it was important to them?'

'They gave it the highest priority.'

'Aunt Rilla said you went to Berlin, too.'

'When I was fifteen. I was already skilled, trained by my father. They thought I would be of considerable use. So, you see, I started my career at your age.'

'You did what I do now?'

'Well,' the Frau Professor laughed, 'we had no computers either. But I wrote up the data for my father.' Her hands twisted themselves round a phial. She screwed it and unscrewed it rapidly. 'I tried to make sure that his formulae were *safe*,' she said, emphasising the word. 'Everything was in such a state.'

'And were they?'

'Not in the end. The Russians took the city over before I – we – could complete his project. They broke into the bunker and burned everything, including all his papers.'

'But you could continue for him,' Mary said, excited. 'You must have remembered quite a lot. You must have known how far he'd got.'

'The records were burned as well. And the formulae

were, naturally, complicated. And there were several. I remembered what I could,' she finished abruptly. 'The rest I had to research all over again.'

'Is that when you got married?' Mary asked. 'During the war, in Berlin?'

'A few months before the end; yes.'

Mary noticed for the first time that Erika Lager did not wear a wedding ring, not even on her left hand. Aunt Rilla had explained that Austrian wives wear the rings on their right-hand ring finger, and switched to the left if they were widowed. 'But you don't wear a ring.'

She looked at her hands, turned them around. 'My fingers are too crippled by the burns. It would make it even harder to carry out my work.'

'Was he very handsome?'

She shrugged. 'A tall, Nordic type. He was an SS officer in the German army. Perhaps he was handsome. It was so long ago.'

'Have you any photographs?'

'There was no time for things like that.'

'Does Aunt Rilla look like her father?'

The tinkle of broken glass as she dropped a test tube brought a frown to the woman's face. 'You asked my opinion about your choice of career. I think you would make an excellent research scientist. You are bright, you work hard, you are dedicated to causes and not to money. You have all the correct qualifications.'

Mary had begun to warm to the funny little woman with the curt manner and the total dedication to her science. She found working with her much more exciting than her studies at school. There were no textbooks, no previous papers, nothing to rely on except the Frau Professor herself, continuing work initiated by her father nearly fifty years earlier. Mary felt as though she

231

was repeating history. She was to the Frau Professor what she, in turn, had been to her father. She wondered why Aunt Rilla had never wanted to do that.

Suddenly she saw Aunt Rilla with Bridget, taking over the doe and her babies, looking after them. She was so good with the rabbit because she *had* helped her mother when she was a girl. What had happened to cause such a rift between them? Why did Aunt Rilla blame her mother for an illness the Frau Professor could not have foreseen or prevented?

For the most part Mary found her generous with her knowledge. She usually took the trouble to explain what she was doing in detail, in spite of the fact that this often held her up. Mary thrived on that. But there were areas which she kept secret from Mary. No amount of pleading could persuade her to share this knowledge.

'The results are not ready yet, Mary. I cannot share my preliminary thoughts with you.'

'I might be able to help . . .'

'You do not understand the creative process. If I talk about such ideas, they might evaporate.'

It seemed a curiously unscientific approach, but Mary could not cajole her into further confidences. Then, almost a week before she was due to return to England, Mary had accidentally brought up a wrong screen as she was about to put in the latest data. This was not a file of the chemical formulae she had occasionally brought up before, but a long list of names and dates, starting in 1956. These data were something she could decipher, could understand. Unable to control her curiosity, Mary had begun to read. She noted lists of female names ordered by year, followed by a date of birth, the name of any child born in the following year, the child's date of birth, the child's name. As Mary scanned rapidly down the screen she saw that all the children were female. Then she heard the Frau Professor's steps dragging along the corridor, about to come into the laboratory. She quit the file as quickly as she could and tried to bring up the one she was meant to work on.

The small figure came up to look over her shoulder. 'What were you doing, Mary?' Her voice was cold, suspicious, the eyes bright.

'Bringing up the current data file, Frau Professor.'

'So why isn't it on the screen?'

A shudder went through Mary as she moved uncomfortably in her seat. The Frau Professor would be so furious if she thought Mary had been spying on her files that she would never let her work in the laboratory again.

'I quit the file when I heard you come in, Frau Professor. I thought you would want me to check the rabbits now,' she said demurely, able to keep the tremble from her voice by using her diaphragm in the way her singing teacher had taught her.

'I've told you before, Mary. I will bring up the data I want you to work on. If you open or close files on your own account again, I cannot have you working with me. Do you understand?' The look was terrifying. 'I thought I had made myself crystal clear several times before.'

'I'm sorry, Frau Professor.' What could be so secret about a list of names? There were no personal details there, just names and dates. And even if she had brought up a screen of formulae, they would be completely incomprehensible unless printed out and studied in depth. Why all the secrecy?

Mary continued to throw all her energies into the laboratory work. Until, quite suddenly it seemed, the very same lethargy that had afflicted Lisl began to take

233

hold of her. She began to feel increasingly sick, particularly just after she had got up. The feeling turned into actual vomiting. She noticed that she brought up a curious white, thick mucous and felt much better immediately afterwards.

At first Mary kept the symptoms to herself. But, as the frequency of the vomiting increased and her weight began to drop, the other girls noticed her increasingly frequent requests to be excused during classes.

The nuns considered it part of proper self-discipline not to ask to leave a lesson in order to go to the lavatory, particularly for the older girls. It was, therefore, also obvious to the teachers that there was something wrong with Mary.

She had been careful not to write anything about her physical problems to her parents. She decided to enlist Erika Lager's help before she mentioned anything to Reverend Mother. 'I have been feeling rather ill in the mornings,' she told her the next time she visited her.

'There's a virus going round.' She sounded casual, off hand. She turned away from Mary and marked up one of the rabbit record sheets.

'I've had this problem for almost three weeks,' Mary said. 'I haven't mentioned it because I thought it was a bug and would go away. But now I'm sick about three times a day. The other girls have begun to comment.'

'Three times a day?' The Frau Professor looked up from what she was doing and bent her full attention on Mary.

'Usually first thing in the morning, and again during the morning lessons.'

'Every day?'

'Every day at least once. Some days it's particularly bad.'

'I think I should examine you, Mary.'

She took her time. She gave Mary what the girl assumed was a very thorough medical examination, testing her blood pressure and pulse, checking her lungs and abdomen.

'I simply cannot find anything wrong with you,' she told her, her eyes looking away. 'But I will take both blood and urine samples, and send them away for analysis. Then we can be sure.' She smiled, 'I know you're missing Lisl. Perhaps we can persuade Reverend Mother that you and I visit her together. That might make you feel better.'

Mary's eyes began to shine at the prospect.

'And now, try to forget your little problems. It is always better to disregard the body and concentrate on the mind. That is where human beings are different from animals – they can think, and they can invent. Concentrate on that and you will find your body will return to its own equilibrium.'

'But I wasn't thinking about my body. Why would I suddenly feel ill when I felt well before?'

'It sometimes happens at puberty, Mary. The hormonal changes take some people by surprise, and give rise to unusual symptoms. I have taken several samples to see whether you need hormone therapy to steady you. Are your periods painful?'

'They can be.'

'And what about the flow, is that heavy or normal?'

'Rather slight, most of the time.'

'Perhaps we need to give you extra oestrogen. You are somewhat underdeveloped.'

'My grandmother thinks I've developed a bit too

235

much! I put on weight last term, you know, though I have lost some recently. And my bosom has become distinctly bigger.'

'Even so, if your periods are slight, there is some sort of imbalance.'

'My periods have stopped.'

'Stopped? Really?' There was a curious sparkle, a subdued excitement Mary could not understand. 'And you haven't mentioned that to anyone?'

'Well, at first I didn't really notice, because I didn't start to menstruate until just before coming to this school, anyway. My doctor in London told me not to expect a regular flow until next year.'

'No doubt he knows.'

'He's known me ever since I was a child.'

'You're still a child, Mary. You're only just fifteen. All these hormonal changes can take their toll.' The Frau Professor swept her hands impatiently away from Mary and walked over to her basin to wash them. 'Roll your sleeve down again, Mary. We have work to do. Just try not to think about yourself so much.'

'This is Herr Doktor Kramer, Mary. I think you have heard of him. He has been the convent's medical practitioner for many years. He comes from Salzburg.'

The doctor smiled and held out his hand. 'How do you do.' The grip was firm and strong, the eyes kind but searching.

Mary had been surprised to find herself summoned to see Reverend Mother right after the last bell, and even more suprised to find this stranger with her. Automatically she curtsied to Reverend Mother, shook the doctor's hand.

'I understand from Sister Marka that you have not

been feeling at all well, Mary. She has noted your frequent need to excuse yourself. That is undoubtedly a sign of illness in your case. It was irresponsible of you not to bring it to my attention.'

'I've discussed it with the Frau Professor, Reverend Mother,' Mary said defensively, 'She has examined me and says she can't find anything wrong.'

'You are in my care, my child. I know the Frau Professor is our first call in case of illness, but only as an adviser. It is she who always insists that we get a second opinion on anything which is causing problems for more than a few days. It is our duty to the girls' parents.'

'The Frau Professor asked you to call in Herr Doktor Kramer?'

'She also brought to my attention the fact that you have not been feeling well. How are you now?'

Mary, tempted to say she was totally recovered, found herself unable to do so under the serene gaze of the faded eyes. 'Much better, Reverend Mother.' The eyes continued to gaze at her benignly. 'Well, I do still feel sick sometimes.' Mary smiled her nervousness. 'But it's getting much better. Just a bug, I expect.'

'I have asked the Herr Doktor to examine you, so that I can send an adequate report back to your parents, child. They have put their trust in me, and I would be quite irresponsible not to make sure that there is no serious problem.'

Mother Theresia was sitting at her desk. She gave a slight sign with her hands and Dr Kramer, who had been standing sideways to the room and looking out of the window, turned and approached Mary.

'I shall remain in the room. But I will not listen, my child, you can rely on that. You can say anything you feel necessary to the doctor, and you can be assured that

237

everything you say will be in confidence.'

'We shall sit down, ja?' The unfamiliar man beckoned her to the other side of the room and invited her to sit on the sofa with him.

The large, high-ceilinged room seemed suddenly vast to Mary. Dutifully walking over to the doctor, she could see Mother Theresia busying herself with papers on her desk.

'You have been feeling ill?' he asked. 'You feels ill, or you brings up the foods?'

'There were a few days when I vomited several times,' Mary admitted. 'But I feel much better now. I really think it's all blown over.'

'Blown over?'

'Vorbei.'

'You feel completely well?'

'A bit tired at times. Occasionally I feel sick, but nothing like as bad as a week ago. I'm all right now, really.'

'Just a few basic tests, Mary. If you have no objections.'

Mary had serious objections. The idea of a strange man touching her was entirely repugnant. She pulled both arms protectively across her breast and stared, dumb with horror, as the doctor pulled out his stethoscope.

He watched her, nodded. 'It will not be necessary to undress,' he reassured her. 'You can keep on your blouse. Please stand, take off your jumper.' He listened to her heart, while she shivered. It took several attempts for him to complete the test. 'Cough, please.' Laboriously he went through the whole gamut of the general tests Erika had also done, his face completely blank.

At last he smiled reassurance, motioned Mary to sit

down again. 'Perhaps you will be kind and roll up your sleeve.'

'What are you going to do?' Mary was near to tears.

'I only wish to take your blood pressure.' He wound a tape round her upper arm and squeezed a bulb attached to it. 'Very good,' he said at last, watching the pressure gauge. 'Everything is fine. I think you are in excellent condition.' He stood to put his paraphernalia away, sat next to Mary again, laid a hand on her shoulder.

She started from him, eyes huge with fear. He withdrew it immediately.

'The physical examination is over. Perhaps we have a little talk?'

'A talk?'

'I understand you have had the troubles last summer. It was serious enough for you to lose your voice.' He smiled. Affable, charming. 'If you have no argument, I will take the pulse.'

Mary leaned her torso slightly further away from him, but allowed him to take her wrist. Her pulse began to race.

'You worry that I mention this incident to you?'

'I try not to think about it.'

'You have to try?'

'Not usually,' Mary said, exasperated. 'Just when people insist on bringing it up. And I prefer women doctors,' she burst out loud enough to startle the nun busy at her desk.

'I am sorry. We still have not enough lady colleagues.' The doctor smiled again but his eyes were veiled. 'Our young women prefer to marry and have the children.' His lips closed tight. 'Now, what about your menstruations? Is that in order? Normal?'

The resentment in Mary's voice would have been

obvious even to a foreign speaker. 'I only had one period before . . .'

'Before that trouble with the boys . . .'

'Before I came here. I haven't had one since.' Sullen eyes jabbed at the doctor. 'Frau Professor Lager says that it's a mixture of hormonal imbalance and acclimatising myself to the thinner atmosphere. She says it could easily be summer before I start again. There's nothing to worry about.'

The doctor pulled a pad from his pocket and wrote something down. 'You look a little pale. We will do tests for anaemia. You are very thin. Is that always so?'

Mary's eyes snatched away. 'Actually, I put on quite a bit of weight last term. The Sisters' cooking is wonderful. But I did lose my appetite, so I've lost some of it this term.'

'You are dieting, yes?'

So he thought she was anorexic, well, bulimic perhaps. No doubt he thought she *made* herself sick every time she excused herself from class. The idea infuriated her. 'I am *not* dieting! You don't eat much if you feel sick a lot. Austrian food is quite delicious. I enjoyed it very much when I first came here.'

'So, ja. I think it is enough. You are free to return to your school work.'

Mary jumped up like a jack-in-the-box. 'Good afternoon, Reverend Mother,' she said, her voice tearful, remembering the required curtsy. In her hurry to get away she almost fell backwards. Kramer gently balanced her by placing a hand on her back and Mary shuddered to her feet.

'Goodbye, Herr Doktor', she said, perfunctorily, holding out her hand. She wrestled to open the right side of the double door; the doctor did it for her.

As she rushed out, she bumped into Renate Scheider-bauer. Had the girl been listening? She was always hanging around, watching Mary, waiting to see what she would do. Mary guessed she was already longing for the time when she would be shown how to take over Lisl's duties.

'What did they want?' Renate demanded, walking beside Mary.

'What do you mean, "they"?'

'Everyone knows Reverend Mother called Herr Doktor Kramer. Just like everyone knows there's something wrong with you.'

'There's nothing wrong with me. Gastric flu, that's all.'

'For goodness' sake, Fullbridey. Slow down! Sister Christa's on the prowl. She'll have us polishing the chapel floor as a penance.'

'He thinks I'm nuts,' Mary said crossly. 'He thinks because I lost my voice over that business in London I'm unstable. As far as he's concerned I've lost weight because I'm bulimic. I expect he's ringing my parents right this minute and telling them so.'

20

Mary hurried from the convent as fast as she could, down the road towards Erika Lager's house. She wished she still had Lisl's bike so that the wind could blow away her memories of the last half hour. She felt contaminated, hated the pictures torturing her mind: the doctor's hand on her wrist, her arm, the appraising look in the dark brown eyes peering into hers. He had been trying to reach her secret places, her private thoughts. She felt this as a violation of her innermost being, an attack on her personal space. She caught great gulps of the cold March air into her lungs, pulled off her headscarf and allowed the icy breeze to catch her hair. She'd stop by the little stream that trickled through the meadow beside the Frau Professor's drive. Perhaps it would not be entirely frozen. She'd splash the clean, uncontaminated water over her face and arms, allow it to sting her skin, to cleanse it. She wanted to be rid of the feeling of being pawed over, labelled unstable by a well-meaning mediocrity.

A glint of colour completely out of place among the grey-white stone, the frosty twigs, the blue-green evergreens at the roadside made Mary hold her breath, then let out tiny bursts of small clouds of steam. Someone, something, was watching her, waiting for her. She stopped, heart hammering. A glint of late sunlight reflected the gleam of a painted shape, concave, curved, dipping down. An ambush? Was someone about to spring on her from the tangle of scrub at the side?

There was no movement. The scuttle of a robin hunting an insect drew Mary's eye towards an indentation in the road. It was the track leading to the footpath stepping down to Kernkirchen more directly than the road, the short-cut she and Jenny had walked down last summer. She walked across the road to look, and found herself confronting the bonnet of a car. It was backed into the overgrown pathway, well hidden from the road. Her heart thudded into her throat. What was it doing there?

She stared at the unusual colour, watched the shadow of clouds drape over it, deepening it to something familiar. Where had she seen that shade before? Nile-green; not factory smooth but sprayed on by an amateur. She recognised the Heldens' Volkswagen which Joseph had restored and resprayed. Maybe it was Lisl?

Mary sprinted towards the car, her eyes now moistening with hope, her lips stretched wide in anticipation. As she reached it, she heard the door open and saw her friend get out.

'Lisl!' she cried. She saw the same Lisl she'd always known: medium brown hair, loose tendrils pointing to high cheekbones, fawn eyes with their gentle expression, rosebud mouth.

The door clicked shut and the car backed further into the track. She recognised Joseph in the driving seat, found the tears blurring her vision, felt all was safe. 'Lisl,' she breathed. 'It's you at last!'

Her friend moved up to her, put an arm round her shoulders. 'Ssh, Mary. Not so loud. We don't want the whole village to know.' She pulled her by the elbow, dragged her into the track and towards the car. 'We'd almost given up on you. Don't you go to the Frau Professor right after school?' Her voice was strained, conspiratorial. 'It's almost dark.'

'Usually I do,' Mary said, her eyes shining happiness. 'This afternoon Reverend Mother called me in to her office, that's all.'

'Has she asked you to do my chores?' Lisl looked wistful, leaned back against the car.

'Scheiderbauer is going to do all that. Not till next term, though.'

'Why are you so late?'

'That old quack from Salzburg was called in to examine me, just because I've got some sort of bug. They think I'm bulimic.'

'You mean Herr Doktor Kramer?'

'That's what Reverend Mother called him. Silly old fuddy-duddy! I *told* him the Frau Professor had done all those tests. I don't like him touching me. He just went on and on.' Mary shuddered.

'The Frau Professor examined you?'

'Just to make sure I was OK.' Mary stared at Lisl. 'She said she'd done the same for you.'

Lisl nodded, tired eyes almost shut, then shrugged and clasped Mary to herself. 'The Herr Doktor's OK, you know; just old.'

'Kept on with loads of those stupid questions,' Mary breathed, her eyes deep. She grinned, remembering jokes she and Lisl had shared. 'Anyway, younger than the Frau Professor.'

'Everyone's younger than the Frau Professor.' Lisl giggled. 'It's just so wonderful to see you.' She slipped her arm from Mary's shoulders, linked it with her friend's and pulled her even further along the track. 'I've missed you dreadfully.'

'You could have fooled me,' Mary said, then laughed out loud in her delight at seeing Lisl again. 'Why didn't you even answer my letters or anything?'

'I couldn't.'

'And your mother wouldn't fetch you when I phoned.' Mary took her arm away and looked into Lisl's eyes. 'I couldn't understand that. What's all the mystery? Were you at death's door or something?'

Lisl's face had taken on a beatific smile. 'Not ill, Mary. Not ill at all. Something wonderful has happened to me.' Her eyes were soft and dreamy. 'You'll never guess. Not in a million years.' She opened the passenger door. 'Get into the car and see what I've got to show you.'

It crossed Mary's mind that perhaps Lisl had decided to join a different order of nuns, a less enclosed one. She'd been away at another convent, had not been allowed to write or phone or get into any sort of communication with the outside world. And now she'd brought the habit to show her, had spread it out on the back seat. Mary looked through the side window, expecting to see the white robes of a postulant, a large crucifix, a wimple.

Instead, she saw a car seat with a baby strapped in it. 'Why, it's a baby!' she said, astonished. 'A tiny one.' She stared at Lisl. 'Your mother's had another baby? She's asked you to look after it for her? Is that why she kept saying you were too busy to talk to me?'

The infant, strapped into a battered seat which had evidently done duty for many years, had its little body wrapped in a duvet coat against the cold, only the small face peeping out. It was pink with health.

'Not my mother's, Mary,' Lisl whispered. 'She's mine, my very own. Her name's Johanna.'

'*Yours?*' Mary's head, craned to look at the child through the glass, shot up to stare at her friend. 'What on earth do you mean, yours? How could she possibly be?'

'I mean I had her – gave birth to her.'

Joseph opened the driver's door as far as he could in the small space. He squeezed out, smiled at Mary and held out his hand across the bonnet. 'Servus, Mary.'

'Hello, Joseph.' The shy smile, the reserve, the handsome eyes brushing over her but not forcing themselves on her, relaxed Mary into friendliness. 'Reverend Mother said you wouldn't be around till Easter.'

'Reverend Mother doesn't know everything about me,' he said gruffly. 'You look terribly peaky and thin. Are you all right?' His fingers were warm over hers but he let them go, smiled gently and turned towards his sister. 'Hold on to her, Lisl. I think she's about to faint.'

'I'm . . .'

'White as a sheet,' he said. 'You and Lisl sit in the car and talk. I'll collect some pine-cones for Mutter's fire. Back soon.' And he strode further away along the track and out of sight.

'Let me push the passenger seat forward. You get in and sit down after I've climbed into the back. I'll sit beside Johanna. Bit of a squeeze to manage it, but we're both slim.'

Mary stood, leaning against her friend, wide-eyed, her mouth open. 'But you couldn't have had a baby, Lisl.' She gulped, caught a cold breath, felt it go through her, cutting her. 'You told me you'd never had a boyfriend. You had a vision of Our Lady. You wanted to become a nun . . .'

'That was true then,' Lisl said, evading Mary's eyes. 'Before I got to know him properly.'

'But . . . But that was only last summer, Lisl. Last August, during summer school.' Mary squeezed into the car, knelt on the front seat, rested her arms on its back and watched Lisl as she bent towards the baby. 'And later, when we climbed up to the grotto, you said you always wanted to stay a virgin. And that was in September. It's only March now.'

'The baby was a bit premature. That happens with teenage mothers.' Lisl, squeezed in beside her daughter, was looking at Mary, eyes shining love. 'Isn't she beautiful? I just had to find a way to show her to you.'

'May I hold her?'

Lisl unstrapped the baby, kissed the little face, pulled the duvet coat into shape and handed her to Mary.

'She does take after you,' Mary marvelled, pushing back the little hood, gazing at the child. 'Your eyes, your mouth, the high cheekbones, even your lips.' She smiled at the baby, stroked her fat cheeks. 'Just like Jenny and her mother,' she said, her forehead creasing into frown-lines. 'And the way you and your sisters look exactly like that old photo of your mother. I've never before come across daughters who look so like their mothers.'

Lisl was putting the hood on the baby's head again. 'She might catch cold.'

'Perhaps it's because most of you come from the same village.' A feeling of unease, of something she had seen before but could not quite connect, tightened Mary's shoulders, tingled down her spine.

'I know,' Lisl laughed gaily. 'Everyone says that, except my mother. She keeps saying you can't tell at this stage. She even manages to see something of Kurt in

Johanna. His mouth, she says. His full lips . . .'

'Yours are the same,' Mary brushed that aside, then jumped, leaned back. 'What did you say?' she whispered.

'Kurt's lips . . .'

'Kurt? You mean Kurt Miller, Lisl?' Mary almost wailed. 'That's what the Frau Professor said. She said *he* was your boyfriend. And Reverend Mother said you were going to get married. I didn't believe either of them. It isn't true, is it?'

'As soon as I'm sixteen.'

'You can't mean he's . . . He can't be! I don't believe it,' Mary said, her voice flat. 'When we met him at your parents' place, and he brought you that rose, you said you couldn't stand him. Don't you remember? We wouldn't let him come to lunch, ran away . . .'

'I said he was crazy about me.' Lisl's voice was low.

'You said it was because you reminded him of Helga.'

Lisl's eyes grew dark. 'He's in love with *me*, he thinks the world of me.'

'How can you keep talking about him as though you liked him? You said you couldn't bear him near you, Lisl. You said he gave you the creeps. How could you . . .' Tears choked the words away. 'You couldn't have done. You could only have got to really know him in the last three months.'

'Don't be so silly, Mary. I told you I've known him all my life. I said we practically grew up together.'

'That's not the same as being in love with him, going out with him. You said he disgusted you, you told me over and over again that he made you sick with his presents and the flowers he brought you, all that stuff. You said you threw it all back at him.'

'That just encouraged him.'

'You told me you'd never had a boyfriend,' Mary insisted, 'let alone actually slept with someone. You said you were a virgin, were always going to stay one. You must remember that.'

'I was!' she cried, then hung her head. 'It isn't like that, Mary.' She put her hand out to Johanna's head and stroked it. 'All childish fantasies. All day-dreams.'

'When we climbed up to the grotto,' Mary pressed on, staring at her friend, 'you'd have been pregnant *then*. How can you say you've had a baby?'

'I could if . . .' Lisl began, then stopped herself again, biting her lip.

'You simply couldn't have.'

'It was at the Braune Rössl, you see,' Lisl said, shifting her eyes, fixing them on the baby, her voice a monotone. 'I didn't realise; I felt dizzy.'

'The Braune Rössl? You went there with Kurt?'

'Not with Kurt exactly. It was after – you know. Before you came.'

'After you had the vision, you mean?'

'You don't understand.' She rocked the infant, kissed her. 'I wasn't quite there. Light-headed, I suppose. Still under the spell of it. I'd just come down from the grotto, you see.'

'And you met Kurt?'

'Not Kurt; Joseph. I'd left the convent, walked along the road to St Walter, not thinking about anything in particular. Joseph was there, going down to Kern-kirchen, to the lake. I walked with him.'

It sounded like a carefully rehearsed recital to Mary.

A grimace as Lisl tried to smile. 'And we came across a whole crowd of locals, young people I've known all my life. We just went along with them, down to the inn.'

'You mean you joined them and got drunk?'

249

'Not really,' Lisl said, her voice now hoarse with tension. 'We were with them, but I just seemed to be out of it.'

'You mean he . . . You didn't know what was happening?' Mary stared, stunned.

'No, no. When we'd been there for a little while I nearly passed out, and needed some air . . .'

'And he took you out, took advantage of you? He's as bad as that?'

'He followed me.' Lisl shrugged. 'He's a man, Mary. In any case, we're getting married as soon as we can so he's behaving very well.'

'He slept with you while you were not quite there, and he's behaving well?' Lisl began to cry. Softly at first, then her shoulders began to shake. 'It isn't true, is it, Lisl?'

'I don't know,' she sobbed and put her head on Mary's shoulder, the baby between them. 'Don't go on and on about it. I don't remember anything. Just that Kurt said he couldn't help himself.' She wept, the tears pouring down. 'I just wanted to tell you about my little girl,' she gulped. 'And about how happy I am.'

'So why are you crying?'

'Mutti says it's post-natal depression. It's quite common, you know. I'll get over it soon.'

'But why won't they let you go out if you want to?'

'They're afraid of what I might do,' Lisl said, her eyes hard. 'They think I might kill myself.'

'Why would they think that?'

'Because I'm depressed; the baby blues.'

'That's silly,' Mary said. 'You wouldn't ever leave your baby.'

'I'm sorry, Mary. I couldn't get away before. My mother watches me all the time, says my place is with the baby and that I'm not to go out gallivanting on my own. Kurt comes round every day and fusses over the two of us. When he isn't doing that, he's working hard for his father so that he can get some money together for us. He's gone out to buy things for Johanna today. It's only because Joseph's home that I could escape for a bit.' She looked at Mary, then at the baby. 'They won't let me see you, or write to you, or even talk to you on the telephone. You'd think you were somehow dangerous.'

'And Reverend Mother wouldn't let me visit you.'

'At least that makes sense. She wouldn't approve of your being friends with someone who's had an illegitimate baby. You're not to consort with unmarried mothers.'

'But if you're getting married, it should be perfectly all right.' She looked hopefully at Lisl. 'It's not true, is it? They know you aren't going to go through with it, and they think you'll run away. Is that it?'

'I have to marry him, Mary. I have to give Johanna a father.'

'Give her one? I thought you said Kurt *was* the father.'

'A legal father, so that she is his legitimate daughter. It's to make sure he's there for her. My parents insist on that.'

'But he's such a macho pig, Lisl! He runs after all the girls, and boasts about how many chase him. Jenny was round him and his crowd as often as she could get away. She told me all about it.'

'It's the way men are around here.'

'Not Joseph.'

'There are always exceptions.'

'Kurt can't be very bright, Lisl. And you're so gifted,

too. How can you possibly marry a man like that? And what about your violin? Let alone becoming a nun.'

'The Little Sisters wouldn't have anything to do with me now. Anyway, I'm not interested in becoming a nun any more. I've got Johanna to look after.' She held her hands out to take back the baby, kissed her, rocked her in her arms. 'And I love my baby more than playing the violin.' She smiled at Mary, strapped the baby back in her chair. 'She's simply adorable, wonderful.'

Joseph opened the driver's door. 'I'd better get you back, Lisl. Mutter will have finished her milking soon and begin to wonder what's up. And you, Mary. Strap in. I'll give you a lift as far as the Frau Professor's. Otherwise you'll be very late and she'll smell a rat.'

21

Mary was disappointed that it wasn't Joseph who was driving the minibus to the airport. Perhaps it was too early, even for him. She had to take the six-thirty flight to change in Vienna for Heathrow. One of the men from St Walter, a member of the team who had helped rescue her the term before, was in the driver's seat. She examined his hair, dark with a smattering of grey, and brought her eyes down to the deep pleat at the back of his grey jacket with the green trim. Somehow the traditional clothes she had admired so much when she had first come to Austria now exasperated her. The man turned round to check that everyone was seated. Even the antler buttons, coloured light beige and a deep brown, appeared to wink at Mary, to glint a menace she could not understand.

Something weird, something unholy, was happening within the convent's hallowed space. She felt threatened without Lisl's friendship, without her presence. She shook herself. Perhaps her feeling of foreboding was simply that Lisl was no longer at the school. But deep down she knew quite well it had to be more than that.

The Nile-green Beetle, with baby Johanna and Lisl in the back, came into Mary's mind. A sweet little baby, her round face pink with cold. Could it really have been

253

true that Lisl and Kurt . . .?

The last visit to the grotto with Lisl came back to her, and she saw again what had startled her so much that day. The silhouette of a figure, emphatic, dark. The remnants of slanting sun had shown light between the legs stretching determinedly away. Not her reflection, for she had been wearing a skirt. Nothing at all like the shadow that had frightened her a moment later.

She was now sure that what she had seen was a man. He had to have been an experienced mountaineer to move away from her like that. Could it have been Kurt? She remembered Lisl looking anxiously around. She might have guessed that Kurt had been there, that he had scaled the mountain from the other side, picked flowers, taken them to the grotto to be there to greet the one he loved. Had he been lurking behind bushes, waiting his chance, and left only because Mary had got in his way? Perhaps Lisl had lied to her. Perhaps she had already been Kurt's lover, tired of him, and taken her friend up with her almost every time to keep him away from her.

Mary did not believe that, but she was sure that the figure had been Kurt. She remembered Lisl's angry look when she had pointed out the freshness of the flowers to her. She heard again how Lisl had insisted they be thrown away rather than left there to grace the statue of Our Lady. It became clearer now why Lisl's family and friends would readily assume that Kurt had fathered her child. But if he had, he must have forced himself on her. It must have happened exactly as Lisl had described, when her mind, her soul, were still wrapped up in the vision. She was not, Mary was sure she had never been, interested in having a boyfriend.

So what had made Lisl so disturbed and tearful? Why

hadn't she simply told her mother that she would not marry Kurt because she did not love him? There had been something else Lisl had wanted to tell her, something on the tip of her tongue she could not bring herself to say. 'I don't know,' Mary remembered her wailing. 'Don't go on about it. I don't remember anything.'

Was it that Kurt had actually – raped her? Something she dared not confide to anyone in case . . . What? It didn't make sense.

Strange that Frau Helden was so keen for Lisl to get married. When they had mentioned Kurt to her that day at the farm, giggled at his boasting about his skill in devouring Marillenknödeln, told her about the roses he had given both of them, there had been no hint of any desire to see Lisl married to him. Instead, Frau Helden had laughed good-naturedly. 'That young man still carries the torch for poor Helga,' she'd said, almost light-heartedly. 'Poor thing! Lisl's so like her, he just can't get over it.' And she had smiled a small, sad smile.

She knew Lisl wasn't interested in him, that she would never wish to take Helga's place. Something was wrong: a mysterious undercurrent Mary knew was threatening Lisl. Whatever it was, Frau Helden wanted to keep it secret, wanted to prevent Lisl from telling anyone.

Mary shuddered as the thought welled over her. Had Lisl's parents been afraid of losing her to the convent? Had they actually put Kurt up to impregnating her? That's what the Frau Professor had implied. How could she help Lisl escape? She could not possibly be expected to marry Kurt. There had to be a way to help her.

'Also, aussteigen!' the driver shouted as they drew up at Salzburg airport. Mary picked up her cases, waved her farewells and checked herself into the departure lounge. She eyed the boxes of Mozartkugeln on display and bought one for her mother. Should she have brought some holy water back for Aunt Rilla? She had been so preoccupied she had not even thought of that. Her eye was caught by bottles of Bailoni liqueur: the sickly sweet of Gold Marillenlikör, the alcoholic strength of Marillenbrandt. Sadly she thought back to the Marillenknödeln, their succulent apricot fillings melting into potato dough. Frau Helden had heaped them on her plate, had been so proud to show off traditional fare. Where were those good times now?

Mary settled back for the trip. She had problems of her own to puzzle out on the journey. Was the Frau Professor's chill tone, her eagle eye after that episode with the computer files, the reason she was so glad to get away? Not exactly glad to get home, since there was very little for her to do there. Glad to get away from the other girls, she finally worked out. To escape from their curious stares, their whispers, their nudging each other every time she passed.

The flight from Vienna arrived on time. She saw Aunt Rilla waiting for her, waving at her as soon as she walked out of the Green channel, rushing to help her with the trolley.

'Your mother has an important session with new clients this morning.' She embraced Mary, then pushed the trolley towards the exit. 'She said you would understand. She simply could not put them off, they were about to kill each other.' Aunt Rilla stopped, smiled warmth at Mary and hugged her. Then her eyes became fine slits as she held Mary away from her and considered her face, her figure. 'Anne mentioned you have not been feeling well, and that the school called Herr Doktor Kramer in,' she said, a small flicker in her eyes.

'I took that with a large grain of salt. Reverend Mother can be quite pernickety. Then I phoned Mutter. She admitted you'd mentioned feeling off. How are you now?'

'I'm perfectly all right, thank you,' Mary answered dutifully, turning away to hide her expression. She no longer felt sick as often as before. In fact there were long passages of time when she did not feel sick at all. She hoped it was all behind her, hoped she would be able to get through meals at home without disruption. Otherwise Daddy was sure to send her off to yet another doctor. 'They all make this silly fuss. I hope you're not going to start.' The disappointment at her mother's absence made her sound more astringent than she felt.

'So you're feeling OK?'

'I had a stomach bug, that's all. The flight's made me feel a bit nauseous, but that was probably the plastic food.'

'Really? Air Austria are usually quite good. Anyway, I hope you did not bother too much. I have made lunch for us both.'

'It's only ten o'clock, Aunt Rilla.'

'For later. A good, nourishing Gulaschsuppe, in case you feel deprived.'

Mary subdued the heave she felt and smiled at her godmother. Could she possibly confide her worries about Lisl to her? Her parents were no use, she was sure they wouldn't even listen. Her mind went back to the time Aunt Rilla had rescued Bridget, when she had taken on both the doe and her babies. Perhaps she would be prepared to help Lisl.

But Aunt Rilla was distracted with asking about her state of health. There seemed to be something on her mind, something she was finding it hard to tell her. Now was not the time to bring up Lisl's problems.

They drove in silence along the M4 spur, then joined the motorway to central London. 'Maybe I should warn you,' Aunt Rilla began uneasily, 'Reverend Mother herself phoned your parents. Herr Doktor Kramer was not entirely happy with your state of health. He thought there might be a nervous disorder.'

'I knew it.' Mary said heatedly. 'Stupid old fool! He thinks I'm bulimic.'

'You didn't like him?' Her eyes, almost hidden behind the deep folds of eyelid, turned briefly to Mary, then back to the road.

'He thought I was making myself sick to lose weight.'

'He actually said that? He is normally so polite and pleasant.'

'He didn't say anything to me. I *told* him the Frau Professor had already examined me–'

'My mother examined you?' Gabriela's foot pressed down on the accelerator and they surged into the outside lane.

'She said I looked unwell,' Mary passed it off. 'Just the usual stuff. Stethoscope and that.'

'Kramer's a gentle old thing. I am sure he is doing his best. Anyway, your father has already made an appointment with Dr Grossmann,' Gabriela finally said. 'I hope you will cooperate. He is trying to make sure last year's problems do not resurface.'

'You mean Reverend Mother told my parents I needed psychiatric help? That creepy Kramer said I was cracking up, didn't he?' Mary twisted in her seat. 'He thinks it's worse than bulimia, doesn't he?'

'Not psychiatric help, Mary dear. Just an assessment. To make sure you do not lose your voice again.'

'At the rate they're all going, they'll achieve just

that,' Mary shouted, her lungs full power. England was no better than Austria. They were all persecuting her. And now there was no way she could broach the subject of Lisl with Aunt Rilla. That would just mean another adult ranged against her.

'In fact that's where we're going first. The appointment with Dr Grossmann is at eleven this morning.'

'We're on our way, you mean?'

'Yes, Mary,' Aunt Rilla said uneasily. 'Your parents thought it best to get it over with as soon as you arrived.'

A terrible thought entered Mary's mind. What if this psychiatrist used hypnotism? What if he wormed out of her that she believed Lisl had been made pregnant on purpose? That there was a plot to stop her friend becoming a nun? If she gave that away, would they actually lock her up?

'You say this friend of yours – Elisabeth – disappeared from the school during the autumn term?'

Dr Grossmann was seated behind his desk. Mary was opposite him on an upright chair. She had refused both the sofa and the couch.

'She didn't come back after the Christmas holiday. They wouldn't say why.'

'Who are "they", Mary?'

'The other girls, the teachers, everyone.'

'You asked?'

'Yes. She wasn't feeling at all well the last time I saw her. I thought she might be really ill.'

'Dead, you mean?'

'All right, I did. There was all this stupid mystery.'

'So what did you do?'

'Tried to talk to her younger sister who's also at the convent. She kept running away.' Mary's eyes glittered.

'They all giggled behind my back and talked in the local dialect, so I couldn't follow what they were saying.'

'Did you try asking anyone else?'

'One or two of the teachers.'

'Nuns, you mean? You felt they wouldn't lie because of their habit?'

'The nuns have a vow of silence except for really important things. A lot of the teachers are lay; the nuns are mostly too old.'

'But you felt the teachers would be truthful?'

'I wanted to find out what had happened, so I asked.' Mary sounded peeved. 'Anyway, it was a waste of time. They just patted my arm and changed the subject.'

'Did it occur to you that Elisabeth might not want to talk to you?'

Mary stared at Dr Grossmann. 'No. We were best friends.'

'It happens.'

'I knew it wasn't that,' Mary said coldly. She hated this man with his silly questions, his supercilious manner. What did he know about her and Lisl? She'd pull rank with the Frau Professor. This man was only a stupid doctor. 'I asked Frau Professor Lager. Elisabeth used to be her assistant.'

'Used to be?'

'She doesn't go any more.' He wasn't even listening properly. She'd just told him Lisl had left the school. 'The Frau Professor asked me to take over.'

'Really? That must have been very exciting for you.'

Mary turned her head away.

'And?'

'And what?'

'Did Dr Lager know what had happened to your friend?'

260

'*Professor* Lager. She said there was absolutely nothing wrong with Lisl . . .'

'Lisl?'

'That's what her family call Elisabeth,' Mary said impatiently. 'The Frau Professor said not to worry about her. It was all because her family didn't want her to go back to school.'

'Professor Lager had examined her?'

'Yes. She said the local families always put pressure on the girls to get married.'

'And you accepted that?'

'You think she's a liar?'

'What I think is neither here nor there.' He opened a notebook and made some notes. When he looked at Mary again his expression was resigned. 'So that's the best you could do, was it?'

'I tried to ring several times. Lisl's mother put the phone down the minute she recognised my voice.'

'So why didn't you visit her? The girl lives locally, you said?'

'Eight kilometres from the convent by road. That's too far to walk without their missing me. Going cross country is dangerous in winter.'

'I see. The school wouldn't give permission for you to go?'

'Reverend Mother said Lisl had changed. Because she has a boyfriend now, she isn't suitable.'

His head jerked up. 'What did she mean by that?'

'The nuns don't let the girls mix with boys during term time.'

Grossmann's smile struck Mary as infuriatingly patronising. 'They think male companionship is a serious threat?'

'They want gifted girls to be able to develop their

261

talents, not just become housewives.'

'So they discourage marriage?'

'No,' Mary almost shouted. This man was clearly an idiot. 'They just want them to have a *choice*. Austrians think women belong in the home.'

'Kirche, Kinder, Küche, eh?'

Mary looked doggedly at the wall behind the psychiatrist's head. A total waste of time. She scuffed her shoes against the chairlegs.

'So – you have lost your friend.' His hands steepled as he looked over his glasses. 'What do you feel about that?'

'Feel?' Mary twisted in her chair, looked at the clock on the wall. 'I miss her.'

The doctor drummed his pencil on his pad. 'You're very hostile, Mary.'

'I didn't ask to come.'

'Your parents are worried about you.'

'Mummy didn't even meet me. She made my godmother bring me straight from the airport.'

He jotted something down, looked up. 'You're keeping something back, Mary. Something important. I can't help you unless you tell me everything.'

'I don't need help.'

'You know that isn't so. You've been feeling ill ever since your friend left the school. Feeling deprived is fine, feeling annoyed is usual, but to start feeling sick enough to vomit several times a day – that needs investigation.'

Mary pursed her lips tight and stared beyond him again.

'What else did you and this Elisabeth do?'

A shrug.

'You must have done something special together.'

262

'Climbed up to the grotto.'

'The grotto?'

'A shrine above the convent,' Mary explained reluctantly. 'There's a festival in October.'

'What sort of festival?'

'The Mothering of the Brides.'

He looked up, his eyes now wide. 'To celebrate motherhood?' Another note was added to the pad.

'The new brides come to pray for a baby.' Mary looked at the doctor, and grinned. 'One couple in ten is infertile now, you know.'

'I do know, Mary. I am surprised that you do.'

'My mother's a marriage counsellor. My godmother has always longed for a baby.' She might as well annoy him if she could. 'She's Professor Lager's daughter, you know. That's how I got to the convent in the first place.'

'So that's why Professor Lager researches infertility?'

'Infertility? She's nothing to do with that,' Mary said bluntly. 'Whoever told you that knows nothing at all about it.'

'I stand corrected. What does she do?'

'She is a molecular geneticist. She is working on self-splicing RNA to form specific ribozymes,' Mary recited, her eyes cold. 'Such ribozymes can cleave the substrate sequence in a predictable manner, that is, they form a set of sequence-specific endoribonucleases.' She paused dramatically. 'Does that answer your question?'

'Very impressive.' Grossmann had the grace to grin. 'Does that mean she can alter the performance of an RNA molecule?'

Mary kicked at the legs of her chair. 'I suppose.'

'So what particular attribute is she working on?'

'It's confidential. Even I don't know.'

'It sounds as though you are learning a lot of biology.'

'Genetics. As a matter of fact the Frau Professor's almost got there,' Mary told him gleefully. 'She's just finishing the last set of corroborative experiments.' She stared at Grossmann, her eyes intent. 'She started aeons ago, helping her father. He'd finished a vital piece of research just as the Russians marched into Berlin.'

Grossmann's eyes veiled. 'Berlin, eh?' His lips twisted. 'He can't have been doing the same work. RNA wasn't known about then.'

'I do know that, Dr Grossmann. He worked it all out without knowing precisely what he was doing. Intuitively.'

'I see.' The dark eyes seemed to accentuate the bulge in his nose. 'Very convenient.'

'It did happen like that. The Russian soldiers blundered into the bunker and there was a fire and it was lost.'

'That does sound a little pat, Mary.'

Her eyes blazed. 'That's what happened. The Frau Professor was there herself. She tried to save his work, and her hands were very badly burned. They were permanently damaged.'

'You always call her Frau Professor?'

Mary tossed her hair back.

'I'll take that as a yes.' The doctor wrote more notes, looked up. 'Were the Nazis interested in this work?'

'Yes. What's wrong with that?'

'Are you saying he was able to identify some genetically transmitted attributes?'

'Yes.'

'So, applied to humans, specific traits might be encouraged to reproduce indefinitely,' Grossmann said, almost to himself. 'That could be a way of furthering the master race, I suppose.'

264

'Master race?'

'The Nazis believed that only people of Aryan descent were worth breeding from. I'm sure you've heard about the Holocaust.'

'They killed the Jews.'

'And Gypsies, and homosexuals, and anyone else whose physical characteristics or attributes they didn't fancy.'

'You mean they exterminated them like vermin?'

'Very graphically put, Mary.' He smiled slowly, his eyes hooded. 'They also bred human beings like animals. They paraded healthy young girls chosen for their Aryan looks naked in front of the cream of their young men. Then they simply encouraged the men to choose partners with a view to impregnating them, quite impersonally, to produce master-race babies.'

Mary shivered. She remembered that Kurt's grandmother had been a Nazi. Did the Heldens want Aryan grandchildren, and were they insisting on Lisl producing them?

'You're cold? Shall I put the heating up?'

'I didn't know about that. That's just horrible.' Her shoulders hunched and she began to breathe deeply.

'You feel faint, Mary? Would you like to lie down?'

'I remember now. They took the Frau Professor's father to Berlin and forced him to work for them.'

'You were told this?'

'My godmother told us.'

'So what happened to him?' The lines between Grossmann's nose and mouth were deep. They deepened further as he looked at Mary.

'He died.' Mary turned towards the window, staring out.

'You certainly know a great deal about all this, Mary.

265

Are you and Professor Lager very close?'

'I told you, I'm her assistant.'

'You are fond of her?'

'She teaches me a great deal. I'm grateful to her.'

Another note. 'But your parents mentioned she examined you and found nothing wrong with you?'

'Exactly. Because there isn't.'

'And did she have an explanation for your symptoms?'

'Hormonal changes,' Mary said airily. 'Quite simple. So this session is a complete waste of time.'

'It's your privilege to think so, Mary . . .'

'You can hardly stop me.'

'. . . but if you want to go back to that school you'll have to humour me. That is the condition your parents insist on.'

A sullen dropping of the head. 'You can *see* I'm perfectly all right.'

'It seems the Reverend Mother told your parents that your school work has deteriorated badly. You have not made the progress in German that you made last term. A very disappointing report all round, Mary.'

'My singing teacher's very pleased.' Frau Professor Weisskopf was excited by the progress she was making, spoke of auditions in Salzburg with Professor Kupfer. The breathing exercises, Mary had noticed, were enlarging her lungs and strengthening the muscles in her abdomen quite significantly. Mary smiled to herself as she made her diaphragm go up and down – she knew exactly how to control her abdominal muscles. She could protrude her stomach, or make it flatten.

'Even she maintains you do not concentrate as well as before.'

'I was upset about Lisl – Elisabeth.'

'Now look, Mary, I know you're still holding out on me. You might as well get on with it. Did you ever come across your friend again? If you did, you must know what was wrong with her.'

'She found a way to meet me.'

'And?'

'She was OK.'

'You'll have to do better than that.'

'Her brother Joseph drove her to meet me in the family car.'

'I'm waiting, Mary.'

Mary fidgeted with her hands. 'There was a baby in the car.'

The psychiatrist swivelled his chair right round, the excitement in his voice barely controlled. 'A baby? Elisabeth has had a baby?'

'I found it very hard to believe.'

'But you did believe her?'

'I got into the car and looked at it. It looked exactly like Elisabeth.'

'And whose baby was it?'

'Hers, of course.'

'I meant: who is the father?'

'Her boyfriend's name is Kurt,' Mary said, her eyes down. 'Kurt Miller.'

'And where does he come from?'

'He lives on the farm next to her parents'. Except in the summer, when he works as a lifeguard on the Kernsee.'

'So she's known him all along. And the convent had no idea she was having relations with him until she became pregnant?'

The satisfaction in the man's voice drove Mary on. 'That's why they didn't want me to see her. I told you, they say it's a bad influence for us to mix with married women.'

'But Elisabeth isn't married, I take it.'

'She's not sixteen yet. Anyway, it's quite common for country couples to have a child first. That way the man knows he isn't marrying a barren woman.'

The doctor's mouth dropped open, then shut again. 'So they are planning to marry?'

'Elisabeth's father would kill Kurt if he didn't.' Her eyes fixed on the floor.

'Old customs die hard.'

Mary kept her lips tight.

'And what does Elisabeth think of all this?'

Mary stared straight at Dr Grossmann. 'She loves her baby.'

'And you, Mary? What do you feel about it all?'

'I think she's very lucky to have such a beautiful little girl,' Mary retorted. 'She says she loves looking after her.'

'You will do exactly as I say, Mary,' her father thundered. 'Dr Grossmann is an experienced man. If he says there is a problem, there is one.'

The Fullbrideys were in their living room. Mary had retired to her favourite perch on the window seat. Her mouth had turned mulish as she leaned out to look at the rose bushes cut back to stumps. Daddy believed in hard pruning of old wood. Mary was always surprised at the luxuriant growth which followed. 'You do pay him,' she said, gritting her teeth. 'He could just be touting for more business.'

Thomas Fullbridey's eyes darted fury. 'This is preposterous! We should never have sent you to that outrageous school. Where did you learn to be so cynical? A young girl like you should not even think along those lines.'

Mary wondered why her father would imagine that her life, though sheltered from young men, was different from life among other groups of people. As the nuns were fond of pointing out, both they and the girls were human beings, subject to their usual weaknesses and strengths. Experience might add to those. Mary did not feel her own had been without trauma.

'I don't know why everyone is making such a fuss,' she mumbled, subdued. She could not afford to antagonise her father, otherwise he would probably not let her go back to Austria. The prospect of spending all her time in her parents' house appalled her.

'A fuss? You call it making a fuss when your examination marks plummet from As to Cs?'

'They're graded from one to four in Austria, Daddy. Threes aren't all that bad. You can't expect me to get ones all the time. No one else does. Last term was exceptional.' She looked aggressively at Thomas. 'Anyway, my singing has improved. Frau Professor Weisskopf said so to Reverend Mother. It takes a lot of energy to use one's voice properly, you know. I expect it tired me.'

Her father put down the *Financial Times* he was using as a shield and looked at his daughter. 'I suppose you have scored there. Well, yes, your voice is much more controlled. But that's not nearly as important as examination results. And I must point out that your voice teacher also says you don't concentrate, that you can't seem to keep even the simplest new points in mind. I find that very strange. You've always had an excellent memory.'

'I can't help my memory deteriorating.'

'It isn't deteriorating, Mary. There seems to be a temporary block. That has to mean there's a specific problem. That's one of the things Dr Grossmann is getting at, and it's what really worries me, my pet.'

Mary could not deny it. When she had first come to the convent she had had no trouble keeping in mind the new techniques Frau Professor Weisskopf had taught her, or any problems in remembering her exercises. Now, not only did she find it difficult to concentrate on her lessons, she could not even remember the words of a new song from one minute to the next.

'I did have a bug, Daddy. All the girls . . .'

'None of the other girls was as affected, I understand.'

'How can you possibly know that? Does it say in my report?' The nuns made it a rule to send the reports straight to the parents without showing them to the pupils.

'We had a full report from Reverend Mother, enclosing Doktor Kramer's diagnosis. He could not find any evidence of infection, but he was still concerned. There's something wrong, Mary.'

'The Frau Professor also examined me. She said I was fine; very healthy, she said. An excellent constitution.'

'Actually, Mary, Professor Lager wrote us a note as well. She insisted there was nothing organic to worry about, but said she preferred to warn us that you had reacted more to the bug than the other girls.'

Why on earth had the Frau Professor gone behind her back? Mary leaned further into the garden and watched a blue tit looking for early aphids. They were all conspiring against her, picking at weak points, trying to take over her life. 'So what does the brilliant Dr Grossmann want me to do?'

Anne went over to Mary and put an arm round her. She wriggled away. 'Nothing very much, darling. He just thought you should have a physical examination. You do have a bit of a tummy, you know.'

Mary looked down at herself. It was true, she had to admit, that since she had lost weight she seemed to have lost it everywhere except her abdomen. She'd obviously forgotten to hold her muscles in. She pulled them tight – her belly was quite flat.

She stood up and showed herself to her parents. 'It's the singing,' she told them confidently. 'You don't understand. The exercises increase your abdominal muscles quite substantially. I can make my tummy flat, or swell it out.' She demonstrated. 'So what does *he* think it is?'

'A purely psychological problem, Mary. Nothing at all to worry about.'

'Then there's no need to go and see another doctor, is there?' Mary had sat down again and was hunched into herself, her arms over her breasts. 'You know I hate having all these examinations. It's so distasteful.'

'He's very worried that you haven't started your periods again. You are fifteen now, Mary. You really should be menstruating on a regular basis.'

'If Dr Grossmann had any sense he'd see it would make me worse,' Mary said, tearful now. 'I'm not even feeling sick any more.'

She saw them exchange glances, her father nod. 'He thinks it best that we check out any minor physical problems first. There could be relatively simple ones like an ovarian cyst, or a polyp in the womb. That sort of thing could lead to trouble if it were not dealt with at an early stage.'

A light dawned on Mary. 'You mean he thinks I've

got an infection, like the one Aunt Rilla had? Is that what you're worried about?'

She saw her mother look startled. 'I hadn't really thought of that,' she said, voice low. 'Anyway, I've made an appointment for you with Dr Jennifer Graham. We felt it best to find a lady doctor.'

'What sort of doctor is she?'

'A lady doctor . . .'

'You mean a gynaecologist, don't you?' Mary shouted hysterically.

'She is very discreet. She won't really bother you more than she can help.'

Even the medicals in Austria had left her feeling uneasy, tainted somehow. 'I don't want to go,' she said, stamping her foot.

Anne held her close, kissed her forehead. 'I'm sorry, darling. We do have to have some tests done, just in case. Now that Dr Grossmann has pointed it out, I – we can both – see that your shape has changed.' She stroked Mary's hair back. 'Your grandmother even spotted it at Christmas. It didn't really show because you'd put on weight all over, but she's got an eagle eye. Now you've lost all that weight again it is quite obvious.'

'You will come with me, won't you, Mummy?'

'Of course I will,' her mother tried to comfort her.

Mary drew back. 'I'm not going with Daddy.'

'Quite right, Mary, my dear,' Thomas said softly. 'You need to go with your mother.'

22

'Anne!' Gabriela tried to stop herself from looking shocked to see her friend unexpectedly standing on her doorstep. 'Did you try to ring?'

'I'm sorry, Rilla,' Mary's mother gasped, clutching at the front door jamb. 'Something terrible has happened. I can't go home just yet. May I come in?'

'But of course.' Gabriela held out a hand and pulled the distraught woman into her house.

Anne seemed to be on the verge of some sort of breakdown. Her normally tidy appearance had a strange nonchalance about it: the dishevelled hair, the lips only half-coated with lipstick, the ungloved hands. Gabriela took in the mismatched buttons and button-holes of Anne's coat, the cavalier way she had thrust her scarf into a pocket.

'I came on the off-chance,' Anne gulped. 'I was too upset to wrestle with a public phone. They're always vandalised.'

'You know you're always welcome,' Gabriela said, helping Anne take off her coat. She looked uneasily up the stairs and, hearing no sound, steered her into the living room.

'I can't believe this is happening, Rilla.'

'Come and sit down and you can tell me all about it.'

Anne sank into an armchair and paused only for more breath before continuing. 'It's about Mary. It's so terrible. . .' Both hands pushed frantically through her hair.

'What on earth has happened? Has she had an accident?'

'It's not an accident,' Anne cried out, tears running. 'I wish I thought it was. We send Mary to one of the best schools in Highgate, and she is almost gang-raped at an exclusive party there. So we ship her off to this secluded, carefully controlled convent *you* stake your life on . . .'

'There's been a problem at the convent? They have expelled her?'

'Expelled? I suppose they will,' Anne said, wiping her eyes. 'But that's not important. As far as I'm concerned all this is *their* fault.'

'What is?'

'We wouldn't send her back anyway,' she shouted. 'After all, we leave her in what we take to be the safest place possible – in the care of nuns. An enclosed order, at that.' Anne pushed wisps of hair back from her face. 'And your mother as well,' she wailed. 'You'd think *she* would be safeguard enough. What more could we have done?'

'What has happened, Anne? Is Mary all right? Where is she now?' Gabriela's eyes began to fill with tears. 'I thought she was happy there.'

'She's pregnant.'

Gabriela's heart constricted at the words. She felt for a chair behind her and sat down heavily. 'You are going too far, Anne. Just because the girl vomits in the mornings . . .' Her voice trailed off. 'How could Mary possibly be pregnant? I know her so well, there cannot conceivably be a boy. She would have mentioned it.'

'Pregnant, I tell you,' Anne howled. 'And not a word from her.'

'I don't believe it! She's still traumatised by that awful experience last June. . .'

'How could she do this?' Anne shouted.

'Hold on a minute, Anne. My mother's upst–' Gabriela began.

Anne interrupted her, pointed an accusatory finger. 'You said she couldn't be safer. You said she would develop her voice, learn German, increase her educational base enormously. You said we couldn't do better for her.'

'There must be some mistake, Anne. What on earth gives you the idea that Mary is having a baby?'

'Idea? It isn't an idea. It's a proved, undeniable, medically established fact. Mary is six months gone.'

'She can't be! It doesn't make sense.' Gabriela got up and began to pace the room.

'Do you suppose I'm making it up?'

'Which doctor maintains this nonsense? Grossmann? For goodness' sake, take her to someone properly qualified to deal with an obstetric problem, not a psychiatrist.'

'We aren't idiots, Gabriela. I took her to a woman gynaecologist two days after her visit to Grossmann.' Anne was quieter now. 'I've just come from there. She phoned to say she had to see us both, it was not something she could discuss on the telephone. Thomas and I have just been talking to her. She's done extensive tests; she even showed us a video of the scan. Mary is carrying a daughter. There was no doubt about it, the picture was very clear.'

Anne suddenly put her head into her hands. Loud,

gulping sobs shook her body, loosened her hair still further. She did not seem to care.

'There has to be a mix-up in the notes. Some simple explanation . . .'

'Simple? What *are* you wittering on about? Whatever the explanation is, it isn't simple.'

'Mary has never mentioned a boy to me.' Gabriela looked at Anne. 'I know it sounds unlikely, but doctors can get the wrong end of the stick. Look what happened about those supposedly abused children up in Cleveland. I think this woman is way out on a limb.'

Anne nodded. 'I thought so too. I thought she'd got the wrong video, was showing us another patient's. But then she showed us the results of all the other tests she'd done – two separate pregnancy tests, blood tests, the scan, the lot. I'm going to take the results to our GP for confirmation, but I already know she's got to be right.' Anne fingered some papers out of her handbag and gave them to Gabriela, who handed her a Kleenex. She blew her nose. 'It all adds up in retrospect.' Her voice sounded almost normal. 'No periods, morning sickness, loss of weight at three months, lassitude, a dislike for foods she used to love, the swelling breasts, even the curious decline in her short-term memory.'

'But she's only fifteen. And she's only had a few periods.'

'Apparently neither of those facts would exclude the possibility of implantation.'

'But it's impossible. She's never, ever, talked about a boy. Mary isn't the sort for one-night stands, for goodness' sake! She'd have let something slip.'

'I know.' Anne sighed, looked helplessly around. 'The only boy I've ever heard her mention without a sneer is Joseph. The one who sang the Ave Maria with her and taught her the folk songs.'

'I know him quite well. He's simply not the type to . . . What's more, he isn't in St Walter during the term. He studies in Salzburg.'

'He was there for the festival,' Anne said coldly. 'You told us how helpful he was about your ankle.'

'Exactly. And I was there as well, Anne. Mary did *not* have secret meetings with him then. No chance at all.'

'He's that girl Elisabeth's brother. Maybe Mary was invited to their farm again.' Anne's tears flowed fast. 'It *must* be him. What have they done to my little girl?'

Gabriela reached over to a shelf and grabbed a box of tissues.

Anne snatched them from her, blew her nose. 'There's something even more peculiar, Rilla.' She took a deep breath. 'The gynaecologist says Mary is still a virgin. That's what puzzled her at the original examination, that's why she didn't jump to any conclusions until she'd run all the tests, and that's why she was particularly careful.'

'A virgin?' Gabriela went over to Anne and put her arms round her neck, kissed her enthusiastically. 'I just knew it. I knew Mary wouldn't have slept with a man. She isn't ready.' She smiled, eyes now moistening. 'Then everything's all right. There's no way she can possibly be pregnant. She's just mimicking it – a phantom pregnancy, that's all it is.' The relief spilled over into tears. 'Mary is almost a woman. The desire for a baby can be very strong.'

Anne shrugged. 'To do him justice, that was Grossmann's original prognosis. We didn't even mention it to Mary, we thought it so absurd. But it is not a phantom baby – we saw the video.'

'Someone else's . . .'

'She's six and a half months pregnant, Gabriela. I've no idea how; I don't really think she's got a boyfriend. The child's afraid of men.'

'So how does this lady doctor explain the virginity away?'

'Says it occasionally happens. Thomas wrote it down, he was so sure it was nonsense.' Anne took out another sheet of paper and showed Gabriela Thomas's neat script.

> *The hymen is intact. Ejaculation near the vulva can result in pregnancy. But there is no question of penetration in the normally accepted sense. Consequently I would rule out anything but a single occasion. Quite unfortunate, but there are reports of such cases in the literature.*

'And how was this supposed to happen without Mary knowing about it? Is Mary supposed to have been like Tess of the d'Urbervilles, sleeping innocently while some boy . . .'

'Dr Graham had some complicated, absurd theory about a fainting fit due to the high altitude she wasn't acclimatised to.'

'And, conveniently . . .' Gabriela stopped.

Anne was crying again. 'I just don't believe that. It's ridiculously far-fetched.' She looked furiously at Gabriela. 'Did Mary say she'd fainted at any time?'

'No.' She turned away from Mary's mother. 'But you really must ask *her* that, Anne. What does she say about it? Have you spoken to her?'

'Not yet; I came here first. Thomas was seething, said he had to get straight back to the office. So we haven't even discussed it. I wanted to talk to you. I haven't got the faintest idea what to do.' Tears welled again. 'How am I going to cope?'

'If that's all that's worrying you, Anne, it isn't a problem. Michael and I will be happy to have Mary here until it's all over.'

'Oh, Rilla, I didn't really mean that. I can't think ahead as far as that. I'm going to ring that old nun,' Anne fumed, dabbing at her eyes. 'Complaining about Mary's report, when all the time . . . And your mother. Your mother said there was nothing wrong with her.'

'Well, there is not, is there?'

The door swung open and Erika Lager stepped into the room. Anne stared at her, mouth open, unable to speak. She looked at Gabriela, questioning.

'I was trying to tell you, Anne. My mother is staying with us over the Easter holiday. She arrived last night.'

'Pregnancy is not an illness, Mrs Fullbridey. Mary is quite fit. I understand that is what your doctor confirmed for you.'

'You were listening, Mutter?' Gabriela turned angrily towards Erika. '*Der Horcher an der Wand hört seine eigne Schand.*' She turned to Anne. 'Eavesdroppers never hear good of themselves.' She looked at her mother stonily.

'I could hardly fail to hear,' Erika pointed out coldly. 'You were both shouting.'

'Rather splitting hairs.'

'I did not like to interrupt.' Erika went to her daughter's drinks cabinet and took out three glasses. 'What we all need is a drink,' she said. 'I prescribe a stiff one. Whisky all right for you two?' She filled the three glasses.

Anne drank deep. 'You're supposed to be a doctor,' she said, aggression oozing out of every pore. 'You saw

Mary every day, and you didn't spot she was pregnant. How d'you account for that?'

Gabriela took the proffered whisky with shaking hands and gulped it down. She glared angrily at her mother, took the bottle from her and sat beside Anne, refilling her friend's glass.

'I see no reason why I should. It is the last thing that would occur to any of us. Herr Doktor Kramer – the Salzburg doctor – did not spot it either.'

'Austrian medicine is clearly way behind British medicine.'

'There *was* a virus going round to account for the sickness . . .'

'What about that girl Elisabeth?' Anne suddenly asked, swivelling round at Erika. 'What was wrong with her, in the end?'

Gabriela's head jerked towards her mother. 'Yes,' she said, 'I'd forgotten that. What happened about Lisl?'

'She had a baby,' Erika said.

'*She's* had a baby?' Gabriela gasped. 'And you didn't even bother to mention it?'

'Why should I?'

'She's Friedl's daughter, Mutter. I know them very well . . .' She frowned. 'Does Mary know?'

'I don't know. I told her Helden was getting married. She has a long-standing relationship with one of the local boys. Not at all the same thing, is it? Quite trite, really.'

Anne was almost choking. 'But if Elisabeth was pregnant, the thought must have crossed your mind about Mary. They were together all the time. She must have . . .'

'I do assure you the two are not connected, Anne.

Helden's baby was born in March. She must have got pregnant before she even met Mary. The two pregnancies are not linked in any way.'

'I'm going to get in touch with the school,' Anne stormed. 'It's *their* responsibility. They must have allowed her to go out on her own.' She stood, irresolute, by the window. 'What on earth are we going to do? A baby. What am I going to do with a baby in the house?'

23

'Aunt Rilla.' Mary smiled at her godmother as she let herself into the Adlers' house. 'I didn't know you were in. I was just going to clean out Bridget's hutch. This is great.'

Gabriela was startled. The child seemed normal, unconcerned. Could she really be taking her pregnancy in her stride like this?

'Why aren't you with your mother, Mary?' Gabriela beckoned her through to the kitchen and unlocked the back door leading to the part of the garden where the rabbit was housed.

Mary walked in. 'Mummy's gone out. You know how busy she is.'

'But it's Maundy Thursday. I would have thought she'd have stopped for the Easter break by now.'

'Meetings all day, she said.' Mary shrugged. 'Loads of new clients, and everyone seems to be having problems. Mummy says marriages are under special strain at Easter and Christmas.' She looked around Gabriela's kitchen and eyed the new curtains she had put up. 'Those are nice and cheerful. I'd love a drink.'

'You're alone all day?'

'I'm going over to Kate's later. Mummy's terribly busy, Aunt Rilla. She went out first thing. The clients seem to flock to her. She told me the Frau Professor arrived yesterday. Is she upstairs?'

'Busy as well. Went off right after breakfast to do some reading at the Patent Office.'

'Anyway, I've got tons of work to get through, but I thought I ought to see to Bridget first.'

'Work? You've taken a holiday job?' Gabriela tried to read Mary's state of mind. Had Anne and Thomas not even talked to the child since yesterday? 'Your father agreed to that?'

'Singing practice, Aunt Rilla. Is your memory deteriorating, like mine?' she asked, her eyes twinkling. 'You know I've got to do my exercises every day. I promised Frau Professor Weisskopf. It's a surprise. I'm going to learn another song all by myself. She'll be really pleased. She thinks I've lost my musical memory, but it was just the bug. I'm fine again.' She walked towards Gabriela's counter top, looked back. 'I'll put the kettle on, shall I? Tea or coffee for you?'

'What?' Gabriela's eyes followed Mary's movements, concentrated on her midriff.

Mary looked uneasy at the distracted reaction, the stare towards her abdomen. She pulled in her belly muscles, and frowned. 'Is something wrong, Aunt Rilla? Have I forgotten something I promised to do?'

'Let's sit down. Much easier.' There was no question that when the girl wasn't thinking of her posture, filling the kettle, for example, she displayed something of a tummy on her slim frame. Could she be pregnant and have no inkling of it? Such a state was not unknown among very young girls. Gabriela thought back over the years. Several of her contemporaries in the village, even one or two of the ones who had attended the convent, had had babies in their teens, without appearing to have grasped that they had been pregnant. Such happenings had been accepted as perfectly normal. Their boyfriends, delighted at this proof of fertility, had, for the most part, eventually married them. In such a close community there would have been trouble if they had not.

'In a minute, Aunt Rilla. I'll just get the mugs.'

Gabriela thought hard. It was likely that Mary did not connect her vomiting with pregnancy. Why should she? If she was still a virgin, she presumably had no idea she *could* be pregnant. Was the gynaecologist correct in her hypothesis? Gabriela could not bring herself to believe in an event as incredible as that. Where could that have happened, anyway? And Mutter had refused to discuss the matter further.

'So what else are you doing with yourself,' she managed to bring out, 'with all this time on your hands?'

'Kate's mother has invited me for lunch. Then we're off to play tennis with her brothers.'

'Tennis? You're going to play tennis?' The shock in the voice was unmistakable.

'What on earth's the matter, Aunt Rilla? Why shouldn't I play tennis?' Mary looked at her sharply, then smiled. 'Oh, I see. You've got tickets for a concert and want me to go with you. That it?'

'Your parents have not had a talk with you?'

The kettle had boiled. Mary, about to pour the hot water into the waiting mugs, their spoonfuls of instant coffee ready, missed her aim. 'Talked to me about what? You mean Reverend Mother has told them I'm not to go back?' Her hand shook.

'I'll do that, Mary. You look as though you might scald yourself.' Gabriela's eyes, now moist, looked directly at her goddaughter. 'So you do know what I'm talking about.'

Mary allowed her godmother to take the kettle. She looked white, the blood draining from her head. 'Are they really angry, Aunt Rilla?' She pulled a stool from under the counter and sank down on it.

'Has no one told you how to take care of yourself in your condition?' Gabriela said, frothing the coffee by pouring the liquid from a considerable height and adding milk. 'Do you want me to put in some sugar?'

'All right,' Mary grabbed the coffee, and sipped. 'I'm not really ill, you know. Just a bit weak after that gastric flu. It wasn't the convent's fault. Everyone had it.'

'Your mother came over yesterday afternoon,' Gabriela explained, dragging out another stool and looking down at her mug. 'She told me then. I could not believe it. I still cannot.'

'I don't know why she's fussing and blaming the school. I haven't been sick once since I got back,' Mary drank the coffee, relaxing tense shoulders. She took two more cubes of sugar and stirred them in. 'I feel very well now.' She blew into the coffee, hesitated. 'Did Mummy say I had to leave right away?'

'We did not go into that.' That was not a consequence Gabriela had thought about. True, of course; Mary would not be able to go back to the Immaculate Conception. 'Have you told your parents what actually happened, Mary?' She took another gulp of coffee, looked at the young girl. 'I still cannot understand how this could be.' She paused, her hand over Mary's. 'Is it really true? I am not interested in what other people say, that proves nothing.' She got up to stand behind Mary and put her arms round her neck. 'And whatever the circumstances, Mary, a wonderful miracle has taken place. You know you can rely on me to support you in anything you want to do. Anything at all, my little one.' She kissed the top of Mary's head. 'I will never let you down.'

'Oh, Aunt Rilla,' Mary said feverishly. 'You know!'

'Your mother was so overcome she came straight over to tell me. To give herself a chance to compose herself, she said. Your father had to get back to the office.'

'*Mummy* told you?' Mary stared at Gabriela. 'She can't have, Aunt Rilla. She doesn't know anything about it. I haven't told anyone except Joseph. Not even Lisl.'

'*Joseph*?' Gabriela gasped, stood back from the young girl and sat down again. 'You have already talked to Joseph?'

'Well, he was there. I did feel a bit funny at the time, and it just slipped out. He promised not to tell anyone else.'

'But your mother knows, Mary. Dr Graham, the tests. She must have discussed all that with you.'

'Dr Graham?' Mary stared at her godmother. 'What would it have to do with her? I thought Dr Grossmann was supposed to do the psychological assessment.' She paused, stared. 'You mean they've had Dr Graham's results?'

'Naturally that is what I mean.' She put the child's chin in her hands and looked into her eyes. 'What else could it be? They talked to you last night, did they not?'

Mary pulled away and absently stroked the coffee mug. 'They didn't say anything special. I went to a concert with Kate and Lauren Saunderson, so I didn't get back till late.' She stared at Gabriela's face, at the moist eyes. 'I did think they sounded strange, sort of distant. I thought it was because I was a bit late.' She grinned. 'It was only fifteen minutes, but they said I should have phoned.' A watery smile. 'They mentioned something about having to talk to me tonight, when Daddy gets home. That's all they said.'

'So what do you think I am talking about?'

'You said it was a miracle, Aunt Rilla. And that's exactly what it was.'

'A miracle?'

'You said "a wonderful miracle has taken place". I thought you knew, somehow. I thought you'd guessed because I told you how much I wanted it.'

'Wanted what, Mary?'

'A vision of the Blessed Virgin, Aunt Rilla. That's what I thought you were talking about. I thought you'd realised that I'd seen her. Just like Lisl did,' she said excitedly, then put her hand over her mouth. 'I wasn't supposed to say. You won't tell anyone, will you?'

'Hold on a minute, Mary. What do you think is going on?'

'The vision, Aunt Rilla. It was in the grotto.'

'But the grotto is closed in winter.' She frowned. 'And you are not allowed there, anyway. You didn't go up there, did you?'

'Not during the winter; last autumn, after the festival. Actually, it was the day you flew back to London. Reverend Mother allowed me to go up because Lisl's parents had taken her home and there was no one else to look after the grotto.' Her eyes glowed with pride. 'I took her place. You remember, she was really ill. She couldn't stand for any length of time, let alone do the climb. I was very worried about her.'

'That's when you had a vision, Mary?' Gabriela stared at her goddaughter. Had the girl been overcome by altitude sickness, gone into some sort of coma or catatonic state? Had Dr Graham's idea been remark-ably accurate? 'You never mentioned it to me before.'

'I haven't seen all that much of you. You were away skiing during the Christmas holidays. And I didn't think you'd approve. You said I didn't need visions.'

'Where exactly did this take place?'

'That's what I'm telling you, Aunt Rilla. That day I went up to the grotto for Reverend Mother, and there was all this damage, and they sent a rescue party . . .'

'You mean you had an accident?' Gabriela stared, appalled. 'No one ever mentioned anything to me about that! Not even you, Mary. Why didn't you tell me about it?'

'It never came up.' Mary smiled. 'Anyway, it wasn't like that. The village team were called out, but only because I was away so long and Reverend Mother got worried.'

'So there was something wrong up there?'

'Storm damage, that's all. Some sort of landslip on the path and in the grotto.'

'You mean you knew there'd been a storm and you carried on alone?' Gabriela's face showed her horror. 'That was most foolish.'

'It was my only chance to see the vision, Aunt Rilla. I knew if I didn't go then I'd never get another chance.'

'So you carried on. I see.'

'It was a test of faith,' Mary said proudly. 'I couldn't move the guard stone. That's when the first sign came.'

'The first sign?'

'That I was going to have the vision,' Mary said breathlessly. Her eyes glowed, her body seemed to swell with vibrancy. 'The sun was shining and I looked up at it, and prayed for guidance on getting rid of that boulder. First there was a sudden mist, and then there was a sort of hissing noise and the light started to zigzag down . . .'

'Lightning! That's terribly dangerous.'

'And there was an enormous flash, and the boulder moved.'

'My God, Mary! You could have been killed.'

The girl did not even hear her. 'It split into bits and scattered all over the place.' Mary focused on Gabriela. 'God opened the grotto for me,' she said artlessly.

Gabriela took one of Mary's hands. 'It was an electric storm, Mary, my dear.'

'And I was sort of catapulted into the grotto. I was a bit stunned. There was water all over the floor, like a sort of lake.' Her eyes looked far away. 'The hymn says "Mary, star of the sea".'

'And?' Gabriela said softly. 'What happened then?'

'That's when I saw it.'

'You saw what, Mary?'

'A huge halo. So glorious, so beautiful. A sort of red glow on the inside, then merging outwards into blue. That's how I knew. The blue; Our Lady always appears in blue.'

'A halo round the sun? Parhelion,' Gabriela murmured, almost to herself. 'That happens in freak weather conditions . . .'

'Not weather, Aunt Rilla. How can you say that? It changed. The colour went and the light turned into an enormous arch, high up in the sky.'

'Was there a noise?'

'It was completely silent.' Mary's eyes were staring. 'And then the most brilliant thing happened. The light blazed against the clouds and turned into two crosses on either side. It was glorious, fantastic. I wish you'd been there.'

'Mary, my dear, you saw mountain phenomena – light focusing on ice crystals . . . Reflections can show like pillars of light.'

Mary's eyes glowed soft, her face transformed by sweetness and innocence. 'Then the light changed. The crosses dissolved, and I thought it was all over, that she wasn't going to appear.' Mary's eyes sparkled. 'It was so wonderful. I went on looking up into the sky – and there she was.'

'What colour was she, Mary?' Gabriela asked gently.

'A sort of blue. Slate blue, and light all round her. Like diamonds surrounding her. So breathtakingly beautiful, Aunt Rilla, so exquisite.'

'Did she speak?'

'Speak?' The question pulled Mary out of her memories, and she frowned. 'Only to my soul. I didn't actually hear anything. Then she faded. A glow of pink spread over the blue and diamonds, and she faded away.'

'St Elmo's fire followed by the Alpenglüh,' Gabriela said softly.

'You have a special name for her? Is that what the brides see when they come each year?'

'I hadn't really thought of that,' Gabriela said sadly.

'So now you know it was a miracle,' Mary said jubilantly, 'just like you said. Now you know that I'm not ill at all. Whatever those tests say, Our Lady wouldn't let me get really ill.'

'Not ill, Mary. You are certainly not ill. But your mother will tell you that the tests showed something very important.'

'I suppose you're going to say they think I'm bulimic,' Mary said scathingly. 'That's stupid. Anyway, I thought

Dr Graham was supposed to be a gynaecologist.'

'She is. Her tests show the physical signs of – something quite different.'

'You look very serious, Aunt Rilla. Is there something *really* wrong with me? Have I got cancer?'

'No, my dear. Nothing like that, you mustn't think that. But it really isn't my place to tell you.' Her hands spread out helplessly.

'Mummy's not here,' Mary said angrily. 'She's never there for me. You say there's something. She didn't bother to tell *me* anything at all, and now I'm supposed to wait?' Mary shouted. 'I want to know. I have a *right* to know.'

'It is your parents' place to tell you, Mary.'

'*What* is supposed to be wrong with me, Aunt Rilla?'

Gabriela walked over to her, held her shoulders. 'Nothing is wrong with you, Mary, honestly. I'll ring your father, ask his permission to . . .'

Mary pushed her away. Then her eyes widened, her mouth dropped open. She gagged, ran to the kitchen sink and vomited. She turned to face her godmother. 'You're saying I'm like Lisl, aren't you? Because I was sick the way she was? You think I'm having a baby?' Mary whispered, her eyes goggling. 'That can't be true. I'm a virgin.'

'We know that, Mary.'

'The Frau Professor's told you about Lisl, hasn't she? You believe what they say about her, too, don't you?' she cried, hurling the mug with coffee across the kitchen floor. 'You're just like the rest of them, and you think I'm the same as Lisl! You think I have a boyfriend . . . you think I did what she said she did.'

Gabriela tried to hold her, to comfort her. Mary tore herself away and rushed out of the kitchen door, down

291

the garden towards the rabbit's hutch.

She would be safe enough for a few minutes. Gabriela picked up her cordless telephone and tapped Thomas's office number while she watched nervously as Mary took the rabbit out of the hutch and hugged her. The conversation was short and to the point. Gabriela put the receiver back in its cradle and walked down to the rabbit enclosure.

'Mary, my dearest, your father has given me permission to talk to you. He can't get away just now.'

Mary sat on the grass at the end of the Adlers' garden, clasping Bridget. 'Those boys,' Mary whispered. 'Those boys at Highgate Ladies . . .'

Gabriela thought for a moment, then brushed that aside. 'It's too long ago, Mary. That was last June. It is April now. The baby would be here.' Gabriela gathered the girl to herself, embracing her and the rabbit. 'Do not worry, Mary dearest, we'll work it all out. I will help you.'

'It's just like Bridget,' Mary said, the tears streaming down. 'I suppose it was the shock.'

'The shock? Whatever do you mean?'

'You said there was an electric storm before the vision.' Mary put her head into the rabbit's ears, kissing them. 'That's how Bridget got her babies.'

'You think you are having a baby because of that?'

'What else could it be?' she wailed. 'Daddy wouldn't believe about Bridget, either.' She looked at her godmother through her tears. 'But you believe me, don't you, Aunt Rilla?'

'You are not a rabbit, Mary. They may be mammals, but they function in a quite different way from you. It cannot have been that.'

'So how could I be pregnant?' Mary sobbed. 'It can't

just happen. I'd know if I'd been with a man,' she gulped, 'wouldn't I?'

'Usually you would, Mary. But there could be circumstances in which a man might approach you without your knowing it.'

'Circumstances? What circumstances?'

'After your vision. Did you black out, or feel fuzzy, afterwards?'

'What's that got to do with it?'

'Dr Graham thinks that, perhaps, someone – well, you know. When you were in a faint.'

'I'm still a virgin. You said you believed that, that you knew.'

'Everyone believes that, Mary. Even Dr Graham. I'm not talking about, well, penetration. Just spilling, you know.'

'But Joseph found me in the grotto. No one else can get up there, not in the bad weather. I know when he turned up – he put his coat over my shoulders. I *wasn't* faint any more. I had the vision ages before he came. It was all over by then.'

'But you *were* alone with him?'

'The others were close behind. He's . . .' She tore out of Gabriela's arms and whirled round, the rabbit scrabbling up her shoulder. 'He's not like that,' she screamed. 'Joseph wouldn't do anything like that. I don't believe you.'

'He's very fond of you . . .'

'I hate you. Hate you!' she yelled. 'You're just as bad as the rest of them, saying such horrible, revolting things. I don't believe he would – he's kind, and good, and saved me.'

'People get carried away . . .'

'It isn't true,' she sobbed. She took the rabbit off her

shoulder, stroked her, faced her godmother, the tears stopped. 'Anyway, he didn't even put his arm round me to steady me when I told him not to. He knew I didn't want it. He wouldn't do *anything* I didn't want.' She held the rabbit against herself, cradled her, rocked her.

'Just think a moment, Mary . . .'

'That's what they made Lisl say,' Mary said, eyes dry and flashing now. 'They made her say it happened with Kurt. Except I know it didn't. Whatever happened to me happened to her as well. That's why she's had a baby.' She turned earnestly to Gabriela. 'She was going to become a nun; she didn't want to get married to anyone. They *made* her say it was Kurt Miller, I know they did.'

'So what do you think happened, Mary?'

'It was the vision, Aunt Rilla. That's what it has to be. Lisl had the vision, and so did I. And we are both virgins, and we both became pregnant. You said it yourself. It's a miracle – two miracles – just like the Immaculate Conception. I'm having a baby the way the Virgin Mary had Jesus.' Mary's eyes began to glow.

'But you are carrying a little girl, Mary.'

'A girl?' Her eyes grew round, her face shone with joy. 'Then I'm having God's Daughter,' she said. 'Now I understand. *That's* what the vision meant.'

24

'So, Mary, they have finally found out.'

Professor Lager had joined Mary in the living room of her parents' house. It was Easter Sunday, and Thomas had suggested a meeting there. Erika had come early; Gabriela and Michael were to join them after mass.

Mary's head jerked up. 'You mean you knew all along, Frau Professor?'

'Naturally I knew. I am a doctor, and I took samples for the usual tests. It was not difficult.'

'But you didn't tell anyone – not even me!' Mary gasped. 'How could you possibly do that?'

'It was to protect you, Mary. What good would it have done had I said anything before? Just think: you might have been urged to have an abortion. Almost certainly, in my view. Your father, for example.'

'He couldn't be so horrible.'

'Perhaps not; we cannot be sure, but I judged that even discussing it at an earlier stage would not have been in your interests.'

'I might have liked to decide for myself,' Mary burst out. 'Had you considered that?'

'Naturally that is always the best solution. But you were only fourteen at the time, Mary. That sort of pressure might have been too much for you. It could have affected both your physical and mental well-being. I know only too well how difficult it is to think at such times . . .'

'So how do *you* think this happened to me? I suppose you think it was Joseph, like everybody else.'

'That is the most obvious explanation, and many people would not go beyond that. But no, I don't.'

'But you were the one who said Lisl had a boy-friend . . .'

'And I still do. Helden is a giddy girl, she already knew Kurt quite well, her case is quite the usual thing that happens in the village. But for you to be having a baby is very different. I know your attitude to men is, shall we say – delicate.'

'So what do you think happened to *me*?'

'I think someone took advantage of you, Mary, when you were not quite yourself, that time on the mountain,' Erika said slowly. 'The altitude, the state of the grotto. There are men who will try to benefit from the situation.'

'You mean like Dr Graham said?'

'It isn't so preposterous. Just think for a moment, Mary. You yourself know no man has been near you. In my view you quite rightly exclude Joseph Helden, and you *are* a virgin. Even a complete stranger verified that. And you are also pregnant.'

'You're saying that someone . . .'

'I'm saying you were not alone on that mountain. People climb up from the other side, you know. They have to be skilled mountaineers, that is true, but the convent is not the only approach. So I believe in your innocence, my dear.' She patted Mary's hand. 'And I believe you when you say it was not Joseph.'

'That's not what happened.'

'So you keep insisting. What other explanation can there be?'

'You'll just dismiss it as superstition, Frau Professor.'

'Try me.' She smiled, 'I am not so set in my ways that I would not consider something out of the ordinary. That is what I do every day in my work. I stand other people's fixed ideas on end, and look at them.'

'I think I am having a baby the way the Virgin Mary had Jesus: I think I'm having God's Daughter.'

'Really? An interesting idea.' Her small, bright eyes swept over Mary. 'What makes you think so?'

'You aren't going to say it's all rubbish?'

'You haven't answered my question yet.'

'I had a vision, you see.'

'An annunciation? An angel to tell you you were having God's child?'

'Not an angel; the Virgin Mary.'

'And she told you you would have a baby?'

'She didn't say anything. But Lisl had one too,' Mary said breathlessly. 'She was the one who said I could have a vision if I wanted to.'

Erika's eyebrows shot up. 'So Lisl had a vision as well, did she?'

'Yes. Hers was before mine. She told me about it, and I believed her. I thought it was wonderful.'

'And where did she have this vision?'

'In the grotto.'

'And you? Was yours in the grotto as well, in exactly the same spot?'

'Yes.'

'At the time of the festival?'

'Not exactly. Hers was before that, and mine was after. Why? Do you believe it could have happened like that? I thought you were an atheist?'

297

'Agnostic, Mary. I keep an open mind.' She paused, looked out at the garden. 'However, I think that if *two* girls were to claim to be virgins, both have a baby, and both of them deny having had a boyfriend, it would strongly suggest there might well be another explanation. But Lisl doesn't say that, does she?' She looked searchingly at Mary.

'No,' Mary said softly. 'She's much too scared.'

'You've seen her recently, have you?'

'You won't tell the Heldens, will you?'

'You can rely on that.' Her eyes were alert. 'So Lisl admits Kurt is the father?'

'She pretends. I know she doesn't mean it, because I know her. And now *I'm* having a child without a man. I think it happened in the same way.'

'We have to look at all the possibilities. The myth of virgin birth is very potent.'

'But you don't believe it?'

'The story was very popular long before Christianity. There must have been some germ of truth there. There's virtually never such a story without some cause. But we do have to find a cause, Mary. It doesn't just happen out of the blue.'

'It's like the mice and rabbits in the laboratory,' Mary said slowly. 'I hadn't thought of that before. They have no mate. *They* come about like that.'

'No, they do not. Not on their own. I make that happen. And, though mice and rabbits are mammals, their reproductive systems differ from those of human beings. I have always stressed that to you, so you know perfectly well it is not the same. What we are missing in your case is the catalyst.'

'The vision was the catalyst!' Mary said, excited now. 'That's why it happened to Lisl, too.'

'A physical one, Mary. For example, the women of Portugal used to think that eating an apple blessed by a priest could make them pregnant. What is lacking in your theory is the substitute for the man's seed. Even the Christian story posits God's contribution.'

Mary pouted, then her eyes lit up. 'Other strange things happen. What about the way mice behave if they're pregnant with a near relative? You taught us that even the smell of an unrelated male's urine will make them abort. That isn't caused by a physical catalyst.'

'It has a different, well-established, cause. The mouse genes governing cell-surface variation are linked to those regulating smell. But I agree about one thing. In your case we do not have all the facts.' She frowned. 'Let's just leave it at that.' She patted Mary's hand again. 'But we must keep my not disbelieving you as our little secret. Otherwise they'll think I'm gullible and won't let you come and stay with me. And that's what I think you should do, you know.'

'You mean you'd have me to live with you, in your house?'

'Why not? It is not entirely unselfish on my part. You can continue to assist me. I can arrange for some of the lay teachers to come over so that you can go on with your lessons and your singing. And then you can try to decide what you want to do once you have had your baby.'

'You think my parents would let me go?'

'They hardly want you here at the moment,' Erika said drily.

'Aunt Rilla would have me.'

'Gabriela would always do her best for you, I know that too, Mary. She is a very loving woman, she would make a wonderful mother. And she has always longed for a child herself.' A slight nervousness showed in the way her hands drummed on the window. 'One thing you can be sure of is that I won't try to take your baby away from you.'

'You think Aunt Rilla would want to adopt her?' Mary's brow furrowed into anxiety.

'Your parents will raise the matter in a few minutes. I merely wanted to alert you to the choices before you so that you could think about them before they come in. You have to grow up quickly, Mary, just as I had to. We are quite alike, you and I. We have both had similar experiences in life.'

The ringing of the front door bell made Erika put her index finger to her lips. They could hear Thomas answering it. He ushered Michael and Gabriela into the room. Anne followed with bottles and glasses on a tray.

'Well, now,' Thomas announced, 'let's all start by having some refreshment. Then I think we should talk about our little problem right away.' He moved to the tray, picked up a bottle of malt, and waved it questioningly at Erika.

'Excellent idea,' she said.

Thomas arranged for everyone to have a drink, took a sherry himself, and stood against the mantelpiece. 'We all know why we're here, and we have all given the matter considerable thought. Mary is in a difficult position, and I want to make sure she does not jeopardise her future.'

'It is for Mary to choose,' Gabriela said softly.

'She's a very lucky girl to have alternatives.' His intonation was judgmental. 'Well now, Mary, there are three possibilities for you to choose from. You can remain at home with us, you can go and stay with

300

Gabriela and Michael until the baby is born, or you can return to Austria with Professor Lager. She has offered to put you up so that you can continue with your schooling there.'

Mary was still perched in the corner of the window-seat. Normally she felt safe there, but today she felt at bay. Precisely how was she supposed to react? Her father was putting her on the spot on purpose, she suddenly realised. He could as easily have brought this up at any other time, but he had chosen not to, and her mother had done the same. Now that she thought about it, she realised her parents had never once discussed the matter when the three of them were on their own. They had used Grossmann as a sort of intermediary to find out her mental state, and now they were using Gabriela and Michael, and even the Frau Professor, to distance themselves from her. Whatever she said, she was bound to upset someone. Was this her father's way of inflicting punishment, or did he have some other motive?

As he drew his lips back and his eyebrows arched into two dark, angled arrows, Mary thought again how very like little horns they were. Did she actually hate her father, or just dislike him?

Dr Grossmann had implied that she was still nervous of men in general. Did this affect her attitude to her own father? She looked towards Michael. He was a man as well, but she was not nervous of him. In fact she liked him. She liked the way he treated her simply as another human being. He did not talk down to her, he did not assume that whatever she said was rubbish, he did not patronise her. She would not mind a father like Michael at all.

Mary felt tears prick at her eyes. She had gone out to buy a loose A-line dress which hid the slight protuberance of her belly. She drew her knees up under the voluminous folds and laid her head on top of them. 'It's very kind of everyone,' she managed to say.

'We all want to help . . .' Gabriela began, about to get up and, Mary was sure, put her arms round her.

Michael, sitting next to her on the sofa, pulled her back and held her there. 'Mary needs to decide this important step for herself, Liebling. Don't make it harder.'

The person she least wanted to hurt was Aunt Rilla. She had been wonderful. She had talked of the miracle of the child she was carrying within her, she had chatted about baby clothes and showed her the matinée jacket she had already started to knit, and it was she who had suggested that the vitamins Dr Graham had prescribed were as much for the baby as for the mother. What was more, Aunt Rilla had been the one to rescue Bridget and look after her. And Bridget was thriving.

But there was something about Aunt Rilla that worried Mary. Could someone be too keen to help? Her pet rabbit, happy in the Adlers' garden, hopped to Aunt Rilla. She no longer seemed to remember Mary at all. Could that happen with her child? Is that what the Frau Professor had meant?

'I have to finish my commitments to my students,' Gabriela said, her face flushed, her voice eager. 'But exams start in mid-June. Someone else can do the invigilating. I can be free to give Mary my whole attention from that time onwards.'

Michael watched his wife, a small smile flickering over his lips. 'You know you are very welcome in our house at any time,' he said, turning to Mary. 'You can

302

change your mind later, if you wish. I shall be away on assignments much of the summer, so you would have Gabriela all to yourself.'

'You're all being so kind,' Mary said helplessly. How could she explain that what she wanted to do was to go back to Austria, but not because of the Frau Professor? She wanted to be able to talk to Lisl, to share the pleasures of motherhood with her. Much more importantly, she wanted to ask her again about Johanna's father. She did not believe the story about Kurt any more than she believed what she considered to be the idiotic story of how she came to be pregnant. Both she and Lisl had been virgins, both had conceived. She needed Lisl to corroborate that. Then the Frau Professor would be convinced, and would prove it to the world.

She also wanted to be near the grotto so that she could try to have another vision. She knew the Blessed Virgin would look after her, see that her physical needs were met. But she needed guidance for both herself and Lisl. How were they to bring up these babies? What was their destiny?

She had been specially chosen; she had always known that. And she would bring her daughter up as God's Daughter. No one believed her, but who had believed the Virgin Mary? She had no intention of giving up her child, even to Aunt Rilla. She had no idea how she was going to support her baby, but she was not going to be parted from her.

So why not stay with her parents? One thing she could be certain of was that they would not try to take over her child. They would put pressure on her to have it adopted. Daddy would find a way. It was not safe to stay at home.

303

'Your mother and I would be happy to engage a nanny,' Thomas suddenly put in, 'then you can go to school just as you used to. And you can come back to see the baby every day.'

A vision of Lisl kissing her little daughter came back to Mary. She didn't want to go to school. She simply wanted to look after her little girl – her name, Mary had already decided, would be Marina – herself. How could anyone choose to do other than look after their own child? Whatever he said now, her father would never stand for that.

'Mary wishes to stay with me,' Erika pronounced in her clear, staccato tones. 'That is quite obvious.'

'You are so noted for your love of children,' Gabriela said bitterly. 'Why should she choose to stay with you?'

'Mary and I understand each other,' Erika said, her eyes alight, her crippled hands clasping the glass, swirling the whisky. 'We have a surprising amount in common. I also had a baby when I was very young – not quite as young as Mary, but only seventeen. And I also had no husband to support me. I think Mary and I will manage very well together.' She put her whisky down. 'We shall continue as before, except the teachers come to us. Well, Mary?'

'You were not married?' Thomas walked over to Erika, his bulk towering above her small frame. 'I thought Gabriela told us you had been married. An SS officer.'

'I was widowed,' she said, her eyes flints. 'Like so many others. I married in January 1945, Thomas.' Her blue eyes glittered. 'The Germans surrendered in May. There was street fighting to the last. Hugo went missing, presumed killed.'

304

'People still married in those times?'

'Why not? Many married because of the times.'

'Was it a legal marriage?'

'Why shouldn't it have been? I was over sixteen. Unfortunately the papers were destroyed. Conditions were indescribable at the time, you know.'

'Was he a German?' Mary suddenly asked. 'Aunt Rilla doesn't look very German.'

Erika drained her glass in one gulp. 'Of course he was German; he was a Prussian, a major in the Waffen SS. Unusually tall. That is why Gabriela is so much taller than I am.'

'How terrible for you, Erika,' Anne said. 'War does such dreadful things to people.'

The little woman sipped more of the whisky from the glass Thomas had refilled. 'The past is the past. I do not dwell on it.' She looked up. 'Well, Mary? Have you decided?'

The girl used both hands to push her loose hair into a tight knot at her neck, and stood. 'I'd like to go back to St Walter,' she said, her voice decisive. 'It's so peaceful there.'

'But, Mary,' Gabriela said, shaking off Michael's hand, 'have you really had the chance to think such an important decision through? Wouldn't you rather be in England for the birth?' Her deep eyes were full of anxiety. 'Suppose there was a storm . . .'

'For goodness' sake, Rilla, the local girls are safely delivered of babies, you know.' Erika knocked back her whisky and held out her glass for more. Thomas looked at her coldly but complied. 'She will be living with me. After all, I know how to deliver a baby if I have to!'

'You are always so busy with your work, Mutter. And

305

what about the Toronto conference? I thought that was in June.'

'I shall not go this year,' Erika announced, sweeping aside this obstacle.

'Not go? But you have never missed that conference before,' Gabriela gasped.

'My paper is not ready yet. I prefer to wait until next year. By then,' she held her glass up to emphasise the point, 'I shall have finalised my results.' She turned to Mary. 'It will not be a sacrifice. You can help me get the data into the computer. That is always so time-consuming. If you continue as you have, perhaps you can even help me do some of the analysis.' She stood. 'Very good. Everything is settled. So,' she continued in a bright tone, 'I leave on Tuesday. It will be best if I take Mary with me.'

'She can come later,' Anne said unsteadily. 'I'd like to take her shopping.'

'Mary should not travel alone,' Erika insisted. 'And she should travel soon. The airlines, quite properly, refuse to take women in the later stages of pregnancy.'

'But that's the day after tomorrow.'

'We need to make a few arrangements,' Erika said smoothly. 'I think Mary would like to be taking part in that.' She smiled. 'We will furnish a nursery, buy the baby clothes, and a crib. Nothing elaborate, just a few things.'

The expression on Aunt Rilla's face, the deep, desolate look in her eyes, cut through Mary.

'And Gabriela will join us as soon as she can,' Erika continued. She turned to her daughter. 'I have an excellent suggestion. Why not find someone to take your place as soon as possible? Then you can be with us before the birth. The child is not due until the middle of July, I understand.'

The tension lifted slightly. 'I'll decorate the nursery,' Gabriela said at once. 'Wait until I get there for that.'

25

'Have you finished inputting those results yet, Mary?' A bank of computer screens blinked at her in the top section of the Frau Professor's laboratory. Her anxiety about her data bordered on the obsessional. 'Put them on both types of floppy, as well as the backup tape. I will also transfer them to the computer in my bedroom.'

'I'm going as fast as I can, Frau Professor. One more file, I think.'

'That's the last batch of results, you know. I am longing to analyse these with the others.' She laughed. 'Excitement can make one careless. We have to keep our heads. Do you know the stage we have reached, Mary? Have you any idea what we are achieving?'

'Second generation results, tested five times,' Mary said without the slightest hesitation. 'All the test animals are showing the required response, but I still don't know what that is, or how you did it. You promised to tell me, Frau Professor.'

'Patience, patience.' The twisted hands were trembling.

'I know the ribozyme allows them to reproduce asexually by effecting changes in the RNA. I know that you have transformed the animal's genetic make-up to produce the ribozymes in its reproductive cells. Are you saying that the new genetic structures are always heritable? That the modified DNA reproduces itself when the animal reproduces?'

'Excellent, Mary. Your understanding has improved enormously. That's exactly what it does.'

'But you said there was a problem with that.'

'Not for most of my work. It doesn't apply to farming, for example. Animals bred for meat are in any case sterilised, or slaughtered before they breed.'

'So it has to do with reproduction?' Mary persisted. The older woman's nostrils widened, and her eyes grew sharp. 'I'm only trying to learn, Frau Professor.'

'I suppose you need to know. The problem was that second generation breeding animals could *only* reproduce asexually. I need test animals which breed asexually, but which do not cut out the cross-over stage.'

'Cross-over?'

'I thought we'd already dealt with that.' She looked sharply at Mary. 'I'd better recap. During the first stage of meiotic division of the germline cell, two sets of homologous – matched – chromosomes cross over with each other to produce two new sets with sections of DNA exchanged between them. This rearranged set of chromosomes forms the basis of a new organism.'

'A completely different one?'

'It is unique, but very similar to the original.'

'Why does that matter?'

'Otherwise the progeny would be identical to the mother and each other. That's obviously undesirable. So I began to look for an antigen to subdue the action of the original ribozyme. I needed to be able to stimulate second generation females to reproduce asexually without losing the cross-over. That is the stage I have now reached.'

309

'Wouldn't it be better to have a catalyst which achieves both ends in the first place?'

'Really, Mary. Naturally it would,' she said snappily. 'My ultimate aim is a completely different ribozyme, one which can engineer an animal which can reproduce both sexually and asexually. It is the one I shall be working on from today.' Her smile reached her eyes. 'I am sure you can understand that both the antigen, and the work on the new ribozyme, will make my original discovery of the utmost importance.'

'And when do you expect to isolate the new catalyst?'

'We will have to wait and see. Years, not months, I'm afraid.' She looked at the computer screen. 'I have reached a phase like this before and seen the results destroyed. It has taken me almost fifty years to get back to square one. That is why I am ultra cautious.'

'D'you think they'll miss the male?'

'This type of breeding female, you mean?' The Frau Professor laughed. 'Not for a single moment. What do they need him for? They are interested in having young, and I can arrange that. So what do they gain from the buck?'

'Nature gains,' Mary said solemnly. 'You taught us at school why we have sexual reproduction. Successive adaptation to a changing environment, you said. Without it an animal species like rabbits could become an anachronism, and simply die out.'

'You see, we are not talking about nature. We are talking about control. Our does are specially bred to reproduce choice genes. You know we have used genetic variation in the past to further our own ends. We have selected very carefully – plants as well as animals. It is called breeding. This is a modern variation.'

Mary turned away from the computer keyboard. 'But if we discontinue the selection process, if we impose only the traits we consider desirable, surely we're not getting the benefits of sexual reproduction?'

'I do not advocate that we get rid of it altogether. I merely suggest that to breed primarily from females which already suit our particular environment, without the uncertain injection of the male's genetic heritage, has remarkable advantages in many circumstances.'

'So we can't get rid of males entirely.'

'Certainly not. As you know, we already interfere substantially in commercial farming. We segregate male calves and castrate them to use for meat production. We select only certain females for breeding, and for producing milk.

'As far as cattle are concerned all we need is a number of first-class bulls. It would be perfectly feasible to produce heifers for outstanding meat production, and then to reproduce asexually from them. The differential in carcass weight would be more than made up for by the simplicity of the system. No laboratories would be required, and no vets. The ribozymes would be produced by factories, and the whole process would be entirely under the farmer's own control. Selective breeding could be reserved for those animals kept for precisely those purposes.'

'Surely that isn't new, Frau Professor? I thought lots of farmers artificially inseminate their cows. That's why one hardly ever sees a bull around.'

She stared at her. 'Haven't you understood what I've been saying, Mary? That is not the same. That system is out of date. The modern version of that system is fertilising cattle ova in the laboratory and reimplanting breeding cows with the chosen embryos. At present,

311

male embryos are selected because they put on more meat. Then, when the resulting bull calves are born, they are sterilised.

'My discovery is an advance on that. It would lead to a much more efficient system. No need to collect ova, fertilise them, then reimplant them. It all happens when the animals ingest the catalyst-encoding DNA. That is why everyone is going to be battering at my door.'

'Oh!'

'What do you mean "Oh"? You don't believe me?'

'I think the baby may have started, Frau Professor.'

'You aren't due till July, Mary. It's only the middle of June.' She noticed the girl's white face, and frowned. 'Well, one can never be sure. Better sit down somewhere. Lie down if you think you would be more comfortable.' She patted Mary's arm. 'When we are sure you are in labour I will contact your mother. We don't want to get her over for a false alarm.'

'I'd better do the backups right away.'

'Good girl.' She watched as Mary deftly closed the open file and initiated the backup programme. 'Make an extra floppy, will you?' she suddenly said. 'It might be a good idea to take one with us if we need to take you off to hospital.'

'I think . . .' Mary got off the stool and leant against a wall, her forehead damp.

'Stop working now.' The Frau Professor sounded concerned. 'I will see to the backups myself,' she added, leading Mary out of the laboratory. 'Let's get you to the bed Glockner prepared for you.'

They walked slowly together across the hall to the downstairs room that had been designated as a nursery, already scoured clean and rearranged for Mary and the

312

baby. The wide, comfortable bed invited her with clean sheets.

'Lie down, my dear. Don't panic. You know what I told you. Just allow your body to guide you, do not fight it.'

'I know.'

'The main thing is to relax. It will be a long time yet. There are sometimes false starts, specially in a first pregnancy. The new mother simply does not know what to expect. *If* you have started, we are still in the very first stages of labour. The baby will take at least six hours to be born. Many first labours take ten or twelve, or even longer.'

'You will stay with me, won't you, Frau Professor? You promise? Right to the end?'

'I will stay with you. I always keep my promises. And I will look after you very carefully.' She patted Mary's arm again. 'Don't worry, child. There's nothing to worry about. You are healthy, and having a baby is not a disease.' She drew a chair up to the bed. 'We will while away the waiting time together. Perhaps it is time to alert your mother. After that, shall we play a game of Scrabble?'

'Let's leave ringing Mummy for now. Maybe a little later. Can we just talk? Tell me how it was when you had a baby.'

The Frau Professor's face became taut. 'I'm not sure that that would be a good idea. Things were quite different then, you know; there can be no comparison. Everything was in such a state of confusion. It was not even a year after the end of the war.'

'You mean Aunt Rilla was born as soon as the war ended?'

'It ended in May . . .'

313

'And her birthday is in December,' Mary said eagerly. 'The 24th. We always celebrate it together at home.'

'Do you?' She looked at her watch. 'That contraction lasted about thirty seconds. Long way to go.'

'Where were you then?'

'When Rilla was born? Here, in St Walter.'

'I mean at the end of the war.'

'Right at the end?' Her small hands curled into fists. 'I've already told you: in what was later to become the eastern zone of Berlin. Working and living in a bunker. It was the only way to be protected from the unrelenting bombing and, later, the mortar attacks from the Russians. Times were quite terrible.'

'You mean you lived under fire from the enemy?'

'We certainly did. The German forces were collapsing on all fronts, the Americans had virtually wiped out the last of Hitler's Panzer troops which were to have defended Berlin against all comers. Even the famous Nebelkrähe – the carrion crows – left the area.'

'Did you see any of it?'

'Early on, all too much. Later, I stayed below. Everything was in chaos, there was hand-to-hand combat in the streets. In our district the Red Army had to fight to take over each building. It was unbelievable. German boys of sixteen were drafted in to help.' She looked thoughtful. 'Most of them were members of the Hitler Youth. They were prepared.'

'Were you a member?'

'It was expected.' Her eyes grew dark. 'Just as my father had to join the Union of Nazi Physicians.'

'So you were Nazis?'

'We were members of the party, because it was required. It did not mean we believed everything they

314

told us. I have always thought things through for myself; brainwashing works only on the weak-willed.'

Mary gasped as a strong contraction surprised her. The Frau Professor looked at her watch again, then made a note.

'That was quite painful,' Mary said, getting back her breath, her voice low. 'Is it going to get worse than that?'

'Just relax, Mary. There are excellent ways of easing the pain when it comes to it. It would be a mistake to start too soon.'

'So go on telling me. It takes my mind off the contractions.'

'It was confusing. Both the British and Americans coming from the west, and the Russians from the east, moved much more slowly than they need have done. Perhaps it gave us false hope. Who can tell now? The battles dragged on, and I concentrated on my work.'

'It sounds very exciting.'

'Not the sort of excitement one wishes for.'

'The work, I mean, Frau Professor. Was your father there with you when the Russians took over?'

'What? N—' She frowned. 'Naturally he was in Berlin. I've told you all that. The Nazis ordered him there.' The quick, constantly moving body sat suddenly still, hunched in her chair, her eyes vacant.

'Tell me what really happened to you, Frau Professor. All the details. You always promised you would, and there was never any time.' Mary winced slightly, but the threatened contraction did not materialise.

The Frau Professor glanced at her watch, then away again. 'It was quite – unfortunate. Neither of us was thinking about the fighting, or about politics. It is hard to believe, with bombs exploding all around us, shelling

315

just outside. But we were working deep underground. It was a freezing winter, one of the coldest on record.'

'Winter? But I thought the war ended in spring?'

The head jerked up. 'I'm talking of the time leading up to the end. The bomber attacks had been raging for many weeks; for months, in fact. We were both so busy with our recent results, so excited by what we had achieved, we simply did not notice what stage the war had reached.'

'Your father must have been thrilled that he had got what he wanted.'

She looked blank, as though she had regressed into the past. 'In a way, yes.' There was a singsong quality to her voice which made Mary look at her. 'You see, he got the results, but he did not understand the implications of what he had accomplished. He was a pure scientist, you understand. He had no thought of applying the consequences of his research.' She paused, a spasm crossing her face. 'I was very fond of my father, you know. I would have had the chance to get away. No one would have stopped me leaving Berlin then, but I chose not to take it.'

'How did he die?'

'He was shot,' the Frau Professor said, her voice short and clipped.

'By the Russians?'

The fierce eyes had glazed over. 'By a firing squad. He died for his country, like so many others in that terrible war.'

'You mean he was killed by the Russians who crashed into your bunker?'

'What?' The eyes had trouble focusing. 'Well, of course, that's what I mean. They all pointed their rifles at him at the same time, and shot him.'

316

'You had to watch that?' Mary whispered. 'How absolutely dreadful! Can you bear to tell me what happened?'

'The soldiers burst into the laboratory, stormed in without warning. I suppose I should have noticed that there was more than the usual commotion going on, but I was immune to that by then. They were savages. They just burst in, had no idea about anything. Started to smash up the place – glass flying everywhere. All I could do was grab my father's notes, cower out of the way, and try to hide them.'

'And did you?'

'There was one of those hollow stools with a lid. I stuffed them into that as soon as I saw the first bayonet coming through the door.'

'And your father? Didn't he try to save some of them?'

She shrugged. 'He didn't get the chance.'

'But you said you didn't save them in the end.'

'They knew nothing. About laboratories, or scientific work, or even lavatories.' She smiled. 'Do you know, they thought lavatories were for washing in?'

'Washing in?'

'They knelt in front of them and used them for washing their faces. Or washed their feet in them.'

Mary giggled faintly. 'But what happened? You haven't told me.'

'They went on smashing things up. Eventually they stopped, caught sight of me.' Her eyes went dull. 'As far as women were concerned they had only one thought.'

Mary's small face turned white. 'You mean . . .?'

'All women: old, young, pretty, ugly,' she rasped. 'It made no difference to them. Where other young women knew what to expect, how to try to protect themselves, I

317

had no idea. I found out later they used their lipsticks to dab on spots of red to pretend they had a contagious disease. I had no lipstick, only a pen. I didn't know that the rape of Berlin had begun. There was no one left to protect me.'

'Except your father,' Mary whispered. 'Or had they shot him by then?'

The bright eyes blinked. 'Yes. He was dead by then.' She sounded flat, depressed.

'He must have tried, whatever the odds.' Mary thought back to Miss Johnson's heroic efforts.

'What could one man do? The SS officers, including my husband, had all left to do their duty.' A proud look in the fierce eyes. 'I was already carrying his child.' She paused, appeared to come back into the present. She smiled faintly. 'I don't know how you got me telling you all this. Even Rilla does not know about the Russian soldiers. It would be better if you did not tell her.'

'I won't, Frau Professor. They killed your husband, too?'

'Yes.'

'And your father?'

'How often do I have to tell you?' she burst out. 'He was shot.'

'You said we had similar experiences in life. I wondered what you meant,' she said softly. 'How could you live?'

'My body lived. My mind fled somewhere else.'

There was a silence. Another contraction began to take hold of the girl, and the Frau Professor made a note of the time. 'Ten-minute intervals,' she said laconically, 'and up to forty seconds. But it will be ages yet, Mary. Try not to tense, it will only tire you. Remember this is a natural process. Your body is equipped for it.'

318

'What happened afterwards?'

'What? Do you really want to hear about all that now?'

'It gives me something else to think about.'

'They simply left me there. I was no more use to them and, being a woman, of no importance.' A wan smile. 'I tried to save the papers.' She looked fixedly at her hands. The scars of burning were still on her palms, thick and unyielding. 'The laboratory was burning, everything wooden was alight. I tried, but I could not save them.'

'That's what you meant, earlier on? That's why you make so many backups?'

'You never know what will happen. I would not like to lose all that work again.'

'What did you do?'

'Found somewhere to hide. I don't remember exactly. I existed in a stupor. Perhaps I just lay somewhere for several hours and people thought I was dead. Or did not care. Eventually I dragged myself into whatever shelter I could find.' She turned her palms towards herself and stared at them. 'No one was left.'

'What happened to your father?'

'His body, you mean? I have no idea. We heard all kinds of rumours of a mass grave. My mother never stopped hoping she would hear where he was buried, that he would have been honoured. They were very close. But I knew better. I knew they would accuse him, even posthumously, of war crimes.'

'And did he?' Mary sounded shocked.

'Commit war crimes? He was interested in his work, and unfortunately for him the Nazis considered it of value. He had no choice but to continue his research. Perhaps he had no choice anyway. He wanted to do it. It is the work I am doing now. All scientific work can be used well, or misused. There is no point in not carrying it out for that reason. The ethics are up to humanity in general. All scientists can do is produce the results of their research.'

'Would the British have imprisoned him if he had lived?'

'I don't think so. He was forced to work for the Nazis. I think that would have become clear.'

A spasm crossed over Mary's face as a strong contraction went through her body.

'Still only forty-five seconds. We have a long way to go.'

'Tell me how you managed.'

'I did not have time to think about what had happened to me. The first priority was food, and it is remarkable how the urge to survive overcomes everything else. I gave no thought to anything apart from finding food to fill my stomach. After that I thought about warmth, and only then about safety.' A hollow laugh. 'Priorities change remarkably quickly.'

'How did you get money?'

'It was not a useful trading tool. I stole what I needed, I made a plan to get away from territories occupied by the Red Army, and I carried it out as soon as I could.'

'You came back here?'

'I worked my way back. And by the time I got here, I knew I was pregnant.'

'Pregnant? You mean from the –?'

'Certainly not,' she snapped. 'I told you I was carrying Hugo's – my husband's – child.' She shrugged. 'How can you understand? There was no time to think, food was scarce, I felt dreadful, I had to fight my way through dangerous territories for hundreds of miles. Worrying about whether I was pregnant or not was the last thing on my mind.'

'So you don't know for sure whose baby it was?'

'It was Hugo's,' she seethed. 'Why wouldn't I be sure? He was exceptionally tall, and strong, with a square jaw.'

'But Aunt Rilla is very dark,' Mary said, frowning. 'Not really German-looking. And she has those slanting eyes . . .'

'The rape must have damaged her; must have affected the chromosomes. This isn't the time to discuss abnormalities.'

'Abnormalities?'

'Never happens to very young mothers, Mary. I shouldn't have mentioned it.'

'What abnormality?'

'Just a slight effect on the chromosomal coding of the cells, that's all. But with it comes a heart of gold. That's the good thing about it all.'

'You mean Aunt Rilla has defective genes?'

'It won't happen to your baby, Mary. Concentrate on that. It is time we concentrated only on that. I'm going to ring the ambulance.'

'You might have phoned me,' Gabriela said, her voice quivering. 'You know very well I wanted so much to be here.'

Erika's Audi chugged swiftly out of the airport and on to the road to the hospital. 'Marina was a month premature. How would you think I could predict when the baby would be born?' she retorted irritably, checking her mirror as she signalled to turn left. 'Anyway, my first priority was to look after Mary.'

'You want to keep her all to yourself,' Gabriela

reproached her mother. 'You've spent more time with her than you ever did with me.'

'You are always so impractical, Rilla. The child was born yesterday; you were due to arrive today. You might have managed to get here a flight or two earlier. What possible difference could it have made?'

'I might have got here in time to be with Mary.'

'I was with Mary. It was not possible even to contact her own mother before you. She was out all day meeting clients.'

'She is not here?'

'I left a message with Thomas's secretary. She arrived earlier this morning. As you know, there are no direct flights. She hired a car and drove over from Vienna.'

'So she's with Mary now.'

'She called in briefly. She's gone to her hotel to rest.'

'Something tells me that being a marriage guidance counsellor is not entirely her forte. She doesn't even want to know about her own grandchild.'

'Oh, I don't know, Rilla. You need a cool head, and to be detached. I think she qualifies on both those counts.'

'Detachment is not one of my qualities,' Gabriela said, resigned. 'So let's get over there. I can indulge myself a little before Anne gets back.'

'I think,' Erika said, her small, elfin face widened by a grin, 'she's put out at being a grandmother. She prides herself on looking young. Probably thought herself safe for another ten years.' A gleeful dart of the eyes. 'I think your grandmother always thought it an advantage that I had you when I was so young. She could have been your mother, after all. She was only thirty-seven when you were born.'

'You'll be telling me next she was my mother.'

Gabriela looked at Erika sideways. 'Was she, by any chance? Did she have an affair during the war?'

'An affair? My mother? Certainly not.' Erika took her eyes off the road to look at her daughter. 'Sorry, Rilla, but I'm afraid not. You are definitely my daughter.'

'You've never talked to me about my father properly.'

'I thought we were going to see Mary.'

'It won't take longer because you talk while driving.'

'Don't you want to hear about Marina?'

'There's something wrong with her?'

'She's rather small, on the delicate side.' Erika looked concerned. 'I think Mary will have to stay on here for several weeks.'

'I understood she was going to do that in any case,' Gabriela said tartly. 'Or did Anne come over with the intention of taking them back?'

'Nothing's been said. No doubt everyone put off making decisions, and the baby's early arrival caught them on the hop.'

'D'you think the Fullbrideys will take them home?'

'They're your friends, Rilla. You should be able to judge.'

'We've hardly seen them lately. Somehow they hold me responsible for the whole thing.'

'*You*?' Erika was astonished enough to swerve the car. 'What on earth could you have had to do with it?'

'I introduced Mary to the convent.'

'That really is nonsense! It couldn't have been a safer environment.'

'Not from their point of view. The child did get pregnant here.' Gabriela looked at her mother reflectively. 'Do *you* know how?'

'As it happens, I have no idea. I've tried talking to Mary, and it's hopeless. She's convinced about the miracle routine.' Erika shrugged. 'She's absolutely hooked on the vision and the hand of God.'

'She told you about the vision?'

'Yes. She seemed to think it would satisfy me.'

'It couldn't have come about like that,' Gabriela said firmly.

'Really? *You* think it could not happen that way? I'd always assumed you believed in the myth of the Blessed Virgin.'

'I believe it as a matter of faith. But God's Son has been born already. And Mary had a daughter.'

'That's the most interesting aspect of all this. Mary believes she has given birth to *God the Daughter*. That is new. All the myths talk of male progeny.'

'Not that old chestnut about the superiority of women.' Gabriela sighed. 'So you believe Mary because she has produced a daughter? Is that right?'

'What? Well, I suppose that does make it more attractive. You don't believe in the possibility of God the Daughter?'

'No,' Gabriela said shortly. 'And presumably you put it out of court entirely.'

'I am always open to new ideas,' Erika said, her eyes glinting. 'Or perhaps it would be more accurate to say, the reinterpretation of old ideas. It isn't only Christians who believed in virgin births. Dozens of the pagan gods were God-begotten and virgin born. Plutarch mentions that the Egyptians believed that the spirit of God was capable of sexual intercourse with mortal women.'

'Are you really saying you accept Mary's version?'

'I'm saying there's no smoke without fire. I think my favourite example is that at one time Spanish women

324

actually thought they could become pregnant by eating a lily. Does that remind you of anything? We can hardly blame Mary if she gets such ideas into her head.'

'Really, Mutter. All this talk. Presumably you don't consider such a possibility?'

'I regard people's beliefs as important as anything else about them. Anyway, I would say that the survival of the myth of virgin birth is entirely due to men's dislike of real women. They prefer a mother who has never allowed sex to divert her from motherhood. That's why the Church maintains the Virgin Mary had no other children. God could not have chosen such a whore.'

'Erika Freud.'

'Actually I just got carried away.' Erika gripped the wheel in a vice-like hold. 'I'm inclined to think the usual explanation is the right one, unless proved otherwise.'

'And that is?'

'Some young man in the grotto. I would guess she has repressed the whole thing. Maybe she was not even really aware of what was going on. The act must be repugnant to her.'

'Because of those boys.'

'She'll be scarred for life.'

'Grossmann didn't seem to think it was such a big deal.'

They were driving through the hospital grounds. Erika spotted a parking place and wrenched the car into it. 'A man! What can he know of such an experience?'

'But she wasn't actually –'

'Only the Fullbrideys could be stupid enough to engage a male psychiatrist. They need a woman skilled in these affairs. This suppression can't possibly be doing Mary any good.'

'You've tried to get her round?'

'I haven't messed about. Too dangerous.'

They arrived at the hospital grounds, parked, got out of the car and walked towards the maternity unit. 'Well, here we are, Rilla. She's in this room.'

Their knock brought a quick, bright response: Mary, surrounded by flowers, her eyes aglow with the thrill of new motherhood, was sitting in a chair by the window. The baby, asleep, lay in a crib beside her.

'Aunt Rilla.'

She was about to get up, but Gabriela rushed over and pushed her back into the chair. 'Mary, my dear, how radiant you look.'

'Isn't she gorgeous?'

Gabriela simply could not help herself. The sight of the tiny, helpless creature in the cot loosed a torrent of frustrated maternal feelings. The tears welled up, all she could do was try to hide them behind the huge bunch of red roses she had brought for Mary.

'The miracle of birth. So tiny, so fragile, so beautiful.'

The baby opened her eyes, wrinkled her forehead. She looked exactly like a tiny image of her mother.

'I think there is no mistake that she is yours.' Gabriela laughed, her eyes betraying a slight unease. 'My goodness, she has exactly the same shape of head, the same gaze, the same shell-like ears. You will look just like sisters as soon as she is a little older.'

'But we are not sisters, Aunt Rilla,' Mary said quietly. Her face had grown older, almost mature. The hazel eyes looked deep. 'I am a mother, not a child.' A soft, caressing smile brushed the baby's head. 'Marina is my daughter. I am responsible for her, and I am going to bring her up.'

26

'I'll get it,' Erika called from her hall through the open door of the kitchen where Gabriela was preparing lunch. 'I'm expecting someone.'

Gabriela knew her mother was paranoid about people coming to the house. She was intensely possessive about anyone who had made an appointment – they were to be greeted only by her. But someone foolish enough to call unexpectedly was sent on their way with shrill admonitions not to disturb her work.

'Michael,' Gabriela heard Erika greet her son-in-law without any sign of enthusiasm. 'I thought you were someone else.'

Gabriela's heart thumped with delight. She was kneading dough and worked rapidly to free herself from the clinging mass.

'I see you're as delighted to see me as ever, Schwiegermutter. I had no idea you were expecting an admirer. I must be a grave disappointment.'

'You talk such nonsense.' Erika ushered him into the house. 'Is Rilla expecting you?'

'Sorry I couldn't warn you I was coming. Just stepped out of the arrival hall in time for the airport bus to Kernkirchen. Albert Helden spotted me there and offered me a lift back.' He grinned. 'Everything happens in seconds in my world.'

'And to what do we owe this unexpected honour?'

'I've finished my stint in Israel, so I thought –'

'Schatzi! What a wonderful surprise.' Gabriela, bedirndled and with an apron dusted white with flour, was free at last to rush out of the kitchen to greet her husband. 'I didn't think you were getting back until after the weekend.' She was conscious that her face, suffused with heat from the wood stove, was bright red. She didn't care, she was radiant with delight.

'That was the theory. In practice I've finished the story earlier than expected. All very satisfactory.' Michael looked smug. 'My editor says I deserve a little holiday. He's given me the long weekend I didn't need in Israel, so I thought I'd jump on the next plane to get me to Salzburg.'

'That's really wonderful.' Gabriela's soft brown eyes slanted love at her husband. 'You're in for a treat – your favourite Rinderbouillon with dumplings. I'm trying to build Mary's strength with nourishing beef broth.'

'So how are mother and child?' Michael looked over Erika towards the open door leading to the nursery.

'Thriving,' Erika said, deadpan. 'What else did you expect? Come in and see for yourself.'

She was about to push into the room when Michael tapped on the door. 'May I come in, Mary?'

'Just a minute,' the young mother called out, flustered, turning away, trying to adjust clothing to hide her breast. 'All right,' she finally said, a muslin nappy now draped around her shoulder.

Michael walked through. Gabriela had painted the room during the fortnight it had been considered wise for Mary and Marina to stay in hospital. Gleaming white walls, freshly washed and ironed chintz curtains, a wicker crib, all glowed their welcome. Mary, comfortable in the rocker Heidi Fluge had always sat in to feed her daughter and granddaughter, smiled vaguely at Michael as she concentrated on nursing Marina.

'Little mother Mary. You look as though it comes naturally.'

The girl, her eyes calm and filled with love for her child, continued to suckle her. She nodded at Michael, put two fingers inside the material covering her bosom, presumably placing the nipple between the baby's lips. 'Marina's rather small, and a little delicate,' she said, watching anxiously. 'But she is getting stronger every day.'

'From here, she looks as though she's doing well. Just like her pretty mother.'

'No need to make a fuss,' Erika announced in her brusque way. 'Don't let her dawdle, Mary. See that she takes what she needs, then put her down. Don't forget to use the pump if she doesn't empty the breast, or you won't have enough for her. She'll catch on fast enough not to play games.'

Michael lifted his eyebrows at Gabriela, clearly surprised to see Mary paying so much attention to Erika, drinking in the words. Gabriela shrugged back at him. She inclined her head, beckoning him towards the kitchen.

'So what's the deal here?' he said, softly, sitting down by the table Gabriela had covered in flour for knocking back the yeast dough rising near the stove.

'Anne came over for a week, Thomas for three days. They've shot off back again, relieved that Mutter laid down the law and said the child needed to stay put for at least two months to get properly established.'

'Is that true?' He tore off a piece of pastry and

moulded it into a ball. 'Or just convenient for every-one?'

'I'm not exactly an expert, but the baby does look small compared to the others born in the hospital at the same time. She weighed in at only two and a half kilos.'

'But they let her go?'

'Because of my mother, I suppose. What's very clear is that Mary and Mutter love the arrangement. They're getting on like a house on fire.'

'Turn-up for the books.'

'Mutter seems to think they have a lot in common. Both had babies very young, both single mothers.'

'And both impregnated in the same way, by any chance?'

'Hardly.' Gabriela frowned. 'My mother's a frightful woman in many ways, a dreadful mother, but she never said she didn't know who my father was.'

'But she's never talked about him, either. Or shown you a photograph. It's hard to believe you are her daughter sometimes, you're so different.' He seemed pensive as he looked his wife over. 'Both physically and mentally.'

'Funny thing is, I asked her if I was Oma's, by any chance.' Gabriela grinned. 'Just the other day. I would have been quite pleased, but she wasn't having any of that.'

'Have you inherited some of your grandmother's features, then?'

'More from her than from Mutter, I sometimes think. Her chin, her hair, her way of thinking.'

He picked up a piece of dough and began to nibble it, then spat it out. 'I'm starving! Are you going to stop cooking and give me something to eat?'

'Just got to finish this bit. I won't be long.'

'And Mary . . . Does she still stick to that original story?'

'She's adamant. She absolutely insists that the baby is the result of a virgin birth.'

'Marina, Daughter of God,' Michael said. He pressed the piece of pastry flat in his hand, curled it round the top and flattened the lower part. 'I give you the Virgin,' he said. But his eyes held more than a joke at Mary's expense. 'She must have some reason for this unbelievable theory.'

'She doesn't stop there. She claims that Lisl's child was brought about in the same way.'

'And what about Lisl? Does she go along with that?'

'Mary hasn't been able to get near her. Not since last March. Mary insists she's too frightened to admit it, that her family are somehow determined to stop her doing that. She's got it in for poor old Friedl. I don't know why, exactly.'

'Has she?' Michael said absently, moulding the dough.

'Because she kept hanging up on Mary, refused to tell her what was going on, I suppose. She didn't tell any of us. I was quite upset myself.'

'A gaggle of virginal conceptions.'

'Actually, that's not what Mary means. That would include test-tube babies and variations on that theme. Mary is talking about conception after praying for a vision, and without the aid of a man. She got the idea from Bridget. She prayed for the rabbit to get well, and she did. But she also had kittens. God works in a mysterious way is the theme.'

Michael put his finger into a large jar of thick plum cheese made from the local Zwetschken and sugar. 'Delicious Povidl,' he said, licking off a large chunk. 'If you don't feed me soon you won't have much of this left. Did you make it, or has Resi been around more than usual?'

'Resi is permitted to make preserves and cakes at home, and bring the booty over. She's a wonderful cook.'

'No better than you.'

'Better at Austrian dishes. I'm out of practice there. But I am graciously permitted to cook the lunch and prepare breakfast and supper.'

'Well, there's a treat for you. Don't let that mother of yours take too much advantage.' He played with the dough again, split it into one large and one small piece, then fashioned them into two similar figures. 'What does the old witch say about that stuff Mary peddles?' The dark eyes looked intently at Gabriela.

'Quite interesting. Bit odd, in fact. Keeps muttering about belief systems or some such rubbish. Says the myth of virgin birth has been around a long time, so there might be something in it. Sounds completely unscientific.'

'It is true. The idea that women were impregnated by gods or spirits was taken for granted in the ancient world.'

Gabriela stopped knocking back the dough. 'Mutter doesn't deny that such a possibility exists – not at all. She says it probably does happen with women, every now and again, just as it does with other animals. But she doesn't believe it would happen twice, within months, in the same area.'

'So what's the official explanation of Mary's child?'

'What it always was. The ejaculation of sperm, by a person or persons unknown, over the unconscious Mary in the grotto.'

332

'The gynaecologist's theory. In some ways it sounds even less plausible than Mary's claptrap.' He laughed. 'Must go down really well with Thomas and Anne.'

'They've all but washed their hands of the whole thing. They contribute financially, but can hardly bring themselves to acknowledge Mary as their daughter. Marina simply does not exist for them. I think they're convinced Mary had a boyfriend and is concealing that. Joseph is the obvious candidate. That's also what the village thinks. Can't say I altogether blame them.' She looked up at Michael. 'What do you think?'

'I don't agree it can be as simple as that,' he said, frowning. 'Why would Mary go on denying it? What would be the point?'

'Perhaps she really doesn't know.'

'So what, precisely, is going to happen once Mary leaves here?'

'Don't ask me.' Gabriela punched down the dough with unnecessary force. 'I think my mother has in mind keeping the two of them here.' She pushed her knuckles hard into the springy mass. 'It's really odd, completely out of character. I don't know what's got into her.'

'Why not suggest to Mary that she come and live with us permanently?'

'Really? You wouldn't mind?' The yearning on Gabriela's face betrayed her feelings. 'No, Liebling. It's too much to ask.'

'I don't mind, Schatzi. We cannot have a child, and you could think of Mary as your surrogate daughter. And you get little Marina as a surrogate granddaughter at the same time. That's got to be a first!' He grinned, then took his wife in his arms and kissed her.

'My fingers are full of dough.'

'Terrible,' he said, and sucked at them. He nuzzled

her ear. 'It would be all right with me, honestly, Schatzi. Thomas can make a decent contribution to their board, but I'm happy to provide the base.'

'You'd settle for that? A baby in the house which isn't yours?'

'A baby in your arms. Mary will be off as soon as the little one is weaned.'

'What makes you say that?'

'She's only fifteen. She'll get over her fear of boys, be excited by what life has to offer. She won't abandon Marina, but she'll be glad to have you take the brunt of being tied down by her. That's why Anne is steering clear.'

'And what do you get out of it?'

'That it would make you happy.' The smile left his face. 'I hadn't given it much thought before. But if you say Mary insists it happened to Lisl as well as to her, we should just test that theory.'

'Are you serious?'

'As a matter of fact I am,' he said slowly. 'It sounds so bizarre. Anyway, there's an easy way to find out.'

There was a peremptory ring at the front door and they could hear Erika rush through the hall to answer it.

'I've brought her for you, Frau Professor. You said you wanted to see her.'

'Come in, come in. Right through to my laboratory. It won't take more than a minute or two.'

'It's very good of you, Frau Professor.'

'Think nothing of it, young man.'

'Who's that?' Michael asked. 'The chap she was expecting earlier on?'

'I suppose so. The villagers all bring their children to her. I think she does the immunisations free. Saves

334

them money and a trip to Salzburg, so they're really keen.'

'What's in it for her?'

'You are so cynical, Michael. Public relations, I suppose.'

'I know that voice from somewhere.'

'Of course you do. I told you, one of the village men.'

A baby began to wail. They could hear the father trying to shush it, could hear Erika's futile 'There, there.'

'That wasn't so bad, was it? I'll be in touch,' they heard Erika's clipped tones as she walked through the hall again. 'Remember me to your parents.'

'She's up to something, I can tell,' Michael whispered at Gabriela. 'Otherwise why all the secrecy? It's usual to bring visitors through to say hello.'

'You and your intrigues,' Gabriela said affectionately. 'You see a deep, dark plot in everything.'

'That was Kurt Miller,' Michael suddenly said. 'I can tell that cocky voice anywhere. What's he doing here?'

'Time for Johanna to have her shots, I expect. She's the right age. Resi's latest gossip is that Lisl is feeling sick again. My mother told Mary she shouldn't visit in case Marina caught a bug. I suppose that's why Kurt brought the baby, and why Mutter didn't want Mary anywhere near.' Gabriela smiled, hugged her husband. 'You're really going over the top about my mother. Why don't you enjoy the break here, and go climbing? You're always saying you never get the chance.'

'As it happens, that's precisely what I'm going to do this weekend. See if I can get hold of the famous Joseph as a guide.'

'But you don't need one . . .'

His eyes went hard as he put his fingers to his lips. 'Don't give that away,' he said. 'I'm on holiday. I like climbing, but I don't know these mountains at all well. You know how dangerous that can be.' He grinned. 'I'd like to talk to him.'

'You think he'd tell you if he was the father?'

'I think I'd find out; my interviewing technique is pretty good. Anyway, this insistence of Mary's about the virgin conception – it's odd, not really like the New Testament story at all. She believes that not only did she have a child without a man, but that Lisl also did. That's very unlike the Christian belief.'

'I suppose that does make it different from the age-old excuse.'

'As I was saying, it's easy enough to test.'

Gabriela laughed. 'It is? Then I'd certainly want to know how. I don't think even my mother's been able to penetrate to the truth of that.'

'Very well-chosen words. But she has missed a trick, our brilliant scientist.'

'She has? And what is that?'

'Genetic fingerprinting. If Marina is Mary's daughter without the aid of man, their DNA "signatures" will prove it.' He smiled. 'And if that doesn't work out, if Marina's DNA shows a paternal inheritance, innocent local men should be willing to supply tissue samples to eliminate themselves.'

Gabriela's mouth dropped open. 'Herr Gott noch einmal! You're brilliant, Schatzi. Absolutely *brilliant*. Mutter can see to that. She's got all the equipment in her laboratory. She does it for her animals.'

'Shh, we're not at home, you know. Walls have ears, as my parents used to say.' He grinned again, eyes dancing with mischief. 'I really don't think we should mention anything to Erika. Let's keep it dark.'

She frowned. 'You mean my mother shouldn't – wouldn't – actually have missed something as obvious as that.' She divided the dough into small pieces, made a deep hole in each one and put a large spoonful of Povidl into it and pinched the dough closed over it. Then she placed the Buchteln – oven-baked doughnuts – ready to rise. 'Clever you. The old dragon might have put that one over on me. I thought she hadn't cottoned on.'

'No chance.' Michael went up behind his wife and put his arms round her waist, kissing the top of her dark head. 'I'll get my editor to have the analysis done in England.' His voice had dropped low.

Gabriela leaned back against Michael as she rubbed dough from her fingers. 'But what about the samples?' she said softly. 'I don't think I'll be able to get hold of blood. And it would be most unwise to involve Mary. She might tell Mutter. But I could get snippets of hair from both of them.'

'Hair is no use without a follicle attached. How about a swab from the baby's mouth or nose? Can you do that?'

'No problem. And Mary?'

'Breastmilk? I heard something about a pump. Or hair from her hairbrush. You're bound to find some strands with follicles attached.'

'Always so brilliant,' Gabriela said lovingly. 'I'll get something suitable from both of them.' She paused for a moment. 'Could there be a problem about using the samples without permission?'

'You're right. I forgot about authorisation. Mary's a minor, of course; and involving Thomas and Anne doesn't bear thinking about,' he said. 'I'm off to Lebanon for a couple of weeks. I think, my dear, I will have to claim that you are *in loco parentis*. I'll send the samples to my editor with a covering note. He'll wheedle it through OK. Past master at it.'

27

'It would be fun to go and visit Lisl, don't you think, Aunt Rilla?' Mary was standing at the big picture window in Erika's living room, pointing out the magnificent view of the mountains around St Walter to the unimpressed Marina.

'Feeling bored, now that Michael has left again?'

'That's not what I meant,' Mary protested. 'You know it isn't. But Lisl's my friend, and she's had a baby just like me.' She turned to face Gabriela. 'I want her to see Marina.'

'You want to show her off, is that it?' Gabriela smiled. 'Why doesn't Lisl come here? She can always leave Johanna with Friedl.' She looked worried. 'I don't like the thought of Marina going out in this weather. The Föhn has just blown up. It's given me a splitting headache and that means there are storms around.'

'You and your weather predictions.' Mary looked longingly out of the window. 'I've rung to ask her time and again. She'll answer the phone – when her mother's not about – but she always makes an excuse about coming over. She's afraid.'

'Worried about my mother, you mean? I thought she was such a favourite of hers. Did they fall out about something?'

Mary shuffled her feet as she eased Marina's arm through the sleeve of a handknitted matinée jacket great-grandmother Fiona had sent. Delighted by her new status, Mary's grandmother appeared to be the only member of her family at all pleased by Marina's arrival.

'I don't think it's anything like that, Aunt Rilla. Lisl started feeling off a couple of weeks into the autumn term. That's why the Frau Professor was so keen that she should teach me how to assist in the laboratory. I don't think they ever had a row. Unless it was over the Christmas holidays. The Frau Professor visited them once, she told me.'

'Lisl hasn't said anything to you?'

'Not since that time before Easter. She won't even talk when I do get her on the phone. Always seems to be worrying that her mother is listening, or will catch her out.' Mary looked at her baby. 'She doesn't even say she'd like to see Marina. She doesn't exactly refuse to meet, but she does put a lot of obstacles in the way.'

'But you're determined to talk to her.'

'You said Frau Helden was a special friend of yours at school, didn't you?'

'My best friend,' Gabriela reddened, embarrassed. 'We have lost touch a bit since Helga's accident.'

'So you'd like a chance to get together with her, wouldn't you?'

'This trip is for my benefit, is it?'

'I didn't mean that; I just meant you'd understand why I'd like to talk to Lisl.' Mary was busy putting a light duvet outfit on her child. 'I just want her to admit that Johanna came about in the same way as Marina.'

'I don't think she's going to do that, Mary.'

'Then I want to know why she's so scared about telling the truth.'

'Perhaps Mutter will keep an eye on the baby. It might be better not to take her. What if Lisl has another infection?'

'It wasn't an infection in the first place, Aunt Rilla. She had morning sickness, just the way I did.' Mary held Marina against herself. 'I'd rather take her with us,' she said possessively. 'Suppose she needs a feed?'

'All right then,' Gabriela agreed. The baby was healthy enough in spite of her diminutive size. 'There's a heater in the car, and I'm sure we can wait the storm out at the Heldens if it does break.'

Erika was ensconced in her laboratory, working at fever pitch. They set out without disturbing her, leaving her a note in case they had not returned by the time she surfaced again. The July afternoon was warm. The sun, high above the mountain tops, gleamed brilliant rays into grey cloudbanks gathering below. A sudden shower drenched the car, glistened the road in front of them, then passed. The brightness of the double rainbow arching over the peaks was magnificent.

'Just like the one that day at your parents' house, when we went down to see Bridget,' Gabriela said in awe. 'Nature can put on some breathtaking performances.'

'It is beautiful,' Mary agreed absently. She twisted her head round to look at Marina strapped in her baby seat. 'She's fast asleep.'

Their reception at the Helden house was muted. Frau Helden, her hair much greyed since Mary had last seen her, waved podgy hands at them, but avoided the customary handshake which greetings normally involved. It was as though she wished to make it clear that there was to be no physical contact with either Gabriela or Mary. She did not even glance at the baby.

'It's been much too long since we had a proper gossip, Friedl,' Gabriela tried out, startled at the lack of response, standing awkwardly on the doorstep.

Friedl Helden did not even smile. 'Lisl had a difficult pregnancy,' she said, tight-lipped. 'I had no time for anything outside the family.' She turned to Mary. 'You keep on bothering her, writing to her, ringing up. I think she's told you, time and again, she's far too taken up to see anyone.' Her nostrils flared. 'I've even had to give up my summer visitors.'

A gust of wind followed by a sudden, drenching shower forced her into hospitality. 'You'd better come into the Wohnzimmer. The baby will catch cold. Perhaps a cup of coffee, and some Strudel?' she said, grudgingly, but she made no immediate move to fetch them.

The living room, cold without the winter comfort of warmth from the big Kachelofen set in a corner at the far end, was bleakly formal. 'Coffee would be delicious, Friedl.' Gabriela smiled at the woman she had known so well, and who seemed like a stranger now. It was as much her fault as Friedl's, she scolded herself. She should have visited more often after Helga's death. But she had found the loss of her Austrian goddaughter too painful, had tried to avoid being reminded. Seeing her old friend's sombre look, her harassed eyes, she felt ashamed about not having been there for her. She had not even looked her up last October. 'Why don't we join you in the kitchen, Friedl?'

'Much too untidy,' Friedl hurried to say and pointed to the upright sofa, the wooden chairs. 'Do sit down.'

Gabriela realised that the physical differences

342

between her and her friend had become substantial. Friedl, married in her late twenties and mother of three, had the stolid, set housewife look and ponderous gait of Austrian middle age. Her dirndl swelled over a large bosom, the apron girdling a wide waist and skimpy over hefty hips. Her arms, strong and muscular, were bare below the white dirndl blouse. Long, plaited hair was wound demurely into a bun at the nape of her neck.

Friedl eyed Gabriela, examining her from top to toe. 'You're looking very youthful,' she said, her dour voice even lower. 'But, then, you haven't lost your figure bearing children.'

The stab of grief prevented Gabriela from answering. A determined smile hid the misting of her eyes. Her arms ached with the void of a child, and she turned towards Mary. 'Shall I hold her for a bit?'

'Thanks, Aunt Rilla.'

'We all get older, Friedl,' Gabriela said softly, 'but you have daughters who are the spitting image of you when you were young. You don't know how I'd love to have that.'

Friedl dropped her eyes. 'The little one is very small,' she finally said as she walked over to Gabriela and slipped the duvet hood from Marina's head. She looked from her to Mary and back again, a sort of hopeless look in her eye. 'How much does she weigh?'

'Nearly three and a half kilos now. She's gained a whole kilo in the first month,' Mary explained proudly.

'So you're a grandmother, Friedl.' Gabriela looked up from clucking at Marina. 'How does it feel?'

'Makes me feel even older. Well, Lisl has taken over a lot of the housework.' Friedl twisted the corner of her apron, stood eyeing them awkwardly. 'I suppose you'll find out soon enough. Another's on the way.' She shifted towards the door.

Gabriela's head jerked towards Friedl. 'Has Joseph got married? Your children are fast workers.'

'Joseph? Of course it isn't Joseph. He's wrapped up in his music and his studies, and he's not the girlfriend type. It's Lisl again.'

'Lisl is having another baby?' Mary broke in. 'So soon?'

'It's the way it goes.' Friedl retreated and firmly shut the door.

'They're practising Catholics, Mary,' Gabriela reminded her. 'I don't know how Lisl is going to cope with it, but I expect she'll find a way as soon as she's safely married.'

'Where *is* Lisl, d'you think?' Mary's eyes were searching the room, looking towards the door. The whole ambience of the house felt false, reeked of deceit, unease. Something was very wrong here.

Gabriela shrugged. 'Hiding upstairs, hoping we'll go away. For some reason Friedl doesn't want us to see her. Maybe Lisl doesn't want to see us. Perhaps she's got fat, or is embarrassed by her new pregnancy.'

Friedl shouldered the door open, carrying a tray before her. She huffed it down.

'You must be very busy preparing for the wedding,' Gabriela enthused. 'Is it soon?'

'As soon as she turns sixteen.'

'That's in August, isn't it? I seem to remember all three of your girls were born in the same month. You planning a large do?'

'Just families,' Friedl mumbled rather than said. The aroma of coffee filled the room. 'Have some of my Apfelstrudel,' she encouraged Mary. Her voice sounded confident for the first time, on firm ground. She even smiled in the warm way Gabriela remembered from their youth. 'You look as though you could use it.'

Suddenly Lisl's glossy nutbrown head peeped round the door. 'Mary,' she breathed, but she did not come in.

The obvious delight in her friend's eyes encouraged Mary to smile friendliness in return. 'Lisl, it's you at last! I've brought Marina to show you.' She took the baby from Gabriela and held her up.

'Lisl!' Frau Helden hissed.

'What on earth's the matter, Friedl? Is Lisl ill?'

'She's in no state . . .'

The girl remained in the shadow by the door. 'Excuse me, Tante Rilla, I'm not properly dressed.' Her voice trailed off, then came back. 'You bring Marina, Mary. Let's take her upstairs to my bedroom. Johanna's still asleep.'

As soon as they had left the older women, the girls broke into a run in their haste to get to Lisl's room.

'Why didn't you come and visit?' Mary shouted after her friend, finding it hard to keep up while carrying her baby.

'It's not that easy, Mary. My mother expects me to do my share in the house now that Johanna and I are living here. She's slowing up.'

Mary noticed Elisabeth was thin, thinner than when she had last seen her. Then she looked towards her belly and could see the swell. 'Why are you doing this?'

'Doing what?'

They had arrived in a large, light bedroom on the first floor. A double bed, its bulky Federbett billowing above it, almost filled the room. At the side stood a wooden cot, intricately carved. Lisl went up to it, absently began to sway it on its rocker legs.

'Marrying Kurt.' Mary did not associate Lisl with marriage. She had been touched by the atmosphere in the grotto, by her vision, just as Mary had. A husband was simply not a part of it.

'What's wrong with getting married?'

Mary, gurgling at Marina, was about to go over and look into the cot when she caught sight of the other side of Lisl's face. 'What's happened to your face?' she cried out, appalled. The skin was black and blue. The ear, double its size and purple, stood out in angry condemnation. Lisl shrugged resigned shoulders. Mary now saw that the corner of her mouth was also swollen. It must be painful for her friend to speak. 'He did that to you?'

Lisl turned that side of her face away. 'It's not uncommon around here.'

'So why are you going to marry him? You don't have to,' Mary cried. 'It's a crazy thing to do.'

'I'm carrying his second child, Mary. What else am I to do?'

'What are you saying, Lisl? You know the first one isn't his. I never believed it when you first told me, but now I *know* it wasn't true. Because it's happened to me, too. We both drank the holy water and we both had visions. You know it was because of that our daughters came about.'

'That's all such nonsense, Mary.' A deep sigh, a heave. 'Just childish nonsense. It can't happen that way, it doesn't make sense.'

'You were a virgin, Lisl,' Mary insisted, her eyes beginning to fill with tears. 'We talked about it often enough. Don't you remember? You said you were happy to keep yourself as a bride of Christ –'

'I've grown up fast. I'm a mother now, I have

346

responsibilities: a daughter to think about, another baby on the way. I can't afford such silly fancies.'

'But you told me yourself, that day in the car.' Mary gulped. 'You cried, and said you didn't really know how it had happened, you couldn't remember anything. As far as I could work it out it was Kurt who maintained he was the father, not you. Are you going to deny that now?'

'The spirit is willing but the flesh is weak,' Lisl intoned. 'We all know that.'

'You mean you *were* tempted to sleep with him?' Mary's eyes had grown into saucers. 'You couldn't have been! He's crude, and coarse, and . . . He forced you, didn't he? It's the only way it could have happened. So what you hinted at in the car was true? You had a baby because he raped you?'

'No, no, he didn't force me,' Lisl insisted, her voice low. 'That's not his style. He's got any number of girls after him. He's so damned good-looking.'

'Let me get this straight. You were actually having an affair with him and you still told me you were a virgin?'

'Not an affair, Mary. Nothing like that. You've got it all wrong. I was a virgin when I drank the water and had the vision. It wouldn't have happened otherwise. It was afterwards that it all began to go wrong. I don't think I knew exactly what was happening around me, I was on a sort of high. And when I'd come down from the grotto – I told you, I met Joseph and we ran into the usual crowd. Kurt joined us at the inn.'

'And you immediately had sex with him? Right then, after the vision? I don't believe you, Lisl!' Mary walked over to Johanna's cot and looked at her. 'She looks even more like you than last time,' she said, a frown crossing her face.

347

'Of course not then; don't be so silly. I told you. I was confused and, at the same time, sort of exhilarated. So I joined in with the others at the Braune Rössl, danced a bit, had a glass of Coke. But I felt woozy, I had to go outside for air. Kurt came after me, said he'd see me home. I was still very dizzy, and he was definitely drunk. He sort of pawed me about, I don't really remember much. It's only natural that it should happen, you know. My mother even asked me if I was all right when I came in, I was so white.' Lisl wiped her eyes. 'I'd no idea what she was thinking.'

'So you don't remember sleeping with Kurt,' Mary said. 'You just assumed what they all said was true.'

'What other solution could there be?'

'A virgin birth,' Mary said, triumphant. 'Just like Marina. Just like the Virgin Mary had Jesus. He was the Son of God, not the son of any mortal man. Johanna and Marina are the Daughters of God.' She stopped, eyes wide. 'They have to be. They can't be anything else.'

'There's no such thing, Mary. Be sensible. There is no way you could have had a baby without a man. You're denying what really happened, making it up.'

'So what d'you think happened to me, then? I know I didn't sleep with anyone. You know I didn't, because I couldn't. Not after that business . . .'

'Joseph rescued you that day, didn't he?'

'You're accusing your own brother?'

'No, I'm not accusing him. It isn't a crime, for goodness' sake! You were frightened, exhausted, looking for a hero. He was the big rescuer. It happens so easily, Mary. Can't you just believe that?'

'He didn't even touch me. I've just reminded you, I can't cope.'

348

'You have repressed it, Mary. Because of what happened in London you can't face up to it.'

'I can do without the amateur psychology, thanks very much. I get enough of that from the professionals.' Mary rocked the cot. 'Why are you lying, Lisl? A lullaby of lies,' she said, staring into the cot. 'The truth is that he hit you because you wouldn't sleep with him. That's it, isn't it?'

'Don't say such things.'

'If you don't back me up, no one else will listen to me, Lisl. Even the Frau Professor said that if it happened to both of us she would believe it.'

'Because of the visions, you mean? Like some of the brides?'

'She says there has to be a catalyst. I think the visions could do that.'

'Does she believe that?'

'I don't think so.' Mary looked at Lisl reflectively. 'She thinks it has to be a physical catalyst.' She put her hand out to Johanna, who grasped it and gurgled at her. 'You saw Our Lady. Did she say anything to you? Did she ask you to bear the Daughter of God? Like the archangel Gabriel asked Mary if she was willing to bear Jesus?'

'I've told you a million times, nothing like that. She didn't speak. She just appeared to me.'

'Was she holding Jesus in her arms?'

'I don't know. I hate the way you keep on all the time,' she snapped.

Mary stopped, looked at her friend, unable to speak. Tears came into her eyes and began to pour down her face.

'Don't, Mary,' Lisl whispered. 'Don't cry.'

'They won't believe either of us if you don't tell the

349

truth, Lisl. They'll go on hounding us.'

'All right, I'll tell you,' Lisl suddenly cried. 'I did have her without a man, Mary. I gave birth to her without having sex,' she cried out loud. 'Without a sperm entering my body. I know I was still a virgin after I came home. And I am still a virgin.'

'Have you told anyone?'

'No one,' Lisl whispered. 'They'd think I was off my rocker.' Her eyes streamed tears. 'I didn't mean to tell you, Mary. It won't do any good. Sometimes I think I'll burst with the knowledge of it. Even Joseph might start to believe them.'

'You've told Joseph?'

'He knows there's something different. He says he knows me and how I feel about Kurt, and he believes I haven't slept with him.'

'But what about Kurt, Lisl? He must know it wasn't him.'

'He was tickled pink. It proved his manhood, and I remind him of Helga. I think he thought he was getting my sister, her child.' Lisl smiled through her tears. 'And, after all, he was pretty drunk. So I just let him assume things. I thought they'd kill me if I didn't.' She suddenly preened. 'Anyway, he's crazy about *me* now. He's never even insisted that I sleep with him, in case he hurt the baby before she was born.'

'Why don't you tell him, Lisl? After all, he can't be jealous of God.'

'He'll kill me, Mary,' Lisl said, her voice level, unemotional. 'He'll kill me because I'm pregnant again. He'll be convinced I've slept with someone else.'

'Whatever would give him that idea?'

'He only comes round during the day, that's why. He can't stand the way Johanna cries at night. He hasn't

350

stayed the night once since she was born.' Lisl's tears were flowing now.

'Does he know you're having another one?'

'No one has said. He knows I've been sick again, because he's seen it. And this time even he must know it wasn't because he slept with me.'

'Oh, God, Lisl! You couldn't even do it to fool him, could you?' Mary whispered. 'I know you couldn't.'

'I just wanted to look after my baby.' Lisl took out a handkerchief and sniffed. 'That's all I wanted to do.'

'Have you told your mother about it?'

'I tried. She gets as angry as Kurt does; angrier,' Lisl sobbed. 'She even hit me herself. I couldn't believe it. We've always been so close before.'

'That's why she won't let you see me? That's why they're keeping you a prisoner?'

'You've got to help me, Mary. Tell the Frau Professor about me and what's happened.'

'Why didn't you say something on the phone?'

'One of my parents was always listening, and I couldn't prove anything. It's different now you say you're the same. You said the Frau Professor might believe us.' She wept again. 'Kurt wouldn't even let me take the baby for her jabs. He just grabbed her without a word. I thought he'd taken her for good. He did it so that I had no excuse to get away, to see the Frau Professor myself.' Lisl grabbed Mary's hand. 'She's very clever. She'll find a way of proving it.'

'She doesn't exactly believe me either. Even Aunt Rilla doesn't, though she knows I'm not lying. But I'm sure they will if we both stick to our stories.'

'Perhaps.' Her eyes looked blank. 'I told you not to come. It's no good, Mary. They won't believe us, it's too incredible.' She sighed. 'Don't come again, they'll

351

only beat me up.' She looked intently at the baby in Mary's arms. 'Well, now you're here, are you going to let me hold Marina, or not?'

Mary's eyes softened. 'Of course,' she said. 'Isn't she beautiful?'

'Adorable. And the spitting image of you,' Lisl whispered, tears falling down her cheeks. 'It really is extraordinary.'

'You were a very long time talking to Lisl, Mary. I had the greatest difficulty keeping Friedl from barging in on you. I had to spout no end of nonsense.'

'I'm sorry, Aunt Rilla. But I did have to talk to her, you know. I was right. Lisl's in real trouble.'

'You're getting a taste for the melodramatic. What do you mean, in trouble? She's in the bosom of her family, she has one lovely daughter, and she's going to have another baby. *And* Kurt is crazy about her, by all accounts.'

'She can't stand Kurt. Anyway, it took ages to get it out of her, but in the end she admitted it.'

'Admitted what?' Was Mary actually becoming unstable? Should she be thinking of contacting Anne and Thomas?

'It's what I said, Aunt Rilla. Johanna was also a virgin birth. I told you Lisl had the vision, too. That's why Johanna is older than Marina. She had it in July. Last year, before the summer school.'

'Look, Mary, you have to stop this nonsense. Friedl is already very annoyed, and you'll have Kurt and Albert after you as well. Let me say this just once more: Lisl and Kurt have a healthy sexual relationship. Johanna is the result of their union, a perfectly ordinary state of affairs between two young people.'

352

'But –'

'Let me finish. The fact that Lisl and you daydreamed about becoming Little Sisters, and looking after the festival, and all that stuff about visions, well, that was perfectly normal at your ages. But you *have* to grow up. You have to put those fantasies behind you now.'

'You don't understand!' Mary cried out, turning to her godmother, her eyes wild. 'Lisl's second one's the same. Kurt has *never* slept with her. He only visits to see the baby; he's never stayed there since Johanna was born. He can't stand the way the baby wakes at night, so he's either in Kernkirchen or with his parents.'

Gabriela sighed. 'You have to stop this, Mary. Even my mother won't be able to protect you if you go on like this.'

'Protect me?'

'The village doesn't like people going on in this way. We aren't in London, it's very labyrinthine here. You have to take account of what people feel.'

'They have to know what's going on.'

'You still insist that both these children were conceived as a result of a vision of the Virgin Mary?'

'Yes. That's what I keep telling you.'

'Well, there you are then, Mary. You've got it wrong. Lisl can't have been up to the grotto since Johanna was born. It's winter. Anyway, she hasn't been anywhere. Her mother told me she was afraid to let her out of her sight. So it can't be a vision this time.'

Mary thought for a moment, looking at Marina, staring out of the Audi's windows. 'I didn't ask her whether she'd had another vision,' she said at last. 'She might have done. But I don't think it has to be in the grotto. She has a statue of Our Lady in her room, with a candle and everything.'

353

'You're going too far with this, Mary. Stop it, or I'll have to ring your parents –'

'Aunt Rilla, you wouldn't – you couldn't – do that! I thought you were my friend.'

'You are as aware of the facts of life as I am. You cannot go on deceiving yourself like this.'

'I'm going to speak to the Frau Professor as soon as we get back,' Mary sobbed. 'Lisl asked me to. She said she was the only one who would help her. I see she's right. I'm not going to tell you anything else. You're just as bad as my father.'

The Audi was approaching the drive of Erika's house. An ancient Citroën Diane was parked in front of it. Its battered body showed that its colour had, at one time, been yellow.

'D'you know whose car that is, Mary?'

'I've no idea.'

'Was my mother expecting someone?'

'Not as far as I know.'

As they drove up to Erika's garage to put the car away, a young man strode out from the terrace at the side.

'It's Kurt Miller,' Mary called out, alarmed. 'What on earth does he want?'

They didn't have long to wait to find out.

'Good afternoon Frau Adler, Mary,' he said, holding open the Audi's door and attempting to help Mary out. When she shook him off, he unstrapped Marina and her seat.

'Give her to me.'

He shrugged and handed the child to Mary. 'I'm sorry to intrude, Frau Adler. I am looking for the Frau Professor.'

'She must be around somewhere. We had the car.'

'I have rung the bell several times. There is no answer. And there is no one in the back.'

'She's working in her laboratory. She's very busy, Kurt. Perhaps she didn't hear. What did you want?'

'She has some results for me.'

'Results?'

'I brought Johanna over. The Frau Professor has taken blood and was going to run some tests for me.'

'On Johanna? Is she ill?'

The front door opened and Erika stood looking out, bright eyes sweeping over the people assembled there.

'What is all this racket? Who was that, banging and knocking at the door? Did you forget your key, Rilla?'

'It was me, Frau Professor. I did ring to start with. I was looking for you.'

'No need to go on so. I was in the middle of a delicate experiment. I can't just run to the door because someone unexpected is banging on it.'

'I'm sorry.'

'I have some vital results to correlate. I explained that last time you were here.'

'I didn't mean to disturb you, Frau Professor. You said you'd have Johanna's results by now.'

'Yes, yes.'

'Are they –?'

'For goodness' sake, man, now that you're here, come in. Don't just stand there, looking absurd. Come through to the laboratory. I'll talk you through them there.'

28

'Have you heard the news?' Resi bustled into Erika's farmhouse kitchen. The woodstove, lit even in summer since it was the only cooker available, made the kitchen an inviting place on rainy days. Resi's strong arms clasped a twenty-five-kilo bag of animal feed as though it weighed no more than a shopping basket.

'Another bomb explosion in New York?'

'A bomb?' She looked puzzled, then brightened up. 'No, not New York. I'm talking about our news,' she said. 'Nothing to do with outsiders; not as far as I know, anyway. That Lisl. She's had an accident.'

'Helden Lisl?' Gabriela asked, the wooden spoon she was using to stir the onions softening in butter stopping in mid-air.

'Who else? Always said she'd come to no good. Putting on airs, playing the violin. Just a country girl like the rest of us.'

'Is she badly hurt?' Mary asked, her eyes round, her face losing colour.

'She had the baby with her on the back.'

'They're both hurt?' The spoon was stirring swiftly, banging the side of the saucepan. A fragrant onion smell suffused the kitchen.

Resi looked at Gabriela meaningfully, and shrugged

stolid shoulders in a gesture of dismissal. 'Dreadful for her poor mother. She's in a state of shock. Can't speak, can't eat. Just beats her breast and says it was all her fault.'

'It's serious?' Mary whispered, her throat dry. But at some level she already knew. Her shoulders sagged as the realisation forced itself into her mind.

'What? I can hardly hear you, little bird.' Resi stared at the ashen face. 'Serious, yes. She was riding that old bike of hers. Used to be her mother's. I always said the brakes would go. That hairpin, dangerous so near the village and all. And the baby's weight at the back . . .'

'What actually *happened*, Resi?' Gabriela almost shouted at her.

'A great skid-mark all across the road. You can still see it, in spite of all the wet.'

'Not off the road?' Gabriela had forgotten the onions. A smell of burning alerted her. She turned and took the pan off the stove. 'Are they . . .?'

'Old banger like that, straight over the sheer drop by the bend. No chance to help them even if there'd been someone there to see it.'

Mary had been listening and watching. She felt faint, dragged out a stool and sat down heavily. 'We were with her only yesterday,' she murmured. 'She was so happy with her little Johanna. She loved looking after her.' She stared from Resi to Gabriela and back again. 'How could it happen? How? Her mother didn't let her go out.'

'I can't believe it,' Gabriela agreed. 'Friedl said only yesterday that she was far too taken up round the house to go out. Anyway, I thought she'd been feeling off again.'

'Which bike was it, Resi? The one I used to borrow?' Mary's voice broke.

'That's the one, they've only got the one between the lot of them.'

'There's never been a problem with that bike before,' Gabriela said. 'And Friedl told me how careful Lisl always is . . . was . . . of Johanna. She would have ridden very slowly.' She stared, the fridge door wide as she forgot what she had gone to fetch. 'Someone coming fast the other way?'

'No car involved, they say. No one else at all. The police – my Hermann's the one who's looking into it – haven't a clue what caused it. They're up there now, measuring the skid-marks and all that.'

'She did have morning sickness badly again. Perhaps she felt ill? Maybe that was it?' Gabriela went over to Mary and put her arm round her. 'Did she say anything else to you, Mary? About leaving, for instance? Anything you haven't told me?'

'You mean she was having another one?' Resi looked put out at news she had not brought. 'No one told me about that.'

The tears began to well in Mary's eyes. She tried to pour orange juice into a funnel on top of the feeding bottle and spilt it over the table.

'I'll do it.' Resi dumped her load on the floor. 'I knew you'd be upset, but you were bound to find out. Best you should hear it at home.' She looked round for a cloth to mop up the liquid. 'Just awful the way poor Friedl has lost two of her girls. You wouldn't credit it, both having accidents. They always say lightning doesn't strike twice, but it does. I said I saw that raven nesting in the church. Horrible things.' She wrung the dishcloth out in the sink. 'Three innocent young lives; the poor little one as well.'

'Four, Resi. Four if you count the unborn one.' Gabriela sighed. 'And Friedl was so proud of being a grandmother. She doted on the little girl.'

Mary stared at the orange juice making a pool on the wood of Erika's old-fashioned kitchen table. The liquid glistened its vivid glow shading into rust, then brown. Mary took her finger and traced the letter L, then smudged the juice across the table surface, dispersing it to seep unobtrusively into the wood. There was nothing but a darkish stain to show where it had been.

Lisl's matter-of-fact words came back to Mary: 'He'll kill me, Mary,' she'd said, as though it was the most natural thing in the world. But Lisl had also said Kurt came over to see the baby. Had he gone there yesterday after he'd talked to the Frau Professor?

Mary, trying again to pour the juice into a sterilised bottle, looked at Resi for the first time that morning. 'Lisl's dead,' she said in a singsong voice. 'Yesterday she was there, and now she's gone.' Her eyes stared through Resi. 'Someone wanted her dead.' Her eyes roamed round the kitchen, refocused on the orange juice. 'First they forced her to lie, and then they wanted her dead.'

Gabriela looked at Resi. 'Go and fetch the Schnapps, will you,' she said. 'From the living room. That'll help a bit.'

Gabriela hugged Mary's shoulders. 'You don't know what you're saying, Mary. This sort of thing does happen. The Heldens all shared that ancient bike. Perhaps the brake-pads were worn down. It only takes a bit of rubble on the road . . .'

'Now there's no one else who'll believe me. Someone deliberately killed her,' Mary said coldly. 'It wasn't an accident. Kurt killed her.' She turned furious eyes on Gabriela. 'I told you Johanna was the same as Marina, I told you Lisl admitted it. She tried to tell her mother, but she wouldn't listen. She asked me to tell the Frau Professor, to see if she could help her. But I couldn't get her to listen to me, couldn't prise her away from that damned laboratory. She always says something terribly important has come up, and she just doesn't hear anything I say.'

'I hear you, Mary. Believe me, I am trying to help.'

'You wouldn't believe me yesterday, you think I'm making it up. And now it's too late!' She shrugged off Gabriela's arms, snatched the bottle now filled with orange juice, pushed Resi bearing Schnapps out of the way and ran towards Marina's room. They heard her crash the door shut with a bang.

'She's going to lose her milk over this,' Resi said, shaking her head, pulling a handkerchief out of a wide sleeve. 'Poor little mite. So thin, as well. Better get the Frau Professor to give her something.'

'The milk has begun to dry up already. Let her be for the moment.' Gabriela took another drink from the coffee she had been sipping. 'There's another cup in the pot. Help yourself.'

'I should get on . . .'

'Tell me what else you know about this accident.'

'There's nothing else to tell.'

'Was it the brakes?'

'They don't know yet. There was a skid, that's obvious. So she must have put her foot down hard and there must have been some braking power. Going too fast and lost control, I expect. Not used to the extra weight behind her. And in front of her, you say. Easy enough.'

'How do they know no one else was involved? Perhaps a tourist coming the other way? Driving on the wrong side of the road?'

'He'd have been lynched by now. You know that road, no side roads until you get to the convent turn-off.'

'Gone beyond St Walter, had she?'

'Exactly. First right-hand bend. People heard her scream, and then the bumping as she fell. Any car driving through the village after that would have been stopped.'

'There's that small track off to the left, leading through Günther's meadow down to Kernkirchen.'

Resi's eyes swivelled. Her hand, holding the cup of coffee she'd just poured, began to tremble. 'Someone local? Deliberate?'

'When did it happen?'

'All they had to do was frighten her . . .' Resi said, her eyes slitting.

'*When*, Resi?'

'Late afternoon. Evening, really. She'd gone to see Reverend Mother. Wanted to show her the baby. That's what Irma heard from Maria Zauner. Sister Christa let it out.'

'Sister Christa spoke to Maria?'

'She was worked up about the accident.'

'What was she doing, cycling *away* from St Walter?'

'Who knows? Going down to Kernkirchen to look for that Kurt, probably. You know he's there all through the summer. Work, he calls it.' Resi grinned. 'Checking up on him, I dare say. Not that it would do any good. That's a real Casanova, that one.'

Gabriela stared out of the window at the wet landscape. 'It's been raining all night.'

'That was much later, afterwards. The road wasn't really that wet when it happened.'

'The rain will have washed out any footprints on the track,' Gabriela said quietly. 'I'm going to go and visit Reverend Mother. Look after Mary for me.' Was Mary right? It felt all wrong, not like an ordinary accident. Something decidedly weird was going on, and it concerned both Mary and Lisl.

Gabriela put on her boots and raincoat, and set off for St Walter and beyond the village to the convent. There was something oddly familiar about this accident, something she vaguely remembered but could not quite bring to mind.

Why did it make her think of Helga? Perhaps because she, too, was engaged to Kurt. 'Kurt killed her,' Mary had stated so confidently just a few minutes ago, as though she knew. Had Kurt also killed Helga? That was ridiculous! Gabriela remembered that he hadn't been anywhere near the Helden place the day her goddaughter died.

Plodding along the well-known road, Gabriela noted that the coarse vegetation of summer was already browning into the first signs of autumn. She screwed her eyes against the sun and looked along the tarmac, trying to see it as she used to see it as a child. Warm, summer sun peeking through clouds caught by the peaks, showers interspersed with hot sunshine, the pervasive scent of alpine meadow flowers, the peaceful grazing of milch-cows, the tinkle of the bells round their necks. Autumn would bring the festival . . . Oma. Her apple cheeks, her ready smile. The memory of her grandmother Heidi slowed Gabriela's step, stooped her back, pricked at her eyes. She could see Heidi's laughing, loving eyes which gleamed their pride every time they

362

caught sight of her. The lump in her throat grew larger as she remembered the carefree laugh, the welcoming arms, the soft, encouraging voice.

'What happened to you, Oma?' Gabriela whispered on the wind. 'What happened to Lisl and Helga? What's going on here? Tell me what to do, who to talk to, how to work it out. I need your help. Show me how to protect Mary and Marina.'

'Grüss di' Gott, Rilla,' a voice floated towards her. 'Your ankle quite healed up now, is it?'

Gabriela blinked into the sun, almost blinded by its brilliance and the reflections from the sodden road. 'So it's you, Magdalena. Yes, thanks. What are you doing here?'

'Just been visiting the reverend great-aunt. I try to come every three months. Didn't know you were around. I thought you only came in October?'

'It's a long story. So you've just been to see Reverend Mother?'

'Left her to have her nap. Afraid she's getting on a bit, her attention lapses after quite a short time. Don't think she can hang on much longer.'

'As bad as that?'

'Seems to be very frail. Sister Christa was moved to speech about it.'

'I rather wanted to talk to her.'

'Sister Christa?'

'Mother Theresia. I think she knows something about my grandmother's death.'

'Your *grandmother*? Jessusmaria, woman! That must have been – well, nearly forty years ago. Same year you got so ill, wasn't it?' Magdalena had stopped in the middle of the road, then moved next to Gabriela at the side as she heard a car approach. 'The middle fifties, for goodness' sake. What on earth do you want to bring all that up for?'

'Did you hear about the accident?'

'You mean that girl of Friedl's? The one who had a baby?'

'Lisl, yes.'

'Looked just like her mother when she was a girl; always gave me a turn. And Helga, too. Ghosts from the past.' Magdalena looked towards the high peaks. 'The baby was killed as well. What a tragedy.'

A refrain ran through Gabriela's mind. Twins; those sisters looked alike enough to be twins. Triplets, counting Ursula.

'Rilla? Are you all right?'

'Sorry, Magda. Lisl was having another one.'

'Already? I suppose that could explain it.'

'Explain what?'

'Maybe she felt faint, you know what they say about preg . . . Well, I suppose we wouldn't really know, you and I.' She broke off, her eyes bright. 'What I mean is it's so sad. I hear that stud she was going to marry cut up rough about the first one crying all the time. Beat her about.'

'Actually, we went to Friedl's yesterday, my god-daughter and her baby and I.' Gabriela paused a moment and looked at Magdalena carefully. 'Have you been recently?'

''Fraid we've lost touch, now I live with Ulrike. Other side of Salzburg, you know. But I met Friedl in the village the other day. Bit cool, I thought. Well, frosty would be a better word. So no, I haven't bothered.'

'Did she say anything about Lisl?'

'I asked about her, congratulated her on being a grandmother, said how wonderful it must be to have a daughter like that to remind one of one's youth. Didn't go down well, for some reason. Probably miffed that the girl shows up how much she's aged.' Magdalena looked at Gabriela taking in every word. 'Why are you so concerned about Helden Lisl? What's she to you?'

'I was her sister's godmother, Magda. I do know them quite well. And something about that accident feels – *déjà vu*. Both daughters having fatal accidents. I can't quite put my finger on it.'

'Come on, Rilla! So we can't have babies, and you're upset that Helden Lisl conceived two in no time at all. Don't brood, you'll just have to come to terms with infertility.'

'It isn't that. Why does everybody always put anything I say down to that?'

'You're too wrapped up in that child you were with last October, you know. The English Mary. They say it was Helden Joseph who fathered the little one on her. Anything in it?'

'I can't talk now, Magda. I've got to catch Reverend Mother right after her nap. Maybe she will remember a few things which have been puzzling me.'

'I'm having lunch in the village, the Goldener Hirsch. Let's have a glass of wine when you're through.'

Gabriela merely waved as she walked faster towards her goal. People had begun to pigeonhole her as a menopausal woman panicking at the ticking of the clock. They thought her demented because she had not been able to have children. Just as they thought that Heidi, in her delirium, had been emotionally compelled to throw herself off the mountain, that Helga had taken risks training the horse, that it had been Lisl's fault that she had fallen off a bike she had been riding successfully for years.

365

Childhood images trickled back to Gabriela, mingled with images of Resi now. Oma had left her with a much younger Resi that fateful afternoon.

'Resi will be here, Rillikins. I won't be long.'

'Don't go, Omi. Don't leave me!'

'It is God's work, my little one. He will keep you safe for me.' He had kept *her* safe, but not her grandmother.

. . . Why do you keep going . . . see to Rilla . . . more in your line . . .

Clean for the Holy Mother . . .

. . . Superstitious rubbish . . . Do it for you if I must . . .

. . . Don't want you and your science in there . . . ungodly . . . a violation . . .

Gabriela, startled, found herself outside Reverend Mother's door. She knocked discreetly.

'Herein!'

The voice calling for her to come in was audible but faint. Gabriela opened the door to see Mother Theresia standing by her window, looking at the mountain rising majestically a short distance away.

'It's you, my child,' she said. A smile lit the faded eyes, then waned. 'You look troubled,' she murmured. 'There seem to be so many problems. Our little Lisl is dead.'

'I heard that, Reverend Mother.'

'They say she did it on purpose. They say she could not stand the father of her child, or cope with a second pregnancy so soon.' Mother Theresia turned to Gabriela. 'They asked me what I thought. I am quite sure Elisabeth did not commit suicide. Her baby was with her, she would never have harmed the little one. I told them to bury her in hallowed ground.'

'You have no qualms? You think it was a genuine accident?'

'It is unthinkable that it could have been anything else. She came to see me, to show me her baby. She asked me to pray for her, said she needed my prayers.' There was a silence. 'She asked me to believe she had never been unchaste.'

'Did she say where she was going?'

'To your mother's. Something about medical tests. I told her not to worry so much.' The old head shook.

'You're sure . . .?'

'I am quite sure. Elisabeth was gentle, loving, innocent – just like Mary Fullbridey. I do not know how either of them came to be with child. I cannot believe that either of them knew a man, and then denied it.'

'Mary insists it is the case.'

'It is a mystery,' the old nun said softly. 'And yet I think we know the solution. Somewhere the answer is staring us in the face, and we cannot see it. We must pray for enlightenment.'

'Mary claims she had a vision.'

'So many young girls see visions. They are not real, though they are real enough to the girls who have them. Such young minds are easily seduced.'

'What I have really come about, Reverend Mother, is to talk to you about my grandmother.'

'Our faithful Heidi.' She sighed. 'It seems all those I have known well are dead.'

'Something about Lisl's death, the circumstances of it, remind me of Oma's.' Gabriela fidgeted with her wedding ring, twisting it to and fro. 'In fact, in some strange way, this curious business with the babies brings my grandmother back for me.' Her eyes filled with tears. 'I hope you won't think me superstitious,

367

Reverend Mother, but I can hear her calling me, telling me something . . .'

'It is your unconscious memories, my child.'

'. . . something to do with the festival.'

'You are angry with God for allowing your grandmother to fall. You think she was doing His work, and yet He let her die. We cannot fathom His ways.'

'It's not His ways I am concerned about. There's something odd about all these accidents. My grandmother crashes to her death when she is a seasoned climber, Helga crashes from a horse when she is an excellent rider, then Lisl crashes from a bike she's ridden successfully all her life, and Johanna is killed as well. None of it should have happened.'

'Innocent lives, I know. It was God's will . . .'

'I'm sick of God's will! Only the good seem to die, Reverend Mother.'

'You are troubled, Rilla. You think I can help you, and I would be only too happy to. What is bothering you?'

'I can't understand why you allowed Oma to go up to the grotto if she was so ill, Reverend Mother.'

'Ill? She was not ill before she went up, Gabriela. I would never have allowed her to go.'

'She was not delirious?'

'You think I would let her climb up there in such a state? I could not have missed such symptoms.'

'But my mother said . . .'

'It is tragic how that illness could strike so suddenly, so unexpectedly.' Reverend Mother sighed. 'She was so eager to make sure all was right for the festival. So terrible for your mother to be up there, and yet not able to save her.'

'You mean my mother was already up there?'

'She always went in those days, before her arthritis took such a hold. So conscientious, our Erika. She insisted on putting meshing over the trough, on inspecting everything herself, the day before the festival. And she always took samples to check that the water was pure.'

'I thought that was something which was instituted the year after that? Because the infection had broken out that year?'

Reverend Mother looked round at her.

'Can I help you to your chair, Reverend Mother?'

Gabriela tried to marshal her thoughts. Was her memory at fault about when Mutter had gone up there? She remembered her mother coming back that day, her face white, her right arm and leg bleeding, bruised. Even so, she had looked beyond her for Oma.

Her mother had just looked at her, one clawlike hand clutching a cheek, standing away from her, by the door, blood dripping from her arm.

'Where's Omi? Is she ill?'

'You have to be brave, Rilla . . .'

'Where's my Omi? What have you done with her?'

'I tried to save her, Rilla. She was delirious, she went up to the grotto. I followed her.'

'What did you do?'

'I tried to save her, Rilla. She was so ill, so hot. She gulped the water, splashed it all over her . . . and then she ran out, slipped.'

'*Save* her? Save her from what? Why didn't you stop her?'

' . . . I tried to hold her, child. Look, I fell down with her, grazed my arms and legs . . .'

'*You*?' She remembered she could hardly contain herself. '*You* were up in the grotto?'

Gabriela brought herself out of the past, bent towards Reverend Mother and offered her her arm.

'Thank you, my child.' The slow, unsteady journey to the chair left Mother Theresia breathless. 'Perhaps I am not remembering it right . . .'

Reverend Mother said Oma had followed Mutter, that Mutter was already up there, that Oma wasn't delirious . . . The blood drained from her face. She shivered.

'You look quite pale yourself, Rilla. Sit down.' She smiled, wistfully. 'I cannot help your grief, but I can give you something of Heidi's. Something I have treasured for many years. It is an indulgence,' she said. 'It would be better if I gave it to you.'

'You have something belonging to Oma?'

'She kept the festival records, Gabriela. In her own hand, although not as meticulously as your mother would have done. Heidi was not trained as a scientist, but she kept the records for the ten years after the war. Then I took over.'

The old nun tried to open a drawer in her desk. Her fingers grasped the handle, were unable to move it.

'Let me do that, Reverend Mother.'

Gabriela pulled out the drawer. It was stuffed with yellowing sheets of poor quality paper, curled at the edges, falling to pieces.

'Take it, Gabriela. In memory of Heidi. It is all in her handwriting.' Mother Theresia slumped back in her chair. 'God be with you, my daughter,' she whispered, waving Gabriela out.

29

'Grüss Sie Gott, Frau Adler!'

The postman's cheerful greeting resounded across from Erika's drive towards the garden at the side. Gabriela and Mary were sitting outside the french windows of the old hunting lodge, on the terrace overlooking the Kernsee. The deep blue lake shimmered in August sunshine, the white sails bobbing like corks on the calm water.

'Sign, please,' the postman said, a huge grin on his face as he rode his bicycle up the path to Gabriela and handed her a pencil.

'Of course, Franz. Your English is getting very good.'

The beam was even broader. 'From London, yes?'

She nodded agreement, eyes blinking at the envelope. 'Michael seems to think his letters are special.'

'He sends good news, yes?'

'I hope so.' Three frown-lines betrayed her nervousness. Was Michael ill? He'd never registered his letters before.

'Goodbye, London,' Franz called, his grey-clad figure wobbling away.

Gabriela ripped open the envelope, hands trembling. She unfolded a single typed sheet, and a five-thousand-schilling note fluttered down. Mary jumped up and grabbed it before the wind could kite it away. Michael was sending her money? What for?

Liebling,
I'm writing rather than phoning because it's safer. Whatever you do, don't show this to anyone, don't leave it lying around. I registered it so that it would be for your eyes only. The money is a cover. Change it to smaller notes, keep them handy. My job makes me melodramatic. That's why I'm still alive.

The results of the genetic fingerprinting are both astonishing and alarming. The two sets of DNA show that Marina's DNA is derived only from Mary's. Marina really is the result of a virgin birth – she has no father. Her body is, genetically speaking, virtually identical to Mary's. At a different stage of life, naturally. The only other example of such a close match is that of identical twins – two embryos split from a single fertilised ovum. Their DNAs are the same. Mary's and Marina's are not, but the variations are insignificant.

It goes without saying that I do not believe this extraordinary business has anything to do with God or miracles. I think the truth lies nearer home. The fact that your mother did not test the DNAs strikes me as highly significant. But what is going on, why and how, I have no idea as yet. But I intend to find out.

I have spoken to my editor. Some aspects of my assignment in Israel have their roots in Berlin. My mind keeps going back to all those discussions about your mother's work with her father. My instincts point me towards ferreting out any records relating to your grandfather's genetic research under the

372

Nazis. So I have done a deal with the paper: I cover the rest of the Israeli story, and start this special investigation there as well. You can contact me at the Hotel Victoria.

PLEASE, PLEASE do not breathe a word of this to anyone – ANYONE. Something most peculiar – sinister – is going on. It has the hallmarks of an extremely important story. I am longing to get into it; I cannot do otherwise. Pandora's box is wide open.

Keep your ears and eyes open. Talk to Mary again about the day she had the vision. See if there's anything else she can tell us.

I cannot say it often enough: be very careful, my darling. Burn this letter, put it in the kitchen woodstove now, rake the ashes to break up any fragments. No whisper of this to Mary, either. I'll be with you as soon as I can.

> *Your adoring husband,*
> *Michael*

Gabriela gaped at the letter, read it again and again. The implications were clear. Mary *had* been right all along. She had been a virgin, she was a virgin still. No man had been involved in any way: there was no spilled seed, no rape, no love affair. Mary's child had not been *begotten* – she had emerged. A ripe ovum, ready for implantation by a sperm, had begun to divide on its own, to burgeon into human life all by itself. How could this come about?

She stared unseeing across the picture-postcard panorama spread out in front of her, shivered in spite of the August sun blazing down. The reason Marina looked so like Mary was because, in a way, she *was* Mary. Some of her chromosomes were, perhaps, rearranged, but they were composed only of her mother's genes. That's why the DNAs were so similar. Marina was both Mary's daughter, and, in a sense, Mary herself. Was this a miracle?

'How's Uncle Michael?' Mary asked. 'Still writing torrid love letters?' Gabriela looked up, her eyes blank. 'Hello, there, Aunt Rilla!' Mary walked over and flicked at the underside of the letter.

Gabriela started, crushed the paper into a ball, and put it into her pocket.

'Really steamy, is it?' Mary giggled. 'You do look het up. I wouldn't try to read your letter, Aunt Rilla, honestly. I was only teasing you. Is something wrong?'

'Wrong? He's got a new assignment, that's all. I thought we were going to have a holiday together, but apparently not. He's already gone.'

'Israel again?'

'Not exactly,' Gabriela said, shifting her eyes.

'Where, then? Back to Lebanon? Are you worried about it?'

'Northern Germany this time. Berlin,' she mumbled. 'That sort of thing.'

'That's where the Frau Professor was during the war,' Mary said brightly. 'She told me all about it.'

'Really? She talked about her time there?' Gabriela looked at her goddaughter with interest. Mutter must really have taken to the girl. 'What did she say?'

'Oh, you know. About the bunker and all that, and the conditions there, and how she worked right up to the last day of the war.'

'So she always said.' A bunker near the Tiergarten, a stone's throw from the bunker Hitler was in. Helmut Fluge's research had been very important to the Nazis.

'She and her father, your grandfather. He was a

374

member of the Union of Nazi Physicians, she said, and she belonged to the Hitler Youth.' Mary stopped, then carried on. 'Only because they had to. They didn't want to be Nazis. The Frau Professor told me the party members tried to brainwash her, but it just didn't work. That only happens with weak-willed people. Anyway, she was much too busy helping her father to worry about politics. He was a genius, she said.'

'I never knew him.'

'He was very brave. He tried to protect her,' Mary said.

'Protect her?'

'Against the Tartar hordes, Aunt Rilla. Funny how she and I are so alike, isn't it?'

'Alike?' Gabriela stared at Mary. 'I would have thought you were quite different.'

'The sorts of things that happened to us,' Mary burbled on. 'Like having a child in one's teens, and having to bring her up on one's own. And the Russians.'

'The Russians?' Gabriela frowned.

Mary shifted from one foot to the other, closed her lips tight. When she looked at Gabriela again her eyes were veiled. 'Burning all the papers.' She shrugged. 'Burning her hands like that. It must have been a terrifying experience.'

'I didn't know you had been burned, Mary,' Gabriela said slowly. The child was keeping something back. Was it connected, somehow?

'Are you feeling all right, Aunt Rilla? You look a bit odd.'

'I'll just have something to drink, Mary. I'll be fine. Absolutely fine. Better than ever before.' Gabriela stood, walked over to the table with its tray of drinks and gulped some lemonade. She stretched to her full height, and smiled. 'And what else –'

'So this is where you are,' Erika announced as she walked out through the french windows. 'I thought you were going to help me, Mary? You are quite fit now. It is not good to sit around doing nothing.'

'She's still nursing, Mutter. And you're not making allowances for the shock. Naturally Mary is still upset. It's only been two days –'

'And you think I am not?' she snapped. 'I have known Helden since she was born. I would have liked to get to know the little one.' Her head jerked back as her eyes flashed. 'As a matter of fact I had already sent a message to her via her brother. Told her she could come to live here at any time.'

'You invited her to *live* here? With the baby?'

'She wouldn't have been able to cope with that frightful oaf.'

Gabriela was silenced. Her mother offering a permanent home to a young woman with a baby? What was happening to her? Was she mellowing with age?

'I only ask for a little help when it is needed. Work takes one's mind off other things.' She smiled. 'When the autumn term starts we can train Scheiderbauer to help. Meanwhile I would appreciate a little assistance with putting the data into the computer, Mary. It can't be that taxing for you, but my eyes aren't what they were. I can hardly see by the time I've spent several hours looking at the screen.' She looked at Gabriela with assessing eyes. 'Is something wrong? You seem – different, somehow.' She looked her daughter up and down.

'Nothing is wrong.'

'She had a letter from Uncle Michael.'

Erika snorted. 'The love-birds. He wants you to come

back right away, I suppose?'

'Not for a week or two, when he's finished the next assignment. Unless I'm overstaying my welcome?'

Erika snorted. 'We should discuss Mary's future before you leave.'

'Isn't she coming back to England?' It had never crossed Gabriela's mind that either Erika or Mary would contemplate her staying on in St Walter for more than a few more weeks. 'I thought I was picking her up when Marina was fit enough. I assumed she was going back to her parents.'

'I could carry on like last term,' Mary said eagerly. 'Stay for another year. I'll be sixteen then, and ready to apply to the Guildhall. The Frau Professor said she didn't mind about Marina.'

'You are willing to have Marina here?'

'Mary is an excellent assistant,' Erika said, her small eyes bright. 'Glockner can always come to help with the baby if we need her.'

'Glockner? You'd have Resi Glockner in the house?'

'Why do you repeat everything I say, Gabriela? Has the heat affected you?'

'I thought children got in the way of research,' she said dourly. 'Wasn't that what you always said to Oma?'

'Marina is a very quiet infant. She is no trouble at all.' The small eyes glinted against the sun.

'But she will be a toddler in a few months.'

'I know how human beings develop,' Erika said, her mouth drawn tight. 'Mary is a young mother and can cope. Your grandmother was finding it too much for her.'

'That isn't true, Mutter!'

'You always make difficulties,' Erika barked. 'We'll discuss it some other time. In any case, I intend to take

377

it easy next year. My research is at the point where I shall be in a position to rest on my laurels for a while. I think I deserve a break.' She took over the chair Gabriela had been sitting on. 'Let's have a drink.' She turned to Mary. 'You don't mind fetching it, do you? A Schnapps for me. Rilla?'

Michael's letter had to be destroyed at once. He didn't even know about the sinister new turn of events. After all, Lisl Helden was dead, and the circumstances surrounding her death were questionable. 'I'll go and get it,' Gabriela said. 'Is the woodstove in the kitchen alight?'

'You know perfectly well it is, Rilla. How else could we cook?' Erika frowned. 'Now what? The soup's already simmering for lunch.'

'Then I might as well get the dumplings ready. And there's something I have to see to right away,' Gabriela said. 'It won't take a minute.'

Mary walked towards the railing overlooking the panorama, thinking about her situation. Scheiderbauer? The Frau Professor could think about Renate Scheiderbauer taking Lisl's place before she'd even been buried? She hadn't even referred to the accident, let alone shown any signs of grief until the subject was brought up.

Perhaps Aunt Rilla had been right about her mother all along. She was a heartless, ruthless woman, not to be trusted, a selfish slave-driver who wanted everything her own way, thought only about her work. Her only reaction appeared to be how quickly she could find someone to replace Lisl. Did that mean she was already thinking ahead, already finding a successor for herself? If she thought it through properly, she would have to admit that she was redundant now. How long would it be before the Frau Professor packed her off? Mary's eyes filled with tears again. She missed Lisl so. And just when everything seemed to be going right, when she had finally persuaded her to admit what had happened, she'd died.

A blinding, biting headache began to bind Mary's forehead. Her breast milk was drying up fast, and she had to supplement Marina's feeds with bottles. The child worked hard to suckle, and nothing seemed to be going into her. Then she was too tired to take the bottle. She was losing weight.

'Aunt Rilla,' she began, walking into the kitchen with the baby in her arms. She had begun to fuss within half an hour of the last feed. 'I think I'll have to bottle-feed Marina from now on. My milk seems to have gone. I might as well stop trying.'

'Oh, Mary, that is sad. Why not have a word with Mutter before you give up entirely?'

'I'll decide,' Mary said. 'She can't make me feed the baby.'

'But of course not. I'm sure she wouldn't . . .'

'If it suited her, she would,' Mary muttered under her breath.

Gabriela stopped making the Semmelknödel she was preparing for supper. Her fingers were sticky, a glutinous mixture of yesterday's shredded rolls, flour and water dripping from them.

'Not those awful dumplings again, Aunt Rilla.' Mary sounded uncharacteristically petulant. 'I think it's all this heavy food which made the milk dry up.'

'There's plenty of salad and vegetables, Mary. I don't think you've been deprived,' Erika said sharply, walking into the kitchen, her glasses falling down her nose. 'I left some notes,' she said, peering round. 'Now, what's

379

all this nonsense? You need to drink more. Water will do, that's all you need to keep the milk flowing.'

'I'm not going on breast-feeding her,' Mary declared. 'I'll give her a bottle now, she didn't get enough at the feed. She gets exhausted trying to suckle something which isn't there.' She grabbed a bottle from the fridge and took it over to the microwave. 'Then I'm going down to the lake for a break. I do nothing but see to the baby.'

'Give her to me,' Gabriela said, quiet but firm, cleaning her fingers. 'I'll give her the bottle. Why not lie down for a bit?' She hesitated, then decided to carry on. 'The requiem mass is tomorrow morning, remember, in the St Walterkirche. I am sure you want to go to that, Mary, so don't make yourself ill.'

'I wouldn't miss that.' She brought Marina over to Gabriela. 'It's just that I never do anything but change nappies.'

'Then go on down to the lake, Mary. It will do you good,' Erika agreed, looking keenly at the girl. 'Perhaps we ought to ask Glockner to take Marina over during the day. Give you some time to get back to your singing and your studies.'

'Glockner? You're suggesting handing Marina over to Glockner during the day?' Gabriela breathed hard as she confronted her mother as soon as Mary had gone to change. 'If that's the best you can think of for the child, she really ought to come back with me. That is outrageous.'

'You mean you want Marina for yourself, to adopt her.'

'Mary does not want that. They could live with Michael and me. Mary can continue a normal, teenage life. I'll see to Marina when she isn't there.'

380

'You have a way of turning yourself into a martyr, just like your grandmother.' Erika shrugged. 'I suppose we need women like you.'

'Women like me? Barren, you mean? Made barren by their mother's indifference.'

'You brought it on yourself.'

'I did?' She stared at her mother. 'What's that supposed to mean?'

'Always putting your hands into the chemicals. I told you they were potent. I told you to wear rubber gloves.'

'What chemicals?' Gabriela asked, nostrils flaring, senses alert.

'You and Friedl – constantly burrowing through the feeds. Slobbering all over those animals. It wouldn't surprise me if you nuzzled some of their saliva, shared their food,' Erika thrust over her shoulder as she left.

Not their food, no. But she and Friedl *had* used their bare hands to mix the feeds. How could that have made them ill? Perhaps some of the liquids had seeped into that cut on her finger, the one which had gone so deep. It had stung. Had her mother added chemicals to the feeds? Even if she had, it didn't make sense. How could she have got an infection from chemicals? And even if she had, how could she and Friedl have contracted the same infection as the women who had gone up to the grotto? The brides had had no connection at all with any of the animals, nor with the chemicals.

'I'm going now,' Mary announced, putting her head round the kitchen door. She had changed into shorts and boots.

'If you wait for a few moments, I'll drive you down,' Gabriela hurried to say. 'Marina is almost through with her bottle. Mutter will be around to keep an ear out for her.'

'I thought you were going to look after her, Aunt Rilla? You know the Frau Professor is too absent-minded. She'll get involved with her work and forget all about Marina. If you don't do it, I can't possibly go.' Mary stood, a mulish look in her eyes, twiddling a pair of sunglasses.

The girl was equipped in socks and Doc Martens. Planning to sail? Was she meeting someone? It began to dawn on Gabriela that she was not, perhaps, quite as reclusive, averse to boys, as she always maintained. Perhaps that was why she didn't want company.

'Drive you down, I said. Not stay,' Gabriela said sharply. 'It is a good forty-minute walk, after all. I thought you wanted to get back in time for Marina's bath.'

'I'll take the short-cut,' Mary said airily. 'By Günther's meadow. I'm quite capable of getting there and back by myself,' she added as she flounced out.

30

'If it isn't the immaculate conception.' The voice came from Kurt Miller, sitting high up in the lifeguard's chair Mary strolled by on her way towards the jetty. 'And where's the little bastard?'

Mary was startled. She had not expected him to be at work, had assumed he would not return to his duties until after the funeral. Was he not even pretending grief at Lisl's death? Had he no thought for little Johanna, the child he had told Lisl he adored, had asserted so confidently was his?

'Grüss Gott,' she said with a quick flash of teeth, hurrying past.

'So, where is she?' Kurt bellowed after her. 'Another little brat with an unknown father.' She heard the sound of running feet behind her, then saw the furious, red face and flashing eyes rounded in front of her. 'A pair of whores!'

Bright red suffused Mary's face and neck as people turned to stare at them. Locals she knew began to titter. Tourists, not understanding what Kurt had shouted or the drama involved, watched with interest.

'Halt's Maul, du Scheisser!' she suddenly heard a strong voice shout out behind them. 'Shut up, you shit!' Kurt whirled back towards her and pushed her roughly out of his way. She turned and watched him vault on to his high wooden chair and looked to see who had dared to shout at him.

Sure footsteps walked towards her. 'Take no notice, Mary. He is not worth even getting annoyed with.' Joseph's golden tenor. He smiled at her, shrugging Kurt away. 'Perhaps he is upset by Lisl's death. I can see how it is with you as well. May I walk with you a little?'

'Hello, Joseph.' Her eyes looked up, then down almost immediately.

'I am fetching a few things for my mother. She is so distraught – I have never seen her like this, not even when Helga died. I suppose it is because they are both gone. She loved the little girl, you know, almost as though she were her own. She will never get over it.'

'I'm sorry, Joseph. It must be so awful for her. And you, of course.'

The lines from nose to mouth were pinched, his eyes drawn, big hollows underneath. 'I told Lisl I would take her anywhere she wanted to go,' he choked. 'I said I never doubted her.'

'Why didn't you bring her over to the Frau Professor?'

'What do you mean?'

'She said she'd sent a message to Lisl via you.'

'The Frau Professor said that? When was that supposed to be? I'm only here because my father asked me . . .' He stopped and stared out across the lake. 'The only thing the Frau Professor talked to me about was the Zahnradbahn. She asked me whether I could possibly get it into working order.'

'But no one uses it,' Mary said, mystified. 'Even in the summer it would only be used by the girl who looks after the grotto once a week.'

'She said she wanted to make sure that what happened to you could never happen to the new girl. Renate Scheiderbauer, she said.'

'How odd; it had nothing to do with the Frau Professor,' Mary said. 'I went up there for Reverend Mother.'

'I explained again, though I thought she knew all about it. The train can only run if an engineer is on the site. It's far too dangerous without that.'

'I can't get it out of my mind, Joseph,' Mary said softly. 'Where was Lisl going that evening? Do you know where she was heading on that bike?'

'No one has any idea. Mutter said Kurt came over late that afternoon. Perhaps she wanted to get away . . .'

'I know about what he does,' Mary whispered. 'Aunt Rilla drove us over to visit Lisl. That's when I saw the bruising on her face; she told me then.'

Joseph looked around. They were alone. 'Shall we walk along the edge of the lake? Away from people?'

'That would be nice.'

'Where is the little one?'

'Aunt Rilla is looking after her. I needed some time to myself.'

'It must be very hard for you.' His soft eyes took in her hair, her face. 'How are you? You look a little pale, tired out.'

'I'm fine. The baby often wakes me up at night, that's all.' Her head, the gold gleaming in the sun, was turned to the lake. 'Did Lisl talk to you, Joseph? Did she tell you anything?'

'About the way Kurt treated her, knocked her about, you mean?' His eyes flashed. 'My father sent for me last time it happened. He and I sorted that pig out pretty well a few days ago,' Joseph said grimly. 'We told him if he laid a hand on her again we'd break his bloody arms for him. I think he got the message.'

Looking fully at him for the first time Mary could see he had a bruise on his face, that his right hand was swollen. His eyes glowed fury. It would not be safe to tell him about her suspicions, that she thought Kurt was actually responsible for Lisl's death, or he might attempt to kill Kurt then and there. Had Lisl confided in him, or had she only said that Kurt was not the father of her child?

'Did Lisl tell you about Johanna?'

Joseph looked away, towards the lake, his eyes slit against the bright reflections. 'Kurt wasn't the father,' he said at last. 'She told me that.'

'Did she tell you who is?'

'She told me about her vision, Mary. She told me Johanna was born as a result of that.'

'I think she was right. You know I had the vision too; you were the one who saw me just after it. And then I had Marina.'

He walked on in silence, his eyes roaming the lake and the sky.

'What do you think, Joseph? Do you think we are both liars?'

'I know you would not lie, let alone about something like that,' Joseph said slowly, deliberately. 'Either of you. But, you must forgive me, I don't think visions bring children about.'

'Lisl was having another baby,' Mary said, tears beginning to swell. 'I couldn't understand that. I never had the chance to ask her. Had she had another vision? Did she tell you?'

'No,' Joseph said. 'That's the point. No vision, no man, just cooped up in that room with Johanna all the time. And a statue of the Virgin Mary, with a little

candle and some flowers. And a bottle of holy water.'
Joseph squared his shoulders. 'My father did not understand. He forbade her to leave the house, and my
mother kept guard. The poor girl was going mad.'

'How did she get away?'

'Crept out while my mother was doing the milking, I
think. Ursula always tried to help her; she probably
kept my mother occupied.'

They walked on for a few moments, both immersed
in their thoughts of Lisl. The happy, loving, pure child
who had dreamed of becoming a nun, of tending the
grotto for the rest of a simple life. Their hands
brushed against each other, joined in mutual comfort.

'I think she might have been cycling over to the Frau
Professor, to ask her to let her stay with her, to get away
eventually. She told me she couldn't go through with
that wedding,' Joseph said at last.

'Kurt was still prepared to?'

'My parents virtually proved to him that there was
no other man. How could there be? He couldn't really
get out of it.' He sighed. 'What is so tragic is that, in
his way, he loved Lisl. Or at least he was obsessed by
her.'

'*Did* you believe her, Joseph?'

'I believed her, I believe you, that you had babies
without sleeping with a man. I have no idea how.'

'Because of the visions, Joseph.'

'I can't believe that. There must be something else.'

'What else?'

'I don't know, Mary. I wish I did.'

'The Frau Professor said she'd believe me if I could
show her that Lisl was the same.'

'Did she?' His eyes sparked. 'That's interesting.'

She began to cry. 'And now they'll all say they were

387

right, I'm making it all up. They say it was you, you know.'

'Me?' Joseph stopped in his tracks. 'Why me?'

'Because you came up to the grotto on your own, because we were alone together for a short time.'

'You mean while you were coming round from your faint,' he said, and laughed. Then his face changed to one large scowl. '*You* don't believe that, Mary, do you?' He looked her in the eyes. 'Anyway, you were already coming out of it when I arrived. You know perfectly well I couldn't have . . . you know what actually happened.'

'I know it wasn't you, Joseph. I know you would never do anything like that.'

Joseph suddenly swung round and pulled Mary towards him, taking her other hand and looking into her eyes. She could not deny the intense, probing look. Almost without realising it he had put his arm round the slight shoulders, hugged her to himself. 'Did you ever have a boyfriend, Mary?'

She shook her head, leaned it against him, sobs racking her, Lisl's gay laugh echoing in her mind.

'Be calm, Mary. Both you and Lisl had a baby without a boyfriend, but there has to be a cause. I always checked that bike. You sometimes borrowed it. Did you have any problems riding it?'

'It was very easy, very comfortable. You think the bike was tampered with?'

'I don't know, Mary. Something strange is going on. I have no idea what it is, but I'm going to find out, I promise. Something is wrong about the way she died. I've lost my sister, and I'm not having anything happen to you.'

'So you know Lisl's death wasn't an accident?'

'If what you say is true, it might not have been,' Joseph whispered. 'Don't talk to anyone about it, Mary; no one at all. It could be very dangerous.' He held her away from him, grasped her shoulders tight, looked into her eyes. 'The last thing I would ever want to do is harm you. I am so sorry – I did not mean to tell you about my suspicions. It is the grief, speaking about Lisl. Don't breathe a syllable, promise me, now? Not even to Frau Adler.'

Without another word they moved apart and began to walk towards the Braune Rössl's car park. The Nile-green Volkswagen stood empty this time. Mary closed her eyes, tried to stem the tears as she thought back to the last time she had been in it.

'I'll give you a lift back,' he said, and held the passenger door open.

Joseph drove back towards St Walter, fast and in silence. He stopped the car at the bottom of Erika's drive, pushed his arm behind Mary to open the passenger side door, brought it back across her shoulders, squeezed, patted her, smiled. His voice, when it came, sounded cracked.

'Better no one here knows you have been with me. Don't even look at me at the requiem mass tomorrow. I shall be staying at home for the next few weeks. Ursula answers the phone when I'm not there. Let her know if you need me, Mary, please. Do not hesitate, do not forget. Remember Lisl. I will always come at once.'

'Another letter from Michael?' Erika looked suspiciously from the envelope in her hand towards her daughter. 'Where is he? That's a German stamp.' Erika examined the postmark. 'Posted in Berlin. New departure for him, isn't it? I thought his beat was the Middle East.'

'The Israeli story led to Berlin,' Gabriela said, taking the letter and putting it in her pocket. 'The world isn't divided according to journalists. Some connection with the story he did last month, I think.'

'Not all that Jewish stuff again. I would have thought even the Jews would consider that had been dealt with.'

'I really don't know.' Gabriela smiled; a veiled, nervous smile.

'You look positively furtive,' her mother said. 'Are you planning to go to Berlin yourself, or what?'

'Not that I know of.' Gabriela turned her back to her mother and tore the letter open.

Berlin, 8 August 1993
Liebling,
This trip has been very illuminating. I have almost finished the investigations here and expect to get away next week. I am coming to pick you up on my way home. And Mary, too, if Marina is remotely fit enough to travel. I think it very important that they leave. Try to get them ready, and Mary used to the idea.

> *Your loving husband,*
> *Michael*

'So? Any news?'

'He'll be through next week, and suggests he travels via St Walter to pick me up.' Gabriela smiled disarmingly. 'It would be a good way to help Mary and Marina back to London.' She went over to the baby and stroked her head.

'But Marina isn't up to such a trip yet, Aunt Rilla,'

390

Mary said instantly, frowning.

'Marina is seven weeks old. She seems quite fit to me.'

'Indeed, what's all the rush? The child is not very robust. In any case, where is Mary going to live in London, and what is she planning to do? I don't believe she has addressed these problems yet.'

'Then it is high time she did,' Gabriela announced, eyes hard on Erika. 'It does not seem entirely suitable for her to stay here.'

'I thought all that had been worked out. Well, Mary? Are you longing to get back to your parents' house?'

'She has another choice. She can come and stay permanently with Michael and me.'

'Really, Aunt Rilla? Do you and Uncle Michael really mean I could live with you all the time?'

'He would be honoured, he said. And you know my feelings on the matter.'

'And you would stay at home to look after Marina while I went to school or whatever?'

'I'd be delighted, Mary.'

'Like Bridget,' Mary said.

Gabriela smiled. 'Not exactly like Bridget,' she said, looking straight at Mary. 'Because you would be living with us. And *you* would be in charge of Marina, not me. I would merely offer any help you need.'

'Bridget? Who is Bridget?' Erika demanded.

'Bridget was Mary's pet rabbit. She had a litter unexpectedly, and Thomas was put out. I offered my home to the new mother and her family.'

'My God, a rabbit!' Erika's eyes slitted in fury as she rounded on Mary. 'You can't afford all this sentimental nonsense, Mary. I am offering you the chance to stay here. You can continue with your lessons as before, and above all you can develop your voice. At the same time you can assist me with my work. Would you really want to give all that up, leave Frau Professor Weisskopf and go to some useless English school?'

'If I go back to London, I don't think Mummy and Daddy would allow me to live anywhere but at home,' Mary said, her lips beginning to quiver. 'They'd insist on my staying with them. I don't think I could cope with Daddy telling me what to do with Marina.'

'Your father would settle for your living with us, I think . . .' Gabriela began.

'Her father will make sure Mary does not embarrass them,' Erika agreed. 'He wouldn't want the baby anywhere in London. Definitely not with you, Rilla. You are only just down the road from them.' She smiled at Mary. 'I am not offering to dandle Marina on my knee, but I will organise someone competent to look after her. Think about what I am offering you.'

'Marina should be brought up in England, Mutter.'

'Twaddle! As soon as Mary starts her singing career she will be travelling all over the world. What's so special about England?'

Gabriela shrugged. 'So now you have choices to make, Mary. In the end you have to be the one who can live with that choice.' She smiled, her eyes soft, her arms cradling the baby. 'I can't offer you luxurious surroundings, or a wonderful singing teacher, or even the chance to take part in exciting research. But I can offer my full attention to your little daughter. And Michael will fill the role of foster-father. You are not offered that in Austria.'

Mary walked over to Gabriela and took Marina. 'It's very kind of everybody,' she said. 'If you don't mind, I'd like to think about it all. Something Lisl said.' Her eyes filled with tears. 'She said she could not afford the way we used to think. She was a mother and had responsibilities. I have to decide what's best for Marina, not what's best for me.'

She hugged her baby to herself and ran out of the room. They heard the door slam shut.

31

Hochwürden took the sprinkler from one of the altar boys, walked round the coffin and sprinkled it three times on each side. Then the parish priest of St Walter took the censer and incensed the coffin in the same way.

Together they intoned the well-known words: '*Requiem aeternam dona eis, Domine, et lux perpetua luceat eis*' – 'Eternal rest grant unto them, O Lord, and let perpetual light shine upon them.'

The small graveyard behind the church of St Walter was full to overflowing. The whole village seemed to have turned out. It had been decided that Lisl and Johanna would be buried together. The coffin was lowered into the ground and a spontaneous sound of sobbing went through the congregation. Gabriela and Mary, filing behind the full complement of the Helden and Miller families, watched each of them throw down a red rose, and then a handful of earth.

Of the two mourning families, only Friedl Helden was not present. Resi, arrived at Erika's house an hour earlier to look after Marina, had warned them not to expect to see her there. She had insisted it was because the grieving mother had completely lost her reason. Herr Doktor Kramer, she had been eager to let them know, had been called in and had injected Friedl with a strong sedative.

Erika Lager was also missing. She maintained that her arthritis was too bad for her to stand for such a long time, and that it made no difference to Lisl now. The real reason, as far as Gabriela was concerned, was that her mother could not tear herself away from the laboratory even for a morning. This time, apparently, she really had arrived at a crucial stage in her research.

Gabriela looked around the familiar faces, the villagers she had grown up with, the Little Sisters, the lay teachers from the convent. She looked at Albert Helden, at Joseph – and at Ursula standing next to them. It took her breath away. It was as if the Friedl she had known at school was standing there. She sighed as she remembered the gay, laughing, carefree girl who had been her closest friend, the one who had comforted her after Oma's death, the one with whom she had spent the rest of her childhood. And now she had had more than her fair share of tragedy herself. How could she ever have presumed Friedl had been more blessed than she? Could anything be worse than losing a child? And Friedl had lost two.

Her eye was caught by Magdalena and her sister Ulrike, and Ulrike's daughter Klara, standing in line, waiting their turn. She gasped: Klara and Ulrike were incredibly alike. Uneasily she remembered the time she had mistaken Jenny for her mother Greti, and as she looked at Mary, standing beside her, Gabriela understood that Mary and Marina were alike in just that way.

The only people to have identical DNAs were identical twins, Michael had said. These women and their girls were not twins; they were mother and daughter. And the reason they looked so uncannily alike was because

395

none of these girls had had an input from a father. Their chromosomal structure was more or less the same.

The ground began to sway as Gabriela realised that Mary was not the only woman this had happened to. It had been happening to St Walter girls for years. It was becoming clear to her that this incredible phenomenon had happened to Friedl, to Greti, to Ulrike – and probably to many others she had not come across recently, or did not even know. And Mary had always insisted it had happened to Lisl, too.

As the sad procession wound around the open grave, she thought back. Friedl had married late for a village girl. She had left the area, gone to work in an office in Vienna and, one holiday when visiting her family, had renewed her friendship with Albert Helden, a young man whose equally young wife had died of leukaemia, leaving their baby Joseph without a mother. The two had married within weeks, but found the children did not come. Friedl had sought medical help, then felt time was running out. And, even though Friedl was no longer a practising Catholic at the time, Albert had persuaded her to attend the festival.

That was the very year she had conceived Helga. After that she had become devout, believing a miracle had taken place. There was another gap. A second visit to the shrine had produced Elisabeth, and another later on had resulted in Ursula. Three daughters, each after a visit to the shrine, uncannily alike.

And Greti, too. She had come back from the States to try her luck at the shrine, taking part in the festival ritual. And she had given birth to Jenny, and had had no further child.

What was the tie between these women and their daughters? There had to be a common thread, a cause other than a miraculous one. It was too pat for that. These results were too regular, too similar, to be real miracles. Whichever way she turned it round in her mind, Gabriela realised the event common to their lives was taking part in the festival of the Mothering of the Brides. That's what all these women shared. But Lisl and Mary were not brides, they had not been allowed to attend the festival. What linked *them* to these women?

Both girls had gone up to the grotto. Was whatever induced virgin births in the air? That could not be so, otherwise the nuns, and any other female attendants, would have become pregnant as well. But there had to be a cause, something which connected Lisl and Mary to the festival pilgrims. Not a miracle – but just the opposite. Something unholy. Unnatural.

'Are you all right, Aunt Rilla?' Mary had put an arm through hers and was pulling her away from the grave-side. 'You look a bit rocky. You might fall in.'

'Sorry, Mary. I'm finding it hard to come to terms with Lisl's death. The poor child had only just started out in life, and the little one had hardly begun. I keep hearing that haunting sound, the way she played the violin . . .'

'I know,' Mary whispered. 'I have to find out what happened to her. I can't believe it was an accident.'

Kurt Miller was standing opposite them, his face a white mask, his eyes staring into nothingness. His father and brothers stood protectively around him, his mother's large black hat waved like a flag of death as she talked volubly to her friends.

'Let's go back, Aunt Rilla. I can't take any more.'

'All right, Mary, but I cannot go without saying something to Albert. Wait . . .'

'I'll come with you. She was my friend, my very best friend. I want to tell him that.'

Walking away from St Walter, away from the sight of Lisl's coffin being hidden under mounds of earth, Gabriela realised that Mary must have the key to the mystery, even if she did not know it.

'There's something I have to tell you, Mary.'

'You want me to leave here.'

'That's true, but first I want to apologise for not believing you earlier. While we were in that sad crowd, throwing earth in poor Lisl's grave, I saw that I'd been wrong, quite wrong.'

'About it not being an accident?'

'About you and Lisl.'

'You believe me about her? Now that she's dead and we can't help her?' Mary said tearfully.

'Yes, Mary, I believe you. And I want you to tell me everything that happened to you. Every tiny detail.'

'I've told you, time and again. I went to the grotto, I had a vision. There's nothing else.'

'You were catapulted into the grotto, you fell into the water there and you felt groggy. But you didn't faint right away, did you? So what did you do?'

Mary began to walk faster, ahead of Gabriela. 'Prayed,' she shouted back at her. 'I prayed to have a vision.'

Gabriela ran to catch up with her. 'And what else, Mary? What else did you do?'

'What else do you think I did?'

'I've said I'm sorry I didn't believe you, Mary. Please help me now. It is important.'

'All of a sudden?'

398

'You want to know who killed Lisl –'

'So you believe me that she was murdered?'

'Perhaps not murdered; driven to death. Yes, I do believe it wasn't an accident.' Gabriela had caught up with Mary, taken her arm. 'Before we get back, tell me what else you did. What was it?'

Mary stopped walking, stood still. 'I drank the water,' she choked. 'And so did Lisl. She said that's what made her have the vision, and she told me to do it too.'

'You drank the water?'

'Just a few drops,' she gasped. 'Was that a terrible thing to do? Was it a desecration of the shrine?' Gabriela put her arms round her shoulders, and Mary began to sob. 'I know I shouldn't have done it. I know it's only for the brides. But I wanted the vision so much . . .'

'Calm down, Mary. It is not so terrible.'

'I pretended to Reverend Mother I was going up to see to the grotto. It was a blasphemy.'

'You did not mean any harm.'

'D'you think God will punish me because I committed a dreadful sacrilege? It was only for the brides, I knew that. Do you think He will take Marina from me?' She began to spin round, then threw herself on the ground, hugging her knees.

Gabriela sat down and embraced her.

'I couldn't bear it, Aunt Rilla. What shall I do? How can I make amends?'

The water, *that*'s what they all had in common. They had all drunk the holy water. Could it be true that it contained a special ingredient? Were the tales of fertility founded in fact, was that why girls came from far and near, was that why they believed? Because it really was true?

Gabriela stood and pulled the desperate child up, hugged her. 'God isn't like that, Mary. He will not harm Marina.'

'How would you know, Aunt Rilla? You've never done anything really wrong,' she sobbed, heaving, covering her eyes.

'Listen to me, Mary. None of this is just a simple miracle. Michael realised we could test whether you were right or not by comparing your DNA with Marina's. If she really was the result of a virgin birth, the genetic fingerprinting would show it up.'

Mary stopped and stared at Gabriela. 'You want to take samples of our blood and analyse them?'

'I also have a confession to make, Mary. I took combings from your hair, and some nose swabs from Marina,' Gabriela explained. 'And I sent them to London for analysis without asking your permission. That's what was in Michael's letter. You were right. Your DNAs show that Marina is –'

'God's Daughter.' Mary gasped. 'I told you, Aunt Rilla! I told you she was.'

'No, Mary, that is not right. Marina is *your* daughter, and only yours.'

'She's the same as Jesus!' Mary cried. 'I had her like the Virgin Mary had Jesus.'

'No, Mary, you did not. Jesus had to have a genetic structure distinct from his mother's. In those days, of course . . .'

'Why are you saying that? What is the difference? I was a virgin, and I had a vision, and . . .'

'The difference is that Jesus was a man,' Gabriela said quietly. 'So he had at least one chromosome that he could not have inherited from his mother. He was a male, and she was a female. We do not need a test to tell us that he had an XY chromosome and she had an XX one.'

'You mean there is no sign of God in Marina?'

'There is a sign of God. All human beings are the children of God. But Marina is not God's only, unique, daughter. She is one of at least two. You said yourself that Johanna came about in the same way as Marina.'

'So God has chosen another way, a new way,' Mary said, but her voice was low. 'You are right, it is different from Jesus – He was God's only begotten Son. Marina is one of two: both she and Johanna must be God's Daughters.'

'Mary, my dear –'

'The world is different now,' Mary went on, becoming heated. 'In Jesus's time only men were important. Now women are just as important. Maybe God intends women to take over the world, to make it a better one. Maybe He is sending His Daughters to show them the way Jesus showed for men. A woman's world, not a man's.'

'And you think that is good?' Tears began to run down Gabriela's face.

'It is the future,' Mary said. 'I always told you I had a special destiny. Now I know what I was specially chosen to do. It is my duty to prepare one of God's special Daughters. I cannot go back on it. When I had the vision, I promised I would do whatever was required.'

'Marina is not the result of a miracle, Mary. Not in the usual sense. You and Lisl both drank the holy water. *That* is what makes this extraordinary phenomenon happen. It cannot be anything else.'

'And faith.'

'It is not a question of faith. It didn't happen just to

401

you and Lisl. The brides drink the water as well. And I think some of them have daughters like yours.'

'But you believe in the festival, Aunt Rilla. You believe in miracles.'

'I believe in true miracles. I don't think this is a true miracle, I think this is a travesty, something quite different. And I think you know it, too.'

'You have lost your faith.'

'No, Mary. It is our duty to make sure that what seems to be a miracle is a true miracle. The Church teaches us that. We have to get some of that water and have it analysed. That's how we can finally know what happened to you, to Lisl, to the brides.'

'The water? You think there's something in the water?'

'Yes. Now, can you think of a way we can get hold of some?'

'Joseph,' Mary said slowly. 'He said anything he could do to help, to ask him. He would be glad to do it; he told me so.'

'You've been seeing him?'

'I came across him yesterday, down by the lake. He was collecting something for his parents.'

'Reverend Mother won't give permission . . .'

'He doesn't need to go that way. He can climb the mountain from the other side, then climb down to the grotto.'

'Not on his own, Mary. It is too difficult.'

'Kurt did it, Aunt Rilla,' Mary said, excited. 'One day when I was up there with Lisl I saw a man. I wasn't sure it was him then, but I am now. Joseph can do anything Kurt can do. He can abseil down to the grotto and fetch some water from one of the troughs.'

'How can we get hold of him?'

'He said ring up, Ursel will answer . . .'

'She isn't at home at the moment. Albert told me she's staying at the convent for the time being. Friedl can't cope with the way she looks so like Lisl. You heard what Resi said.'

'It must be awful for her,' Mary whispered. They walked in silence. 'But I know how we can get hold of him. He practises the organ in the chapel,' Mary announced. 'We could talk to him there.'

'Then I had better do it. Tongues will begin to wag if you go, and that won't help.' She thought for a moment. 'We need some sort of container. Something small enough to post, something which won't get broken. A bottle is no use.' She smiled as she thought how to do it. 'I know, we'll use one of those stainless steel phials my mother uses in the lab. She won't miss one.'

'Like the one you used that time when you brought me the holy water? You remember, before I ever came here?'

'I'd forgotten that. At least we know it won't leak.'

'The Frau Professor is terribly fussy about them, Aunt Rilla. She went on and on at Resi for mixing them up one day, when she was dusting or something. She locks the lab now, won't allow anyone into it.'

'You're sure to be in there updating the data files,' Gabriela said confidently. 'She's bound to pester you to do that later. You can pinch one then.'

Suddenly Mary seemed to panic. 'Let's get back now, Aunt Rilla. I have to see that Marina is all right.'

'Not a single word of this to anyone, Mary. You may be right, and Lisl was murdered. If that happened because of the way Johanna was born, it means you and Marina could well be in great danger. Promise me you won't say a word to anyone. Not even to my mother.'

'I promise, Aunt Rilla. I definitely promise you that.'

32

'Schatzi! I'm over here.'

Michael's strong, lithe body was striding out of Salzburg airport, a bulging briefcase clutched under his left arm. He turned at the sound of Gabriela's voice, pushed the suitcase on the trolley out of the way and let the handle of the briefcase slip into his left hand. He hugged his wife, love overshadowed by a look of compassion, of care.

'I've brought my mother's Audi. Driving back will give us a chance to talk,' Gabriela enthused. 'I could hardly contain myself waiting for you.'

'There is a lot to talk about.'

'You sound very grave. You got the water?'

'Every drop arrived safely. An excellent container.'

'And? Were you able to find something which would shed some sort of light on what's been happening?'

'Nothing. No sign of unusual substances of any kind. Minerals, plenty of them, as you would expect when you analyse water from a mountain stream. No, there's nothing there which could cause such a phenomenon.'

'You're sure? You went to the right place?'

'I went to the top laboratory. They tried all kinds of sophisticated tests, looking for any number of microscopic components. Nothing.'

'But it *has* to be the water. There's nothing else it could be.'

'I don't know about that. I do know there has to be some sort of catalyst – based on a formula, a chemical concoction – that can produce a child like Marina. But it isn't in the sample you sent. It did come from the grotto, I presume? Not from the source stream?'

'Absolutely. From one of the troughs in the grotto.'

'Then we'll have to think again,' he said, his eyes puzzled.

'I can tell from your face: you've found out something else, something awful. Is it really terrible?' Gabriela whispered, hardly able to breathe.

'Terrible? No, not necessarily. Unexpected, perhaps, though with hindsight it all seems obvious.'

'I see.' She breathed in deep. 'The car's just over there.'

'I'll drive.'

'If you prefer.'

Michael heaved his suitcase into the boot and settled himself into the driving seat.

'So what did you find out?' Gabriela felt a paroxysm of anxiety, her chest muscles constricting. She was glad Michael was driving.

'I think I'd better set the scene from the beginning, Schatzi. It is not a nice story. We are talking of events in early 1945, towards the end of the war. The stench of defeat was all around for the Third Reich, Berlin was under threat from the Russians on the east and the Allies on the west. The Nazis were at bay; what had been one of the most monstrous regimes in history was squirming in its death throes, lashing out where it could. I'm reminding you of all that because I think it had a vital effect on what happened.'

'Get to the point, Michael. Was it true that my grandfather worked in Berlin?'

'Quite true. I found a register of licensed laboratories, and one of the research scientists mentioned by name is Helmut Fluge. Several scientific papers written by him are also mentioned. He was installed in an underground lab only a stone's throw from Hitler's bunker.'

'Liebling, we know all that. My mother always insisted that my grandfather's work was very important to the Nazi cause.'

'But Helmut Fluge wasn't working for the Nazis. He was doing his best to prevent them from benefiting from his research.'

'So he wasn't a Nazi? What Oma always told me was right?'

'Not just that he wasn't a Nazi; he did what he could to resist. His bravery was quite remarkable.'

'But how could he do their research and . . .?'

'That's the incredible thing. He hoodwinked them.' Michael drove in silence for a few moments.

Gabriela's hands went cold. 'Fooled the Nazis?' She began to rub them, trying to bring back some warmth. 'Well, go on, Michael.'

'And for that he was condemned as a traitor. There can be no doubt about it. The records show that he was shot by a firing squad for betraying the Third Reich. The charge was withholding essential information about a scientific discovery. He was shot on 12 March 1945. That was the seventh anniversary of the Anschluss with Austria. A bitter irony.'

'But – But my mother always said . . .' She stopped and looked at her husband, but he was looking grimly at the road ahead, his mouth tight. 'She always said he was

407

in the bunker with her to the last, that he tried to protect his work from the Russians, and that they shot him for that.'

'I'm sorry, Liebling. The entries detailing his execution are unassailable.'

'A traitor?'

'You can be proud of that.'

'But what on earth was he doing?'

'Grab hold of something, Gabriela. It's uncanny. He was working on parthenogenesis – virgin birth. No doubt he intended the results to be used only on animals: for testing beneficial drugs, or as a method of increasing the yield on farm animals, for example. But the Nazis had different ideas.'

'But that's what my mother does,' Gabriela said, frowning. 'She breeds animals parthenogenically to test her work on degenerative diseases. So do lots of other scientists.'

'I'm sorry, my pet, but I don't think that is the only thing that Erika is working on. I think that her work on diseases is merely a by-product, or perhaps a cover. I'm almost certain that her *actual* interest is parthenogenic reproduction in mammals. It is not merely a means to an end.'

Gabriela shivered.

'But that's another story, and I'll give you my theories on that in a little while. To get back to your grandfather. He worked many years before the unravelling of the genetic code, the discovery of DNA, let alone RNA enzymes – ribozymes. So we have to accept what I could dig up in the archives, which was simply the assertion that he had found a catalyst for parthenogenic reproduction in several species of mammal.'

'What species?'

408

'Cattle, sheep, pigs. Several rodents.' Michael shrugged that off. 'That's not the point. The point is that he was able to apply it to man – well, woman. Somehow he worked out a combination of chemicals which can catalyse the cleavage of RNA molecules in secondary oöcytes. What was even more remarkable was the *way* in which he achieved it. The organism can breed asexually by simply *ingesting* the catalyst.'

'I can't really follow all that.'

'I had to mug it up as well. I'll try to explain it very briefly. The germ cells in the ovary, before the onset of puberty, are called primary oöcytes. They contain four distinct sets of maternal chromosomes which, eventually, split up. The original cells are actually produced in the foetus within the first few months of life, and stay in a state of suspended meiotic reproduction. At puberty one of these cells ripens each month, and its meiotic process is reactivated to produce a viable daughter cell called a secondary oöcyte. This cell is unique, with the full complement of forty-six human chromosomes, made up of the original genes but arranged in a new way. Normally this cell meioses – splits – a second time. However, your grandfather was able to use it as the basis for mammalian parthenogenesis.'

'So how does it happen?'

'He found a way of stimulating the secondary oöcyte into reproduction on its own. Without knowing what he was doing; just doing it.'

'What does that mean, exactly?'

'It means that he had found a way of vivifying the female ovum *before* union with a sperm. This is possible because the oöcyte already has two distinct sets of homologous chromosomes, but they are both maternal. And, as I said, he did this not mechanically, as had been done in laboratory animals up till then, but simply by feeding the organism the right substance.'

'You mean the female simply eats something?'

'Exactly. In other words, he could cut out the need for cumbersome surgical procedures: removing cells from the ovary, stimulating them, then reimplanting them in the womb. That was the accepted method of inducing asexual reproduction in laboratory animals – still is. And, anyway, those may develop in a different way from human beings. But he managed to achieve parthenogenesis without any of that, and in human beings as well as in animals.' The car swerved slightly. 'An awe-inspiring discovery.'

'But how could he possibly have come across such a substance?'

'I don't think he came across it, I think he concocted it. Perhaps he noticed that the women who attended the St Walter festival each year were more likely to become pregnant than the average. Maybe that was the basis for his formula.' Michael concentrated on the traffic now building up. 'I presume there are materials somewhere in that grotto which stimulate the sex cells. There must have been something there in the first place, because the Nazis built an expensive Zahnradbahn to get their women up there. Somehow he must have isolated an additional element, or elements, which produced mammalian parthenogenesis.'

'Some sort of mineral, I suppose.'

'I have absolutely no idea.'

'And my grandfather really discovered a formula to achieve this in human beings?'

'Yes. But I don't think *he* applied it to humans. I think the Nazis did that. The result was that a post-pubertal virgin ingesting it could start a baby without a sperm fertilising the ripened ovum. She would then bear a child which would, naturally, have almost the same DNA as hers. There would be some variations because of the crossover when the secondary oöcytes were formed.'

'I don't know about all that scientific stuff, but the result sounds exactly how Mary claims she had Marina. That certainly is awesome.' She looked ahead, unseeing. 'I still don't understand. Why were the Nazis so concerned?'

'The master race. Don't you see? If they could find the very best examples of Aryan womanhood, they could reproduce them indefinitely. Think what it would have meant: within one generation they could readily produce ten or eleven genetically similar women who, in turn, could be bred to increase the number of such women. More importantly, they thought they could use this method to increase the master race rapidly enough to displace all other races.'

'Of course.' Gabriela suddenly said. 'I understand it now. The final solution could be used to get rid of Jews, Gypsies, homosexuals and then anyone at all who didn't fit their ghastly measurements. And these new Aryans would take their place.'

'Better than that. They didn't even need to eliminate the less obviously undesirable. All they had to do was crowd them out.' He gripped the steering wheel. 'We can only be thankful that genetic engineering as we know it had not been discovered then. They would undoubtedly have used it to eliminate any traits *they* considered undesirable. What a world that would have been. Even Huxley's *Brave New World* would have been better than that.'

She turned slanted eyes to Michael. 'They would have

411

eliminated people who look like me. I don't fit into the Aryan mould.'

He put a hand on her shoulder, squeezed. 'There was a snag to the brilliant plan.'

'A snag?'

'Parthenogenesis can reproduce only females, by definition.'

'Easy enough to collect a few studs and have them impregnate all the "correct" females!'

'That's where he had them, the cunning old devil. That's exactly where he had them on toast.' Michael grinned, jubilant. 'He didn't produce just one formula. The first one induced parthenogenic issue, but that *issue* could only reproduce parthenogenically.' He saw her frown. 'What I mean is, an organism which had been produced parthenogenically could only, itself, replicate in this way. And it could only replicate identically.'

'I'm afraid that doesn't make any sense to me at all, Michael,' Gabriela snapped. 'In spite of my mother's valiant attempts, I seem incapable of coping. Due, no doubt, to my less than adequate intellect. You'll have to translate that into ordinary language for me.'

'It means that once a germ cell begins to reproduce by means of stimulation with such a catalyst, the resulting offspring can only reproduce parthenogenically.'

'Applied to people, Michael.'

'For example, a young girl, a virgin like Mary, could start a baby without sleeping with a man.'

'A virgin conception, yes,' Gabriela broke in, impatient.

'Let me finish, Rilla. The girl herself could go on to have other babies – with, or without, a man. But her parthenogenic *daughter* would only be able to have a

412

child in that way – not in the normal way.' She was still hesitating. 'Applied to the example of Mary, it would mean that Marina would be able to have children only by the self-fertilisation of one of her own ova. All her ova would reject sperm.'

'You mean a child like Marina would be doomed to be infertile?'

'Not infertile, no. She could have a baby the way Mary had her, but only in that way.'

'I think I see.' She turned saucer eyes on him. 'A quite terrible idea.'

'That's only a theory in Marina's case. We still have to look into that. But that was the catalyst your grandfather allowed the Nazis to take over.'

'And they found out, and killed him for that?'

'I am guessing that your grandfather came up with at least two formulae: one like the one I have described, another which produced normal women parthenogenically. And then, I think, he held out on the Nazis. He made sure that the formula they got hold of produced progeny which could *only* reproduce parthenogenically.' Michael chuckled with glee. 'A clever lad, that grandfather of yours. I only wish I could have met him.'

'What would be so wrong with that, from the Nazi point of view?'

'Not what they were after at all. Such a formula would not lead to an increase in Aryan males. On the contrary, it would, after a short time, lead to a race of female clones who would be bound to degenerate quite quickly.'

'Why would that be?'

'Because the same DNA would replicate through the generations. It would get tired, and mutate. Eventually

413

it would succumb to degenerative disease.'

'And we all have unique DNAs, so that doesn't happen.'

'Exactly. Anyway, somehow they must have found out he had another formula, one without this terrible defect, and that he was keeping it from them. I'm pretty sure *that's* why your grandfather was shot.'

'Didn't they test these sorts of discoveries in concentration camps?'

'I'm afraid they did. I take it that's where they tested the formula on humans. But that was hardly Helmut Fluge's fault. What could he do?'

Gabriela stiffened beside him, grabbed his arm.

'You think it was immoral of him?'

'There wasn't time for them to find out about the parthenogenic daughters like that. So how did they know?' she whispered. 'How did they know he was cheating them?'

Michael's head had turned towards her. She grabbed the wheel to steer it. 'We can't afford to get killed, Michael.' There was steel in her voice.

'Erika,' he said, his voice hoarse. 'She was the only one who would have known, apart from him.'

'She must have turned him in,' Gabriela said, the tears running down her cheeks. 'She's ruthless enough to have done a thing like that. When she talked to Mary, she boasted she'd been a member of the Hitler Youth. Weren't they encouraged to put the bloody Fatherland above all else? Betray their parents if necessary?' Her voice lowered, turned hard. 'She told me often enough how she assisted him, was his right hand. I take it she turned her own father in. At the tender age of seventeen.' Her voice rasped and broke.

'How can we know, Liebling? Perhaps they knew

already, from the test animals, just the way he did.'

'How could my darling Oma have produced such a viper? She's an inhuman monster.'

'She was brainwashed, Rilla, like all the other young people,' Michael said softly, his hands now firm on the wheel, heading on the main road towards Kernkirchen. 'An ambitious, academically brilliant girl. She must have seen the convent as suffocating, hated her mother's – and other women's – role in life, resolved to do much better.' He put his right hand on Gabriela's. 'The poor old thing. If it weren't for the horrific consequences I'd feel quite sorry for her.'

'Then you are much more forgiving than I am. I hate her guts.'

'So there's a little bit of her in you after all.' He grinned.

Gabriela's eyes glowed fury.

'Try to calm down, Liebling.' He stroked her hand. 'There's something else I want to tell you about before we get back. Something you need to know. I think I found out about Hugo Lager, too. Again, mostly guess-work.'

She sniffed, blew her nose. 'My father? What about him?'

'There is no record of a marriage between Erika Fluge and Waffen SS Major Hugo Lager on 26 January 1945. Or any other date that year.'

'So she wasn't even married.'

'She was. I turned to the records of the year before. Your mother married on 14 October 1944.'

'She married someone else?' Gabriela stared at her husband. 'Why would she lie about that?'

'She *did* marry Hugo Lager. But that's what I thought: why has she lied all these years?' He smiled at

Gabriela. 'So then I had one of my hunches. I looked at the dates of death.'

'Death?'

'26 January 1945 was the day your mother was widowed. Her husband was on duty in Berlin. Missing, presumed dead.'

Gabriela's eyes blinked. 'I see.' She stared at Michael, saw him eyeing her. 'Is that significant?'

'When is your birthday, Rilla?'

'You know as well as I do, 24 December.'

'From January to December is more than the gestation period, my pet. It proves you are not Hugo Lager's daughter.'

'My God!' Gabriela whispered.

'There's more. As far as I can unearth, a unit of Ivans burst through to the laboratory your mother was working in. I take it they saw a young girl, and raped her.' He put his hand out and patted his wife.

'You think I'm the result of that rape,' Gabriela breathed, white.

'I think you may be.'

She stared out of the car, silent, while Michael drove. 'In a way, you know, I think I already sensed that,' Gabriela said. 'A reference Mary made to the Russians. I realised there was more to it at the time, but I didn't connect.'

She closed her eyes, shuddered. How could she have missed such an obvious clue about her own mother? Russian soldiers had . . . of course they had. Drunk with victory, any woman they came across was raped. So that's what it was. She was the child of a rape, not the son of a proud SS officer. *That* explained her non-Aryan looks.

She should have guessed long ago. It explained so

416

much: her mother's antipathy to men, her instant rapport with Mary. Erika had not been able to come to terms with the alien sperm which had invaded her body. Perhaps leaving her daughter with Oma had been a wise decision. A feeling of deep sadness ran through Gabriela. She sighed.

'Really? Not such a terrible shock, then.'

She knew who she was at last. Her eyelids were not due to a chromosomal defect in her genetic make-up. She was of mixed race – Aryan and Mongoloid. 'That's why I have slant eyes.' Gabriela laughed, a bitter laugh. 'She always said conditions at the time, the terrible privations, led to physical "weaknesses" in me. The bloody witch!' A horrifying thought struck her. Had her mother actually wished her barren, because she could not cope with her obviously mixed parentage?

'Water under the bridge, Liebling.'

That's where the muscular frame, the Asiatic hair, the sallow complexion came from. Gabriela stared out of the car windscreen, overwhelmed by her mother's past, the implications, the lies. She turned her pinched face to Michael.

The Braune Rössl loomed ahead, inviting by the lake. He parked the car, helped his wife out and ordered Schnapps. 'Let's have some lunch.'

'I couldn't eat,' she wailed. 'How can I ever see that woman again without wringing her neck?'

'Try to think what she must have gone through.'

'How did she get away?'

'Who knows? The spectacle as she crawled out of the bunker must have been horrific. It is amazing how the spirit to survive takes over. I take it she crawled her way towards the west and, somehow, back to Austria. I would imagine that the idea of pregnancy did not even occur to her.'

'And by the time she got here, it was too late for an abortion.'

'True, but even if it hadn't been, where could she have gone for that? It was only legal in Berlin at the time, by special dispensation from the Bishop. Certainly not in Catholic Austria. She had to go through with it.'

'And then I was born. That must have been quite a shock.' She put her hand on Michael's. 'Resi once told me something, you know. She said when my mother first saw me she'd called me a Mongol baby. *Resi* thought she meant a Down's syndrome child. But my mother was right, a Mongol baby is exactly what I was – am.'

'A Tartar, mein Schatz. A beautiful, enchanting, loving Tartar baby.' He looked quizzically at his wife. 'What, exactly, is your mother doing at the moment, Rilla?'

'She's completely wrapped up in that lab. We only occasionally see her; she just asks for food to be sent in. Every now and again she surfaces to ask Mary to input data into the computer.'

'I think I can guess what she is working on.'

'And that is?'

'She has always said she is carrying on her father's work, and I think that is quite right. She has been trying to re-create the formula he refused to give the Nazis, the one that got destroyed.'

'And you think she has?' She frowned. 'There's nothing really wrong with that, is there?'

'There wouldn't be if she had applied her research only to animals. But I don't think she did. I think she found similar formulae years ago, and decided to test

418

them out on human beings. What I think your mother
has been doing is using the shrine, and the festival, as a
means of testing her secret experiments on human
beings.'

Gabriela gasped. 'You mean the brides?'

'Yes.'

'Deliberately?' Gabriela whispered, her eyes unfocused. 'She managed to get the stuff into them without
their knowledge or consent?'

'I think so. It is a perfect cover. Only the brides, or
other married women, are allowed to go. And only they
are allowed to drink the water.'

'But there's nothing *in* the water.'

'Or whatever. We have to assume the catalyst is in
some other practice connected with the shrine. We'll
find out what, don't worry!'

Gabriela began to cry, softly at first, then uncontrol-
lably. 'Those innocent girls. How could she do that?'

'Take it easy, Liebling. We can't change the past but
we'll sort it out, stop it ever happening again. The clever
part was, no one would suspect anything, since brides
get pregnant in the normal way of things. Just think. A
religious festival which was meant to work fertility
miracles for the faithful. And *only* the brides and other
married women were allowed to drink the blessed
water, or whatever, on pain of excommunication. It was
brilliant, and she used it to the full, refining as she went.
So she was able to formulate her catalysts, and test them
out, year after year. And then it all went wrong.
Somehow Mary and Lisl ingested the formula, and it
worked on them. With devastating results.'

Gabriela began to cry again.

'You have to be strong, Rilla. We have to stop it, but
we need to find out all we can first. We are almost

certainly dealing with a mad woman, but a brilliant, completely ruthless one.'

'But *how* is she doing it?'

'I don't know yet, but we'll get there. Anyway, there was at least one glitch – with devastating results – in 1955, the year your grandmother died and the year of the so-called infection which could never be traced. I think that was caused by one of her formulae.'

'My God, Michael! You think it was because of *her* I became infertile? My own mother caused it?'

'I don't know how it could have affected you, you didn't take part in the festival –'

'Do you know, she actually told me how that happened. She said it was my own fault I got it,' Gabriela gulped.

'*Your* fault?'

'Because I mixed the animal feed with my bare hands, without wearing rubber gloves. She always said I shouldn't. And I had a rather deep cut on one of my fingers that year. Do you think that's what it was? Her formula somehow got into my bloodstream? That's why it was so bad for me, much worse than for Friedl?'

'So then . . .'

'Reverend Mother said there was nothing wrong with Oma.' Gabriela suddenly exclaimed. 'She said when she went up to the grotto she was perfectly fit, and that my mother was up there already. Oma must have worked out what was happening, Michael, what Mutter was doing, and how she was doing it. I think she killed Oma! My God, Michael, I think she murdered her own mother . . .' She stopped, staring ahead of her. 'I always sensed there was something wrong, always knew those quarrels I overheard meant something significant. And then Reverend Mother told me about my mother being up there *before* Oma, and I thought she was too old and had muddled it all up. But she was right.'

'It's worse than I thought.' He shuddered. 'It's grotesque, horrific. That would mean she is a murderess as well. We have to sort it out, and do it fast. God knows what other damage she has done.'

33

'Isn't that young Helden standing over there?'

Michael and Gabriela were still not quite ready to brave Erika. They remained sitting on the terrace by the lake, watching the boats drifting in afternoon sunshine. Joseph was on the jetty, leaning against a rail.

'So it is. I didn't realise he'd be around. I thought he was based in Salzburg.'

'He helps his parents out during the summer, and he has commitments at the summer school. This year his parents need him more than ever. Friedl is devasted by Lisl's death. She's in a deep depression.'

'Your letter did say there'd been an accident. So much has been going on it slipped my mind. Let's call him over,' Michael said, standing up. 'Hello there, Joseph.' He waved, then beckoned towards their table. 'In any case, I owe him a run-down on the water analyses. He did a good job, getting hold of the sample.'

'Küss die Hand, Gnä' Frau,' Joseph said, coming up and kissing Gabriela's hand. He clicked his heels at Michael.

'I am so sorry about your sister, Joseph. What a terrible tragedy. And the little one, too. How did it happen?'

'We had so much to talk about,' Gabriela mumbled

apologetically. 'The trip to Berlin brought up so many things.'

'I do understand. I know you were on Lisl's side.' The young face had matured five years in the last two weeks. He turned to Michael. 'Lisl and Johanna were killed while riding my mother's old bike. The baby was strapped in the pannier at the back. According to the police, Lisl must have lost her balance and toppled over the mountainside.'

'My deepest sympathies.' Michael's voice was low.

'Thank you.' Bleak eyes darkened, the mouth set into determination.

'I am sorry I couldn't be here for the requiem mass.' Michael beckoned to the waiter. 'So, let's drown our sorrows. What will you have?'

'A Spritzer would be very agreeable.' Joseph looked at Michael intently. 'Have you had the water analysis results?'

'Very disappointing. So far we've found nothing out of the ordinary, nothing at all. The lab tried a whole series of tests. There is a large content of minerals in the water – hardly unexpected in a mountain spring. But nothing untoward: no unexplained microorganisms, no bacteria, no known viruses, nothing unusual that even the most advanced modern technology could determine.'

Joseph's eyes, so eager to start with, gradually lost their lustre. 'Once Frau Adler had pointed it out to me, told me that both girls had drunk the water, I could see it had to be that, Herr Adler. There is no alternative.'

Michael's head jerked upwards. 'I've just told you, Joseph. There was nothing in that water.'

'Could the phial have affected it, Herr Adler? Should we try again with a glass container?'

423

'No. It's nothing like that.'

Gabriela suddenly stood up. 'I think I've got an idea.' she cried.

Joseph pulled her back. 'Please, Frau Adler, let's keep it to ourselves . . .'

She sat down, her eyes excited, her voice lowered and coming out in gasps. 'I took some holy water from the chapel in a phial, just like the one we used for the sample, as a present for Mary. Months before she came here. She gave some to her rabbit, because it was unwell, and – the rabbit had a parthenogenic litter.'

'Rabbit, Rilla? What on earth have rabbits to do with –'

'You don't understand. The phial, Michael. The phial was from my mother's laboratory. She was ill at the time, and Resi got in there and mixed the used and unused phials up. There could have been chemical residue in that phial. There must have been. *That*'s why Bridget got pregnant.'

At first both men simply stared at her. 'That's it.' Joseph suddenly hissed. 'That's absolutely brilliant. It *is* the water – the *trough* water.'

'But that water's been tested, and . . .'

'But my point, Herr Adler . . .' He was about to speak again when a young man passed them. 'Servus, Joseph.'

'Servus, Fritz.' He turned his head in all directions, nodded and smiled at several people nearby, raised his arm in jovial greeting. His eyes returned to Gabriela.

'Perhaps Frau Adler would enjoy a ride around the lake? The *Grosse Austria* is about to dock.'

'A boat ride? Well, of course not, Joseph,' she began, then saw the signal in his eyes, felt Michael's shoe touching hers. 'An excellent idea.'

'If we walk briskly we can catch her,' Joseph said, leading the way at a lively pace. He did not slow down until they were standing on the landing stage. Streams of tourists, cameras swinging round their necks, were trooping off the little steamboat. 'It's warm enough to sit outside. I'll grab some seats in the stern – on the lower deck,' he called, sprinting towards the gangplank.

He skirted little knots of people waiting to board, put on the determined air of a member of staff, nodded a greeting at the man just starting to check tickets. Charming, apologetic, he flashed a message with his eyes and wriggled through. The Adlers waited decorously for their turn to board and joined him.

'Our voices will carry back in the wind,' he greeted them, smiling engagingly. Michael and Gabriela settled on either side of him. 'The engines will start in a moment. Can I get you a drink?'

'Let's not waste time,' Michael said. 'We have to get back to Erika's as soon as this trip is over. She'll kill us for keeping the car.'

'Something Lisl drivelled on about,' Joseph began, a break in his voice as he spoke his sister's name. 'Last July. I ran into her, just after she'd been to the grotto. She was giggling, on a high, waving a phial about.'

'A phial? She was carrying a phial?'

'Exactly. Just like the one you gave me to put the sample in.' He swallowed, then went on, his voice low. 'She wasn't quite herself, terribly hyper. I asked if she'd gone to fetch a water sample for testing, and was she going to the Frau Professor's? But she said no, that didn't happen till just before the festival. Well, I didn't take much notice, but she suddenly started babbling, saying she had a secret, something very special.'

A tear came into the corner of Joseph's eye. He

wiped it away with his handkerchief. 'I wasn't that keen to listen, but she burbled on, said how she always did it for the Frau Professor, and only she and Helga and the Frau Professor knew about it. No one else at all.'

'Yes?' Michael prompted gently. 'What secret?'

Joseph planted his legs wide, his elbows on his knees, his head held in his hands, and breathed hard.

'Well?'

'The Frau Professor had given her a phial full of purifiers to add to the water in the troughs. Exactly the same amount in each.'

'Really? What for?'

'To make sure there would be no recurrence of the terrible virus which struck in 1955, she said.'

'Purifiers, eh?'

'Yes. We all know that the grotto water has been tested every year since then. What Lisl told me, what none of us knew, was that the Frau Professor had always added purifying chemicals to it. Stirred them into the troughs before the festival. Just to be safe, she told Lisl.'

'She always did that? By herself?'

'Until her arthritis caught up with her and she could not do the climb. So first Helga, then Lisl, did it for her. She swore them to secrecy. She said if anyone knew purifiers were added to the water, their faith in the festival would be destroyed.' His shoulders shook. 'And then she said . . .'

Michael put his arms around Joseph's shoulders.

'. . . that the Frau Professor never gave away secrets, and Helga was dead and couldn't.' He shook Michael's hand away. 'And then she realised what she'd told me, asked me to swear not to tell a soul. I promised. I never even remembered until Frau Adler mentioned the phial and the rabbit.'

'Purifiers,' Michael said. He looked at Gabriela. The tears were streaming down her eyes.

'So that's how she did it.' Gabriela sniffed, then blew her nose.

'Maybe. But I've just told you both. The tests are all negative . . .'

'With respect,' the young man said, 'let me finish. I see you understand exactly what I suspect. No doubt the lab was looking for pathogens . . .'

'No, Joseph, I already had my suspicions. The tests looked for pathogens *and* other components on a microscopic level. The lab was extremely thorough.'

There was a silence. The boat rocked on, slicing the lake.

'You know, I think I have the answer,' Joseph said at last. 'I think I know why they didn't come up with anything. There *wasn't* anyone to add the stuff this year. Lisl was virtually locked up, and now she's dead.'

Dead. Michael and Gabriela looked towards each other, locked eyes, then looked away.

'And the Frau Professor asked me about starting up the Zahnradbahn. I wondered what that was about. Perhaps she was planning to add the stuff herself. Anyway, Lisl went up last July. *That's* when she drank the water, and had her vision. After she had added the chemicals.'

'Exactly. Johanna was born in March,' Gabriela said.

'How do you know?' Michael wanted to know. 'Just because she said she'd put purifiers in the water?'

'It wasn't only that. She was on this odd high,' Joseph explained. 'She never takes drugs, never drinks alcohol – never drank.' He stared into his hands. 'We joined a crowd of young people, went on to the Braune Rössl, danced, the usual thing. All quite innocent. I noticed

427

she stuck to Coke.' He put his head into his hands. 'Then she went out to get some air. I didn't see that Kurt Miller followed her. He's always been after her since Helga died. You know the rest.'

'I'm completely confused, Joseph. Why are you so sure that Lisl being on a high ties in with drinking spiked water?'

'Because it's the way Mary was as well.'

'Mary?' Michael's voice was raised again, but he lowered it. 'But I thought you just said Lisl . . .'

'When I went up to rescue Mary in October, she was coming out of a faint. I didn't really take much notice at the time, but now I realise it wasn't an ordinary one. She was like Lisl, as though she were on a high. I think she drank some of the water remaining in the second trough. That was only a short time after the festival. The chemicals would still have been in that water.' Joseph looked at Michael. 'The autumn storms had been quite fierce. Rain pouring through had silted up the pipe leading to the second trough, so it still contained whatever water was left after the festival. It hadn't been significantly diluted or disturbed.' He looked from one Adler to the other. 'You understand now? Mary drank what the brides drank, what my poor Lisl drank.'

'I still don't quite see . . .'

'My little sister was very religious, very devout. She meant no harm. I am sure she swallowed only a few drops of the water – she thought of it as holy water. More potent then, because she'd just added the chemicals. That's why she had a vision.' He did not even try to stop the tears now cascading down his cheeks. 'She got more than she bargained for. She got pregnant before Mary because she drank the water earlier. She got sicker because it was more potent. That theory explains it all.'

'And when the brides fall pregnant no one is surprised,' Michael said softly. 'And they're the only ones allowed to drink the water. And they drink it soon after the "purifiers" have been added. So that's how it was done. How very clever; diabolical almost.'

'I don't get pregnant,' Gabriela pointed out. 'Not everyone does, you know.'

'But you slipped the last time you drank the water, Frau Adler. Maybe you felt a little nauseous?'

'Only because of the heat,' she began, then stopped. 'It was a curious feeling, yes. And Magda said about the taste . . .'

'Erika always told you why it couldn't work for you, Rilla. She told you the truth. You have no oöcytes, primary or secondary.' He put his hand behind Joseph's back and patted his wife.

'Anyway,' Joseph sighed. 'There's worse to come.' His voice was so low that Michael had to bend down to catch the words. 'Lisl was pregnant again, you know.' The young man swallowed back more tears and turned to Gabriela. 'Mary told you that, didn't she?'

'Friedl told me; she said I'd find out soon in any case. She looked distraught about it. I thought she was worried about Lisl's health.'

'So soon?' Michael said, bewildered. 'That may be odd, but it was hardly the same thing. Kurt was in evidence by then.'

'He never went near her,' Joseph said slowly, carefully. 'Sexually, I mean.'

'How can you possibly know that?'

'Said the baby put him off his stride. So all he did was beat Lisl up.'

'You talked to him about it?'

'He broadcast it to the whole house, to the whole village. Said mothers were impossible as lovers. Made no secret about it. And Lisl, too. Lisl insisted it was true.'

'But how did she get up to the grotto again? I thought your parents wouldn't let her leave the house. Anyway, you've said it yourself – there's nothing in the water this year.'

'The reason it happened again,' Joseph said, lifting his head, looking from Michael to Gabriela and back, 'was the holy water in her room.'

'She had some there?'

'She told me she'd filled a little bottle with holy water. It was standing in front of a statue of the Virgin, with a bowl of flowers and an everlasting candle. Perhaps she wanted to pray for another vision, you see. Before Johanna, I mean. And afterwards,' he gulped, 'afterwards she prayed to the Virgin to deliver her. I think she may have drunk some of that water as well.' Joseph put his head in his hands again. 'And in a way that's exactly what happened. She has been freed: from Kurt, from my parents, from life . . .'

Michael put his hand on Joseph's shoulder. 'Courage, Joseph. We'll see to it that whoever did this to your sister gets their desserts.' He paused a moment. 'Let me get this straight. Each year, before the festival, Lisl or someone else would go up and add something to the water in the trough –'

'Troughs.'

'– the troughs to make sure there were no bacteria there. We tested for that. The number of coliform bacteria did not exceed the standards set for that particular type of water, and we did many additional

430

tests to isolate and culture suspected compounds not normally found in water.'

'That is what I keep trying to tell you, Herr Adler. You were testing pure mountain water. It hadn't had any chemicals added to it. All you are saying is that it didn't need purifying in the first place.'

'I know. What I'm getting at is that we can't prove any of this.'

'All we have to do is get hold of the holy water Lisl had in her room,' Gabriela said eagerly. 'I'm sure Friedl has left it . . .'

First Joseph smiled, then the eyes grew dark, stared at her. 'I'm sorry, Frau Adler. My mother has thrown it out. She was so angry, you see, so distressed. She could not bear anything to remind her of Lisl, and she blamed the Virgin Mary.'

'You're sure? She actually threw holy water away? It doesn't sound like her at all.' Gabriela looked upset. 'She's so devout.'

'Not any more. She smashed the statue, said she can't believe in a God who did this to her child and grandchild. Then she poured the water down the lavatory.'

'So what are we going to do?' Gabriela asked. 'How are we going to prove anything?'

Suddenly Joseph stiffened. 'Helga,' he said. 'My sister Helga. She was the Frau Professor's assistant before Lisl. I remember now. She had a bottle of the stuff in her room. She secreted it in a perfume bottle on her dressing-table. My mother keeps that room exactly as it always was. I think we are in luck at last. I think some of that water may still be there.'

34

'Helga,' Gabriela said hollowly as she and Michael got back into the Audi. 'Poor little Helga. Friedl always said she'd locked herself in her room, and refused to come out, and wouldn't eat. Maybe she knew. And finally Albert coaxed her out with the horse, and when she rode him she fell off.'

'Because she'd drunk the water with the chemicals added?'

'Not necessarily. Who knows? Perhaps she tried to tell her mother and she refused to listen. We can't exactly ask Friedl now.' She sighed, then grabbed her husband's arm. 'Oh, Michael. When Helga was concussed, they called my mother. She came at once. I always remember how pathetically grateful Friedl was. And then she said she'd make sure Helga was not in any pain, that she'd inject an analgesic.'

'An analgesic for a concussed patient?' The Audi's gears complained at the rough handling. 'But that's absurd.'

'The wrong thing to do, medically?'

'Crazy! That confuses the issue when the patient comes round. You can't tell whether their reaction is due to concussion, or to the drug.'

'You mean she killed Helga,' Gabriela said, her voice

almost matter-of-fact. 'An innocent young girl.'

'Bit of an assumption, Rilla . . .'

'She injected her with something,' Gabriela said dully. 'No one could understand why Helga died.'

'Was there a post mortem?'

'There had to be. But there was nothing . . . and . . .'

'And Lisl's dead as well.'

'Yes,' Gabriela said. 'But my mother can't have killed her. She wasn't anywhere near Lisl; she couldn't have been. She was in the lab, I know she was. We were in the house with her, there was no way she could have gone out without our hearing the car, and she can't walk that far . . .'

'Lisl knew the incriminating secret,' Michael said. 'A potent reason for getting her out of the way.'

Gabriela opened the car window, leaned out, breathed hard. Michael slowed down, but she shook her head. 'Forget it, Michael. Just reaction. Had to have some cold air.' She leaned back in the seat. 'I've thought of something else.'

He kept his eye on the road, negotiating a hairpin bend. 'What?'

'The second generation.'

'The what?'

'She said she had got to the second generation, Michael. She was madly excited by it.'

'What second generation? What are you talking about?'

'Johanna, Michael. I wrote you I thought all Friedl's daughters were parthenogenic, that's why they're so alike. If I'm right, *Johanna* is the first of the second generation of human parthenogenesis. That we know of, anyway. *That's* why my mother is so excited. That's

433

why she wanted Lisl and Johanna to come and live with her.'

'So Johanna's DNA would have fingerprinted as identical to Lisl's,' he said, thinking aloud. 'Not just derived from it and without paternal input. That's why she did those blood tests on Johanna. Remember, when Kurt Miller brought her over?'

'I remember. And when Mary and I got back from Friedl's that time, the day Lisl had her accident, he was there, trying to get the results.'

'I suppose it all fits,' he said slowly. 'I take it she's working on data she obtained from testing Johanna's blood. That's why she's even more absorbed than usual. That's also why a woman who doesn't like children invited two young girls with babies to live with her: so she could observe them at first hand. Did she really think she'd get away with it? She must be mad; stark, staring mad!'

'But if all that is right, she wouldn't want Lisl dead. So who killed her?'

'Maybe it was a genuine accident. She was already pregnant again . . .' Michael lurched the car wildly round the next bend. 'My God, Rilla! That poor girl.'

'We've got to get back to Mary,' Gabriela cried. 'Drive faster.'

'No need to panic. I don't think your mother is dangerous to Mary. She needs her; she wants her and Marina, to observe them on the spot. And she is too preoccupied with writing up what she has gleaned from Johanna to think about anything else.' He looked grave. 'Just consider it from Erika's point of view. Presumably Marina is quite different from Johanna. Marina is the result of a new concoction imbibed by an ordinary woman. Johanna could have been Lisl's clone; depends

434

which formula Erika was able to reconstruct. Either way, she now has experimental material right on her doorstep. I don't think for a moment that she will try to kill Mary or Marina.'

'As long as Mary doesn't let on she knows.'

'She's not a fool.'

'She's a young girl.'

'Motherhood is bound to make her cautious, Liebling. You warned her, didn't you?'

'Of course.'

'So relax. What we need now is proof. All we have so far is conjecture.'

'And how are we going to get that? Apart from the water in Helga's room, and that's already nearly three years old.'

'There will be some evidence of what Erika has been working on, in her files or in her published work. The water is a long shot, but it might work. Our best bet would be to find some records of what has happened as a result of that festival throughout all these years,' Michael said as he and Gabriela drove past the drive leading to Erika's house.

'Where are you going, Michael? We've got to get back!'

'To the Convent of the Immaculate Conception. They must have some records we could persuade them to let us have.'

'I wouldn't feel comfortable, Michael. Let's go back now . . . please?'

'But . . .'

'Anyway, there's no need. Mother Theresia gave me my grandmother's records, as a memento,' Gabriela said, putting her hand on Michael's.

'From after the war until she died?'

435

'Exactly. And I did glance at them. There was nothing particularly remarkable. Statistically speaking – and I know all those figures about fertility only too well – the incidence of births was just a little above average.'

'Those records might give us an idea of what we need,' Michael agreed, 'and they would be better than nothing. But what we really want is the records from 1956 to 1993. Properly analysed, they must reveal everything. Did any of the nuns keep them?'

'Mother Theresia said she did.'

'Let's ask her now.'

'But she won't . . .'

'I'll talk to her, Gabriela. I will tell her that I have reason to believe someone is abusing the shrine, tampering with a holy place. We have to tell her, we have to let her know that this may have been happening for years. She will understand at once that I am serious.'

'I've got to get back to Mary first, Michael. Whatever you say, it is too dangerous to leave her without warning her about Mutter and what is going on. You go back later, and see Mother Theresia on your own.'

'Resi says she saw you boarding the *Grosse Austria*,' Erika greeted them. 'Is that true? You spent an hour gallivanting around the lake on a pleasure boat instead of bringing back my car? I needed it to get to Salzburg. I have some extremely important results I wanted the lab to process for me right away. I don't have time to waste.'

'I haven't seen my little Rilla for ages,' Michael said easily, opening his suitcase and taking out a parcel. 'We're here now, Schwiegermutter. I can't see any evidence of disaster.' He flourished the parcel at her.

'Look what I've brought you from your favourite city.'

'You are not a stupid man, Michael. You know exactly what I mean.'

'I will take your results . . .'

'You don't suppose I sit around waiting for other people, Michael. I sent for Kurt Miller. He has taken them for me.'

'In that case I will give you the presents I brought for you.' Michael smiled at her. He handed her two lithographs of Berlin, one of the Brandenburg Gate before the war, the other of the Kupferhalle concept by Albert Speer.

She took them, her fingers curling around the frames. 'Presents for me? Well, that's new.' She stared at him, her eyes slit, then turned her attention to the pictures. 'Not bad. Quite good, in fact. I always thought Speer's plans for rebuilding Berlin were wonderful. How on earth did you get hold of them?'

'Amazing what you can find when you search for it.'

Her eyes still held suspicion, annoyance. 'What were you doing there, anyway?'

'Part of that Israeli story I was on a few weeks ago,' he lied easily. 'Checking out a Jewish woman who managed to survive. Well, half-Jewish, actually. They weren't always rounded up.'

'They were in Berlin.' Erika's eyes flashed, then hooded. 'I think you must have got your facts wrong. Could have happened in Essen, or Bonn, or even Hamburg. Not in Berlin. It was, after all, the Reich-shauptstadt. We couldn't – they couldn't possibly have tolerated that.'

'Perhaps you can help me flesh things out a little,' Michael purred at her. 'You were actually there part of the time.'

She turned her back on him. 'Well, don't just stand there. Come in, come in. Let's have a drink on the terrace. Where's Mary got to?'

'She's feeding Marina. Anyway, she isn't your maid, Mutter.'

'Maid?' She rounded on Gabriela. 'What are you talking about? Her legs are younger than mine, and she hasn't got arthritis. She can get us a drink without everyone making a song and dance about it.'

'Allow me,' Michael said affably. 'Schnapps? What about you, Rilla? A glass of Gumpoldskirchner?'

'You're looking very pleased with yourself.' Erika had walked out on to the terrace and tried to move a small, heavy metal table over. Michael put down the drinks and helped her, adjusting a sunshade. 'You've just completed a story successfully, I take it. Is there really still this interest in what happened during the war?'

'Very illuminating, actually. One thing about the Germans is their incredible thoroughness, their neatness. You would hardly credit it, but the most amazing evidence has been archived.' He smiled. 'I came across someone who had survived the period after the war by collecting old documents. With so many of the public buildings burned and bombed, very little was left intact. She was only a child at the time, but she made a living by piecing bits of paper together for the occupying forces.'

'That's where one hears such nonsense. The Germans are not keeping anything back. The Nazi party was not Germany.'

'Did you come across evidence of the final solution? See any attacks on Jews?'

'Me?' Erika looked puzzled. 'I wasn't there till the

summer of 1943. That was years after the Kristall-nacht started the pogrom against German Jews, you know.' She paused as she thought back. 'I was working in the laboratory all the time, going between my lodgings and the bunker. Mostly during the blackout. It was a dreadfully cold winter, and there was no heat and very little to eat. In the end I slept in the laboratory. At least it was reasonably warm.'

'They gave you a bed?'

'I settled for the floor. You can't have any idea what conditions were like. Wave after wave of bombers, shelling from the Russians. There was nothing I could do except bury myself in work.'

'You spent all your time there? And your father as well?'

'What's this interest, all of a sudden?'

'Just the way I am, Erika. It's what I do.'

'Hmm. Well, all I know is that the reports about the Holocaust are wildly exaggerated. All that business of the extermination camps was so unnecessary. There were much better ways of raising the level of racial purity.'

Gabriela had half-risen from her chair and was evidently about to expostulate, when a look in Michael's eye deterred her.

'Indeed. What, in particular, do you have in mind?'

'My father, you know, was a geneticist.'

'You have mentioned it.'

'A great geneticist. One of his achievements was the non-surgical abortion of foetuses. Useful if they were affected by the rubella virus, for example. As you know, that can cause severe dysfunction, and lead to blindness.'

Michael turned away as his eyes grew sharp. 'Non-surgical abortion?' he said, only a slight tremor betraying his interest.

'He worked out a formula which a pregnant woman could take in her first three months. A hormonal mixture. It had the effect of loosening the embedded foetus and shedding it. No harm done to the mother, or any risk of infection.' She sighed. 'It was one of the formulae which were destroyed.'

'Was that his only invention?'

'He also worked out a formula for stimulating the ripening of ovarian cells,' Erika said. 'But that has been worked on by others now.'

'No wonder the Nazis wanted him to work for them.'

'At least they understood the value of what he was doing. Tragic about the Russians. Those Ivans were the most stupid, the most idiotic oafs you can imagine. Men on the rampage, with only two basic instincts. To fill their bellies and to discharge their penises.'

'Was he working on anything specially significant to the Reich?'

'Increasing the vigour of Aryan stock, getting rid of genetic imperfections. We didn't know what we know today. At that time we confined ourselves to diseases.'

'And if you isolate a potentially defective foetus . . .'

'Then you can abort it.'

'You'd also abort its soul, its brain. No Steven Hawking, for example.'

'That's just sentimental rubbish. A Hawking would turn up eventually. In my opinion we'd have many more. We could select for the highest intelligence once we have isolated the genes for it. It is remarkable how, unless there is selective breeding, animal stock, including humans, reverts to the average. Mendel's laws.'

'But inbreeding is notoriously–'

'That's the whole point. A small gene-pool is always at danger because recessive characteristics can emerge unchecked. My father was brilliant. He found a way to isolate those all too few outstanding individuals without damaging the gene-pool.'

The silence was intense. She looked at them, and frowned. 'You don't believe me?'

'Of course we believe what you say, Erika. He'd worked that out, had he?'

'Precisely.'

'And he was about to let the Nazis have the results?'

'So that's what you're getting at.' She laughed. 'He knew the city was about to fall,' she said, eyes shining. 'His results were quite safe from the Nazis. We both knew that.'

'And now you've rediscovered what he had just perfected,' Michael announced. 'That's what you were going to present to the conference in Toronto, isn't it?'

'Quite right,' Erika said. 'I have now. I hadn't quite got there in June. I have reached the first stage. We have the means to propagate the type of animal breeds we need. Farming will be transformed. My formula is of immense importance.' She lifted her glass. 'You do not seem impressed. I'm going to drink to it. Then you'll have to excuse me; I still have a great deal to do.'

'You do that,' Michael said amiably. 'I need a walk after sitting in an aeroplane all day. I'll see you all later.'

35

Mary was in the nursery giving Marina her two o'clock feed. Erika had refused to join her and Gabriela for lunch and had disappeared into the lab. Gabriela walked into the nursery, a sheaf of yellowing papers in her hand.

'It's really hard to believe, Aunt Rilla. She's such a brilliant scientist, and she does try to do good. She's always talking about the importance of her work to the human race. Why would she experiment on innocent women like that?' Mary was crying, the bottle shaking in Marina's mouth.

'Shall I do the feed?'

'I'll manage,' Mary sniffed. 'I have to grow up. What did the tests show, Aunt Rilla?'

Gabriela came to sit by Mary. 'I'm sorry, my dear. I know you've grown fond of her. I told you already. There's nothing in the water we sent to Berlin. But we're pretty sure chemicals were added . . .'

'So you can't prove it; you're just guessing. I just can't believe she would do a thing like that. And for so many years . . .'

'Keep your voice down. You know there's something. Marina is here, and the DNA results are conclusive proof . . .'

'But the Frau Professor,' Mary whispered. 'How can you say something like that about your own mother, Aunt Rilla?'

'Believe me, Mary, it's the last thing I would want to prove. What can I do? Michael did ferret out some damning circumstantial evidence in Berlin. So now we have to substantiate it.'

Mary had calmed down a little, holding the baby against her shoulder, patting her back. 'And how are you going to do that?'

'Reverend Mother gave me Oma's records, as a souvenir. She had no idea what has been going on, that they might be used as evidence. But I think they might give us a few clues. I've written them up as tables, and you could help me to look them over. You know I'm liable to get the figures muddled up.'

'Where's Uncle Michael?'

'He's gone to see if he can persuade Reverend Mother to let him have her records since 1956. Gives us a chance to see what we can make of these. They're relatively simple, easy for us to collate. Maybe we can give the analysts something to look for.'

'I'm almost through with the baby. I'll just put her down.'

Mary deposited Marina in her cot and followed Gabriela to the small study beyond the living room. She spread the papers out on the table.

'I've looked through them. There doesn't seem to be anything at all out of the ordinary, but Michael insisted that the records must hold some clues. We have to try to figure it out.'

The data ran from the year 1945 to 1955, when Heidi Fluge had died. The rows of names and figures seemed innocuous. Lists, fortunately not too long, of the women who had attended the festival, and the children born to them within the following year. Because the numbers were relatively small and the brides were all local girls, Heidi's records were complete. The girls had been very keen to supply the data, to keep in touch. They had a reputation to keep up. The high fertility rate among the St Walter girls made them very desirable. Men came from far and wide to try to win brides from the area.

There were long tables of names on the yellowing sheets. Beautifully inscribed birth announcements were bundled together with them. Gabriela had listed only girls married less than a full year, the children born to them within that year, and the gender of the children.

Register: 1945–1955
THE MOTHERING OF THE BRIDES

1945:	30 brides	27 births:	15 boys and 12 girls
1946:	35 brides	31 births:	16 boys and 15 girls
1947:	38 brides	35 births:	19 boys and 16 girls
1948:	41 brides	38 births:	19 boys and 19 girls
1949:	43 brides	41 births:	21 boys and 20 girls
1950:	48 brides	46 births:	23 boys and 23 girls
1951:	49 brides	48 births:	23 boys and 25 girls
1952:	51 brides	50 births:	24 boys and 26 girls
1953:	64 brides	63 births:	31 boys and 32 girls
1954:	87 brides	87 births:	43 boys and 44 girls
1955:	103 brides	103 births:	51 boys and 52 girls

By 1955, when Gabriela's grandmother had died, the number of brides coming to the festival had increased to well over three times the number in

1945. Recorded births had equalled the number of brides for both the last two years. No wonder news of the festival had spread, no wonder the whole thing had taken off.

'Anything odd about the numbers, Aunt Rilla?'

'Not really. They escalate quite quickly. In the last two years every bride had a child.'

'Does it say that?'

'It says 103 births for 103 brides. A one-to-one correspondence.'

'Some of them might have had twins,' Mary pointed out. 'Do the records show which woman had what?'

Gabriela smiled happily. 'As a matter of fact, they do. There were two multiple births, but it doesn't really come out on my list. I can see you would make an excellent scientist, if that's what you want to be.'

'Even without that, there *is* something strange here, Aunt Rilla. Something very strange.'

'Really? Apart from the incredibly high conception rate, it all looks perfectly normal.'

'If you don't mind, I'm just going to go over the figures again.'

'You think I can't add?'

'Nothing like that, though I'll check all the figures on my calculator just to make sure. What bothers me is the ratio between boys and girls.'

'They're never identical, Mary. It is just chance.'

'More boys are born than girls, Aunt Rilla. Males are less stable than females, so some die in their early years. Nature ensures equal numbers by arranging for more males to be born.'

'Are you sure? It always seems to me there are more women around than men.'

'Only in some countries, and in certain age groups.

The balance of the sexes in the developed world is blurred because women live longer than men. But at birth the difference is significantly weighted towards boys.'

'Well, there you are, then,' Gabriela said happily. 'That's exactly borne out . . .'

'Not in the later years. The proportions there are wrong.'

'Not meaningfully, Mary. The sample is too small statistically.'

Mary stood above the table, looking at the old sheets of paper, at Gabriela's list. 'The actual dates of birth are there, aren't they, Aunt Rilla? We could pull those out?'

'Of the mothers, you mean?'

'The month the babies were born in. Those are the relevant details.'

'They are? More girls are born at a certain time of year?'

'Not that I know of. But the babies born *before* late April of the following year were unlikely to have been conceived at the festival. Most of the conceptions would result in births in the following June or July. So what we need to do is break the births down into those occurring before and after June of the following year.'

'You are getting a clever little thing!'

'The Frau Professor herself taught me,' Mary said, her voice on edge. She peered at the figures, began to scribble, check additions with her calculator. 'And I can see that these results are rather scary.'

'Scary?'

She showed Gabriela the list she had just made, sorting the figures into neat columns, underlining the

446

last one. 'Look, Aunt Rilla. I've broken the register down into births after June.'

Register: 1945–1955
THE MOTHERING OF THE BRIDES

Date	Brides	Births	Total boys	Total girls	Late boys	Late girls
1945	30	27	15	12	12	11
1946	35	31	17	14	13	12
1947	38	35	19	16	15	13
1948	41	38	19	19	14	14
1949	43	41	21	20	16	17
1950	48	46	23	23	17	19
1951	49	48	23	25	17	19
1952	51	50	24	26	19	20
1953	64	63	31	32	24	25
1954	87	87	43	44	35	37
1955	103	103	51	52	41	46

'You can see what's happening,' Mary said, pointing her finger at the rows. 'The girls have begun to outnumber the boys from 1949 onwards. After that the increase is noticeable, and constant. It *has* to be significant.'

Gabriela stared at the columns. 'That is extraordinary.'

'Do you think Reverend Mother ever spotted that?'

'Not for a moment. I don't think anyone has ever collated those figures, you know. I think they just assumed that what counted was the number of births, not the gender of the children. After all, why should they?'

Mary began to chew her pencil. 'You know what it

447

reminds me of, Aunt Rilla?'

'Reminds you? Are you trying to tell me this has been happening somewhere else? How could these figures remind you of anything?'

'I once brought up one of the Frau Professor's data files, one I have never been allowed to work on, by mistake. I tried to read it before she came back, but all I caught was a list of names.'

'No doubt she keeps the records too, Mary. That's not very remarkable.'

Mary looked solemn. 'Not like these lists. The ones I glimpsed included only female names. I wondered about that at the time. Now that *is* significant.'

'You think the later births will all be female?'

'No, Aunt Rilla. Everyone would have noticed that. I think the list I saw was one of her private lists. I take it she knew which births were normal, and which parthenogenic.'

'How could she know that? Because the babies looked so like their mothers?'

'Not very reliable for tiny babies. Perhaps she took blood samples . . .'

Gabriela stood up, almost capsizing the table. 'The jabs, Mary! That's why she does the immunisations free. It gives her a chance to take blood samples for analysis. That's how she knows.'

'That's brill, Aunt Rilla!'

'Better not get carried away. You only glanced at the screen, you said. And we can't use that as evidence,' Gabriela said brusquely, sitting down again. 'What I was going to suggest was that we could break the numbers we have down even further. We can compare the pre-June births.'

Mary grinned. 'I see you're catching on fast your-self.'

Register: 1945–1955
THE MOTHERING OF THE BRIDES

Date	Brides	Births	Boys	Girls	Late boys	Late girls	Early boys	Early girls
1945	30	27	15	12	12	11	3	1
1946	35	31	17	14	13	12	4	2
1947	38	35	19	16	15	13	4	3
1948	41	38	19	19	14	14	5	5
1949	43	41	21	20	16	17	5	3
1950	48	46	23	23	17	19	6	4
1951	49	48	23	25	17	19	6	6
1952	51	50	24	26	19	22	5	4
1953	64	63	31	32	24	25	7	7
1954	87	87	43	44	35	37	8	7
1955	103	103	51	52	41	46	10	8

'In the early births the boys outnumber, or equal, the girls in every single year,' Gabriela said, awed. 'It has to be meaningful.'

'The later figures show a very remarkable ratio between boys and girls born after June,' Mary said, doodling around the numbers. 'We'll have to get Uncle Michael to send them back to England for a proper statistical analysis.'

'So that's where you are,' Erika said, bursting into the room. 'Such a lovely day, I would have thought you'd be outside.' She walked straight towards them, lifting her glasses to her eyes.

'Did you need some more help, Frau Professor?' Mary asked, jumping up, leaving Gabriela to gather the papers together. 'I think Marina will sleep for another hour.'

'What have you two been up to? You look quite conspiratorial.'

'We're making a timetable,' Gabriela said, bunching the papers together. 'Reverend Mother gave us some of her sheets.'

'Timetable? For Mary, d'you mean?' She came closer, looking at the sheaf in Gabriela's hands. 'What's that old stuff? It looks familiar, somehow.' She frowned. 'That's the paper Reverend Mother always uses. Have you already talked to her?' She turned to Mary. 'I would have expected you to discuss it with me first.'

'I did just mention it to her,' Gabriela lied quickly. 'She gave us a couple of blank sheets. Just to see how it would work out if Mary stayed here. She would have to work very hard.'

'And what is wrong with that? Arbeit macht frei, as they used to say.'

That had been the slogan written above the concentration camps.

'I would say your work practically kept you a prisoner,' Gabriela said to her mother, looking intently at her. 'I hope you won't try to do the same for Mary.'

Erika smiled at Mary. 'I could use some help.' She turned, petulant, back to her daughter. 'You have always had a chip on your shoulder, Rilla,' she said. 'Make sure you look after Marina when she wakes up. You're very good at that.'

'I have never allowed my records to be used for secular purposes,' Reverend Mother said. Her eyes, though old, were sharp. 'I need to know a little more before I can possibly contemplate letting you have them, or even a copy of them.'

'Of course, Reverend Mother. I do understand that. I have just come back from Berlin. My findings there are very disturbing. Unfortunately I'm positive they have a bearing on what has been happening on your doorstep.'

'Happening here? The only thing of consequence is Elisabeth Helden's unexpected death. How could that concern you, Herr Adler?'

'Only peripherally. I was referring to the Oktoberfest.'

'What possible connection could there be between our parochial little festival records and Berlin?'

'Professor Fluge's work there, during the war. I went to examine what papers there were which have survived from that time.'

'I don't understand, Herr Adler. You are working on a story which concerns Professor Fluge, and began during the war? And for that you expect me to allow you access to my private papers?' She smiled. 'I think you are under some sort of misapprehension. I only have records from 1956 onwards.'

'I know, Reverend Mother. But I have reason to believe that Professor Fluge's scientific discoveries are connected with Mary Fullbridey's extraordinary pregnancy.'

'Really? You think you can throw some light on that?'

'I think perhaps I can. May I bring one or two things to your attention? My mother-in-law was in Berlin at that time.'

'Helping her father, yes. She was a brilliant child.'

'Brilliant enough to understand exactly what he was doing and how to use that research in the modern world.'

'And is that not a good idea?'

'It depends. Perhaps you do not realise that Erika Lager had some terrible experiences during and after the war.'

'Of course we all know that. We were not exactly immune from them here.'

'In her case she was unfortunate enough to fall into Russian hands. I think she was raped by soldiers in Berlin.'

'I see,' she said slowly. 'You mean Gabriela is the child of that rape. That would explain her looks. I often wondered.'

'My point is that I do not think Professor Lager ever came to terms with that. I think it has left her with a warped mind. And a permanent hatred of men – all men.'

'Really?' She stared at Michael. 'I had no idea. We have all heard terrible stories of that time. But I don't see how that . . .'

'Rilla's possible father is not important, except to explain what may have happened to her mother's mind. What I wanted to know from you, Reverend Mother, was what *you* thought at the time. My point is that I think the rape unhinged her mentally. Have you noticed any evidence of that?'

'No, Herr Adler, I have not. As far as I'm concerned, Erika Lager is a highly intelligent, ethical, completely sane human being. Brusque, off-hand, impatient – but sane.'

'I think she has never recovered from seeing her daughter that first time, Reverend Mother.' His voice was low. 'I think she has been experimenting with reproduction since then.'

'She's a geneticist. That's not a secret.'

'With human reproduction.'

'Trying to increase fertility?'

'Parthenogenic human reproduction. Virgin births.'

'But surely . . .?'

'Let me assure you that it is, in theory, possible. My point here is that I think she has been doing experimental research on human beings.'

'In Salzburg?'

'Using the unwitting brides who come to your festival as her test cases.'

'Herr Adler, you are letting your imagination run away with you! That simply is not possible.'

'I'm afraid it is. I think Erika Lager has been adding carefully constructed chemical formulae to the water in the troughs, and that she has been using the brides who drink it to test these concoctions.'

Her headdress jerked up, her hands grasped the desk. 'Herr Adler, you can't mean that. That is a terrible accusation. It would be sacrilege, both religious and scientific. I don't think . . .'

'I can't prove it as yet, but I strongly suspect it. Elisabeth Helden and Mary Fullbridey, Reverend Mother – think what happened to them. Both of them. Elisabeth was pressured into saying a man had been involved.'

Mother Theresia sat back in her chair, her shoulders hunched. 'Elisabeth did come to see me. She said she wanted to show me her little girl, and to assure me she had never been unchaste. She was so touching, so sweet. All she wanted was that I should not think badly of her. I assured her I did not.'

'And Mary, Reverend Mother. Mary is an innocent virgin.'

'You think Erika added some potent chemicals . . .'

'A catalyst. Laboratory records show it can be done on animals. We need your help to prove our case, and I think you need ours. Your order, the Church, will be accused of faking miracles if we do not expose this travesty of scientific work. Only you can make it possible for us to prove what has been going on all these years.' He paused. 'You have kept accurate records, I understand.'

'I pride myself on that.'

'A professional statistician can prise the evidence we need out of them.'

'How could Erika have done this? I mean, from a practical point of view?'

'She adds chemicals to the grotto water before the festival each year.'

'No, no, Herr Adler, I would not allow . . .'

'She did not tell you. She pretended to collect a sample of water for testing. In July, and again in October, just before the festival. We think she added the catalyst to the first trough in July, and to the second just before the festival. When her arthritis made her too unfit to climb up, she sent Helga, and then Lisl.'

'And they didn't tell me? Why did they add something to the water without telling me?'

'Erika Lager told them it would destroy the brides' faith in the festival.'

The nun took her crucifix and gazed at it.

'You always know who fetches the water sample?'

'Of course I know. The child who looks after the grotto. Elisabeth Helden for the last two years, following on from her sister Helga. This year it will be Renate Scheiderbauer. All very reliable girls.' She frowned. 'Would you like me to send for Scheiderbauer?'

'No, no! It is vital that we keep this discussion between us a secret. Just between you and me.'

'A secret?'

'So that we can actually work out what has been happening without rousing suspicions. Find incontrovertible evidence.'

'You really think something so evil has been going on?'

'I'm very much afraid it has.'

'You can connect this with your own mother-in-law?'

'Connect it with her research. That is my point, Reverend Mother. She is not in her right mind, and I believe she has used that festival as an adjunct to her laboratory for many years.'

'Used it for purely worldly purposes? That's what you're saying?' The old woman got up, stomped over to the window, looked up at the mountainside. 'That is a heinous crime against God and the Church. What can I do to help?'

'Let us have your records since 1956.'

'That will be useful?'

'If we could have them analysed, Reverend Mother, I think we could learn a great deal. You see, if we can find something which does not correlate with the normal course of fertility . . .'

'It is a holy shrine. Many of the births are miracles.'

'If that is all it is, it would be good to establish that.'

Mother Theresia went over to her desk again. 'Open the drawer, Herr Adler. I have kept the records carefully. Please make some copies, and return the originals

455

to me. I do not think it can do any harm to let you have them.'

'I think you two have done marvels with these figures,' Michael said, his voice flat, his eyes hard. 'I'm very impressed. But actually I think there's one more thing we can get out of them.' He looked from Mary to Gabriela. 'Marina's safely asleep, isn't she? Let's go back to the study.'

'You've worked out something worse, haven't you?' Gabriela asked nervously.

'I've worked out an answer to something which has been bothering me. You said you had not started to menstruate regularly, didn't you, Mary?'

'Well, yes.'

'And Lisl? Can you remember about Lisl?'

'I don't know. Most girls start earlier than I did.'

'But she didn't mention it?'

'We can find out from Friedl,' Gabriela put in, then shook her head. 'No, we can't. She isn't up to that.'

'Ursula would know,' Mary said. 'I remember Lisl talking about Ursula being very late, just like her.'

'But what has it got to do with all this?' Gabriela asked.

'If Mary wasn't menstruating, she wasn't likely to have a ripened ovum which would respond to the catalyst.'

'I don't know what you're getting at, Michael.'

'Another of Helmut Fluge's formulae. He was able to stimulate the ripening of ova, remember. We're nearly there. I want to show you in black and white.' He pulled the sheets towards him. 'You have a look at the data with one more variable. I've highlighted all the births *after* July.'

THE MOTHERING OF THE BRIDES

Date	Brides	Births	Boys	Girls	Late boys	Late girls	Early boys	Early girls	Post July
1945	30	27	15	12	12	11	3	1	1
1946	35	31	17	14	13	12	4	2	2
1947	38	35	19	16	15	13	4	3	3
1948	41	38	19	19	14	14	5	5	2
1949	43	41	21	20	16	17	5	3	3
1950	48	46	23	23	17	19	6	4	3
1951	49	48	23	25	17	19	6	6	4
1952	51	50	24	26	19	22	5	4	5
1953	64	63	31	32	24	25	7	7	3
1954	87	87	43	44	35	37	8	6	7
1955	103	103	51	52	41	46	10	8	9

Gabriela and Mary sat side by side and looked at the figures.

'They're all girls,' Mary said, awestruck. 'All the ones after July are girls.'

'That's why no one's spotted it,' Gabriela said. 'If they broke the figures down at all – that is if they had had them, of course, which as far as we know they did not – they would have assumed the ones after July didn't count.'

'You see what's been happening,' Michael said. 'She must have added sufficient hormones to stimulate the ripening of the ovarian egg cells. These begin to develop at puberty, and the first meiotic division for each one is concluded a short time before that egg's ovulation. One of these cells becomes a secondary oöcyte, the other is rejected and is not used.'

'The polar body,' Mary said. 'Normally the secondary

457

oöcyte meioses into a mature ovum, the haploid cell which will fuse with the sperm to form a zygote. We learned all that in biology.'

'You obviously have the makings of an excellent research scientist, Mary. I can only surmise, but I think that Erika's catalyst encourages the secondary oöcyte to begin its first cleavage – split – on its way to becoming a separate human being. At the same time, I think she may have added something which destroys any sperm which happens to be present. If there *was* no secondary oöcyte, her hormones would produce one.' He smiled. 'Presumably the catalyst remained in the body and ensured that egg cells ripened in this way were fertilised.'

'That's why there were a couple of pairs of twins in these late births,' Mary suddenly said. 'Because two ova ripened at the same time.'

'That's also why Helga, Lisl and Ursula were all born in August,' Gabriela said slowly. 'Friedl always said how strange that was. She had that infection, of course. I think it made her infertile until the hormones stimulated her ovary into production.'

'It all fits. God only knows what else is going on,' Michael said, shuffling the papers together. 'We have to stop her, somehow. We have to stop her fast.' He put the papers into his briefcase. 'I'm going to take Mother Theresia's records to Salzburg, copy them there and courier them to my editor. I'd better do it now, before everything shuts for the weekend.' He stared at Gabriela. 'I'll have to purloin her car, Liebling. I hope you won't object. It's in a good cause.'

36

'What are you doing, Mary? What is that thing?'

'It's a baby-carrier, Frau Professor,' Mary said, an embarrassed smile on her face. 'Michael brought it back from Berlin for me.'

'Why on earth are you dressed in that dirndl?'

Mary was packing travelling essentials for Marina and herself. She had not expected the Frau Professor to come out of her laboratory. 'I'm just sorting out my clothes,' she said nervously as she tried to hide the small carry-on bag she was preparing for Marina. The dirndl was pure romance. She wanted her last full day in Austria to be traditional, and she wanted to leave Salzburg dressed like a local. Furthermore, the dirndl was a very convenient garment for travelling in. Her figure had filled out to that of a young woman, and her other clothes felt tight.

With luck, the Frau Professor would not notice that her car was missing. Michael and Gabriela had driven off in the Audi, carefully shutting the garage doors. The plan was to drop Gabriela off at the convent, where she hoped to enlist Mother Theresia's help for the time when Michael's investigations led to Erika being questioned by the Salzburg authorities. Gabriela would return from London at that point.

Michael, meanwhile, would drive to Salzburg and arrange for Mother Theresia's records to be copied and couriered out, and to collect plane tickets for Mary and Marina. The Adlers' tickets were booked for the early morning flight of the following day.

'In a flight bag?' The Frau Professor's sharp eyes narrowed. 'Where are Michael and Gabriela?'

'Gone to see Reverend Mother, Frau Professor.'

'I see.' She watched as Mary put a rattle and a dummy into the pocket of the carrier. 'Why don't you say you're packing? So you have decided to leave with Gabriela after all. Well, well; she will finally have her child.' Her nostrils flared. 'You might at least have talked to me, Mary. What were you intending to do? Crawl off like some sort of fugitive?'

'I'm sorry, Frau Professor. I was going to explain . . .'

'When Michael and Gabriela returned, you mean. You are afraid to tell me on your own.' Her eyes glittered into points. 'What did you think I was going to do? Keep you prisoner?'

'Of course not.'

'I'm disappointed in you, Mary. You will be going back to a humdrum, suburban existence. Both your considerable talents may well be asphyxiated. How can you choose that over what I am offering you?'

'And what are you offering me, Frau Professor?'

'But I have told you repeatedly, haven't I? I spelled it all out for you. We will find a woman to look after Marina while you prepare yourself for the life worthy of you. You can decide what that is to be. You have a glorious voice and an excellent brain. You could continue to help me with my research, take over from me when my powers are spent. That is what I offer. The proposal is still open.'

'Help you?' Mary suddenly burst out, unable to contain herself. 'Help you cheat and lie, help you use human beings as guinea-pigs?'

'What on earth are you jabbering about?' She walked over to the crib.

Mary threw the baby things she had been sorting into a jumble as she dived towards her child. 'The sacred shrine,' she snarled. 'The festival of the Mothering of the Brides. Only you aren't content with normal forms of mothering, are you? You meddle with God's way, you pollute the water in the troughs – the water those innocent women think is holy, blessed – and produce fatherless daughters, not the children they are entitled to.'

'So you've finally worked that one out, have you? Michael! I should have known, all those questions about Berlin.' The little woman put her arms out to pick Marina up. 'The little one is an unexpected outcome.'

Mary pushed her aside, snatched up her sleeping child and backed away.

'You think I am going to injure her?'

'You are not even going to touch her!'

'In case I contaminate her, I suppose.' Erika paused, looking at the young girl hugging her child to herself. 'Who else knows about this? Apart from the brilliant journalist. Gabriela, I suppose? That's why she was so reluctant to let me know he was in Berlin,' she said, almost to herself. 'I was too absorbed in the latest work to think about it. History repeats itself.'

'How could you do it?' Mary rocked Marina, who had begun to fret. 'How could you?' She sobbed. 'You, of all people. You know what it is like to be raped . . .'

'Exactly. Raped by men, forced to carry their seed.'

461

A look of triumph. 'No woman need put up with that ever again. Not now.'

'How could *you* do this to women? Don't you understand what you have done? You have violated them as much as those Russian soldiers violated you. You have abused unsuspecting women. You have used their bodies for your ends, not theirs.' She kissed her child as she cried, then held her away to look at the features which would develop so like her own.

'You don't understand, Mary. You are too young. They don't count. They are just the vessels we need to confirm –'

'Don't count?'

'Ignorant peasant women. What does it matter? They will have other children. Only the first one –'

'You mean they *all* have parthenogenic children now?'

'Unless the embryo is already well established. My hormones abort early embryos and stimulate a new follicle,' Erika explained proudly. 'I have made enormous strides.'

'You mean that even if there are sperm present, they cannot fertilise an ovum?' Michael's hypothesis had been remarkably accurate. 'So practically all the brides have parthenogenic daughters now?'

'Only since last year. After the hormones have done their work, the ribozymes set mitosis in train – the viable secondary oöcyte splits to reproduce itself into a new human being. Just to remind you what happens.' Her lips contorted into a terrible grin. 'In case you have forgotten everything I taught you.' The hands clawed at air as Mary backed away from her. 'You don't know everything, you know. You are just guessing. You can have no idea of the amount I have achieved.'

'We've analysed the records your mother kept.'

'My *mother's* records? I would have thought you'd get the latest ones from the old nun.' She laughed out loud. 'What do you think those early ones can tell you? They are completely out of date. You cannot imagine –'

'I don't want to know!'

'You stupid, foolish child, haven't you grasped the implications even now? Marina is a very special human being.' She looked at Mary carefully. 'And, don't forget, she was your choice, not mine. I did not force her on you, or even wish for it. You drank the water of your own volition. That was *your* doing.'

'I know,' Mary agreed, her voice low. 'It was a terrible thing to do. I am responsible. And I am going to make amends for that.'

'Really? And just what are you going to do?' The sneer distorted her face.

'Make sure you cannot continue with scientific work. Destroy your formulae.'

'You're going to leave this new species in the lurch, are you? You do not consider them to be human beings?'

Mary stared at the little woman. It was not going to be as simple to set things straight as she had thought.

'And what about my work on degenerative diseases? Are you intending that should be destroyed as well?'

'Some of that has merit, I suppose, but it hardly makes up for the evil you have done. That's much too big a price to pay. And it isn't all good, anyhow,' Mary shouted.

'You don't think ridding the world of a genetically transmitted disease like cystic fibrosis is purely to the good?'

'There's a terrible downside. You must know that.

463

We can't know what we are throwing away. Genetically transmitted diseases we see as physically bad may be linked to valuable attributes. We can't know!' she cried. 'How can we judge?'

'Your thinking is hardly analytical, Mary.'

'I'm trying to think of what's right for posterity, not what's expedient for the immediate future. We're talking about people, not philosophy!'

At first Erika merely shrugged, then her eyes brightened. 'Mary, just listen to me. You cannot throw it all away. Marina is one of a new breed of women.'

'Exactly,' Mary sobbed. 'Something which should not be tolerated. A new race of women who, if they breed, can only do so asexually.'

'You assume that . . .'

'Because of your work with the rabbits,' Mary said. 'It's true, isn't it?'

'It's true of Lisl Helden's generation. But the second generation, Johanna's generation, is different again.'

'Are you saying that *all* those girls, the ones who were parthenogenically brought about around the time Lisl was born, are doomed?'

'Doomed? Certainly not!'

'They are denied their proper reproductive capacities. That is your idea of a new race of women?'

'It was a mistake,' Erika said. 'It is impossible to achieve great discoveries without making mistakes along the way. How could I know that this would happen? Unfortunately the early formulae my father used had that regrettable defect. The antigen, the way to reverse the process and allow these women to reproduce sexually as well, was the formula he had just completed when the Russians took over Berlin. It was destroyed; that was the tragedy. I didn't know right away what was happening.' Her sharp eyes were clear. 'How could I know it would affect human beings like that? I didn't think it would. I told you I'm working on a new formula for rabbits. That new formula is one which can be utilised as a base to produce a new formula for human beings. I'm sure of that.'

'Too late for poor Lisl and the girls like her. Like Marina.'

'But that is why, Mary, I need you to help me carry on. That is why I had to carry out the experiments and have to continue. You know what I am working on now will go far beyond that. My new work will enable women to reproduce normally, or parthenogenically, as they choose.'

'Why would any woman choose such a horrific method of reproduction?'

'Because,' Erika said, a gleeful smile on her lips, 'because then women will call the tune. They will be able to reproduce themselves without a man, and do it indefinitely. A great-granddaughter can show her genetically similar forebear just how she would have been living in the modern world. These women will, to all intents and purposes, be immortal.'

'And will this be available to every woman?'

'Certainly not. Such a trait needs to be very carefully controlled.' A look of triumph. 'In any case, sexual reproduction is necessary for importing new genetic material. The parthenogenic process is useful only for those carefully selected beings who are as free from genetic damage as can be ascertained. The three thousand million letters of the DNA complex will be decoded within the next decade. That's when we can make an informed choice. That's when this method will become invaluable.'

465

'And who is going to make the choices?'

Erika shrugged. 'The society we live in will do that. In any case, the number of mutations, beneficial or harmful, has begun to decline because we interbreed on a global scale. We already know that economic advance combined with the enormous strides medicine has made mean that human beings are almost at the end of their evolutionary road. We are as close to biological Utopia as we are ever likely to get. So we no longer need sexual reproduction in the way we used to.'

'That isn't true –' Mary began.

'At last we can rid the world of all those misbegotten beings,' Erika murmured, almost to herself. 'The educationally subnormal, criminals, homosexuals – all the undesirables. Just think, Mary. We have it in our power to form a race of women . . .'

'Totally without men, you mean. A travesty of humanity,' she screamed. 'None of those so-called undesirables can hold a candle to your type of criminality! You think you're God.'

'Goddess. Exactly; we no longer *need* men, though we may prefer to keep them. At times they can be quite agreeable,' she said, as though considering it for the first time. 'Just think; we can select the finest Aryan stock, the best of womanhood.' She smiled, her face softening as she thought about her work. 'You could think of Marina as a new messiah, one of a race of new messiahs. Not God's daughter, Mary. Nothing to do with God. *I* made her.'

'The devil, more like! What have you done to my baby?'

'I have done nothing, Mary. She is you, just you. Not God or devil, just another version of yourself. Whatever talents you choose not to use, your daughter can use

466

instead. She can turn back the clock. She is your immortality.'

'You are totally demented – deranged,' Mary whispered.

'Deranged? Really, Mary, I thought you were intelligent enough to be able to cope with new ideas. The product of pure woman – for woman.'

'You are much worse than those Russian soldiers you called savages –'

'All they could do was force me into reproducing one of them.'

'– worse than the boys who tried to rape me,' Mary shouted. 'Having a child after that would have been terrible, but at least it would have been natural.'

'Natural?' Erika cackled. 'Natural? I don't know what you think that means. Is it natural to send men to the moon, to save diabetics by the injection of insulin, to perform caesarian sections to save a baby's life? Is it natural to split the atom to make energy? Natural means nothing.'

'It's different . . .'

'Of course it's different. But we cannot go back. It is now possible to reproduce the human race asexually. My father discovered how, and withheld his latest work because he wanted to crush the Nazi cause.'

'He tried to hide it from the Nazis?'

'They found out. The only way I could save his latest formula was to accuse him. Hugo told me they knew . . .'

'You betrayed your own father?'

'I could not save him whatever I did,' she said hollowly. 'I loved him. So I saved myself in order to save his work. I thought he was the most wonderful human being in the world. You do not know what

467

anguish I went through. I wish I could have reproduced *him*. But all I produced was Gabriela. A Tartar child, a mongrel.'

'So why didn't you take the formula yourself, Frau Professor?'

'Because I am flawed,' she said, her eyes staring ahead. 'Because I killed. I am not worthy. My mission in life is not to breed, but to work.' Her mouth set hard.

'Killed? You mean you killed your father?'

She stared beyond Mary. 'Such a daughter would have been just like me, Mary. Don't you see the power of it? Don't you know I would have known exactly how she would behave? She would have shown up what I have managed to hide for decades.' She walked towards Mary, who backed away towards the laboratory. 'It was only because you and that silly Helden disobeyed the tenets of a superstitious religion that you have caused such difficulties.'

'Difficulties? You mean *exposed* you?'

'It won't matter. I have found the antigen, I will refine the formula. I am nearly ready to give women genuine choice in their children. No doctor is needed. It is the most significant discovery since birth control. I have made it possible for us to have a woman's world, a world without the need for a single man.'

'But there is a snag,' Mary said.

'And what is that?'

'This race will die out. It cannot survive. You taught me that yourself.'

'Not necessarily. Women will always have children by men as well. That is built into their very nature, they will not be able to resist it. I do not think humans will change for some time yet, and, by then, who knows? A woman will have found how to adapt to that.'

468

'This particular woman is having nothing to do with you! I am taking my daughter away; I am going to teach her the difference between right and wrong. And I will work to repress your evil research.'

'You are a fool, Mary Fullbridey! A stupid, sentimental fool. You have not even understood what I have done for you. You can use both your talents: your voice and your brain. Because Marina is your alter ego.'

'I think you are the fool, Frau Professor. With all your brilliance, what have you achieved?' Mary paused. 'I will tell you. You betrayed a father you loved, and lost him. You were responsible for the terrible infection which killed your mother and made your daughter infertile. You neglected your child when she was young, and so alienated a loving daughter. And you are responsible for the rape of hundreds of women. You are suggesting I follow in *your* footsteps?'

'I can see you do not wish to,' Erika said, stepping towards Mary.

Mary noticed a blank expression in the woman's eyes and instinctively backed right away, out of the door, along the hall towards the laboratory.

'You don't really think I'll let you betray me, do you? I did not allow my own mother to do that,' she screamed.

Was she actually going to try to do her and Marina physical damage? Mary looked desperately around. There was nothing she could defend herself with. But the woman had arthritis. Even with Marina in her arms she should be quicker on her feet than the Frau Professor.

The laboratory door stood open, the key in the lock outside. Mary dodged ahead, just out of reach. She moved swiftly to the furthest part of the laboratory, the

Frau Professor in pursuit. She seized her chance, rushed ahead of the woman following her, crashed a computer monitor on the floor behind herself and sprinted away and out. She slammed the door shut, locked it and took out the key. She prayed she would not have too long to wait for Gabriela and Michael to return. They had to leave tonight.

37

Joseph had, as agreed with the Adlers, collected the perfume bottle from Helga's room. He went straight back to Kernkirchen and posted it to London for analysis.

'Ursel's at the Braune Rössl, Joseph,' the girl at the post office told him. 'My sister came in and said she saw her there. That Kurt Miller is getting at her. Him and his crowd. Thinks he's God almighty, the stupid oaf.'

'Thanks, Hannah. I'll give her a lift back home.' He strode out. It was late afternoon; the sun was sinking fast, the tourists had abandoned bathing for the day. Only a single lifeguard remained on duty. Kurt Miller and the others must be getting together for their evening meal. He headed for the inn, glanced in the bar and saw no one he recognised. He continued down the spiral staircase into the Weinkeller in the Rössl's underground rooms.

'Well, look who's here.'

He could see Kurt and several of the young men who always crowded round him, surrounded by their retinue of young girls. A whole crowd was gathered at one of the long wooden tables set against the far wall of the spacious cellar. Joseph made out about twenty young people sitting there.

The Weinkeller was the room the locals used. The tourists, enjoying the terraces and the formal dining rooms, kept away from the basic wooden tables and benches. The place was too dark for them, too intimidating.

One of the older generation of Kernkirchners was playing a zither. The young people sitting on the bench were shoulder to shoulder, swaying together to the rhythm. They were enjoying the music, humming and singing the folk tunes the old man plucked out.

'Servus Hans, Georg, Kurt.' Joseph waved amiably at the heads nodding at him and walked towards the bar. His eyes had not adjusted to the low level of light. He let them range from girl to girl to see if he could distinguish his sister Ursula.

'Our expert folk musician,' Kurt yelled above the singing. A hush came over the group, the singing petered out and the zither sounded almost plaintive. 'So what about a song from you, then?' He snickered. 'Or do we have to pay?'

'We all have to earn a living,' Joseph said, keeping a fixed smile on his face. Kurt's tone sounded dangerous.

'Some of us manage it without sucking up to foreigners the whole time,' Kurt continued. 'Some of us find our old friends good enough company.'

'Another Viertel, Kurt? Are you drinking white or red?' Joseph flicked his eyes at the waitress passing with her tray full of glasses.

'Well, if you're buying,' Kurt smirked, 'make it a litre of red and a litre of white.' He grinned. 'All on our lonesome, are we?' he went on, eyes veiled. He put his right hand out, pulled a very young girl sitting next to him on to his knee, put his arm round her neck and

472

kissed her. She giggled happily, her long hair wound in two braids around her head in the typical Gretchen-frisur. Kurt slipped the pins out and two strong, nut-brown plaits hung down her back. 'Almost as good as Lisl's,' he said, the determined smile on his face unable to hide the pain. The telltale moistness in the corner of his eyes alerted Joseph to trouble.

He nodded to the waitress, agreeing the two litres of wine, and looked anxiously around the table from face to face. At last he spotted Ursula sitting at the far end. He had to get her out fast. There was going to be trouble tonight, he could feel it in Kurt's attitude, could sense the fury in him. 'I thought I'd join you,' he said amiably. He looked at his sister, and swivelled his eyes towards the stairs.

'Come on, come on! You don't have to play around with *her*, you know. We can find a girl for you if you're too shy.' Kurt turned to a young girl sitting between two older ones. 'What about Gerda here? She should be young enough for you, Joseph, old friend.' He leered. 'We all know you like them young.'

'What's that supposed to mean?'

'Just a manner of speaking. Life's so much better with a little playmate, isn't it?' He bent the girl on his knee backwards, pulled her chin towards him and kissed her long and hard. 'This one's a corker. Thought I'd try one from a different stable this time.' He waved at Ursula and winked. 'Not that your Ursel isn't as pretty as her sisters.' The eyes grew cold.

Ursula turned her head and looked at her brother uneasily. Joseph blinked his eyes rapidly, indicating she should not speak.

'Devil of it is, she's so much like Lisl it can be quite scary.' The dark eyes glowered, then suffused with

473

grief. 'And my little Helga. Now that one was a saint, a real saint.'

'So how is Eva?' Joseph asked, stung into rage. Kurt's sister had recently had an illegitimate baby while living in the States for a year.

'Eva? Eva has had a baby in the normal way. She doesn't deny it. An American, a black one, at that. But not a virgin birth, like some we could mention.' Kurt's fleshy lips drew back into a snarl. Joseph fought hard not to react. 'Not brought Mary the virgin, then?' Kurt cackled. 'Some of us have seen such wonderful miracles in St Walter. Not just the one, nothing like that. My pure betrothed Lisl had a child which wasn't mine, you know,' he confided to all and sundry, his lips tight.

'I thought you said Johanna was your daughter, Kurt. I thought that's what you were only too keen to tell us all,' Joseph said, his eyes flinting.

'Fooled me there, didn't she? When I was in my cups. You Heldens all stick together when it counts. Tried to catch me for her, didn't you, old Albert and you!' He turned in fury. 'But I caught her out, the bloody little slut. The second time, that was too much even for a simpleton like me. What did she take me for? What do *you* take me for? The village idiot, that's what you think?'

'You know you were the only one . . .'

'I knew I hadn't fathered the latest one, blast you,' he shouted, drowning the zither and quelling further conversation. 'Never got in the mood with the yelling brat in the room. She didn't even deny that I hadn't been near her.' He banged his fist down on the table. 'That really was the limit.'

'You've got it wrong, Kurt.'

'Got it wrong, have I? The English Mary did the

474

same. Quite unbelievable.' He laughed hollowly. 'Who'd have thought we had such saints in our midst?' His fists had curled into tight balls. 'Tried to lay it at your door, did she, Joseph? I saw you creeping off round the lake together. Bloody little slut. Tried to . . .'

'Halt's Maul!' Joseph yelled. 'She's not a slut. She's a sweet, innocent girl caught up in that fiendish racket that's going on.' He glared all round the table. 'What makes you think you can judge like that? What right d'you have?' He gulped down a glass of wine. 'Our poor little Lisl was just as innocent.' Out of the corner of his eye he could see Ursula slipping out from the bench, a shadow by the wall. He needed to give her time. He poured more wine into his glass, twisted it absently. 'Everyone hounded her,' he went on, almost to himself, 'even my mother.' He could see Ursula edging up the spiral staircase.

'Didn't stop her trying to catch me,' Kurt said, nodding his head, drinking more wine.

'And all the time what both of them said was true,' Joseph cried out, tears in his eyes. He put the glass down and stared at the table in front of him. 'They were both innocent, both as pure as snow.'

'You've really got it bad, Joseph. Take my advice, find yourself a nice little local girl. That fucking festival makes sure we have plenty of them.'

'What do you mean?' Joseph's eyes, lack-lustre before, glinted at Kurt.

'Everyone knows we've got more girls than boys in Kernkirchen and St Walter. All the other villages are jealous as hell. *And* you can tell exactly how they'll turn out. The spitting images of their mothers.' Kurt guffawed. 'Helps you to weed out the ones that are going to turn into old dragons.' He turned back to

Joseph again. 'Bloody hell, man, you're good-looking enough. They must be queueing up for you. What the devil's holding you back? You don't need to settle for the little bitch –'

'Don't you say that about Mary!' Joseph bellowed. 'You say that once more, and I'll wallop you so you won't be able to sit on that damned lifeguard's chair, I can promise you.'

'Miststück! She's a whore, a slut, a bloody little liar –'

'She's as innocent as Lisl was. You just said it yourself, you damned stubborn fool. How in God's name do you think my sister got with child again? It wasn't you – you said so, she said so, we knew so.'

'I'm not the only man . . .'

'No one came to the house. Do you suppose my father would let it happen? You know what he's like. Or are you now accusing *him* – or me?'

'I was surprised,' Kurt said, pouring another drink. 'But then again, these girls . . .'

'It's been proved.'

'Nothing can be proved, Joseph.' Ursula, standing quietly half-way up the stairs, her eyes wide, suddenly shouted at her brother. 'Lisl is dead. Let her rest in peace.' Her face crumpled and she ran up the rest of the stairs and away.

'It wasn't me,' Kurt suddenly roared. 'I know it wasn't me. The Frau Professor offered to do a blood test when I took the brat for her shots. She took samples from her and me, and then she told me. Johanna was not my daughter. Her tests proved she couldn't be.' He knocked back another glass of wine, poured more and gulped that on top of it. The tears in his eyes were brimming over. 'I loved my Lisl,' he sobbed. 'I worshipped the ground she walked on. She

476

was the living image of my little Helga.'

'The Frau Professor told you Johanna wasn't your daughter?'

'Exactly. Said not to have anything more to do with Lisl, her child was not mine and I should get the hell out of it.'

'The bloody bitch.'

'You saying the old woman made it up?' Kurt sneered. 'I'm not as much of a fool as all that, you know. I made her show me. I made her explain to me which blood group goes with what. Even I could see there was no way she could be my daughter.'

'She was telling the truth, all right.'

'Fucking hell, what's that supposed to mean? Lisl has a child which isn't mine, and yet she's innocent?'

'It wasn't any man's.' Joseph knocked the carafe over in his fury.

'The Immaculate Conception. The Blessed Virgin Elisabeth.'

'The virgin Elisabeth. You never slept with her and neither did anyone else.' He dabbed at the spreading red wine.

'You got a point somewhere here, Joseph? Or are you just drivelling in your cups?'

'She had a child without a man, and so did Mary.'

'Come on. Pull the other one!'

'Herr Adler had Mary's DNA analysed.'

'DNA? What the fuck –'

'Genetic fingerprinting, Joseph?' Gerda broke in from across the table. 'What did it say?'

'It showed Marina has no father.' He swilled the wine around the glass but didn't drink it. He intended to keep a clear head.

'*No* father? What's that supposed to mean?'

'It means Mary became pregnant, but no man was involved in it.'

'She had her like Our Lady had Our Lord?' Gerda whispered.

'No, not like that.'

'Thought we were going to add blasphemy to our little collection,' Kurt snarled.

'Jesus was the Son of God. With Mary and Lisl it wasn't just no man; not even the Holy Ghost. Marina, and Johanna, are the daughters of the waters of the grotto. The grotto has no sons.'

There was complete silence.

'The grotto?' Gerda whispered. 'You mean they drank the water only the brides are allowed to drink?'

'Yes. They thought it was pure and blessed.'

'That's why so many of the brides have girls?'

'And she spiked it, the old witch,' Joseph sobbed. 'That's how it happened. She bloody spiked it.'

'I'm not that stupid,' Kurt insisted. 'She was carrying another one, and she never got to that bloody grotto again.'

'The holy water, Kurt. Remember she had some by the statue of Our Lady in her room?' Joseph sobbed again. 'I think she took it from the grotto. Maybe that's what did it the second time. My little sister – my sweet, innocent little sister.'

'She didn't say anything when I put it to her straight. All she did was . . .' Kurt stared into his glass, his eyes dull. 'You're sure? This isn't some sort of trick?' he asked, looking at Joseph.

'I'm sure. Would I make up a thing like that? I'm going to arrange to have her body exhumed, have her tested, and Johanna, and the unborn one. It's not too late,' Joseph said.

'Bugger that,' Kurt said, pushing the young girl off his knee. 'Bugger that for a lark. If that old witch added stuff to the water, she's in cahoots with the devil. She's got to be destroyed. And that protegée of hers as well.' He looked around at his companions. 'Leading young girls astray, making them breed only girls – what sort of world is that? Bloody women taking over the world. We'll put a stop to that; I'm damned well going to put a stop to it before it goes any further. I'm going to burn that witch!'

Joseph froze. What had he done? He'd given away the secret, told the whole of Kernkirchen what was going on. How could he have been such a fool?

'Bring me some coffee!' Kurt yelled at the waitress. 'A whole pot of coffee. I'm going to need my wits about me. First I'm off to the bog.' And he strode away to the Herren, several of his friends in tow.

479

38

Joseph shuddered. The hairs on the back of his neck stood on end. Could he avert a tragedy? What would Kurt plan? If he could get into his mind, work out what his strategy might be, he might be able to stop him. He hesitated, then vaulted up the twisting staircase and over to the public telephones on the main floor. He picked the receiver up: out of order, as usual. He cursed the tourists who did not know how to use the Austrian system, and tried the second phone. This time there was no sound at all, not even a dialling tone. Kurt had made his first move. The line was dead.

Should he alert the receptionist? No time to explain. Joseph turned on his heel and ran out into the car park. Kurt's next ploy would almost certainly be to invade the small telephone exchange serving Kernkirchen, to rip the connections out. The girls, even the supervisor there, would not argue with him. What then?

If he could spot Kurt's car, if he could open the bonnet and pull the wiring out, he might get a small headstart. That could be worth a try. First Kurt would try to sober up. Then, all too quickly, he'd marshal his followers, steal vehicles if he needed them, lead them to Erika Lager's Schantze.

The Citroën Diane . . . Joseph searched the car park

with narrowed eyes but could see no sign of Kurt's battered jalopy. He ran frantically between the rows of vehicles, then saw the light increase as the Rössl's doors opened and several young men rushed out. He had to get away before they caught him.

He turned to where he'd parked his father's old Beetle, just a few yards from where he was standing. He cursed himself for painting it such a distinctive colour, began to sweat when he could not see it. Where was it? Surely no one would have stolen that . . .

'Joseph,' he heard a voice. 'Get in!' The Volkswagen was driving towards him, brakes screeching it to a halt, Ursula in the driving seat. He crashed in as she began to pull out towards the road.

'That's him. Over there,' he heard Kurt bellow. 'Let's get him!'

Joseph leaned over his sister to grab the steering wheel. 'Put your foot down hard.' he hissed at her. He had begun to teach her to drive, but she was still a novice.

He swerved the car towards the lake. 'Foot right down. I'll steer.' Squealing tyres swirled the circle around the tables on the terrace, charged for the figures running towards them. They scattered, gave way, hurled missiles. The noise of stones being thrown had the effect of making Ursula's foot stamp down harder on the accelerator. The last stone to hit cracked the back window.

'I think he might have killed Lisl,' he roared. 'He's charging round like a wounded bull. We've got to get to Mary before he tries to kill her off as well.' Joseph allowed his sister to take over the wheel. 'Fast as you can get the old wreck to go.'

'He's got a better car.'

'Not much. I think I know exactly what they're going to do. First off they'll fire the Schantze – easy to make that old wooden structure go up in flames – then they'll smash their·way through to the laboratory, wreck it so nothing's left. But we've got a little time. Before they come after us they'll demolish the telephone exchange so no one can call for help. Then they'll collect petrol in cans.'

'What about . . .?'

'Herr Adler will try to fight them, and he can't win. I've got to get them all out of there. Step on it, Ursel! Use the horn in case someone is coming the other way.'

Kurt would not risk a bodily attack on Erika. She might be small and old, and with only the Adlers and Mary to protect her and her laboratory, but she knew all these young men well, had brought many of them into the world. She would be able to sway them with words. Kurt would fire the buildings before she had a chance to speak. A very satisfactory way to eliminate a witch. With phone lines cut, the fire brigade would arrive too late.

'We've got to have a counter plan. Slow down by the Frau Professor's drive to let me out. Can you manage to drive straight on to the convent?'

'I've done all right so far.'

'Try to explain to Reverend Mother, then go on up into the chapel belfry and ring the bell, Ursel. Hard as you can. The St Walter men will know something is very wrong and come to help. I'll see that Mary and the others get away in the Frau Professor's Audi.'

'Where are they going to go?'

'In the opposite direction, past St Walter and on to Alpenbach. Their phone lines are on another exchange.'

482

'And what about the Sisters, Joseph? Won't he be mad enough to want to smash the shrine? He's got to go through the convent for that.'

'Pray, Ursel. I'll follow you as soon as I can. You can run away home, while I go on ringing the bell. Park the Beetle at the narrow bit of the track to the convent, run the rest of the way up. They'll heave the car out of the way eventually, but there isn't much space. It'll mean we gain some precious minutes.'

No time to think, no turning back. Ursula slowed by Erika's drive and Joseph hurtled out. He sprinted towards the house, across the terrace. He banged on the french windows.

No answer, nothing stirred. He ran across to the garage, raised the up and over door. No car. Were they all out? Unlikely. Someone had to be there with the baby.

He ran towards the front, pushed his finger on the bell and heard the rings echoing. No one, nothing. He ran to the back, drummed on the laboratory windows.

'Who is that?' A strong, suspicious voice shouted from inside. The Frau Professor.

'Joseph Helden, Frau Professor. Let me in. I have to talk to you. Bad news.'

The voice floated back. 'I am locked in. I cannot reach the windows. Smash the glass and climb into the house to let me out.'

'Who locked you in?'

'Don't stand there talking . . .'

The terrace french windows opened. Mary stood just inside, Marina in her arms. 'What are you doing here, Joseph? Has something happened to Aunt Rilla?'

'She isn't here?'

'She's at the convent.'

483

'And Herr Adler?'

'He's gone to Salzburg. We're leaving tomorrow. Why are you in such a state? What's wrong?'

'Why is the Frau Professor locked in the lab?'

'I had to, Joseph. She found out I was leaving. And why. She knows Uncle Michael is on to her.'

'Kurt Miller's after her, Mary. He's found out, too.'

'Found out? Found out what?'

'About Lisl and the baby. I let it slip. He knows about Johanna.'

'What's he going to do?' Mary whispered, her arms tightening round her child.

'He called her a witch; he'll get some friends together. He's coming up behind me, fast. He'll set fire to this place, Mary. He'll kill the Frau Professor if he can.'

'Kill her? You really think . . .'

'He'll destroy the laboratory, annihilate her work. We've got to get you all away from here.'

'I had to lock her in.'

He went over to the laboratory door, unlocked it, let Erika Lager out.

'Calm down, Joseph. He's just a numbskull.'

'He's good at killing, Frau Professor. I'm pretty sure he killed our Lisl. He's got nothing to lose. Sling on a coat and some sturdy shoes. We have to run.'

'Joseph,' Mary cried out. 'We can't take Marina . . .'

'We need something to wrap the baby in. Come on, we'll use the short-cut round the back to sneak Marina into the convent.'

Mary turned huge eyes towards him. She held out the baby-carrier for him to put on.

'A gang of men?' she whispered. She held her baby in her arms, her eyes blank, and rocked her to and fro. 'They'll kill my baby!'

He grabbed her elbow. 'Come *on*, Mary. We have to run. Put the baby into the carrier on my back.'

'No,' she suddenly cried. 'No one is going to take her.'

He tried to take the child, but Mary would not let her go. When he turned to Erika Lager, she was no longer there.

'Frau Professor! Where are you? You have to help me get them away. He'll kill all of you. Don't mess about!'

'I'll be there in a moment, Joseph,' he heard her voice from the laboratory.

'Leave all that, Frau Professor. We have to run.'

The french windows were wide open and he pulled the terrified girl through. 'Look at the road from Kernkirchen, Mary. See those lights flickering along it? Listen to the hooting. They're coming fast. We have no time to lose. You *have* to come with me.'

Her eyes, huge saucers of terror, filled with tears, begged him to let her go.

'Frau Professor! You too!' He rushed into the laboratory. She was stuffing computer disks into a bag. 'Give me those, and leave the rest. You don't have a hope if they find you here.'

'No, Joseph, these are for Mary to look after.' She shut the bag and walked up to Mary. 'Take them,' she said. 'Base your research on them. I have included everything, even the next stage. These are the rabbit antigen formulae. They will be needed.'

'Antigen?' Mary, dazed, stared at the Frau Professor.

'The second generation, Mary. The second generation, once started, cannot stop breeding.'

'Can't stop?' So that's why Lisl had become pregnant again so soon. Not the holy water. The effect of that first dose.'

'You have to carry on where I left off, Mary. It all depends on you now. It is not what I intended.'

'Intended,' Mary sobbed. 'Kurt Miller is right, you are a witch. What you have done has to be destroyed. You've started a new race of women who, if they breed, cannot stop.'

'Yes,' the old woman said dully, 'Lisl was pregnant again.'

'Girls like her will go on reproducing like an assembly line? Until they die of exhaustion? That is your great new race?'

'It's only true of her generation. But the second generation, Johanna's generation . . .'

'Will I have . . .?'

'Not you, Mary. Only the ones like Lisl.'

'And Marina,' Mary choked.

At first Erika merely shrugged, then her eyes brightened. 'Mary, just listen to me. You cannot throw it all away. I am just finishing the new work. You have to carry on for Marina's sake. Take the disks – for your child's sake!'

Mary took the bag from her as Joseph spurted into action again, trying to pull the Frau Professor along with him. 'There isn't time for all that talk.'

She pulled away from him. 'I will stay here, Joseph. My work is done. You go. Look after Mary and Marina.'

'Tell Mary what to do, Frau Professor. Tell her to come with me.'

She walked out to the terrified girl. 'He is a good man, Mary. There are some. The only way to save yourself and your child is to go with him. Look after the disks. The convent will shelter you until help arrives. Say goodbye to Gabriela for me.'

486

'You won't come with us?' Joseph asked again.

'I'll keep them here as long as I can.'

Mary stood, catatonic, unable to move. The hooting of the cavalcade up the mountain road was threatening nearer, the lights flickering on and off around the hairpin bends.

'I would never harm you, Mary,' Joseph said softly. 'Trust me. Just this once, trust me. We will go to Reverend Mother. She will look after you.' He tried to put his arm round the girl clinging to her child.

She backed away, and grasped at the railings overlooking the panorama to the lake.

'You have to save Marina, Mary. If you do not save her, she is lost,' he said. 'They think she is the offspring of a witch. They'll kill her as well as you and the Frau Professor.'

'They'll kill Marina?'

'Yes.'

At last she put her child in the carrier on his back and gave him her hand. Together they ran out into the dark, across the alpine meadow, towards dark trees, dense woods.

39

'The grass is too long, Joseph. I can't move properly,' Mary gasped. 'It's dragging at my dirndl.'

'We can't go by road, Mary. It would be madness. Why don't you hitch it up? I've seen my mother do it.'

The long, wet vegetation was dragging Mary back. 'Do you know how?'

'Sides together at the back, up and tuck some of it over the apron strings, I think.' He looked back at her. 'Try to follow in my tracks. I'll flatten the grass a bit.'

Mary stopped to hitch the skirts out of her way, then followed at a brisker pace. 'What are we going to do?'

He turned back, funnelled his hands around his mouth, spoke softly. 'There's a short-cut through the woods beyond this meadow. Then I know a fairly short, stiff climb to the convent car park.' He turned back. 'Don't speak out, Mary. The sound echoes.' He waited for her to catch up. 'They'll realise the Audi isn't there: at first they may think everyone is out. That could hold them up a few minutes, but I think they'll set fire to the house anyway.'

'It's getting really dark. How are we going to see?'

'Don't worry, I'll find the way. I've done it often enough. Hold on to the baby-carrier and stay close behind me.'

'Is it far?'

'Not in distance, no. The trees will shut out what light there is, but they'll also hide us. We'll be OK, I promise. No noise, remember,' he whispered as he started off again.

Progress across the meadow was slow but steady. As they got to the woods, Mary stopped and pulled at Joseph's arm.

'Wait while I tie these disks into the apron,' she said, breathless, determined. 'I won't be able to climb holding them.' She fumbled in the dark. 'The Frau Professor,' she cried out, sobbing. 'She'll be killed.'

'Shh, Mary, quiet. We have to try to save Marina.'

'What's going to happen to her?' She felt unable to move.

'She doesn't want to go on, Mary,' he said, voice very low. 'Come on, we have to hurry.'

'Why is she giving up? It isn't like her.'

'She's worked out what she wanted,' he tried to comfort her. 'She said she had done as much as she could; you would continue her work.'

'I can't see.'

'Just keep hold of Marina's carrier,' Joseph hissed at her. 'They must be almost there by now, the cars sound very close. We have to get deeper into the woods or one of them might spot us. You want to save the baby, don't you?'

The tears were streaming down her face. 'All right.'

'It's not that far. You can do it. Hold on tight.' He took her hand and pulled her through the scrub. 'Please, no noise. Our lives depend on that.'

The firs, dark sentinels guarding the mountain, concealed the threesome as they inched their way towards the spur leading to the convent. As Joseph groped his way, they could hear Kurt and his followers screeching their cars into Erika Lager's drive. The shrill explosion of broken glass, the thud of stones, followed almost immediately. It sounded like a mob.

Joseph stopped to brush a branch away, and they stared back: five sets of headlights blazing at the house, more coming up the road.

'Can you climb up this bit?' Joseph whispered. 'I can't help you while I'm balancing Marina on my back.' He stopped. 'That stuff you're carrying's too bulky, too much of it. You'll have to ditch it.'

'No. We'll never find them again. She entrusted them to me. I have to take them, I have to preserve the new formula.'

'It's really that important?'

'Without the Frau Professor's work it will take years to reach this stage again. I have to do it for Marina, and the other girls.'

'So wait here, then. I'll take the baby and come back for you.'

'It's not beyond me to climb a short distance, Joseph. Lisl showed me how to climb.'

'In daylight, and a way you knew and without a great lump of stuff in front of you.'

'You go on, fast as you can,' she gasped. 'Take Marina into the convent and come back for me if I haven't managed it.'

The child began to whimper.

'Anything you can put into her mouth?' Joseph whispered. 'Keep her quiet?'

'Hold still.' She went behind him, fished the dummy out of the pocket of the carrier, put it in Marina's mouth. The child sucked avidly. 'Just go,' she urged him. 'Fast as you can.'

He began the ascent, the child now quiet. As he forged higher, the sky began to lighten, a yellow glow reflecting back from the clouds. More sounds of breaking glass, of explosions, of yelling across the meadow. The Frau Professor's house must be alight.

He stopped, looked back for Mary. She was right behind him. 'Can you see what's happening?' he whispered.

'The whole house is ablaze.'

'Concentrate on the climb, take your time. They won't find us here, they can't know where we are.'

'How far to go?

'Far enough.'

The sound of shouts, of men running across the meadow, came nearer. They froze against the mountainside.

The pealing of a single bell drowned out all other sound. It began slowly, then increased into a steady rhythm which fired their heartbeats. Ursula must have reached her goal. The bell's ancient demand would alert the village of St Walter that the convent needed help. It would also tell Kurt that they were intending to shelter there.

They inched their way further upwards. The sound of shouting retreated, then died away in the distance.

Mary pulled at the carrier, and Joseph stopped. 'They'll know we're there,' she whispered. 'They'll finish off what they've started, then come after us.'

'We've almost made it,' Joseph whispered back.

At last they reached the ledge leading to the convent car park. There were no cars. Ursula must have left the Beetle to block the drive. The big stone building, silent, dark, loomed ahead of them, huge portals closed.

'There's no one here,' Mary whispered, lying next to

491

Joseph on the car park gravel. 'No one to rescue the Frau Professor,' she sobbed.

'She's beyond help, Mary. It was her choice. Ursel must have told Reverend Mother what's been happening. The villagers will come, I know they will.'

Joseph slipped off the carrier. 'Hold her,' he said. He sprinted across the gravelled drive. His footsteps, scattering stones, sounded like bullets. He pulled the bell-handle hard, but there was no sound of footsteps, no attempt to open the door. He pulled again, longer this time, and harder. As he pulled, he could hear the chapel bell continuing its message of distress, drowning him.

There was no way to storm the convent. The stone fortress stood, wooden shutters barred against the world, the huge doors tight. Joseph began to bang. He thought he could already hear the engines of several cars as they reversed out of the Schantze's drive and prepared to churn along the road towards St Walter. Would the villagers stop them there? Not such a cavalcade. He guessed that Kurt would carry on and leave the rest to finish off the Frau Professor's house and laboratory. By now he must have worked out that Mary and the child had escaped, that he still had work to do.

His next step had to be this house of women. It had all happened in the convent's grotto – his Lisl had been impregnated here.

The creak of bolts being drawn. The doors opened a small crack and Gabriela's face peeped out. 'Joseph, is that you? I was waiting on the balcony upstairs.'

Mary, clasping Marina, hurried across the drive. Joseph turned back and took Marina from her, pulled her along, pushed Gabriela back into the convent and began to close, then bolt, the doors.

'Where is my mother?' Gabriela gasped, eyes dark

and looking beyond the door. 'Why aren't we waiting for her?' She stared at them. 'What have you done with her?' She took the infant from Mary, cradled her. 'She's hiding somewhere in the woods because she couldn't do the climb?'

'She stayed behind,' Joseph gasped. 'I'm sorry, Frau Adler. I could not force her . . . I had to think of Mary and the child. Her arthritis . . . I – it was all my fault,' he stammered, unable to go on.

'She's *there*? With *them*?'

'She wouldn't come, Aunt Rilla.' The tears were streaming down Mary's face. 'We tried, really we did. She wouldn't leave. She gave me her disks and told us to go.'

'They'll be here in no time,' Joseph suddenly said. 'They'll hoist the Beetle out of the way and charge their cars up here. There's a can of petrol in the boot. I'm going to set it alight, so that they can't move it. Then they can't use their cars as battering rams against the convent doors. It will win us a little time.'

'They'll kill you, Joseph!'

He was already drawing the bolts. 'Bolt them after me, and push that chest against them. Don't open them again.' He turned. 'Hang a rope down from the balcony, on the left side. Watch out for me there.'

'They're almost here . . .' Mary sobbed.

'I have to do it.' And he was gone.

'Let's get up to the balcony,' Gabriela said, carrying Marina, leading the way. 'We need to find something for him to climb up.'

They raced up the stairs, and into Mother Theresia's room.

'Joseph has gone to set his car alight,' Gabriela explained to her. 'It will stop them using theirs as weapons. We need a rope to help him climb back in.'

'You know how to get to the Sisters' quarters, Rilla.' The old woman's voice was calm and strong. 'Tell Sister Christa what you need, she will find it for you. Then ask her to assemble the community and say I would like them to join me here.'

Mary opened the windows to the balcony and looked out. 'I can see headlights flashing along the road,' she told them. 'He won't be able to get back.'

Gabriela put the infant on the sofa, rushed away, was back within minutes with a rope. They walked out on to the balcony and fastened the rope above one of the pillars. Nothing but darkness, and the flashing glimpses of headlights, of hooting along the road.

'Why is he taking so long?' Mary whispered.

They stared at the dark tunnel of the drive carved out of rocks and looked to where they knew Joseph was. And then it came: a bright orange light overwhelmed the dark, sputtered, died down, then leapt high. They could see Joseph, his figure backlit, sprinting away from the flames and towards the balcony. He hurled himself across the car park, crossed to the left of the balcony and grasped the rope Gabriela had secured. He climbed up fast, then pulled it up after him.

The bell had stopped tolling. They could hear Ursula running along the corridor from the chapel, up the stairs. She burst into the room. 'I'm sorry, Reverend Mother, I had to come. I have an idea, I think . . .' She stopped, stared at Mary. 'You're wearing Helga's dirndl,' she gasped.

'For God's sake, Ursula,' Joseph began. 'The bell –'

'No,' she said, standing firm, '*you* go and ring the bell. I know exactly what to do. Mary, take off your dirndl, change into my clothes. I know how to stop him.'

494

They gawped at her.

'Hurry up, Mary. It's our only chance.'

'Very good, Ursel.' Reverend Mother nodded her head. 'Fetch the crucifix, Joseph.'

'The crucifix?'

'The metal crucifix from the chapel. Bring it here. Mary, take your child through the Sisters' quarters, and out through the back.'

'What are you going to do, Reverend Mother?'

'Gabriela, you go with Mary and Marina. Hide in the bushes behind the convent. Mary can show you the old track up to the grotto. Hide there until help arrives. We will go out on to the balcony.'

'But . . .'

The old woman turned. 'I have survived the First World War, kept the Nazis at bay in the Second. Now I will deal with Kurt Miller and his companions.'

'I'll deal with them –' Joseph cried.

'That is not the way, Joseph. Fetch the cross. Then I need you in the chapel to ring the bell, fast and furious as you can. I want only women here. Sisters, line up behind me.'

Mother Theresia stationed herself on the balcony, her community behind her, Sister Christa and Sister Marka on either side.

Joseph returned with the crucifix. 'Over here, Joseph. Help us stand it high on the balcony balustrade. I will hold the centre. Sister Christa and Sister Marka will stand on either side of me to hold the cross-pieces.'

The black figures, only the whites of their wimples and faces showing, lined up on either side, the rest of the community standing behind their Superior.

'I want you steady at the back, Sisters,' her voice rang out. 'Just stand behind me. Joseph, go back and toll the chapel bell. Do not stop. God will send help.'

There was no mistaking the noise of engines revved along the road, headlights fluttering back and forth along the hairpin bends. The cars screamed to a stop as the Beetle exploded.

The Little Sisters of the Immaculate Conception stood firm.

There was a short silence. Then the noise of men scrambling up the drive, the sight of blow-torches alight, making the men look darker and larger than they were.

'They're on the balcony!' a loud male voice cried out.

A torrent of oaths as young men streamed along the drive, an army of torches, the burning remnants of the Beetle illuminating them from behind.

'Sisters, help me hold the cross up high,' Mother Theresia said, her voice softer now. The three nuns balanced the heavy metal on the balustrade.

Kurt Miller advanced towards the convent, a blazing firebrand in his right hand. He swung it menacingly from side to side.

'We'll get you witches,' he roared. 'She-devils and she-devils' brats!'

'Stop, in the name of God!' Mother Theresia called out, her voice high and disappearing in the noise of men and flames.

The cross began to sway as she and the nuns reeled, veils flapping, the long habits swinging from side to side, the chink of rosaries on wobbly knees. The chapel bell rang out again, slowly at first, then tolling into loudness.

'She's a witch disguised as a nun,' Kurt's loud voice shouted. 'One of Satan's tricks. They're all witches and the witches' brats!' he bellowed. 'Up those pillars and on to the balcony. Form a pyramid of men and let's get them.'

496

The lights in the room behind the nuns lit up to full brightness and a young figure, her hair free, danced out.

The group of dark sisters behind the trinity of nuns parted to allow the figure through. She ran forward, began to wave her arms, went up to the balustrade, cried out, 'What are you doing, Kurt? What's this I see?'

There was silence as Kurt looked up.

'Helga,' he croaked. 'My Helga!'

'Is that my sweetheart I see down there? Is that the man I promised myself to?'

The nuns drew back as the girl stepped further out, beside the cross. Sister Paula stepped forward, helped her from behind, up on to the balustrade. The figure lifted her hands up high. The white blouse gleamed in the torchlight, the dirndl dress swirled as she swung it from side to side.

'Kurt? Are you there, Kurt?'

'My little Helga,' they heard as Kurt Miller dropped the firebrand and raised his arms. 'It's a miracle. She is alive!'

'I am alive, Kurt, yes.'

'I'll catch you, Helga, my love. Jump!'

'What about Lisl, Kurt? What have you done to my sister Lisl?'

He froze, then turned, arms still upheld, towards the men behind him. And as he did so, his companions started to melt away.

'It wasn't my fault,' he cried. 'I didn't mean to do it. I tried to stop her! She wouldn't listen to me.'

'You killed her, Kurt,' the young girl's voice rang out. 'You are a murderer. You killed my innocent sister.'

The number of torches grew less, dimmed, as several

of the men behind Kurt began to walk towards the drive and away.

'It isn't true! She was a witch; I had to defend myself . . .' Kurt had turned back again. He stood, apart, gaping at the figure teetering on the balustrade. 'How can it be?' he shouted, angry again. 'My Helga is dead. What *are* you? Where have you come from?' He picked the torch up again. 'Another witch from hell!'

The figure stood still. 'I'm Helga reborn,' she cried out, the young voice carrying. 'I've come to haunt you, Kurt. I've come to revenge my sister Lisl.'

'God will forgive you, Kurt,' Mother Theresia's voice rang out as the three nuns moved in unison to hold the cross upright. 'Put your trust in Him.'

As Kurt looked up, the cross began to sway.

'They're all witches!' he bellowed, picking up his firebrand and brandishing it again. 'They've brought back the dead! Let's burn them!'

The men behind him stood irresolute. One tried to grasp his arm. 'Let's leave it, Kurt.' But Miller jerked him away.

The bell tolled on. 'They're nuns!' another cried out. 'Look at the cross.'

The crucifix, unstable on the balustrade, lurched from left to right and back again. Mother Theresia tried to steady it. 'I can't hold it,' she cried as the metal, top-heavy, slipped from their hands. It toppled over and crashed down.

A single shout, a cry, and then the thud of metal on flesh, on stone. Then silence, interspersed with the continuing tolling of the bell.

Mother Theresia clasped Ursula's skirts, stared over the balustrade. 'Step down, child,' she whispered.

The men behind Kurt stayed still.

The Little Sisters of the Immaculate Conception made the sign of the cross and began to chant the *Nunc dimittis*: 'Now Thou dost dismiss Thy servant, O Lord, according to Thy word, in peace. Because mine eyes have seen Thy salvation which Thou hast prepared before the face of all peoples.'

The bell tolled on, the young men melted away, leaving the inert, spreadeagled figure of Kurt Miller on the gravel.

40

Gabriela and Michael sat in the convent hall, benign pleasure showing on their faces. The annual prizes for the summer school were being presented; they could see Joseph standing on the platform next to Sister Marka, his strong frame alert.

'And now we come to the prize-giving for our beloved St Walter Folk Singing Competition,' Reverend Mother announced. 'This music scholarship, instituted by Mother Theresia in 1993, has been outstandingly successful. We attract some of the most up-and-coming young voices in the world. I will now announce the winner for 2008.' Mother Christa took an envelope from Sister Marka, opened it and read the contents. Her smile swept across the sea of young faces at the front, then moved towards the back where expectant parents and friends waited. 'I see that this year we have cause for a double celebration. Our winner is Marina Fullbridey, the daughter of Mary Fullbridey, the very first winner of our acclaimed competition.'

Gabriela's eyes filled with tears.

'Why are you crying, Liebling?' Michael put a comforting arm around her shoulders. 'I thought that's what you had prayed for? It is wonderful news.'

'Hoped for,' she said.

500

Mother Christa looked towards the second row. 'Don't be afraid, Marina. Your voice is one of the most promising I have heard in many years. We hope this will be the beginning of a great career for you.'

The fourteen-year-old stood and advanced towards the platform. Her sweet, innocent face, her honey-blonde hair matched by the hazel eyes, glowed with achievement. She mounted the platform to accept the prize Mother Christa was handing her.

She took the certificate and looked at the framed picture Sister Marka was offering. A hand-painted copy of the triptych altarpiece she had seen in the convent chapel made her gasp. It depicted the Virgin and Child, with the two central scenes from the Annunciation on either side. Two further scenes were also shown: the birth of Jesus, and the parable of the wise virgins.

'As you know, the first prize is the offer of a place at the Convent of the Immaculate Conception for a year. This includes singing tuition from an outstanding teacher, which such an outstanding talent requires to bring her voice to full perfection. We are delighted to be able to offer Marina this chance. We hope that she will take it.'

Marina smiled, nodded her head, eyes sparkling.

'And now, Marina. Which is your favourite song? We would like you to sing that for us.'

'*Das heilige Wickelkind*,' she said, her head held high, her eyes clear. 'That was the song my mother sang here fifteen years ago, in this very spot. She could not, unfortunately, be with us today. As some of you may know, she has just won the Nobel Prize for her work in the genetic field in which she is an expert: changing the chromosomal structure of harmful genetically transmitted mutations. She gave up her singing career to dedicate herself to helping girls like me achieve our rightful heritage. And she has gone on from there to conquer much genetically transmitted disease. She has her reward.

'Today, I would like to sing a song for my true mother – the one who dedicated her life to bringing me up, the one who nurtured me, the one without whom I would not be here.' She stood and looked towards the back, blew a kiss towards the Adlers. 'I hope you will applaud the real winner today – Frau Gabriela Adler.'

As Joseph, flanked by two young sons, walked towards the spinet and strummed the introductory chords of 'Holy Babe', Marina drew in her breath, waited for the right note and began to sing. Her voice, soft at first, found its strength. She sang the first verse like an angel.

To Gabriela it seemed as though the years had never passed. The glorious voice rose high – and it was Mary's voice.

There was no sound at first, just a stunned silence. But when the applause did come, shouts of 'encore' filled the room. No one could mistake the feelings of the audience. Marina and Joseph looked at each other, he strummed another chord and she began to sing again. Her voice filled the hall, the minds, the souls of everyone there.

The shrine had, after all, performed its miracle. That glorious voice would soon be heard in concert halls and opera houses around the world.

EMMA LORANT

CRADLE

— OF —

SECRETS

Her dream of twins turned into a nightmare

When Alec and Lisa Wildmore move to the pretty Somerset village of Lodsham, they anticipate a rural idyll. Newly pregnant, with one adorable toddler already, Lisa is confident that the countryside is the best place to raise her family; she embodies the good life of the caring 'nineties.

But the sun-dappled tranquillity of the Glastonbury moors is deceptive.

Childbirth brings identical twin boys, despite a scan showing only one baby. When it becomes clear that this is only the start of a terrifying chain of events she is powerless to prevent, Lisa realises she is in the grip of a phenomenon as sinister as it is inexplicable.

Of course she loves her children – blond, blue-eyed and enchanting – and is determined to protect them from any dangers that might attend their unusual genesis. And a rash of 'accidents' convinces Lisa that there are dangers indeed.

Whom can she trust with her cradle of secrets? Alec assumes she is suffering delusions brought on by post-natal depression. Previously friendly villagers adopt a hostile curiosity. Can she even trust her own maternal instincts? Or is Lisa Wildmore losing her mind...?

FICTION/THRILLER   0 7472 4358 1

A selection of bestsellers from Headline

HARD EVIDENCE	John T Lescroart	£5.99 ☐
TWICE BURNED	Kit Craig	£5.99 ☐
CAULDRON	Larry Bond	£5.99 ☐
BLACK WOLF	Philip Caveney	£5.99 ☐
ILL WIND	Gary Gottesfield	£5.99 ☐
THE BOMB SHIP	Peter Tonkin	£5.99 ☐
SKINNER'S RULES	Quintin Jardine	£4.99 ☐
COLD CALL	Dianne Pugh	£4.99 ☐
TELL ME NO SECRETS	Joy Fielding	£4.99 ☐
GRIEVOUS SIN	Faye Kellerman	£4.99 ☐
TORSO	John Peyton Cooke	£4.99 ☐
THE WINTER OF THE WOLF	R A MacAvoy	£4.50 ☐

All Headline books are available at your local bookshop or newsagent, or can be ordered direct from the publisher. Just tick the titles you want and fill in the form below. Prices and availability subject to change without notice.

Headline Book Publishing, Cash Sales Department, Bookpoint, 39 Milton Park, Abingdon, OXON, OX14 4TD, UK. If you have a credit card you may order by telephone – 0235 400400.

Please enclose a cheque or postal order made payable to Bookpoint Ltd to the value of the cover price and allow the following for postage and packing:
UK & BFPO: £1.00 for the first book, 50p for the second book and 30p for each additional book ordered up to a maximum charge of £3.00.
OVERSEAS & EIRE: £2.00 for the first book, £1.00 for the second book and 50p for each additional book.

Name ....

Address ....

....

....

If you would prefer to pay by credit card, please complete:
Please debit my Visa/Access/Diner's Card/American Express (delete as applicable) card no:

Signature .... Expiry Date ....